W9-BVA-132

CROSS
HER
HEART

ALSO BY MELINDA LEIGH

MORGAN DANE NOVELS

Say You're Sorry

Her Last Goodbye

Bones Don't Lie

What I've Done

Secrets Never Die

Save Your Breath

SCARLET FALLS NOVELS

Hour of Need

Minutes to Kill

Seconds to Live

SHE CAN SERIES

She Can Run

She Can Tell

She Can Scream

She Can Hide

"He Can Fall" (A Short Story)

She Can Kill

MIDNIGHT NOVELS

Midnight Exposure

Midnight Sacrifice

Midnight Betrayal

Midnight Obsession

THE ROGUE SERIES NOVELLAS

Gone to Her Grave (Rogue River)

Walking on Her Grave (Rogue River)

Tracks of Her Tears (Rogue Winter)

Burned by Her Devotion (Rogue Vows)

Twisted Truth (Rogue Justice)

THE WIDOW'S ISLAND NOVELLA SERIES

A Bone to Pick

Whisper of Bones

CROSS HER HEART

MELINDA LEIGH

 Montlake

Published by Montlake, Seattle

www.apub.com

Amazon, the Amazon logo, and Montlake are trademarks of Amazon.com, Inc., or its affiliates.

ISBN-13: 9781542006927 (paperback)
ISBN-10: 1542006929 (paperback)

ISBN-13: 9781542006941 (hardcover)
ISBN-10: 1542006945 (hardcover)

Cover design by Shasti O'Leary Soudant

Printed in the United States of America

First edition

For Charlie, Annie, and Tom.
You are everything.

CHAPTER ONE

Grey's Hollow, New York, January 1993

"911. What is your emergency?" the lady asked.

Bree was shaking so hard. She could barely hold the phone to her ear. "Mommy and Daddy are fighting." A slap sounded down the hall, and Bree flinched. "Would you send the police?"

"The police are coming," the lady said. "I'm going to talk with you until they arrive."

"OK." Bree sniffed and wiped her nose with her sleeve. Snot was running down her face. She hated to cry in front of Daddy. It just made him madder, but she couldn't help it.

"What's your name?"

"Bree," she said in a small voice. She didn't think Daddy would hear her, but if he did, then Bree would get the same as Mommy. She looked down the hall. Her parents' door was open, and Daddy was yelling. She couldn't hear all the words, but she knew he was saying mean things and calling Mommy names. She heard another smacking sound and her mother started to sob. "He's hitting Mommy."

"Where are they?"

"In their bedroom."

Erin came out into the hall. She held her stuffed bunny by one ear and dragged him as she walked toward Mommy and Daddy's room.

"Erin, don't go in there!" Bree called as loud as she dared, but it came out as a whisper. She didn't want Daddy to hear.

"Who is Erin?" the lady asked.

"My little sister," Bree answered. "Erin, come here!"

"How old is she?"

"Four. I'm eight. I have to look after her. Mommy said so."

"You're eight years old." The lady coughed.

Bree went down the hall toward her sister, but the phone cord wasn't long enough. "I can't reach her." She held the phone tight. She didn't want to put it down. She yelled, "Erin!"

Her sister turned her head. Erin wasn't crying, but her eyes were real big, and she'd wet her pajamas. When her sister turned around and walked toward her, the air whooshed from Bree's chest, and stars danced in front of her eyes. She pulled Erin down the hall and into the kitchen with her.

"I got her," Bree said to the lady.

In the third bedroom, the baby began to scream. His doorway was right across from Mommy and Daddy's. His crying made Bree's tummy hurt. Daddy would get madder.

"Is that your sister crying?" the lady asked.

"No. I got a baby brother." Bree didn't want Daddy in the room with Mommy, but she didn't want him to come out either. "I have to go get him. I have to make him be quiet." Bree turned to her sister. "Stay here."

Before she could go to the baby's room, Daddy came into the hall. His face was red, and his eyes were small and mean. Mommy was right behind him. Her mouth was bleeding, and her neck had red marks all around it.

"Stop." Mommy grabbed Daddy by the arm. "I'll get him."

Daddy spun and slapped her across the face.

Bree yelled, "Stop hitting Mommy!"

But he didn't. He smacked her again.

The baby screamed, and Daddy turned toward his room.

"What's happening, Bree?" the lady asked.

"Daddy's gonna get the baby." Bree didn't know what to do. She was so scared, her belly cramped, and her legs shook. Her sister crawled under the kitchen table. "Please send the police."

"They're coming, Bree," the lady said. "It's going to be OK."

"Stop it!" Mommy jumped on Daddy's back and started hitting him. "Don't you touch him."

Daddy spun real fast, knocking Mommy into the wall. She fell off his back onto the hallway floor. He turned away from the baby's doorway. His face was dark, madder than Bree had ever seen him. He lunged toward Mommy, his fingers curling around her arm and yanking her to her feet. Then he dragged her back into their room.

"I have to go. I have to get the baby now." Bree put the phone down. She could hear the lady talking as she tiptoed into the baby's room. Red-faced and screaming, her baby brother stood in his crib, his little hands hooked over the top rail.

"Shhh." Bree picked him up and put him on her hip. "You got to be quiet."

As she carried him out, she looked into her parents' room. Daddy held Mommy against the wall with one hand. In the other, he held a gun. Bree froze for a second. Her whole body went cold, and she almost peed her pants.

Then she backed away and ran down the hall as fast as she could. The baby stopped crying as he bounced on her hip. He buried his face in her shoulder and hiccupped. She hurried past the phone on the floor. The lady was calling her name, but Bree didn't have time to talk to her.

She stopped next to the kitchen table and called Erin.

Her sister crawled out from under the table. "Bree?"

"Come on," Bree whispered. "We got to hide."

"I'm scared," Erin said.

"I know where to go. It'll be OK." Bree grabbed Erin by the arm and pulled her out the kitchen door.

Erin resisted. "Promise?"

Shifting the baby aside, Bree drew a tiny *X* in the middle of her own chest. "Cross my heart."

She turned toward the door again. This time Erin didn't resist.

It was dark in the backyard, and the porch was icy under her bare feet. The wind blew right through her pajamas. But she kept going, down the steps and around to the loose board under the porch. She pulled it back and held it while Erin wiggled through the hole. Then she pushed the baby into the darkness and crawled in after him. Bree pulled the board back into place. She'd hidden here before plenty of times when Mommy and Daddy were fighting.

Under the porch, they were out of the wind, but it was still cold.

Bree looked between the boards at the dark yard. In the shadow of the barn, Daddy's dogs barked from the kennel. The lady had said the police were coming. The wind came through the spaces between the boards. Bree couldn't hear Mommy and Daddy fighting anymore. *What's Daddy doing?*

"I'm cold." Erin's teeth chattered.

Bree pulled her sister closer and shushed her. The baby shivered in her arms and whimpered. His face scrunched up, like he was gettin' ready to cry. If he did, Daddy might hear. He might find them. Bree wrapped her arms around his little body and rocked him. "Shhh."

A door slammed, and Bree jumped. Heavy boots stomped overhead. She couldn't tell if the footsteps were inside the house or on the back porch. Had the police come? Maybe it was gonna be OK. Just like the lady said.

A gunshot blasted. Bree jumped.

Mommy!

Her hands tightened on the baby, and he began to cry. Another door slammed. Bree wanted to run to the sound, but she was too afraid. She heard more footsteps, more yelling, then another gunshot.

Bree closed her eyes.

Even without seeing what happened, she knew that nothing would ever be OK again.

CHAPTER TWO

"This is the building." Bree Taggert pointed to a line of brick rowhouses occupying a North Philadelphia block. "We're looking for twenty-year-old Ronnie Marin."

Fellow homicide detective Dana Romano slowed the vehicle and coughed into her fist. At fifty, Dana was long and lean. A few gray streaks highlighted her short, messy blonde hair. Crow's-feet deepened as she squinted through the car window. "Is this his place?"

Bree checked her notes. "No. Ronnie's aunt lives here. The last time he was arrested, she bailed him out. Then he skipped on his bail, and she was out a thousand dollars. I'm hoping she knows where he is and holds a grudge."

The previous week, a nurse had been beaten, raped, and strangled on her way home from the night shift in the ICU. A Laundromat surveillance camera had caught the killer dragging his victim into the alley where her body had been found. In less than twenty-four hours, the killer had been ID'd as Ronnie Marin from North Philly. Ronnie had a rap sheet as long as the Schuylkill Expressway.

Bree had been working her way through Ronnie's known contacts. So far, she'd found no sign of Ronnie, and no one had admitted to seeing him.

Dana had been out sick for the past week and was catching up with the investigation. She pulled the blue Crown Vic to the curb behind a pile of snow as tall as the vehicle. "Remind me what Ronnie's last offense was?"

"Robbery." Bree scanned the dark street but saw nothing alive. In the trash alley that ran next to the home, black ice shone in the glare of a streetlamp. "He did eighteen months. Before that, vandalism and simple assault. He's only been out for two months."

Bree turned the dashboard computer to show her Ronnie's mug shot.

"A quick progression to murder," Dana said.

"Nothing teaches a criminal to be a better criminal like going to prison."

"Maybe Ronnie left town."

"I doubt it. All his connections are here. This is his turf, and he's worked hard to be a BFD in his neighborhood."

Dana shrugged. "What do we know about the aunt?"

"Ronnie's aunt is fifty-seven. She's worked for the same commercial cleaning company for the past eighteen years and has no criminal record."

"Can't pick your family." Dana paused, her face reddening. "I'm sorry, Bree. I didn't mean anything by that."

In the four years they'd worked together, Dana had never brought up Bree's parents' deaths, though Bree had heard plenty of whispers behind her back from other cops in the division. But then, when your father murdered your mother and then killed himself, you had to expect people to talk about it.

"It's all right. I know it." And Bree had mostly come to terms with her own family's past long ago, at least as much as anyone could under the circumstances. She'd also made tragedy and violence a permanent part of her life when she'd become a cop.

Whatever. She'd had more than enough therapy as a kid. She was done with it. After she'd turned eighteen, she'd decided to stop analyzing herself. Some damage left a permanent mark. There was no changing that. She'd shoved her childhood into a dark corner of her memory and moved on. At thirty-five, the last thing Bree wanted was to drag those memories into the light.

She stepped out of the vehicle. Frigid wind whipped along the icy street and stung her cheeks. Despite the cold, she unbuttoned her black peacoat for better access to her weapon.

Coughing, Dana joined her on the cracked sidewalk. She shoved her hands into the pockets of her knee-length parka. "Damn, it's cold."

Just after the new year arrived, an Arctic blast had frozen Philadelphia solid. The cold snap had persisted, nothing had melted, and the week-old snow had grown gray and dingy. But then, city snow was pretty only until the following rush hour.

Bree skirted a patch of shiny black ice. "You should go home when we're done here. You sound like a dying seal."

"No way. I can't stare at the walls of my crappy apartment for another day." Dana cleared her throat, then pulled a cough drop from her pocket, unwrapped it, and popped it into her mouth. "My mother keeps stopping by. Hovering and shoving soup at me all damned day. I've been taking the meds, and the doc says I'm no longer contagious. It's time to get off my butt and back to work."

"What are you going to do after you retire next month?"

"I don't know. My cousin wants me to work night security for his flooring store." Dana paused on the sidewalk to hack.

"Because everyone wants to work the graveyard shift in their retirement."

"Right?" Dana coughed again.

Sighing, Bree waited for Dana to catch her breath. When she'd finished, Bree led the way up three cracked concrete steps. A white wrought iron railing edged the stairs and stoop. Bree and Dana automatically flanked the doorway as best they could to avoid standing dead center and knocked on the door. When no one responded, Bree knocked louder.

Footsteps sounded inside, and a tiny middle-aged woman answered. Bree recognized Ronnie's aunt, Maria Marin, from her driver's license photo. Her complexion was sallow and wrinkled, and she wore her dark brown hair scraped into an unforgiving bun. At eight o'clock on a Tuesday evening, most people would be settling in for the night. Mrs. Marin would be getting ready for work.

Bree lifted the badge she wore on a lanyard around her neck. "I'm Detective Taggert, and this is Detective Romano."

Dana nodded. "Ma'am."

Mrs. Marin's dark eyes went wide, and her mouth puckered before she smoothed out her features. *Fear?* The skin between Bree's shoulder blades itched. Dana shot Bree a side-eye. She'd seen it.

Is Ronnie inside? Or is Mrs. Marin simply afraid to talk to the police?

Bree glanced over Mrs. Marin's shoulder but didn't see anyone. "We'd like to talk to you about your nephew, Ronnie." Bree lowered her voice in case the neighborhood had ears. "May we come inside?"

"No." Mrs. Marin shook her head, fear flashing into her eyes again. Her gaze shifted hard to one side, as if she was trying to see behind her without turning her head. *Is Ronnie listening?*

Bree persisted. "Have you seen Ronnie in the past few days?"

"I don't have to talk to you." Mrs. Marin took a step backward and prepared to close the door.

"No, ma'am, you don't, but your nephew killed a woman." Bree wasn't giving anything away. Ronnie's photograph had been shown on the news the previous night. "Every officer in the city is looking for him. It would be better for Ronnie if he came in with me willingly." Bree let the implication hang that surrendering to her would be safer for Ronnie's health.

Ronnie had committed a vicious murder. His face had been caught on a surveillance video. Clearly, he was no criminal mastermind. The PPD was going to find him. Given his established stupidity, Ronnie would resist and/or run.

Mrs. Marin hesitated for two seconds, then shut the door in their faces.

Dana stepped off the stoop. Rock salt crunched under her boots. She coughed, covering her mouth. "He's in there."

"Yep." Without looking back, Bree walked toward the car.

Dana paused on the sidewalk. "We can't prove he's inside."

"Nope." Bree inhaled. The cold air bit into her sinus passages. "Let's pull around the corner and see if we can get a line of sight on the back door. Knowing we found him is going to make Ronnie want to bolt ASAP."

"We'll need another unit to watch the front door."

They stepped into the vehicle and called for backup. Then Dana drove around the corner and parked alongside an overgrown hedge at the mouth of the alley that bisected the block. The alley was full of shadows, but they could see straight down the middle. Each rowhome had a tiny cement patio enclosed with various types of fencing. Chain link was prominent. But each back door was raised three steps high, and Bree had a clear visual of each rear exit. Most units had lights above their doors. Mrs. Marin's home was the third from the corner. Bree had barely located her unit when the back door opened, and a head poked out. Ronnie surveyed the neighborhood.

"And there he is." She slid lower in her seat, waiting for Ronnie to step out of the house.

"We should wait for backup."

"No. I'm not letting him go."

Dana gave her The Look.

"Don't. You saw what he did. I want him off the street where he can't hurt anyone else." Bree reached for the door handle as Ronnie came out of the house and closed the door behind him. "I'll do the running. You head him off in the car."

"I don't like you going off on your own." Dana shifted into drive.

"You will be right behind me. You just had bronchitis. You won't be able to keep up."

They both knew that Dana could never keep up with Bree anyway.

Dana grumbled in agreement. "When you get a newbie to train, make them do all the running."

Bree didn't want to think about taking on a new partner. Trust didn't come easily to her.

Dana sobered. "Be careful, Bree. Ronnie is a dangerous little shitbag."

"Yep." Bree slipped out of the car. Dana drove away to circle the block. Bree peered around the hedge. Ronnie was heading up the alley. As if he knew she was behind him, he broke into a hard run.

Shit!

Bree sprinted after him, but he reached the end of the alley, turned right, and disappeared behind a wooden fence. Fearing an ambush, Bree stopped at the corner and put her back to the fence. Drawing her weapon, she rounded the corner gun-first. Her heart hammered against her breastbone. Despite the cold, sweat ran down the center of her back, soaking her shirt. But Ronnie wasn't in sight.

Emerging on the next street, she caught her breath and scanned the surrounding brick rowhomes for her suspect. *Where is that little bastard?*

"Bree!" Just ahead, Dana had angled the Crown Vic across the intersection. She pointed out the open vehicle window to the alley on the next block. "That way!"

Following her partner's direction, Bree pivoted on a patch of ice and ran. Behind her, she heard the peel of tires as Dana turned the car. She'd try to cut off Ronnie's escape on the next block, and she'd call for more backup. No doubt there were additional units in the area.

Bree slogged through a snow bank and ran past a dumpster just in time to see her suspect climbing over a six-foot chain-link fence.

She bolted forward. "Stop! Police!"

As she expected, Ronnie ignored her and kept running. Bree didn't bother to yell at him again. She'd save her breath for the chase.

In her peripheral vision, she caught the swirl of red-and-blue lights as a black-and-white unit passed the intersection. Her black athletic shoes skidded on the salt-dusted blacktop. She jumped onto the fence, and it rattled under the impact. Hooking her hands at the top, she hoisted herself over and dropped to the asphalt on the other side.

Spying Ronnie just twenty feet ahead of her, near where the alley dumped onto the main street, Bree stayed on him. She ran three days a week. The initial sprint had been painful for her cold lungs and muscles, but now she was warming up. Her stride lengthened, and she gained on Ronnie.

Dana should be at the other end of the alley to block his escape. But Ronnie looked over his shoulder, saw Bree right on his tail, and made a hard right, jumping onto a square bin next to a rickety wooden fence, poising to leap over it.

Bree was barely five feet behind him. She lunged forward and reached for the back of his jacket.

Almost.

Ronnie's hands hit the top of the fence. She grabbed his hood just as he gathered his muscles to vault over the top. A heavy body hit the wood on the other side. The deep bark of a large dog echoed. Ronnie couldn't stop his momentum in time, but Bree's grip on his hood clotheslined him. Grabbing at the fabric at his throat, he fell to his knees and hit the fence face-first. Bree slammed into the fence next to him. Her cheek smacked the top board. The giant head of a white pit bull appeared as the dog leaped a second time. Its powerful jaws snapped inches from her eye. She felt the dog's breath on the side of her face, and dog spit splattered her cheek before the big beast hit the ground again.

A memory intruded, teeth sinking into her flesh, the phantom pain bright and sharp as if thirty years had not passed. Terror jolted her heart, and she flung her body backward off the fence. She slipped off the bin and landed on her ass in six inches of snow. Ronnie fell on top of her in a pile of sprawled limbs. Something jammed hard into Bree's gut, knocking the wind from her. But she barely registered the ache in her ribs.

Where's the dog?

The pit bull hit the fence again. The weak boards rattled, creaked, and shifted as the dog threatened to break through. Bree heard low growling and heavy breathing. Dog tags jingled as the animal raced back and forth along its side of the fence. Approaching footsteps pounded on the pavement. Backup was here. But Bree's adrenal system didn't believe the danger had passed. Her pulse pounded through her veins. She fought to catch her breath and stem the panic scrambling through her chest, gathering momentum like an eighteen-wheeler barreling down the PA Turnpike.

The fence will hold.

But Bree couldn't breathe. She tried to roll to her side, but Ronnie's heavier body pinned her to the ground. A pair of big, black cop shoes appeared next to her face, and the weight was lifted off her. Still her lungs were locked up, and she gasped for air.

"I got him, Detective Taggert," a voice said. "You can let go now."

Bree inhaled, her lungs inflating, her eyes focusing. The shoes belonged to a beefy uniformed cop. A second patrol officer appeared next to the first. The dog huffed, but it was safely behind the fence.

"Bree!" Dana's voice jolted her. "Let. Go."

Bree blinked down at her hand. Her knuckles were scraped and raw from the impact with the fence, but her fingers were still clenched tightly in Ronnie's hood. The fabric pressed against his windpipe, and his head was craned backward at an unnatural angle. She opened her fist and released him.

"Shit, Taggert," Cop Number Two said. "You ran him *down*."

The two uniforms flipped Ronnie onto his face, handcuffed him, and hauled him away. Another black-and-white parked behind the first.

Dana extended a hand. "You OK?"

Nodding, Bree let her partner pull her to her feet. Her knees trembled, but she sucked it up and forced them to straighten. The other cops would blame her breathlessness on the chase. She hoped.

Dana's face was serious as she raked her eyes over Bree. "You're sure you're not hurt?"

Bree glanced around, aware that the other cops were watching her. Their scrutiny felt hot on her face. She rubbed her solar plexus. "Got the wind knocked out of me. I'll be fine in a couple of minutes."

"OK." Dana steered her out of the alley to where she'd parked the car and opened the passenger door for her. "Sit down and catch your breath."

Bree sat sideways, her feet in the street, and sipped from a water bottle she'd left in the car. Then she wiped her clammy palms on her thighs. Now that the incident was over, impending bruises were making themselves known. Her tailbone throbbed with every beat of her heart. But it wasn't the aches and pains that rattled her, and it wouldn't be the killer she'd chased that gave her nightmares.

It was the dog and the memories its snapping teeth evoked.

She shuddered, then took three deep breaths and did what she did best. She compartmentalized. She shoved that horror show back into the deep, dark hole where it needed to stay. She'd just gotten her heart rate and breathing under control when the phone on her belt vibrated. Bree looked at the screen. She'd missed a call while she was chasing Ronnie. She read the voice mail notification, and her heart did a double tap.

Erin?

"What's wrong?" Dana narrowed blue eyes at Bree.

Bree stared at her phone. "My sister called."

"When was the last time you talked to her?"

"A couple of weeks ago. You know my family is . . ." Bree searched for the word. "Complicated."

"Uh-huh." Dana was more than a coworker. She was Bree's closest friend.

"We talk on the phone, but I haven't seen her since she brought the kids to Philly last summer." The last time Bree had visited Grey's Hollow had been for Erin's wedding four years before.

"I remember." Dana was a history geek. When Erin and the kids came to town, she'd played tour guide, walking them through the Constitution Center, Independence Hall, and other sites. "Did she leave a voice mail?"

"Yes." Bree's finger hesitated over the "Play" button. She should wait until she got home to listen to her sister's message. Unexpected news from Grey's Hollow was never good. Bree's heart began to thud again, fresh sweat gathered on her palms, and all her careful compartmentalizing went to hell. "Could you give me a minute, Dana?"

"Sure. No problem." She turned and walked back to the cluster of cops at the alley entrance.

Planting her feet firmly on the pavement, Bree stabbed the "Play" button. Her sister's voice was breathless and hurried.

"Bree? I'm in trouble. I don't know what to do. I don't want to give you the details in a message, but I need your help. Please call me back as soon as you get this."

Worried, Bree pressed the "Call Back" button. Her sister's line rang three times and connected to voice mail. Bree left a message. "It's Bree. Sorry I missed you. Call me back."

She lowered the phone and stared at it. She'd missed her sister's call by only a few minutes. Where could Erin be? Bree played the message again. Her sister's rushed words knotted in her belly.

Frowning, Dana walked over. "Everything OK?"

"She's not answering her phone." Bree called her brother, Adam, but the call went immediately to voice mail. She left him a message. Next, she dialed the salon where her sister worked, but the receptionist said Erin was off tonight.

"Try her later," Dana suggested. "She could be in the shower."

Bree drank some water and called Erin again. Still no answer. She replayed the message, tilting the phone so Dana could hear.

Dana's blonde eyebrows lowered. "Your sister doesn't seem like the type who gets in trouble."

"She isn't. Erin's a *head down, go to work, raise her kids* kind of person. She doesn't have time for trouble." Bree rubbed the edge of her phone with her thumb. "But just her calling me for help means it's something major. We're not as close as I'd like."

"Not your fault or hers that you weren't raised together."

Erin and Adam had been reared by their grandmother in Grey's Hollow. Bree had been farmed out to a cousin in Philadelphia.

"My childhood isn't my fault." Bree tapped her phone screen and stared at the lack of notifications. "But the decisions I've made since reaching adulthood are one hundred percent my responsibility."

"What are you going to do?"

As children, Bree and her siblings had survived a nightmare together. Despite the three hundred miles between them, they would always have a special connection. They were particularly tuned in to trouble, and Bree could sense from Erin's voice that something was wrong. Really wrong. Erin's tone wasn't *I'm late with the mortgage payment.* She had sounded scared.

There was only one thing Bree *could* do.

She finished her water and stood. "I'm going home."

CHAPTER THREE

With a flicker of apprehension, Matthew Flynn rang his friend's doorbell a second time. Once again, chimes sounded inside the small ranch-style home. But no footsteps approached the door.

Justin should be home. He should be expecting Matt to pick him up for his Narcotics Anonymous meeting, as he had every Tuesday night for months.

At Matt's side, his German shepherd, Brody, whined. Matt glanced down at the dog. Brody's ears were up and his posture stiff.

"What is it, boy?"

Brody whined again and pawed at the concrete stoop. A former sheriff's department K-9, Brody had sharp instincts honed by years of training and practice. The dog barked once. Normally, he was happy and excited to see Justin. His tail should be wagging. His posture should be relaxed.

Something was wrong.

Matt might not understand the signals, but he trusted his dog. Brody's senses of smell and hearing were far superior to any human's. And he always seemed to have a sixth sense as well. When they'd been a working K-9 team with the sheriff's department, Brody had saved Matt's ass more times than he could count. Matt had learned the hard way that he could trust the dog more than he could most people.

He swallowed a lump of pure bitterness. Three years ago, a shooting had ended both their careers. Matt wished the way his future had been ripped out from under him could be described as simply as it had been summed up in the press release. The reality had been anything but. He knew he had to let go of his anger. The sheriff had sent Matt and Brody through the wrong door of a warehouse, and they'd been caught in friendly fire when deputies exchanged shots with a drug dealer. Whether the former sheriff's actions had been deliberate or accidental didn't matter anymore. The man was dead. But letting go of his resentment was proving harder than Matt anticipated.

He opened the storm door and tried the wooden door, but it was locked. Backing away from the door, he scanned the front of the house. Justin's Ford Escape sat in the driveway. A For Sale sign was displayed in the windshield. Justin would not be driving for a long time. Four months before, he'd been arrested for driving while ability impaired by drugs. As a second DWAI offense, the charge was a class E felony in New York State. Justin's wife had asked him to move out. Since then, Justin said he was committed to staying sober and earning back her trust, but there were days when all he talked about were his failures. He battled depression along with his addiction.

Concerned, Matt backed away from the door, his breath fogging in the freezing January night. The exterior and interior lights were on. Justin was on a tight budget. If he wasn't home, the house would be dark.

Matt pulled out his phone. Twenty minutes ago, he'd sent Justin a text, letting him know he was on the way. Matt had been running a few minutes late and hadn't waited for an answer before leaving his house, but now the lack of one felt wrong. Justin usually sent back a thumbs-up. Matt sent a new message. I'M OUTSIDE.

A minute ticked away with no response.

There was only one thing to do. Matt had to go in.

He'd known Justin since they were kids. His friend had been on a downward spiral, set off by a car accident, chronic back pain, and a subsequent addiction to OxyContin. Justin had fallen apart, but he seemed determined to get his life together. Matt would do everything he could to help, including driving him to NA meetings and breaking into his house if there was even a slight chance that his friend could be in trouble.

Possible scenarios ran through Matt's head. Addiction relapse and suicide were among them.

"Come on," he said to the dog as he turned away from the house, but Brody didn't immediately follow. The dog focused on the door and whined again. The sound he made was plaintive, high-pitched, and barely audible. "We'll try another door."

Obedient but clearly reluctant, Brody followed him around the side of the house. Their footsteps crunched in the ice-crusted snow. The patio door was a glass slider, and it was open. Matt stuck his head inside. The den and kitchen were at the back of the house. The kitchen was empty but brightly lit. Two open cans of Coke sat on the counter next to a pizza box. In the den, a couch and coffee table faced the TV. Light flickered from the TV mounted on the wall. A local news station played on the screen.

Where is Justin?

Worry snowballed in Matt's gut. As if channeling his master's anxiety, Brody dug into the snow that had drifted against the base of the slider.

"Yeah, no worries, buddy. We're going in." Matt pulled a leash from his pocket and snapped it onto the dog's collar. Then he stepped into the kitchen. A few clumps of snow fell from his boots. He wiped his feet on the mat and led Brody inside, leaving the door open behind them.

The shepherd panted and paced at the end of his leash. Matt brought him to heel with a single German command. *"Fuss."*

"Justin?" he called. Nothing moved. The tiny house felt eerily still. Brody pulled toward the hallway that led to the bedrooms. Matt held him back as he strained at the end of his leash.

The dog whined again. Matt flipped a light switch in the hall. The laundry room and bathroom were empty. Matt peered into the spare bedroom, which contained only a stack of boxes Justin refused to unpack, claiming the move was temporary.

Brody pulled harder.

"Fuss." Matt repeated the command.

Brody obeyed but his body posture remained tense. He was acting as if he were back on active duty in a high-stress situation.

The master bedroom lay ahead. Matt debated taking the dog back to his vehicle, but he wasn't armed. On the remote chance there was an intruder in the house, Brody would know, and the dog would have his back. Matt listened for a few seconds, but the only sounds were the low voices of the news anchors on the TV in the den. Brody wasn't acting as if there was a threat, but the dog was agitated, whining and shifting his weight from side to side in lieu of pacing. His head bobbed and weaved like a professional boxer.

"Justin?" Matt called out, hesitant to invade the privacy of his friend's bedroom. But Justin's depression made him walk down the hall. The room was lit only by a small bedside lamp, but it was bright enough that he could see what lay in the middle of the room.

A dead body and a lake of blood.

Matt flinched.

He didn't need to feel for a pulse. From the size of the deep-red stain on the carpet, he knew the person was dead. No one could survive that much blood loss.

The body was too small to be Justin. Matt used the flashlight app on his phone to better illuminate the body. Shock washed over him. It was a woman. She wore boots, jeans, and a sweater. Long, dark hair streamed out from under a knit cap.

He moved a few steps to the side and shone the light on her face. Matt inhaled sharply.

Justin's wife, Erin, stared back at him with empty hazel eyes.

What is she doing here?

Brody whined, a thin, plaintive sound. Matt put a reassuring hand on the top of the dog's head as he called 911 on his cell phone.

In rural areas, deputies wore multiple professional hats. Several deputies, including the current chief, also served on the county search-and-rescue team. Others were on the dive team. Several were volunteer firefighters. Matt had been an investigator and, later, a K-9 officer. As he gave the dispatcher the address, he put aside his emotions and viewed the scene like the detective he'd been.

Erin was on her side, her body curled around itself. From the size of the wound, Matt suspected she'd been shot. Blood covered her hands, which were near the wound in her chest. She hadn't died immediately. She'd known she was bleeding out. She'd clutched the wound, maybe even tried to stem the bleeding. The heart stops beating at death, and it had taken a minute or so to pump a fatal volume out of her body. It must have seemed both a long and short minute to her. Matt took in the size of the bloodstain. It had been a futile effort. He hoped she'd lost consciousness quickly.

An image from their wedding flashed into his mind. Justin and Erin posing for a photo with her two kids. He closed his eyes for a second. Justin had mentioned that the kids hadn't seen their father in years. No one even knew where he was or if he was alive. They could be orphans.

The 911 operator gave a response time of four minutes. Matt took two minutes to snap pictures of the rest of the room with his cell phone camera. He was no longer a deputy. Since the former sheriff's death and the airing of the corruption in the department, many other deputies had left. There were a number of new hires, and of the longtime deputies, Matt didn't know who he could trust. How many had known of the former sheriff's crimes?

He was certain of only one thing. This would be his only chance to record the crime scene.

Justin hadn't planned to live here long and hadn't invested in much furniture. The bedroom held a bed, a chair, and a nightstand with a lamp. A purple puffy coat lay across the chair. It looked too small and feminine to be Justin's. *Erin's?* He snapped a picture, then took photos of a dark red smear on the doorframe and another on the wall.

On the floor in front of the bathroom door lay a towel. Matt stooped and touched the corner. Damp.

Matt ducked into the bathroom. Another damp towel hung over a rod mounted on the wall. He used the sleeve of his jacket to open the medicine chest, noting the extra toothpaste, a tube of mascara, and a lipstick on the glass shelf. In the cabinet beneath the sink, he found a hairdryer, a round hairbrush, and a box of feminine hygiene products. As he photographed everything, he wondered if the female items belonged to Erin or another woman.

A siren approached.

"Time to go." He led Brody back out the way they had come into the house, taking more pictures on his way out. He followed his own tracks back to the sidewalk and waited, noting and filing details in his head. The front door had been locked. The back slider had been open, as if someone had rushed out of the house.

Who killed Erin? And where is Justin?

Two hours later, emergency vehicles clogged the street. Swirling red-and-blue lights reflected on the snow. A county CSI van was parked behind the sheriff's department vehicles. The medical examiner had been the last to arrive. Uniformed men hustled back and forth from the house to their vehicles. Each doing his job, focused on a specific task. At the base of the driveway, a rookie manned the crime scene log, recording every person who set foot on the scene.

Standing on the sidewalk next to his SUV, Matt had never felt like more of an outsider.

Grey's Hollow Chief Deputy Todd Harvey approached. Before the shooting, Matt had worked with Todd for years and was 80 percent sure he was trustworthy. Todd stopped in front of Matt and crouched to pet the dog. "How's retirement, Brody?"

Brody leaned in for a scratch behind the ear. With a final pat, Todd straightened. "How long have you known Justin?"

"We went to grade school together."

"You knew the victim too?"

Matt nodded. "But not as well."

"Since he lives here, and her address is a rural route outside town, can I assume they were separated?"

"Yes." Matt took a deep breath. The facts were the facts. "Justin and Erin married four years ago. I was the best man in their wedding."

"Did they have any kids?"

"She has two, but they aren't Justin's." Matt's stomach cramped with pity.

Todd scraped a hand across his jaw. "Shit."

Yeah. Shit.

Grief choked Matt as he pictured the children.

"How old are they?" Todd asked.

Matt cleared his throat. "Luke is in high school. Kayla is still in grade school."

Todd pulled a small notepad from his pocket. "I'll loop in social services. I also have to notify next of kin. Do you know who that might be?"

"Erin's parents are dead." Matt remembered Erin's family from the wedding. The story of her parents' deaths stuck with him. "She has a brother and a sister. The sister lives in Philadelphia, but the brother is local. Erin kept her maiden name, so you should be able to find him."

Todd made a note. "How long has Justin lived here?"

"Four months, since his second DWAI." Matt suppressed a pang of guilt. Todd would already have Justin's record, but Matt still felt disloyal giving him the information.

"Was their breakup volatile?" Todd was definitely focused on Justin as a suspect. The spouse was always on the list, but a good detective didn't go into an investigation with any preconceived notions that could influence how he viewed the scene and evidence. Then again, most of Todd's experience was as a patrol officer and supervisor. He'd never been an investigator. How many murders had he handled?

"No." Matt shook his head. "Erin didn't want the drugs in the house with her kids. He didn't blame her."

"So, he wasn't angry at all after his wife kicked him out of his house?" Todd sounded incredulous.

"It's her house, not his."

Todd pressed his lips together. "Do you know why she was here this evening?"

"No." Matt's gut twisted. "I talked to Justin yesterday. He didn't mention it."

"OK." Todd turned as the medical examiner gestured from the doorway of the house. "I need to get back to it. I'll probably be here all night. I need you to come to the station in the morning and sign a statement."

"Sure." Matt's fingers stroked Brody's head. The dog leaned against his legs, his weight nearly buckling Matt's knees. He leaned into the dog to counter the pressure.

Todd turned away. Matt pictured the scene. Questions about Erin's presence ran through his head. What had she been doing there?

"Did you find her cell phone?" Matt called after him.

Todd walked away without answering. Would he shut Matt out of the case?

Matt looked down at Brody. As usual, the shepherd's brown eyes looked right through him. Brody whined again.

"I know. I'm worried about Justin too."

As a friend, he worried that Justin could be in serious trouble. As a former investigator, he knew that Justin would be a primary suspect, and as a former deputy, he worried about the chief deputy's lack of investigative experience and Matt's 20 percent uncertainty about his honesty.

With or without the chief deputy's cooperation, Matt would find out what had happened.

Chapter Four

He lathered his hands and arms to the elbow, then rinsed thoroughly and repeated the process twice more. He'd worn gloves, but he didn't want to take any chance that blood, gunshot residue, or other trace evidence clung to his skin.

When he was finished, he dried his hands on a paper towel and tossed it in the trash. Flecks and streaks of dried blood spotted the front of his pants and his shirt cuffs. He stripped off his clothes and stuffed them in a paper grocery bag.

He hadn't realized there would be so much blood.

That sounded stupid. Of course a bullet wound bled. But the amount had surprised him. Blood had poured out of her, forming a puddle. It had expanded rapidly under her body, spreading across the pale carpet in a thick pool, like he'd spilled a full gallon of red paint. And the smell—metallic, like coins, blended with the scent of gunpowder, resulting in an odor that was pungent and nauseating.

The whole experience hadn't been what he'd expected.

But it was done. She'd been an obstacle, and he'd removed her. In that way, her death had been her own stubborn fault. She'd known exactly what she was doing. He'd warned her multiple times, but she'd refused to listen. Instead, *she'd* threatened *him*.

As he remembered her disrespect, fresh rage boiled inside him.

Yeah, she'd gotten exactly what she'd deserved.

She'd brought this on herself. All she'd had to do was shut her fucking mouth and do what she was told. But no. She'd thought she was better than him.

And now she was dead.

She'd be silent forever.

He showered, lathering and rinsing his body multiple times. He'd taken precautions. There was little chance of him carrying evidence on his body. But he couldn't stop himself. He scrubbed his skin until it was raw, as if washing his body cleansed his soul. Then he dressed. He cleaned the soles of the boots with oxygen bleach. He'd drive a few towns over and drop them in a donation bin the next day.

He grabbed his bag of clothes and the jacket he'd worn and went outside. The yard was empty, and the cold night air already smelled of smoke. In living rooms nearby, people sat in front of fireplaces and enjoyed the warmth of cozy fires.

His fire would be less cozy and more of a pyre.

He dumped his clothes in a barrel used to burn leaves and other natural debris. He added paper and set the pile on fire. The fabrics were mostly cotton blends and burned well.

The flames consumed their fuel and died down. He added some dried wood and let the fire burn until embers turned to ash. As the orange glow died out, the anger in his heart cooled.

It was over.

Nothing stood in his way. Now he could have what was his by right. The life he'd worked hard for. The life he deserved.

No one else had better get in his way.

Chapter Five

Bree exited the interstate. A few minutes later, she passed the sign welcoming her to Grey's Hollow and fished a roll of antacids from the console.

As usual, being in her hometown felt surreal and slightly nauseating.

After her sister's call, Bree had finished her reports so she would have the next two days off. She'd arranged for a neighbor to feed her cat, packed a bag, and headed north at two in the morning. She'd driven on autopilot for five hours. As she neared Grey's Hollow, the familiar scenery dragged her back to the childhood she'd worked so hard to forget.

She'd tried her sister's number several times. Every time, Erin's number switched to voice mail, and the knot in Bree's belly tightened. On the bright side, anxiety kept her from falling asleep.

She sipped her cold coffee. Her sister lived on ten acres in upstate New York. Erin had wanted her kids to have room to run and raise animals if they wanted, all the things she'd perceived as stolen from her own life after their parents' deaths.

Perception was everything. Bree had lost all those things as well, but she wanted nothing that reminded her of her childhood. But then, she was older and had clearer memories than her sister or brother. Erin could recall only snatches of their life before, and she denied remembering anything about the horrible night that had destroyed their family. Adam had been an infant. He had no memories of their parents at all.

Bree followed the GPS directions. She'd visited her sister's place only a couple of times. She spotted the mailbox, which looked like a black-and-white cow, and turned into the driveway. A layer of snow and ice covered the rutted dirt and gravel. Behind the house sat a small red barn. Barbed wire enclosed the pasture. The last time she'd been here, it had been summer. Everything had been green. Flowers and horses had dotted the grass. It had been peaceful and lovely. Now the icy scene was bleak and lonely.

And there were two sheriff's department vehicles parked in the driveway.

Bree stared, the coffee in her mouth turning sour. Disbelief flooded her. She didn't want to think about the possible reasons.

She pressed the gas pedal. Her Honda bounced and slid all the way up to the house. Bree got out of the car and walked up the wooden steps onto the porch. The front door was closed, and she shielded her eyes to stare through the glass panes in the door. There was no one in sight.

She hadn't buttoned her coat, but fear numbed her to the temperature. The sheriff would not be searching Erin's house unless a major crime had been committed. Her gaze was drawn to the porch swing her sister had installed herself. Snow covered the wooden seat, and ice-coated chains suspended it from the ceiling. The chains squeaked as it swayed in the wind, the pitch of the metallic sound grating on Bree's nerves.

She heard movement inside the house. Bree tried the knob, and the door opened. Erin's place was small for a farmhouse. But Erin had fallen in love with the wraparound front porch and the picturesque barn. She used words like *cozy* and *homey*.

"Hello?" Bree called out from the doorway, not wanting to surprise the deputies or intrude on the scene. But she scanned everything she could see. The front door opened into a large wood-floored living room. On one side, a set of french doors led into an office. The stairwell ran up the far wall, and a hallway led to the kitchen at the back of the house.

Boots stomped on the stairs, and a uniformed deputy descended. Stepping out onto the porch, he motioned Bree to move backward.

He touched his hat. "Ma'am, can I help you?"

Bree showed her badge. "This is my sister's house. Why are you here?"

"I'm sorry, ma'am," he said in a measured voice. "You'll have to ask the chief deputy."

"Is he here?"

"No, ma'am."

"Where are my sister and her children?" Bree asked.

The deputy repeated, "You'll have to ask the chief deputy."

"Has Erin been arrested?"

The deputy deadpanned.

"I know. I'll have to ask the chief deputy. Where can I find him?"

"At the sheriff's station."

Bree turned and scanned the property, her nerves gnawing a hole in her gut.

Why are two deputies searching Erin's house?

The thought of her sister committing a crime was ludicrous. Erin was as Goody Two-shoes as a person could be. But something had happened.

Bree followed the porch around to the back door. Cupping her hands around her eyes, she looked through the windows. The entire back of the house was kitchen. At seven thirty in the morning, Erin should be drinking coffee and getting the kids ready for school, but the kitchen was empty. A hallway led to the front of the house. At the end of the hall, Bree could see lights and a deputy moving around in the living room. Other than the intrusion of the deputies, the house looked normal, with nothing to indicate a physical altercation had occurred.

Who else could Bree call? When Bree had seen them over the summer, eight-year-old Kayla hadn't had a phone, but Luke had been bent over his most of the trip.

If you were a better sister and aunt, you'd know your nephew's number.
But Bree wasn't, and she didn't. She saw Erin and the kids once a year when *they* visited *her*. She hadn't been able to put aside her own issues to see them in Grey's Hollow.

Her boots thudded on the porch as she walked back to the front of the house. The deputy had gone back inside. With ten acres of land, Erin had no neighbors in sight. The closest house was a half mile down the road. Bree pulled out her phone and called her brother again. Her call switched to voice mail, and she left him another message. Adam not responding didn't alarm her. He often neglected to charge his phone. He was an artist. If his creativity was on, he might disconnect for days. He had a habit of taking off for weeks at a time to paint. He might not even be in town.

There was only one way she could get immediate answers. With one last glance at the closed front door, Bree slid back into her car and drove toward the sheriff's station. The town of Grey's Hollow was too small to fund their own police department and relied on the county sheriff for law enforcement.

The dread in her chest expanded until it constricted her lungs. She would not breathe easily again until she saw her sister and the kids with her own eyes.

At seven forty-five, the day was brightening, but the overcast sky clouded the sunrise. Bree turned into the entrance of the Randolph County Sheriff's Station in Grey's Hollow. She stepped out of her car, gave two reporters delivering live updates a wide berth, and walked into the squat, brown brick building. Looping the strap of her small crossbody purse over her head, Bree approached the counter separating the lobby from the front office. Two men in suits conferred on one side of the lobby.

More reporters?

Something was definitely going on.

An older woman in a heavy cardigan greeted her. "Can I help you?"

Bree said, "I'd like to speak with the sheriff."

Forget the chief deputy. She'd go to the top.

The woman took off her reading glasses. "Regarding?"

Bree swallowed, lowered her voice so no one but the woman would hear, and watched for a response. "Erin Taggert."

Recognition lit the woman's face. She knew Erin's name. Bree's belly cramped.

This was not good. Not good at all.

"Your name and agency?" the woman asked. The woman correctly assumed Bree was a cop, which Bree would totally take advantage of.

"Bree Taggert." She pulled her badge from her pocket. "Philadelphia homicide."

The woman clearly noticed that Bree's last name matched Erin's. Something that felt uncomfortably like pity crossed the woman's face, but she quickly wiped it away. "Wait here, please, Detective." She turned and walked down a hallway.

The door behind Bree opened, and a man entered, a German shepherd at his side. The man moved like a cop, but Bree's attention fixed on the dog. *A K-9 team?*

Bree's anxiety grew. She'd been waiting all night for answers but now dreaded getting them. The dog's presence wasn't helping. She moved to the end of the counter, as far away from it as she could get. With some distance between them, Bree breathed a little easier. Her attention shifted to the man. In his midthirties, he was six three, a lean two hundred pounds, and broad shouldered. With piercing blue eyes, reddish-brown hair, and a couple days of stubble on his heavy jaw, he reminded her of a Viking. He was also familiar. She knew him from somewhere. She met his eyes, and he recognized her too.

They had definitely met before, but where?

Nerves had short-circuited her brain.

He opened his mouth, but before he could speak, the woman returned. "Detective, you can come on back." She ushered Bree to an open door marked with the word SHERIFF. Bree barely noticed several uniformed deputies working on computers as she passed their desks. "Chief Deputy Harvey is acting sheriff. We don't have an actual sheriff at the moment."

Bree hesitated at the threshold. She knew instinctively that once she crossed it, her life would never be the same.

A man around thirty sat behind a huge desk. He rose as she entered, shook her hand, and gestured toward a guest chair. "I'm Chief Deputy Harvey."

They both sat. His chair was as jumbo-sized as the desk, and he seemed lost in it.

"My name is Bree Taggert." Bree pulled out her badge again. "Philadelphia homicide."

"Are you related to Erin Taggert?" He leaned an elbow on the arm of his chair.

"She's my sister." Bree pulled her hand into her lap, her fingers curling around her badge until her knuckles turned white. She told him about Erin's message the previous night and finding the deputies searching the house this morning.

"I'm afraid I have some bad news for you. Your sister was killed last night. I'm sorry for your loss."

The news fell over Bree like frost. Her body went cold, her brain numb. For a full minute, she just sat there, staring at the chief deputy. His mouth was moving, but she heard no words, as if her head was full of static.

He got up and walked around the corner of the desk to crouch in front of her. "Ms. Taggert?" He raised his voice. "Are you all right?"

Bree startled as her hearing returned in a rush of sounds and sensations. "Yes. I'm sorry. I, um . . ."

She didn't know what to say or do. Her mind felt like a vacuum. *Erin is dead?*

It didn't seem possible. The deputy left the office for a minute and returned with a bottle of water. After twisting off the cap, he handed her the bottle. She took it but didn't drink. Her throat was so dry that she was afraid she'd choke.

"Are you sure it's my sister?" Bree's voice was barely audible.

"Yes. The medical examiner has positively identified her." He perched on the corner of his desk.

"Where are the children?"

"With your brother."

Who hadn't answered his phone all night. Bree suppressed a flash of anger. She had no right to be upset with Adam. He'd been with the kids when they'd needed him. Bree had been hundreds of miles away. Besides, Adam was distracted on a good day. He'd had his hands full last night.

"What have the children been told?" she asked.

"Last night, I told them their mother had been killed." His face creased with sadness. "I didn't give them any details."

Bree closed her eyes for one full breath as she reeled in her sorrow. When she opened them, her words grated against her vocal cords. "I want to see her."

"Of course. I'll find out when the medical examiner will release the body. Do you have a funeral home in mind?"

Bree flinched at the word *body*. Of course there would be an autopsy. "I want to see her ASAP."

He leaned back and crossed his arms over his chest. "I'll give you the ME's number."

"Thank you." She shook her head, not in response to his statement, but to clear it. "How did my sister die?"

"She was shot."

"Where and when?"

"At her husband's house. Can you tell me why they were separated?"

"He had a drug problem." Bree absorbed his answers. "Where is Justin?"

"We don't know."

What does that mean?

Did Erin's husband kill her, like their father had killed their mother? Emotions clawed for a hold. Bree's compartmentalizing skills were failing her. She latched on to her anger for stability. "Why was she at Justin's place, and who found her body?"

The chief deputy returned to his chair, putting some distance between them. He leaned his elbows on the desk and considered her for a few seconds. "Her body was found by a friend of Justin's. We don't know why she was there."

The man with the dog she'd seen in the lobby flashed into her head, and she remembered him from the wedding. He'd been Justin's best man. Matt. Matt Flynn.

The chief deputy said, "Look, Ms. Taggert—"

"Detective Taggert," Bree reminded him.

"Detective Taggert," he corrected. "I know you're upset. But this is not your jurisdiction, and I can't allow a member of the victim's family to be part of this investigation."

"But you can give me the consideration of keeping me informed." Bree's words sounded cold, and she clung to the icy feeling in her gut. When it thawed, the pain would break through, and she wanted no part of it.

The chief deputy nodded, but his eyes narrowed. "Here are the facts I can share. Your sister was shot inside the home of her estranged husband, Justin Moore, yesterday evening between seven thirty and eight thirty."

Bree knew there were other questions she should be asking, but her mind felt sluggish with shock.

"Do you have any other suspects?" she asked.

"We are just beginning our investigation." The chief deputy shifted forward. "When was the last time you saw your sister?"

"She and the kids came to Philly in August, and we spoke on the phone once or twice a month." Which now seemed so . . . inadequate.

Grief bubbled in Bree's throat. She swallowed it.

Not yet.

Keep it together.

But her control felt as weak as a single silk thread.

"What about Erin's pickup truck?" Her sister had driven a white farm truck, an older model F-150. Bree hadn't seen it at the house.

"I put a BOLO alert out on the vehicle," the chief deputy said.

"Do you think he's driving it?"

"It's a reasonable theory. It's her only vehicle. Now it's missing and so is he."

Bree thought if Justin had killed Erin and driven off in her truck, he would have dumped it by now. Anyone with two brain cells would assume law enforcement was searching for the vehicle.

"I assure you that we are looking at all of the evidence," the chief deputy said. "I will share more information when I am able." His chair squeaked as he shifted his weight back, signaling that he was finished. "I'm going to have more questions for you. I'll need your contact information."

Bree gave him her cell number. She was going to have more questions for him too, once she got her act together.

"Where are you staying?" he asked.

"I don't know yet," Bree said. "When will Erin's house be released?"

"I'll let you know. Hopefully, the deputies will finish searching it today, but I make no guarantees. I don't know what they'll find."

But Bree already knew he wasn't a hands-on investigator. If this were her case, she would be searching the victim's house herself, and not only to find physical evidence. A detective could learn a lot about a person by studying their personal space. She kept her criticism to herself. Ripping apart his investigative procedures would not make him more cooperative.

"The horses will need to be fed and watered this evening," she pointed out.

"Yes. If we aren't finished with the house, one of my deputies will take care of it. Same one who saw to them this morning."

"Thank you." Bree stood too quickly. The blood drained from her head, making her light-headed. She braced herself with one hand on the arm of the chair for a few seconds.

"You don't have any idea what kind of trouble your sister was in?" the chief deputy asked.

Bree shook her head. "Erin didn't get into trouble."

But as she said the words, she knew they couldn't possibly be true.

Chapter Six

Matt watched Bree Taggert bolt from the station. Her face was as pale as the ice on the sidewalk, and she was moving like the building was on fire.

Or she was trying to get as far away as possible from the news of her sister's death.

Empathy swelled in Matt. He knew her history. Bree had lost both her parents in a horrific tragedy. Now her sister had suffered the same fate.

Matt had remembered Bree instantly. She had an interesting face, lean and serious, with hazel eyes that seemed to shift between green and amber according to her mood.

Had she recognized him? She'd moved as far away as possible when he'd walked into the lobby. He thought back to the wedding. At the time, he'd thought the attraction between them had been mutual, but maybe he'd been wrong.

Behind the counter, Marge Lancaster waved a dog biscuit. "Who has a treat for Brody?"

Brody drooled and turned to Matt.

Matt led the dog behind the reception counter. "Go ahead." Marge was going to give Brody the treat no matter what Matt said. She generally did as she liked. The chief deputy might be acting sheriff, but Marge ran the show.

She held out the biscuit.

"Setzen," Matt commanded.

Brody sat and took the treat gently from her hand.

"What a pretty boy you are." Marge stroked his head. The dog's tail thumped on the floor as if he knew Marge was flattering him.

Matt shook his head. "You spoil him, Marge."

"Like you don't." She arched a penciled-on eyebrow. "Not that it matters. He earned it."

"Yes, he did." Matt would be dead if it weren't for Brody. Still, Matt was diligent about keeping up with the dog's basic obedience. A ninety-pound canine needed manners.

"Hier." Matt headed for Todd's door. Brody fell into step beside him, but he stopped at every desk to say hello. Since his retirement, he'd turned into a freaking ambassador.

Inside the chief deputy's office, Matt jerked a thumb at the closed door. "That was Erin's sister, right?"

"Yes." Todd rubbed a hand down the center of his face. He'd shaved and put on a fresh uniform, but the long night had left shadows under his eyes. "She didn't know her sister is dead."

"How did she take the news?" Matt took a seat facing the chief deputy. Brody lay next to his chair, resting his head on Matt's foot.

Todd frowned. "I don't think she's fully processed it yet."

"I'll bet she hasn't."

"How well do you know her?" Todd asked.

"Not well. We met during Justin and Erin's wedding." But both of them had gone to the wedding solo. They'd been seated together. They'd talked. They'd danced.

Todd flattened his palm on a closed folder in the center of his blotter. "She's a homicide detective with the Philly PD."

Matt had been an investigator back then too. They'd had a lot in common. If she hadn't run out of town the day after the wedding, Matt would have called her. But then, considering her reaction to him today, maybe it had been for the best they hadn't seen each other again.

"She's going to be a pain in my ass." Todd tapped on the folder.

"So am I," Matt said.

Todd sighed. "I'll tell you the same thing I told her. You are too close to the case. You have a relationship with the primary suspect. I cannot let you take part in the investigation, but I will keep you as informed as possible."

"So, Justin *is* the primary suspect," Matt said.

Regret creased Todd's face. "I shouldn't have said that."

"It's not a huge revelation. The husband is always a suspect, and Justin is missing. Do you have any other suspects?"

"I can't answer that."

So, that's a no.

"Have you considered—"

"Matt," Todd cut him off. "You're not a deputy anymore."

Matt breathed. Frustration and anger rose in his chest. Todd was going into the investigation assuming Justin was guilty, not to find the truth.

Todd sighed. "I'll tell you what will be in this morning's press release." He consulted a paper on his desk. "The bullet that killed Erin Taggert was a 9mm. Justin's father is missing a Sig Sauer P226 9mm handgun."

Damn.

Justin had been convicted of a felony. He couldn't legally possess a weapon. If he'd wanted one, he would have needed to find another way.

"Mr. Moore didn't know it was missing until we talked to him," Todd continued. "He kept it in his nightstand. It's possible Justin stole it from his father. Did he say anything to you about a weapon?"

"No."

Todd frowned. "Do you know Erin's family's history?"

"Yes."

"The case is already getting media attention. They're calling it the Déjà vu Murder."

"Then the press has decided Justin is guilty."

"I can't control the media," Todd said.

"But you could at least say that you have other lines of investigation."

Todd's gaze went flat. "I'll be issuing a press release later this morning. At this point, I don't have any other theories. The fact is that Justin's soon-to-be ex-wife was shot in his house, and there are no signs of forced entry."

"I can't believe Justin would kill anyone, let alone Erin."

What if Justin was also dead? What if he'd been kidnapped by Erin's killer? What if she'd been killed because of something Justin had done, like owed money to a drug dealer? He'd purchased his oxy from someone. Had she walked in on a drug deal?

Matt didn't express his alternative theories, which all involved Justin still using drugs and would not imply he was innocent.

"You have to admit the cases are eerily similar," Todd said.

"Erin's parents died twentysomething years ago," Matt said. "I highly doubt there's any connection."

"No." Todd looked toward his window. The shade was down, blocking the view and most of the light. "You're right. The similarities are *probably* coincidence."

Matt suppressed his frustration. Todd was going into this investigation with a preconceived theory, which would influence how he viewed the evidence. It happened even to experienced investigators.

Todd bowed his head and pinched the bridge of his nose. When he lifted his head, he handed over the folder. "Please read your statement. I need to get back to work."

Matt reviewed and signed the statement Todd had prepared from the previous night's interview. He put his hands on the arms of the chair, ready to rise.

"You know," Todd said in a quiet voice, "I was surprised when the sheriff made me chief deputy. The job should have been yours. You had more experience."

Matt hesitated, surprised at the admission.

Despite his exemplary record, instead of being promoted, Matt had been given a K-9 and put back on patrol. The sheriff had acted as if the reassignment had been an honor. Brody had been Randolph County's first dog. But Matt knew the job had really been a demotion. The old sheriff hadn't wanted Matt around. He'd wanted him back in the field.

Back in the line of fire.

Stop!

Matt had no proof the sheriff had been out to get him, and every time his mind went off on the conspiracy theory, he felt like he needed to wear an aluminum foil hat.

He lifted a shoulder. "Considering how things worked out, it doesn't really matter now."

"No hard feelings then?"

"No." Matt's old grudge was reserved for the dead sheriff. But if Todd fucked up this case, Matt would hold *that* against him.

"I'll call when I have more questions for you."

"Sure." Matt pushed out of the chair. Brody followed him from the room. Marge was busy helping someone in the lobby, so they didn't stop to say goodbye. Matt pushed out of the station and walked toward his Suburban. The wind blew ice dust across the parking lot. He spotted Bree Taggert leaning against the door of a Honda Accord. He stopped a few feet away. Her face was still pale, her eyes lost, and she was shivering. She wore jeans and a black hip-length coat but no hat, gloves, or scarf.

"I'd like to talk to you," she said. Her lips were slightly bluish. Had she been standing out here the entire time he'd been in Todd's office? He glanced at the building. Two reporters exited the station and headed for news vans parked on the other side of the lot.

"Let's get out of the cold." Matt gestured toward his vehicle.

Her gaze kept dropping to Brody. "Can we meet somewhere?"

"The diner?" he suggested.

"Too public."

"Are you OK to drive?"

"Yes."

"Then follow me." Matt turned and opened the rear door of his Suburban. Brody jumped into the vehicle. Then Matt slid behind the wheel. His house was ten minutes from the station. He drove with one eye on the rearview mirror, making sure her Honda stayed behind him.

He lived in a restored farmhouse on twenty-five acres. He pulled into his driveway and parked. Behind his house, barking sounded from the kennels. Matt and Brody climbed out of the SUV and walked to the front door. Bree parked next to his vehicle and followed. She kept her distance. Inside the house, Matt led her back to the kitchen and sent Brody to his crate.

Brody trotted across the tile and disappeared into the bedroom.

"You don't have to cage your dog," she said.

"It's fine. Brody doesn't mind his crate. It's his den, not a punishment." Though Matt hadn't used it often since the dog retired, but he sensed the dog made her nervous.

She walked a circle around his kitchen.

Matt started a pot of coffee. "Have you eaten?"

"I'm not hungry, but I'd appreciate some coffee." She stripped off her wool coat and hung it on the back of a chair, along with a slim purse. Standing at the french doors that overlooked the backyard, with its kennel and dog runs, she rubbed her arms. "How many dogs do you have?"

"There are six in the kennel, but only Brody belongs to me." Matt came to stand beside her. "When I built the kennels, my goal was to train K-9s. Before I could get the business going, my sister filled the kennel. She runs a dog rescue organization." He handed her a mug.

She wrapped both hands around it. "Thank you."

"You don't like dogs?" he asked, glancing sideways.

Her brows drew together.

"I was bitten as a child." She clamped her mouth shut as if embarrassed by the admission, but he could tell there was more to the story. She stared down at her coffee. "The deputy said you found my sister."

"Yes. I'm so sorry."

She nodded, a short choke sounding deep in her throat. She swallowed. "Can you tell me about it?"

"I was supposed to drive Justin to his NA meeting. He didn't answer the door, so I went in. I found her on the bedroom floor." Matt didn't give details. She'd ask when she was ready to hear them.

She shuddered and closed her eyes for a few seconds. When she opened them, she'd composed herself. "But Justin wasn't there?"

"No," Matt said. Did she think he'd helped Justin get away?

"Why was Erin at his house? And where is Justin?"

"I don't know." Matt pictured the scene.

Bree's eyes narrowed. "That makes no sense."

He shrugged.

She was quiet for a few minutes. "You're no longer with the sheriff's department?"

"No. Brody and I were shot three years ago."

"I'm sorry to hear that." She gave him a sympathetic look. "What do you do now?"

"It was friendly fire, so there was a settlement. We won't starve." Matt flexed his hand. The pink scar in the center of his palm stretched as he opened his fist. He'd taken a bullet in the back too. Ironically, that one hadn't hit anything vital. The nerve damage in his hand was permanent. "I can't shoot with my right at all. Unfortunately, it's my dominant hand. No more law enforcement for me."

Overshare.

He cleared his throat. "Is there anything I can do for you?"

She shook her head. "I called the ME's office. They'll call me when I can see Erin." Her voice faltered. She looked away, her eyes troubled.

"Let me go with you," he offered. "No one should have to do that alone."

She glanced up at him. For a minute, he thought she was going to turn him down.

"Thank you. I'd appreciate that." She took a long, shaky breath. "I haven't seen the kids yet. I don't know what to say to them."

"All you can do is be there," he said.

"On that note, I should go." She turned and set her mug on the kitchen island. Pivoting to face him again, she said, "What's going on with the sheriff's department and this chief deputy?"

"They haven't had a sheriff for some time. The previous one was corrupt and committed suicide. Since then, the department has lost half its deputies."

"Chief Deputy Harvey didn't run for office?"

"No," Matt said. "He doesn't want the job. So far, neither does anyone else. The whole department needs to be rebuilt."

"Do you have any faith in his ability to solve my sister's murder?"

Matt was honest. "I don't know. I think he'll try, but he doesn't have much investigative experience."

She met his eyes. "Do you think Justin did it?"

"No," Matt said with no hesitation. "He isn't the violent or abusive type."

"Addicts can be unpredictable."

"Justin took all the responsibility for their separation. He was determined to stay sober and win Erin back." Matt paused. "He still loved her."

"The evidence against him is strong."

"I know."

Bree pressed a knuckle to her mouth for a moment. Lowering her hand, she straightened her shoulders. "I'm going to find the truth, with or without the chief deputy."

"I want to find Justin. I don't think he killed Erin." Matt could think of no scenario in which Justin would harm his wife—or anyone else. Justin's nature was not violent.

"The significant other is always the primary suspect. Statistically, there's a good chance he's guilty," she challenged. "My father killed my mother."

"I know," Matt agreed. "But Justin isn't your father, and Erin wasn't your mother."

"You're right." She lifted her coat from the back of the kitchen chair. "But the facts remain the same, and Justin looks damned guilty."

He blocked her path to the door.

Irritation crossed her face and one eyebrow arched.

"Do you *want* him to be guilty?" he asked.

She exhaled and met his gaze. The thing he'd liked best about her was her no-bullshit attitude. She did not play games.

"No," she said. "The kids already lost their mom. Knowing their stepdad killed her would make matters even worse for them."

He'd expected her to be honest and direct, but her answer surprised him. "I'm not sure the chief deputy will look for other suspects."

"He won't find what he isn't looking for," Bree finished.

"I think we should work together." He held up a hand. "Let me explain. You would put Justin at the top of your suspect list. I'd put him at the bottom. We both want to solve your sister's murder. You know your sister and your family. I've known Justin since grade school, and I have the local connections."

Plus, he had absolutely no doubt Bree would be working the case, and he didn't like the idea of her chasing a killer alone. She could be the best homicide detective in the world, but she needed someone to watch her back. As did Matt. She was also smart and, he suspected, very good at her job.

She squinted at him. "You want to find Justin before the sheriff's department does. Are you afraid they'll shoot him?"

They shot me, so yeah.

But he chose his words carefully. "I want to know the truth."

Her lips pursed. "So, our goal is the same, but our motivations conflict."

"Yes. We balance each other, and our chances of success are better if we put our heads together."

She snorted. "That makes sense in a weird way."

"So, you'll work with me?"

"I'll think about it."

"Fair enough," Matt said. "Take my number."

Bree pulled her phone from her pocket and entered the numbers as Matt gave them to her. A second later, his phone vibrated in his pocket. He glanced at the screen. She'd sent him a text.

"Let me know when you're ready to go to the ME's office," he said.

Her eyes misted. "I will."

Their eyes met for a few seconds. Was she thinking that the ME was probably conducting an autopsy on her sister at that moment? As a detective, she knew what all that procedure entailed.

Her chin came up, and she blinked to clear her eyes of any unshed tears. No. Matt knew she wouldn't allow herself to wallow in the negative. She'd focus on finding who had killed her sister.

CHAPTER SEVEN

Bree didn't remember the drive to her brother's place. Her mind was on her discussion with Matt. But suddenly her Honda was bouncing down the dirt road that led to the converted barn Adam had lived in ever since he'd barely graduated high school. He was one of the smartest people she knew, but his intelligence wasn't conventional, and he'd despised school. His graduation was one of the rare life events that had pulled Bree back to Grey's Hollow.

The barn sat in the middle of a large, snow-covered meadow. Adam's ancient Ford Bronco was parked out front. The lane had not been plowed, and Bree crossed her fingers that her car wouldn't get stuck. She made it to the end, parked, and climbed out into the cold. There were no trees to break the wind, and it whipped snow dust across the emptiness. For a couple of seconds, she turned her face into a freezing gust, wishing it would numb her emotions as well as her skin.

What would she say to them? How were the kids handling their grief? How could she support them when she couldn't even handle her own emotions?

The front door opened, and a tall, gangly figure stood in the doorway. At first, Bree thought it was her brother. But he stepped outside, and the light fell on his face. It was her fifteen-year-old nephew, Luke, who appeared to have grown several inches since she'd seen him in August. He suddenly looked more like a man than a boy.

His body might be maturing, but his eyes were all lost-child. Bree walked toward him without thinking. Her arms went around him. His body shook as she held him.

"Who is it?" a small voice asked.

Luke was taller than Bree now, and she had to move her head to see her niece. Kayla's eyes were red and swollen, her face pale and blotchy. Bree opened one arm to include her in the embrace. The three of them stood in the doorway, with Bree blocking the wind.

When she pulled away, her face was wet. She wiped her cheeks and scanned the kids. Physically, they seemed fine. The damage was only visible in their eyes. But she recognized the look as a reflection of her own pain, a sorrow that would never heal.

"Where's Uncle Adam?" Bree asked.

Luke jerked a thumb over his shoulder. "His studio."

Bree herded the kids inside. Snow had blown across the threshold. She kicked it outside with her foot and closed the door. The interior of Adam's place was one big room. A king-size bed stood in one corner, with a kitchen, sofa, and TV on the opposite side of the space. A partial wall separated his studio from his living quarters.

Pizza boxes, clothes, and art supplies littered every surface. Bree rated the disaster as a Category 4, which meant Adam was in the final stages of a painting. In the next day or two, the debris would spread to the floor. When he was finished, he'd do nothing but eat and sleep for a week before shoveling out the chaos and beginning all over again.

Dropping her coat on the back of the sofa, she walked to the studio and peered around the partition. Light poured from a picture window onto a huge canvas. Adam squinted at it. He was twenty-eight, but his face was lean and unlined. He could pass for a college student—until you looked into his eyes. Those were old-soul.

He wore ripped jeans and a paint-splattered sweatshirt from the University of Pennsylvania, Bree's alma mater. His hair was shoulder-length and streaked with gray paint. His brush was loaded with gray as well, and he applied it in broad, possessed strokes to a canvas the size of a classroom chalkboard. Bree studied the painting. It was abstract, but she could see the transition. Bold blues and angry reds swirled violently in the background. But the top layer had gone gray. It was fury and sadness, layered in pain. Without asking, she knew the gray had taken over during the night, after he'd learned of Erin's death. Not that the underlying layers were anything approaching happy. His paintings never were. To Bree they'd always seemed as if terrible emotions were exploding on his canvases. Was this how Adam purged his demons?

He'd been an infant when their parents had died. He couldn't possibly remember. *Right?*

But holy hell, darkness was a part of him so heavy she sometimes wondered how he shouldered the weight.

If she were naming this particular painting, she'd call it *Every Shade of Sorrow.*

"That sweatshirt is older than Luke," she said.

Adam didn't respond for a few seconds, then he turned his face toward her. His eyes echoed the emotions in the painting. For the Taggerts, tragedy was a family trait, carrying through the generations along with their brown hair and hazel eyes.

"Bree." He crossed the ten feet between them and hugged her hard. Releasing her, he held her at arm's length and frowned. "I got paint on your clothes."

Bree looked down. Gray splotched her sweater, as if his mood were transferrable. "I don't care."

She glanced over her shoulder. The kids had settled on the couch, where she assumed they had been before she'd arrived. Kayla was watching TV. Luke huddled over his phone.

Bree turned back to Adam. Red Bull cans lined the windowsill. "Have the kids eaten?"

Adam blinked and turned to the window for a few seconds, as if just realizing it was midmorning. "We had breakfast." He ran a hand over his scalp, then pushed his hair out of his eyes. "If you're hungry, there's leftover pizza in the fridge."

His gaze—and his attention—had already returned to his painting.

Bree rubbed his arm. He looked thin, but then he always lost weight when he was working. "You need to eat too."

"OK," he said absently.

She doubted he'd remembered what she'd said. He was in *eat and sleep only when unavoidable* mode. Leaving the studio, she went to the kitchen. More Red Bull cans cluttered the counter next to three empty pizza boxes and a box of Cheerios. The milk was sour, but miracle of miracles, she found eggs and cheese that hadn't expired. She scrambled them and took a plate to Adam. He set it on the windowsill, promising to eat. Bree grabbed a trash bag and cleaned the counter, then set plates on the breakfast bar for the kids.

What should she say to them?

Kayla picked at her food in silence. Luke shoveled the entire plateful down in less than two minutes. He washed it down with water and set the glass down. "When can we go home?"

"Hopefully, later today." Bree reached out and took one of Luke's hands and one of Kayla's. "I don't know what to do, but I want you to know I'm here for you."

Kayla began to cry. Bree rounded the breakfast bar and hugged her.

"I want Mom," Kayla sobbed.

"I know." Bree pressed her head to the child's.

The girl lifted her tear-streaked face. "Why did this happen?"

"I don't know, but I'm going to find out," Bree said.

"Last night, the deputies said Justin did it." Luke's words were tight.

"They told you that?" Bree asked, angry.

Luke shook his head. "No, but I heard them talking."

"No one knows what happened yet," Bree said. But Matt had been right about the deputies and their preconceived theories.

"But Mom was at his house, and he's gone." A muscle in Luke's face twitched, as if he was working hard to maintain control.

"What else did they say?" Bree asked.

"That's all." Luke shrugged. "But I want to know more."

And Bree wanted a few choice words with the deputies who'd talked about the case within earshot of the victim's kids.

"Justin is missing," Bree clarified as much as a reminder to herself as to inform the kids. "Until he's found, we don't know what happened."

Emotions churned in Luke's face. "But you'll tell me the truth?"

"I will," Bree promised. Luke was almost an adult. She would not treat him like a child.

She considered Justin and the odds that he'd killed Erin. Bree's own father had been a chameleon, friendly and amicable when outsiders were present, a bully with his family. Maybe Justin had the same ability to put up a pleasant facade. If so, the kids should have seen both sides of him. She doubted he could have hidden his true nature from the people who lived with him for four years.

"Did you like living with Justin?" Bree asked.

Kayla nodded.

Luke shrugged. "He's OK."

"I didn't want him to leave," Kayla sniffed. "He was nice to me. I miss him."

Bree remembered Justin as a seemingly even-tempered man. Erin hadn't wanted to make him move out, but she hadn't felt as if she'd had a choice. "Did you ever see him be mean to your mom?"

"Nope," Luke said.

"Did they fight?" Bree asked.

"Sometimes." Luke toyed with his fork. "But it was usually Mom yelling at Justin, and him saying he was sorry. He felt bad about the drugs. He wanted to stop. He just couldn't."

"Addiction changes a person," Bree said.

Luke didn't respond for a few seconds. "Justin was kind of a pain, always wanting to do stuff with me. But he was never nasty to me or anything."

Erin had said Justin tried too hard, and Luke had resented the pressure. Luke blew his hair out of his eyes, and Bree saw conflict in them. The teen had given Justin a hard time, and now he regretted it.

"Neither one of you were ever scared of him when he lived with you?" Bree asked.

Both kids shook their heads.

Kids had good instincts. As a child, she'd been terrified of her father. Maybe Matt was right about Justin too. Maybe he *was* innocent, and Bree couldn't separate her own past from the present. She might be as prejudiced as the chief deputy.

Bree's phone vibrated, and she glanced at the screen. Her heart dropped.

The medical examiner's office.

She pasted a bland expression on her face. "Excuse me. I need to answer this."

Swiping "Answer," Bree walked out the front door and closed it behind her. Thankfully, the morgue assistant didn't expect her to hold a conversation but simply told her the autopsy was complete and she could view her sister's body.

Bree hung up the phone. Nerves rattled inside her. Did she go solo or take Matt up on his offer? Nausea turned her stomach at the thought of going alone. It wasn't weakness. She wasn't a robot. Seeing her sister's body *should* disturb her. Her hands trembled as she texted him.

He texted back in a few seconds. Pick u up in 10.

As cold as she was outside without her coat, the last thing she wanted to do was go inside. Should she tell the kids? She wanted to be honest with them, but there were details they did not need to know.

She schooled her face and went inside. "I need to run a few errands."

"But you just got here," Kayla protested, her lip quivering.

"I know, and I'm sorry." She hugged her niece.

"I want to go home." Luke frowned at the studio. Adam had not emerged.

"Me too," Kayla said.

"Let me take care of some business, then I'll see about getting you home. I need you to hang here with Uncle Adam for a little while longer, OK?"

The kids nodded, but they looked disappointed.

"Luke, do you remember Justin's friend Matt Flynn?" Bree asked.

"Yeah," he said.

"I need to talk to Uncle Adam for a few minutes. If Matt comes to the door, would you let him in?"

"Sure." Luke nodded and bowed over his phone.

A news report interrupted Kayla's TV show. Bree saw her sister's photo and Justin's on the screen. Under the images, a headline read ESTRANGED HUSBAND WANTED IN WIFE'S DEATH. Kayla stared, her eyes wide open with horror.

"The Taggert family has a long history of violence and tragedy," the journalist began.

Rushing to grab the remote from the table, Bree pressed "Guide." A grid of channels replaced the news report. She tossed the remote to Luke. "Can you put a kids'-only channel on, please?"

"Sure," he said, but the pain in his eyes told her that the damage had been done.

Bree went into her brother's studio to let him know she'd be leaving for a while. Adam stared at his painting.

"Adam," Bree said.

"Yeah," he answered without looking at her.

"Look at me."

"What?" He blinked away from his work.

Bree sighed. "I have to go out. Keep the TV on channels that won't play the news and try to distract the kids."

"How do I do that?"

"Interact with them." Bree stopped, realizing her voice had sharpened. "Look, I know how you get when you're painting, but they need you. Not just to be in the same house, but to *be* there."

"OK. I get it." His eyes drifted back to the canvas. "I'll be finished with this section in a few minutes."

No, you won't.

Someone cleared his throat, and Bree turned to see Matt standing in the doorway.

"I'll be back as fast as I can," she said to her brother's back. She returned to the kids and put on her coat. "Lock the door after I leave."

She followed Matt outside and waited until she heard the deadbolt slide into place before she climbed into his SUV.

She could barely juggle the kids and their grief for a few hours. How would she help them get through Erin's funeral? And what would happen afterward? Bree put the future out of her mind. This afternoon was going to be hard enough. She was going to have to deal with one task at a time. Unable to converse, she stared out the passenger window as he drove.

The medical examiner's office was in the municipal complex, not far from the sheriff's station. The ride was short, and she was nowhere near ready when they arrived.

But she doubted it was possible to prepare to view her sister's body.

After climbing out of the SUV, she stood on the sidewalk for a few minutes, letting the chill sink into her bones.

Matt stepped out of his vehicle and stood next to her. "There's no rush. Take all the time you need."

Bree doubted an additional ten minutes would make any difference. "Let's go."

They went inside. Matt walked up to the reception counter and spoke to the woman behind it. Before Bree could blink, they were ushered into an office. It felt like time was speeding up, moving too quickly, out of her control.

An African American woman in clean black scrubs moved out from behind the desk. "I'm Dr. Serena Jones. I took care of your sister."

Matt did the introductions, but Bree's hearing sounded muffled.

Dr. Jones turned to face her. "You can see your sister on a monitor—"

"No." Bree cut her off.

"I didn't think you'd take that option, so I had your sister moved to a private room," Dr. Jones said as if Erin were her patient instead of a corpse. "This way."

The sense of impending doom grew heavier with each footstep down the tiled hallway. Bree kept her eyes on the back of Dr. Jones's shirt. They went into a small room. In the center of the space, a sheet-covered body occupied a gurney. Dr. Jones walked around to the opposite side of the gurney and faced Bree over her sister's body. Matt stayed at Bree's side.

The doctor waited until Bree lifted her eyes to hers and nodded. Then Dr. Jones folded back the sheet to reveal only Erin's face. She carefully smoothed the sheet above Erin's collarbones, covering the wound that had killed her and the autopsy incision. Either Dr. Jones or her assistant had taken care to arrange Erin's hair to cover the scalp incision.

Bree tried to block all the autopsies she'd witnessed. It served no purpose to imagine the insult that had been inflicted on her sister's body. Erin wasn't in there anymore. What lay on the table was just a shell. Organs had been removed and examined, then stuffed back into the body in a plastic bag. But as Bree stared down at her sister's face, it didn't feel as if that mattered. Erin's eyes were closed, her face waxen and gray. Her cheekbones were sunken and stood out in sharp relief, as if her body had deflated when her soul left it. Until that moment, her death had felt abstract. Now reality and grief struck Bree like a full-body blow.

Once, when Bree had been a patrol officer, she'd been shot in the ribs. Her body armor had absorbed the bullet, but the impact had knocked the air from her lungs. Her legs had folded like an accordion ruler. The sight of her sister's face felt like a similar punch.

Matt's hand under her elbow saved her from hitting the floor. She closed her eyes for a few seconds and breathed through her mouth. She appreciated that neither Matt nor the ME said a word until she'd regained her balance.

"I know that you're a homicide detective," Dr. Jones said in a soft, low voice. "I'll answer questions about your sister's death. But I want you to let yourself be a human being first."

As if Bree could have formed a coherent question.

She'd delivered death notifications. She'd escorted family members to the morgue. She'd held their hands during this exact instant. But the shock and power and overwhelming nature of the moment had been lost on her.

Until now.

Waves of grief, helplessness, and anger threatened to upend her balance again. Dr. Jones moved a chair from the corner and set it next to Bree.

Three breaths later, Bree recovered her voice, though it rasped as if she smoked two packs of cigarettes a day. "Tell me the truth. Did she go quickly?"

"Yes," Dr. Jones said without hesitation. "She was unconscious within seconds and gone within a minute or so."

She didn't specify how many seconds, but if she had suffered, it hadn't been for long. Bree thought of Erin lying on the floor, bleeding out, thinking of the children she'd never see again.

The kids would want to see her, and Bree would have to let them. As a child, she'd been denied the chance to say goodbye, and she still resented being shuttled to the side, being told to hush when she'd asked questions, being treated as if she were an afterthought rather than the focus of adult attention. She would not do that to Luke and Kayla. They could choose to see her or not.

"Could I have a moment alone with her?" she asked, glancing at the doctor, then Matt.

"Yes. Her body is ready to be released to the funeral home of your choice." Dr. Jones walked toward the door. "We'll be in the hall when you're finished."

"Take whatever time you need." Matt followed the doctor from the room.

Alone, Bree cupped her sister's cheek. The skin was cold, lifeless under her palm. Bree did not lift the sheet. She did not examine the wound. She gave her sister the respect she deserved.

"I'll do my best by the kids." Bree started with the thing that was most important to her sister, then added, "And I *will* find out who did this to you." She drew an *X* in the center of her own chest like they'd done when they were children. "Cross my heart."

CHAPTER EIGHT

Matt had never met the new medical examiner. She was a recent hire to replace the former pathologist, who'd moved to Wyoming.

He leaned on the wall next to the door.

"Can I get you some water?" Dr. Jones offered.

"No, thanks." Matt didn't think he could swallow anything without it coming right back up. He'd seen dead bodies as a sheriff's investigator, but he could still picture Erin alive and smiling.

And that made all the difference.

As an investigator, he'd tried his best to keep his personal life separate from his job. When you'd attended the victim's wedding, that wasn't possible.

The door opened, and Bree emerged. Her eyes were dry, devastated, and determined.

"Can I ask you some questions?" she asked the ME.

"Yes." Dr. Jones led them back to her office. Matt and Bree sat in chairs facing the desk. An autopsy was treated as confidentially as other medical records. As next of kin, Bree was entitled to the results, but the official report wouldn't be available for months.

"Are you sure you want to do this now?" Dr. Jones asked.

Bree nodded.

"All right." The doctor leaned forward, resting on her forearms and giving Bree her full attention.

"She was killed by a single gunshot?" Bree asked.

"Yes. She sustained a penetrating cardiac injury," Dr. Jones said. "Many gunshot wounds to the chest are survivable these days. Your sister was very unlucky. A 9mm bullet lacerated her coronary artery, causing massive hemorrhage. Blood loss would have been rapid."

Matt pictured the lake of blood under Erin. She had lived long enough for a large volume of it to pump out of her body.

"Is there anything else of note in the preliminary report?" Bree asked, her voice strained.

"No. Other than the bullet wound, she was in overall good health." The doctor frowned. "She had sex shortly before she died, but I found no evidence intercourse was not consensual. There were no significant bruises on the body. Her last meal was pizza, eaten an hour or two before her death."

Bree's face was as white and still as marble as she digested the information.

The ME set her clasped hands on her desk. "Why don't you go home and process today? Call me if you have more questions, and I'll call you if I get more information."

Results of some reports, like toxicology screens, wouldn't come back for weeks or months.

Bree nodded. "Thank you."

Her voice was flat, seemingly emotionless, but Matt could see her struggling. Her hazel eyes were misty, the green deepening as sorrow flooded them. She swiped a single tear from her cheek with a trembling finger, then shoved her shaking hands into her coat pockets. Matt couldn't imagine the shock, horror, and grief building in her. He felt like he was intruding on a moment that should be private. Her sister had been murdered, her life ended in a violent act. Bree should be allowed the space to cry in peace. In similar circumstances, Matt would be bawling.

The doctor ushered them to the door of her office. Matt followed Bree through the corridors until they emerged from the building. Outside, she stood on the sidewalk for a few seconds, her face turned to the cold wind. The open edges of her coat flapped, but she didn't seem to notice the freezing temperature.

Matt opened the passenger door of his SUV. Bree climbed into the seat. He rounded the front of the vehicle and slid behind the wheel. He started the engine.

She turned toward the passenger window. "Why was my sister at Justin's place?"

"I think your sister was there regularly." Matt adjusted the heat vents to give Bree maximum airflow and turned on the passenger seat heater as he pulled out of the lot. "I noticed a few things in Justin's bathroom while I was waiting for the deputies."

"Like?"

"There was an extra toothbrush, a woman's hairbrush, makeup, feminine hygiene products." Matt turned onto the main road.

Bree's brows knitted together. "Those could belong to any woman."

"This is true. You don't know which brands she used?"

Bree shook her head.

"Are you going to take the kids back to their house?" he asked, stopping at a traffic light.

"Yes. That's where they want to go."

"Then we can compare the brands in her bathroom to the ones in Justin's."

"Sounds like a good plan." But Bree sounded distracted and exhausted. Maybe she'd had enough for the day. She'd exhibited unbelievable strength that day, but how much could one person handle?

Matt drove to her brother's converted barn and parked.

She reached for the door handle. "Thank you for your help today."

"Anytime." Matt covered her hand and gave it a single, quick squeeze before releasing it. "I mean it. I can't imagine what you're going through."

Nor did he want to. He'd rather run into a hail of bullets than experience the kind of soul-deep loss Bree was handling.

Nodding, she opened her mouth to respond but seemed unable to get the words out. She swallowed, the motion taking time, as if she were eating a dry sandwich with no drink.

Her phone buzzed. She read the screen, then cleared her throat. "It's the sheriff's office." She answered the call. "Bree Taggert. Yes. Thank you." She lowered the phone, exhaling hard. "The sheriff's department has released Erin's house. I can take the kids home now. I'll be busy with them tonight. Can we touch base tomorrow?"

Does that mean she wants to work together?

"Sure." Matt didn't press. "Call me if you need anything."

With a quick nod, she slipped out of his vehicle and walked to the door. Matt watched her disappear inside. He ran a few errands, then drove home on autopilot, unable to get Bree's troubled eyes and quiet courage out of his head.

His sister's minivan was parked in front of his house. He left his SUV and went around to the kennel. His younger sister, Cady, was walking an overweight black-and-white pointer mix around the backyard. At the sight of Matt, the dog lunged and nearly dragged Cady off her feet, which was quite a feat. Cady had rowed crew in college. She was strong and nearly six feet tall in her winter boots.

Matt ignored the pulling dog. "She needs leash manners, but otherwise she is a real sweetheart."

Cady stepped on the leash, tethering the big dog to the ground so she couldn't jump on Matt. "Sit, Ladybug."

The dog planted her butt on the ground, but her entire body was still wagging.

Matt rewarded her with some ear rubs, and he could have sworn she smiled. "I thought that name was ridiculous for a sixty-pound dog, but she's so goofy, it suits her."

"She should be a fifty-pound dog." Cady tugged her hat over long hair that was more strawberry than blonde. "I really want to place her soon. How'd she do at the park yesterday?"

"Great. She's good with other dogs. Loves kids. Not touchy about anything. No reaction to running, screaming, or sledding except for a wagging tail stump." Some idiot had docked the mutt's tail, and they'd done a poor job of it.

Cady smiled. "How does she do with Brody?"

"Fine, but her housebreaking needs work. She peed in the house twice."

"I'll take her home with me and work on it."

"Good idea. Once she's away from the kennel environment, she's super chill." Matt rubbed behind the dog's too-small ears. Kennels were loud and stressful.

"Ladybug, heel." Cady turned and walked toward her minivan. The dog waddled at her side. Cady opened the rear hatch. The dog tried to jump into the van but missed the step and fell flat on her face.

"Oh, no. Are you OK?" Cady checked Ladybug's face, then scooped up the ungainly dog's butt and helped her scramble inside.

Matt tried not to laugh. He followed his sister to the van and gave her a hug. "Thanks for the entertainment. I needed it."

She opened a plastic dog crate, guided Ladybug inside, and secured the door. "I saw the news report this afternoon. They showed Justin's mug shot."

Matt wasn't surprised with the media's choice of photo. A mug shot implied guilt.

"I can't believe he shot his wife." Cady closed the hatch and walked around to the driver's side.

"I don't think he did."

"The reporter used the words *person of interest*, but they presented him as the only suspect." Cady opened the door and climbed into her van. "I know you're going to get involved. Don't do anything stupid. Love you."

Matt stepped back. "Love you too."

She closed the door and drove off.

Matt walked through the kennel and made sure the heater was working. Cady had fed and watered the dogs, and the kennel was clean. Some dogs rushed to him for attention. Others cowered in the back of their space. He spent time with each dog. Full dark had fallen by the time he left the kennels and strode toward the house.

He fed Brody and took him out back to do his business. "What do we do now?"

Brody wagged his tail.

"Want to go for a ride and see Mr. Moore?"

The dog trotted to the front door, and Matt snapped the leash to his collar. One of the reasons Justin had chosen to rent the house near the tiny business district of Grey's Hollow was its close proximity to his father's auto shop. He could walk or bike to work. Justin had lost his job at the bank when he'd been charged with a felony.

Brody rode shotgun, and Matt cracked the passenger window for his sniffing pleasure. Ten minutes later, his headlights swept across the entrance to Moore's Auto Repair. A handful of cars occupied the lot. Matt parked, stepped out of his vehicle, and waited for Brody to jump down. Matt picked up the leash, and they went into the office.

At six forty-five, business was winding down for the day. Mr. Moore stood at the register, explaining a bill to a customer. He acknowledged Matt with a wave and a worried frown before turning back to his client. Two more people waited in line to be checked out. Matt and Brody wandered to the window overlooking the actual shop. One of the four bays was empty. Two vehicles sat on lifts in the others. In the farthest from the office, a single mechanic bent under the hood of a Toyota Camry.

By seven o'clock, Mr. Moore escorted the last customer out. After locking the exterior door, he shook Matt's hand and patted Brody's head. "Matt, I'm so glad to see you."

"I want to talk to you about Justin."

"Yes, of course. I was planning to call you tonight." Mr. Moore glanced through the glass at the mechanic, who was still working. "Let's go into my office." He led Matt into a cramped room with a cluttered metal desk. Mr. Moore closed the door, and Matt pulled a plastic chair to the front edge of the desk. Brody lay at his feet.

Mr. Moore's eyes were bloodshot. He was a tall man, but his stooped posture made him appear shorter. His office chair squeaked as he collapsed into it. "The police came to see me." His eyes misted. "I didn't know what to tell them."

"Tell them the truth."

Anger flushed Mr. Moore's face. "They act like Justin shot Erin. He would never hurt that girl. He loves her."

"I know it."

Mr. Moore removed his baseball cap and ran a hand through his thinning gray hair. "Justin is weak is all. He can't kick those drugs."

"He's trying," Matt said. "What happened with the gun?"

Mr. Moore bowed his head. "I don't know. It was in my nightstand the last time I looked."

"Do you remember when that was?"

Mr. Moore squinted at the ceiling. "A few weeks ago."

"The gun wasn't in a safe?"

"No. I wanted it handy." Mr. Moore examined a line of grease under his thumbnail. He sighed, a long, heavy sound weighted with regret.

"Are you sure Justin took it?"

"No, but he was the only other person in my house recently."

"When was Justin last there?"

"He comes for dinner a few nights a week. His budget is really tight. I can't afford to pay him what he was making at the bank. I wish I hadn't told the police it was missing, but they asked if Justin had access to a gun, so I checked mine. I was surprised it was gone, and I wasn't thinking straight."

"No, you did the right thing."

Justin had grown up in the auto shop. He'd said he was grateful for the job, but Matt had seen him scrub his fingertips raw to get the grease stains out from under his fingernails.

"Why do you think Justin took the gun?" Matt asked.

"That's why I wanted to talk to you. I didn't tell this to the cops, but Justin was afraid."

"Of what?" Matt asked.

"I'm not sure, but he's been jumpy for the last week or so, checking the parking lot on the security camera feeds before he left the shop, stuff like that." Mr. Moore propped his hand on his hip. "I didn't tell the deputies because I was afraid Justin was buying drugs again. *Should* I tell them, even if it makes him look more guilty?"

"Don't lie to the authorities, but you don't have to volunteer information," Matt said. "I'm going to look for Justin."

Mr. Moore exhaled. "I was hoping you'd say that."

"Do you know where Justin bought his drugs?" Matt asked.

Mr. Moore shook his head. "Here's another thing I didn't tell the deputy: when he was using, Justin carried two phones, his regular one and one of those cheap prepaid models."

"For buying drugs," Matt said.

A burner, or prepaid phone, could be purchased without supplying personal information, making the user anonymous.

Mr. Moore hung his head. "That's what I assumed."

"Do you know if he currently has a burner phone?"

Mr. Moore looked away. "He did. He has a red case on his regular phone, and the other day I was putting out some trash and saw him using a black one in the parking lot. It looked smaller too, and it was bone-cold outside. He could have made calls from the break room or borrowed my office."

"Did you hear any of the conversation?"

"Only a couple of words. He said, 'Hold on, Nico,' and waited for me to go back inside before he continued his conversation." Mr. Moore paused, the lines in his craggy face deepening. "The only time he was ever secretive was when he was using."

"You didn't say this to the deputy who came to interview you?"

"No. He didn't ask." Mr. Moore set his cap back on his head. "I don't know what to do, Matt. Do I trust the sheriff's office or not? On the news, it sure seems like they've pegged Erin's death on him."

Because that's what the evidence suggests.

"You're in a tough spot," Matt said. "Can you think of anywhere Justin would go if he needed to lay low for a few days?"

"I've been thinking about this all day, but I just don't know. He likes to camp to clear his head, but not in this kind of weather."

Matt made a mental note to check Justin's garage for his camping gear. He stood. "I'll do what I can."

Mr. Moore wrung Matt's hand. "Thank you. I know you'll do what's right."

"Do you have a key to Justin's house?" Matt wanted to search the premises after the sheriff's department released the crime scene.

"I do." Mr. Moore took a key off his own key ring and offered it to Matt. "Here."

Matt slid the key into his pocket. Then he and Brody left the auto shop and returned to the SUV. Matt made the short drive to Justin's house. The door was still sealed with crime scene tape. So, he couldn't go inside. He parked at the curb.

"I'll be right back," he said to Brody.

He walked up the driveway and shone his flashlight through the small windows at the top of the garage door. Matt had helped Justin move in. He remembered setting boxes labeled CAMPING GEAR in the garage near the wall, next to Justin's mountain bike. The boxes were gone.

Matt returned to his vehicle. He scratched Brody's chest. "Where would he camp in this weather?"

Brody had no answers, and neither did Matt. Driving and hiking to Justin's favorite spots would have to wait for daylight.

Matt pulled out his phone and scrolled through his contacts. He paused on a name and number he hadn't called in years. Kevin Locke. Would he even respond? More importantly, did Matt want to reconnect with his old confidential informant? Matt no longer had a badge or backup. What else was he going to do? He needed to find Justin, and he had exactly one lead to follow: the drug dealer. The clock was ticking. The fact that Justin had taken his camping gear made Matt think his friend might still be alive, but law enforcement all over the state was looking for him. When they found him, civilian and officer safety, not the suspect's, would be the priorities, which was exactly how Matt would handle the situation if he were still a deputy.

He sent the text. HOW R U?

The response came back before he could blink. SOSO.

Same old, same old. Code for "meet me at the usual place."

Matt drove to an industrial park on the outskirts of Grey's Hollow. He cruised around the buildings. The warehouses closest to the street looked to still be in use, but the buildings at the rear of the complex were clearly vacant from the number of broken windows that fronted the buildings like missing teeth. The parking lot hadn't been plowed beyond Building One. But most of the overhead lights still worked.

"He didn't give a time," Matt said.

Brody pricked his ears and tilted his head.

"I know." Matt hadn't liked dealing with CIs when he'd been an investigator. But sometimes it was necessary to deal with low-level scumbags to catch high-level scumbags, and Kevin had always been well informed.

Matt's nerves prickled like tacks on his skin as he drove to the back of the lot and parked in the shadow of a building. The outside chill seeped into the vehicle. His hand ached from the cold. He removed heavy gloves from the rear seat pocket and put them on. He started the engine to warm up the vehicle twice. With his thick fur, Brody curled up on the passenger seat and went to sleep. Matt grabbed an extra fleece from the back seat and layered it under his coat. Then he settled in to wait.

CHAPTER NINE

Bree opened the front door, wiped her boots on the doormat, and stepped into the living room. The kids pushed past her and bolted up the steps to their rooms. She let them go. Adam's house was all one room. They hadn't had any alone time to process their mother's death.

She dropped her overnight bag on the floor next to the steps and walked through the kitchen. Unlike Bree and Adam, with their grim moodiness, Erin had been an optimist, and her house reflected her attitude. The decor was cheerful, from the bright-yellow walls to the checkerboard floor tiles to the whimsical accents. A napkin holder in the shape of a black-and-white cow sat on the table. A cow clock hung on the wall. Unshed tears pressured the backs of Bree's eyes. She breathed until the sensation passed.

The kids weren't the only ones who hadn't had the time or space to grieve Erin's death.

Bree turned to the wide window that overlooked the barn. A light from over the door shone on the icy barnyard. She wandered around the lower level, stopping in front of a bookshelf full of framed snapshots. Bree touched the frame of a picture of Erin, Bree, and the kids standing in front of the Liberty Bell. Bree remembered Erin begging another tourist to take the picture and Bree telling her that's how she'd get her phone stolen. Erin had left her wedding photo on the top shelf, a candid shot of her and Justin clinking champagne glasses. Women who hated or feared their exes didn't keep their wedding pictures around.

Bree turned from the photos and returned to the kitchen. They'd missed dinner. She found a box of macaroni and cheese in the pantry and filled a pot with water to boil.

Luke walked through the kitchen and tugged on a pair of boots by the door. "I'm going out to feed the horses."

"All right. Can you write down what they eat in case I need to do it?"

"Already written on the feed bin."

"Great. I'll make something for us to eat."

He glanced back. "I'm not hungry. Maybe later."

"OK. It'll be here when you want it." Bree didn't know what else to say.

He turned and stared at her. "Am I going to school tomorrow?"

"Do you want to?"

His face was blank. "Is Kayla going?"

"I don't know." Bree rubbed her temple. "Why don't we see how you both feel in the morning? If you want to take some time off, that's fine. But if you'd rather stick to your normal routine, that's OK too. I don't think there's any one right answer here."

He looked relieved. "OK. I might go. Be better than sitting around here and doing nothing."

Inactivity left too much time for thinking. That she understood all too well.

"You let me know," Bree said.

"OK." He grabbed a jacket from the coat-tree and went out back.

Bree made a mental note to contact both kids' school counselors in the morning. She needed professional advice. Of all the things she'd done in her life, this was the one she couldn't screw up. How these kids managed their mother's death would stick with them for the rest of their lives.

What happens after the funeral?

Decisions would have to be made. Had Erin left a will?

Bree rubbed an ache in her forehead. She needed to go through her sister's desk.

Would Bree have to track down the kids' father? Thoughts of Craig Vance taking charge of Luke and Kayla sent a chill straight into Bree's bones. Had he and Erin made any formal custody arrangement?

She doubted it. Erin had been in full avoidance mode as far as Craig was concerned. He had been her drug, and like an addict, she couldn't be around the source of her addiction without risking a relapse.

Bree's headache intensified. There was no point addressing the worst-case scenario until it happened. Unfortunately, that was where a homicide detective's brain went every time. While she waited for the water to boil, she searched the kitchen drawers, but found nothing interesting. A basket of mail contained mostly bills and a few coupons, nothing abnormal. Bree turned to a whiteboard calendar mounted on the wall. Her sister had marked it with her work schedule, Luke's basketball practices, and Kayla's Brownie meetings. Bree stared at a square marked *K violin lesson.*

Bree had started playing the violin at the same age, right after her parents had died. Kayla was the exact age Bree had been. So many parallels between Erin's kids' lives and Bree's past. Too many. Would they end up like Adam and her? Aloof or able to maintain only a few close personal relationships?

The water boiled. Bree cooked the mac and cheese, then went upstairs to look for Kayla. Her bedroom door was ajar. She sat on her bed, crying silently, hugging a stuffed animal that looked half pillow, half pig.

Bree tapped on the doorframe. "I made mac and cheese. Do you want some?"

Kayla shook her head and picked at a thread on the stuffed pig's seam. Bree walked to the bed and sat down beside her. The little girl launched herself at Bree, burrowing her face in Bree's shoulder and sobbing in great heaves. Her tears soaked into Bree's sweater as she wrapped her arms around her niece, rubbed her back, and let her cry. Bree's heart broke all over again.

Ten minutes later, Kayla sniffed and straightened. Bree plucked tissues from a box on the nightstand. She handed a fistful to Kayla to dry her face.

Kayla wiped her nose. "Can I sleep with you tonight in Mommy's bed?"

"Sure, you can." Bree had planned to sleep in the guest room. She hadn't been prepared to use her sister's bed, but she'd just have to deal. If that's where Kayla wanted to sleep, that's where they'd sleep. She thought of Luke. Had he come in from the barn? "Can you try to eat something?"

Kayla nodded and scrambled off the bed.

Downstairs, Bree filled two bowls with mac and cheese, now cold. "Can you nuke these for thirty seconds each? I'll be right back."

Kayla put a bowl in the microwave and pushed buttons. Bree stepped into her sister's rubber boots by the back door. She grabbed a jacket before trudging across the backyard to the barn. The sliding door was partially open. Bree slipped inside without making any sound and walked down the aisle. The last stall door was ajar. Bree peeked inside. Luke stood next to the bay horse, his arms around its neck, sobbing into its mane.

Bree's breath hitched. She backed away, giving Luke his privacy. At his age, he might be embarrassed. She went back to the house and ate with Kayla. The mac and cheese tasted like glue. Luke returned in a half hour, red-eyed and quiet. Bree heated his dinner without comment, but watching the kids' misery, she'd never felt so helpless.

They were all exhausted. Luke did the final barn check and went to bed by nine o'clock. Bree kicked off her shoes, stretched out on the bed, and turned on the TV to wait for Kayla to finish in the bathroom. Kayla emerged in her pajamas and climbed into bed.

What seemed like a second passed, and Bree jolted. A movie she didn't recognize played on the TV. She checked the clock on the nightstand. It was just after midnight. Her sidearm dug into her hip. She'd fallen asleep in her clothes. What had woken her?

A bang sounded from somewhere in the house.

Bree's nerves stood on end as she listened intently. Luke was probably getting a snack or a drink of water. She slid out of bed, leaving Kayla snoring softly, and tiptoed to the door in her socks. The hallway was dark, but Bree didn't turn on any lights. She slid along the hardwood to Luke's room and eased open the door. By the light of the moon streaming in the window, she could see his head on the pillow.

He hadn't woken her.

She retreated to the hall. Something squeaked downstairs. The hair on the back of Bree's neck stirred.

She drew her gun. A movement from Luke's room caught her attention. He was standing in the doorway in flannel pajamas and a T-shirt. Putting a finger to her lips, Bree walked to him, leaned close to his ear, and said in a soft voice, "I heard something downstairs. It's probably nothing, but stay with your sister while I make sure."

Bree eased down the steps as Luke slipped into the master bedroom. She paused on the bottom step, then peered around the wall into the living room. Her gaze probed every dark corner of the room, but she saw nothing.

Old houses settle, right?

After checking the coat closet, she started down the short hall toward the kitchen. At the entrance, she paused, putting her back to the wall and glancing around it, careful to minimize her appearance as a target. A dark figure stood at the kitchen island. Using a small penlight, he was looking through the contents of a drawer.

The room was dark, but to Bree, the size and shape looked male. Was it Justin? She couldn't tell.

He froze. Then his head whipped around. Bree had made no sound, but he must have sensed her presence. He wore a ski mask, but Bree felt his gaze on her.

Bree's gun was already pointed at his center mass. She remained partially concealed behind the wall. "Freeze."

Instead of obeying, he bolted for the door. *Damn it.* Bree couldn't shoot him in the back. She didn't see a weapon in his hand, and a man running away could not be considered a threat. She sprinted after him, but her socks slid on the floor. She wasted a few precious seconds trying to gain traction. When she reached the back door, he was already halfway across the yard. Bree shoved her feet into a pair of boots and ran out into the yard just as he disappeared into the barn.

She sprinted across the crusty snow, the boots sliding as she stopped at the barn door. She glanced around the barn doorframe. The aisle was dark, but a huge shape rushed her.

She sprang backward as a horse galloped out. Its shoulder brushed hers and knocked her on her butt. The remaining two animals were right behind the first.

Bree sprang to her feet. Wind blew through her cable-knit sweater, but underneath, her skin was damp with adrenaline sweat. Leading with her weapon, she slipped into the barn. The aisle was empty. The back door gaped open. Had he left, or was he hiding?

Looking up, she scanned the loft but couldn't see most of it. There was only one way up, a ladder nailed to the wall. To climb it, she'd have to put her gun away.

Not happening.

But she listened for sounds overhead as she crept down the aisle. Straw rustled.

Bree's belly cramped.

She moved to the first stall, putting her shoulder to the wall. She spun, sweeping her aim from corner to corner. From a narrow window set high in the wall, moonlight streamed across the bedding.

Clear.

Bree eyed the third stall door on the opposite side of the aisle. Sweat dripped down her back, chilled her skin, and lifted the hairs on the back of her neck. She eased across the wide dirt corridor, her eyes adjusting to the dimness.

Squeak.

A small, light-colored shape darted out from under the stall door, right across the toe of her boot. Bree jumped backward, purely on reflex, her heart protesting with a skipped beat as she identified a rat bigger than her tomcat. The rat scurried down the aisle. Its long, skinny tail disappeared into the feed room.

Bree shuddered, then turned back to her search.

What spooked the rat?

She crept toward the third stall door. The moon had risen on the other side of the barn. The stall on this side was darker. Pressing her shoulder to the wall, she prepared to sweep around the doorframe. Something scraped above. Bree looked up. Bits of hay and dust rained down on her, followed by a whole bale. She turned and blocked her face and head with her arms as it crashed down on her upper back. The impact knocked her to the ground. She landed on her hands and knees, the wind whooshing out of her.

Out of the corner of her eye, she saw a man jump down into the aisle and run toward the rear door. Shaking hay out of her face, she scrambled to her feet and raced after him. Lungs aching, she rushed out of the barn.

Where is he?

She spotted his dark form on the snowy landscape as he used a tree stump and a fence post to scramble over the barbed-wire fence. Bree set after him. Fueled by the knowledge that this could be the man who'd killed her sister, Bree stretched her strides and began to gain on him.

As she neared the pasture fence, he was only thirty feet in front of her. She leaped onto the tree stump. Her rubber boot slipped on a patch of ice. Her momentum carried her forward, and she landed on the barbed wire. A sharp sting lanced her ankle. The old post broke, and wire snapped, coiling at the sudden lack of tension. Bree got a knee under her body and pushed forward. But the loose wire had tangled around her legs. Kicking and pulling only tightened its hold. Barbs gripped her jeans and dug into her skin, but Bree barely registered the pain.

Caught, she watched the man who might have killed her sister escape into the trees.

She rolled to her back and stared at the sky for a long minute. She could no longer hold back her grief, frustration, and fear. Sobs racked her body, and tears overflowed her eyes. She'd lost her parents and the cousin who'd raised her. But Erin's death was different. Bree was supposed to protect her little sister.

Emotions gripped her heart as tightly and as painfully as the barbed wire wrapped around her ankles. Grey's Hollow had caught her in its grip, and it would never let her go. She heaved in a deep, painful breath that felt as if the air were scraping in and out of her lungs, leaving her raw and vulnerable and hollow. A slideshow of her sister's face, from babyhood to last August, raced through Bree's mind, each image leaving a mark, like the tracks of fingernails in flesh.

The cold seeped through her sweater, and she began to shiver. The breakdown lasted only a minute or two. Her sobs slowed, and she caught her breath.

She sat up and wiped her face on her snow-covered sleeve. Ice pellets tumbled down the front of her sweater. Enough crying. She had work to do.

She'd catch the bastard who had killed her sister. But she couldn't do it alone. She needed help.

She pulled out her phone, called 911, and gave the dispatcher the address. Ignoring the man's request that she stay on the line, Bree ended the call.

She carefully untangled the wire from around her ankles. Unwinding the wire proved much harder than getting caught in it.

Bree nicked her fingers working the barbs free of her jeans. When the last point was extracted, she climbed to her feet.

Cold and wet, she made her way back to the yard. Thankfully, the horses hadn't gone far. They were nosing through the snow behind the house. Bree put them away and trudged up to the house.

Luke stood at the kitchen door. He held a shotgun in his hands, the muzzle tipped toward the floor. Kayla's white face peered out from behind him.

"Here's how he got in." Luke pointed toward a circular hole cut in the glass pane above the deadbolt latch.

Bree climbed the porch steps. She opened the flashlight app on her phone and shone it on the glass.

Kayla's eyes widened.

"Don't worry." Bree squeezed her shoulder. "It's not going to happen again. I'll make sure of it."

Kayla nodded, but she looked only slightly less scared.

"I'd better take that." Bree motioned toward the shotgun. "The sheriff's department is on the way."

"It's Mom's." Luke handed her the gun.

But Erin hated guns.

Bree took the 20 gauge. "When did she buy it?"

"A couple of months ago. We took a safety class together and a shooting one too."

"That's good." She unloaded the weapon and slid the shells into her pocket. "Where does she keep it?"

"There's a safe under her bed," Luke said. "She gave me the combination. I thought I should get it out in case whoever broke in came back."

"You did great, Luke." Bree patted his shoulder. "Are you OK, Kayla?"

Nodding, Kayla clung to her brother. Bree returned the shotgun to the safe, then hugged both the kids as they waited in the living room.

Red-and-blue lights swirled in the driveway as a sheriff's department vehicle parked.

Bree opened the front door. "I'm a police officer, and I'm armed." She greeted the deputy, showed him her badge, and summarized the incident. She pointed to the trees behind the property. "He ran into the woods."

"There's a road back there. We'll check it out." The deputy used his shoulder mic to call for another unit. When he was done, he asked, "Do you know how he got in?"

"Through the back door." Bree led him to the kitchen.

"I'll check the rest of the house and dust for prints," the deputy said.

Still holding on to her brother, Kayla shivered. While the deputy went to work, Bree washed her hands and put Band-Aids over the cuts on her fingers. Then she made hot cocoa for all three of them. No one was going back to sleep just yet. She settled the kids in the living room with cocoa and some cookies she rooted out of the pantry. Luke turned on the TV and let Kayla choose a Disney movie.

Bree went into the office and closed the french doors. The kids could see her through the glass. She didn't know how to comfort them but sensed they needed her presence more than words.

She began making plans. Keeping the kids safe was her first priority, and there was only one person she could call in the middle of the night for help—Dana. Then Matt's face popped into her head.

Maybe there were two.

As she pulled out her phone, she thought about her sister's shotgun. After what had happened to their parents, Erin had been determined that there would never be a firearm in her home. There was only one reason she would have bought a shotgun.

She'd been afraid.

But of whom?

Chapter Ten

Matt sat in the driver's seat of his SUV, impatiently watching for his CI's vehicle. Brody whined. His head turned toward the road.

Matt touched the dog's back. "Good boy."

A minute later, he heard the rumble of an approaching engine. He straightened as headlights swept across the snow. His body had stiffened in the cold. Under the glove, his hand felt like a frozen claw.

A pickup truck turned into the parking lot. It drove in a slow, careful circle to the right side of the lot and stopped.

Matt turned his headlights on and off three times in rapid succession. The truck answered with two blinks.

Kevin.

"Here we go." Matt started the engine again and cruised toward the center of the lot. Cold air blew from the vents.

Brody whined again.

"It'll be OK."

The dog cocked his head as if he questioned Matt's opinion.

Not wanting Kevin to see the dog, Matt commanded him to lie down in German. The dog complied, but his posture remained alert as Matt lowered the window.

Matt commanded him to stay, then he climbed out of the SUV. The temperature had dropped into the single digits, and the air felt like tiny daggers to his eyeballs.

Kevin stepped out of his truck and swung a handgun to point at Matt's chest. "What the fuck do you think you're doing texting me?"

Matt raised his hands in front of his chest. "Whoa. I just needed to talk to you. I'll make it worth your time. Since when do you carry a gun?"

"Fuck you." Kevin spat. The hand that held the gun trembled. "I haven't heard from you in years. You're not even a cop anymore. What do you want?"

Matt didn't move. He didn't want to spook Kevin any more. The CI had gotten twitchier since Matt had seen him last.

"Nothing. I swear." Matt kept his voice calm. "We've known each other ten years, man."

"But you want something from me, right?" Kevin accused.

"You're right," Matt admitted. "But I'll pay you for the information, as always."

"Fuck you." Kevin raised his arm, the gun pointing straight at Matt's face.

Matt's heart stuttered. Sweat broke out under his coat. How could he deescalate the situation?

Before he could react, dog tags jingled. Brody flew out of the SUV, took one running stride, and took Kevin to the ground. The gun went flying, skittering across the ice-crusted snow.

"Help! Help!" Kevin screamed, trying to cover his head with his hands. "Don't let him kill me!"

Brody stood on Kevin's chest, his bared teeth inches from the CI's face. Matt kicked the gun away before calling off the dog. Brody didn't move at first, and Matt had to issue the command again. The dog looked disappointed as he backed, stiff-legged, off Kevin's chest and returned to Matt's side.

Matt picked up the leash. "You can get up now, Kevin. The dog won't hurt you as long as you don't do anything stupid."

Kevin climbed to his feet and swayed on shaky legs. Looking closer, Matt could see Kevin was gaunt. He'd been consuming more drugs than food. He was twenty-four years old but looked much, much older.

"What happened to you, Kevin?" Matt asked.

Kevin studied the ground. "What do you want?"

"I'm looking for a local dealer, sells oxy."

"Everybody sells oxy."

"Goes by the name Nico," Matt said.

Kevin blinked up. Fear brightened his eyes for one second before he shut it down. "Don't know him."

Yes, you do.

"Are you sure?" Matt reached into his pocket and pulled out two twenties. He held them up.

"Sorry." Kevin shook his head. "Can't help you."

Kevin was obviously afraid of Nico, but he was also an addict. And an addict could always be bought, because he valued his high more than his life.

Matt added another twenty. "How about now?"

Kevin licked his chapped lips. "I wish I could."

With a twinge of guilt, Matt added one more bill to his bribe. He wanted to give Kevin just enough cash to have a small party, but not enough to last long. He wanted Kevin to need to come back for more.

Kevin froze. His shoulders slumped, and he nodded almost imperceptibly. Matt held the cash out, and Kevin reached for it. Brody growled low in his throat, and Kevin snatched the bills and stepped back.

"This Nico is bad news?" Matt asked. He must be for Kevin to hold out so long.

"Yeah." Kevin fingered the cash in his pocket.

"What can you tell me about him?"

Kevin chewed on his lip.

"Do you know Nico's last name?" Matt asked.

"Nope. Doubt that's his real first name."

"What's he look like?"

"Skinny dude. Bald. Cold eyes." Kevin shivered. "He don't look like much, but he'll fuck you up." The wind picked up and whipped around them. Kevin shifted his weight. "That's all I know. I gotta go."

"I need to find Nico."

"No way." Kevin took two steps backward and began to turn away.

"I'll pay you two hundred dollars to help me."

Kevin stopped.

"Tell him I want to buy some oxy."

Kevin looked at the ground and shook his head. "You still look like a cop. He'll kill you."

"Don't hide it then. Tell him I was a cop. I was shot, and now I need oxy." The best lies skated as close to the truth as possible.

"No promises." Kevin shrugged, retrieved his gun, and started toward his pickup.

"Hold on, Kevin." Matt opened the back of his SUV and took out a protein bar and a bag of almonds he kept for emergencies. He offered them to Kevin, who blushed, looked away, and pocketed them.

"Save some of that cash for food," Matt said.

Kevin nodded. But they both knew he wouldn't. He slid back into his car and drove off, accelerating too fast and fishtailing out of the parking lot.

Matt and Brody settled back in the SUV. Matt rubbed behind the dog's ears. "Thanks for having my back."

Brody wagged his tail.

Matt's phone vibrated. He dug it out of his pocket. Bree's number showed on his screen. He checked the time on his dashboard clock. One thirty. Unease rushed through him as he answered. "Bree?"

"Yes. I'm sorry to call so late, but someone broke into the house." The edge to her voice alarmed him further.

"Is everyone OK?" Matt pressed the gas pedal. His Suburban leaped forward.

"We're fine. But the kids are scared. I think they'll feel better with an extra adult in the house."

"On my way." Matt dropped the phone in a cup holder, turned onto the road, and gunned the engine. He arrived within fifteen minutes of her call and parked next to a sheriff's department vehicle. She must have been watching for him, because she opened the door before he knocked.

"Thanks for coming." Her gaze dropped to the dog at his side.

"I brought him for a reason." Matt rested a hand on Brody's head. "His senses are a thousand times sharper than ours. We can't install a security system in the middle of the night, but no one will sneak into this house while Brody's here."

"I know how valuable K-9s are. My issue with dogs is mine to deal with." But she moved away from Brody as she stepped aside to let them into the house.

The kids were watching TV. Their eyes were shadowed. Kayla was curled into a ball. She spotted the dog, sat up, and smiled. "Brody."

The dog trotted across the room, jumped onto the couch, and curled up between the kids. He wagged his tail and preened while Luke and Kayla petted and fussed over him.

"Before Erin and Justin split up, Brody and I came here for dinner now and then," Matt said.

Bree locked the door and led him back to the kitchen. She wore jeans, a sweater, and her Glock.

He leaned on the island. "Where's the deputy?"

"Looking for the intruder." Bree pointed toward the back of the house. "Who ran into the trees." The bright light over the kitchen island brought out the dark circles under her eyes.

"When did you sleep last?"

"It's been a couple of days," she admitted. "I'll try to take a nap later."

"Brody and I can stay all night. Is there anything else you need?"

"Thanks, but I have a friend from Philly coming tomorrow—now today—with some of my things."

A friend?

Matt suppressed the quick burst of irritation. Bree's *friends* were none of his business.

"Do you think it was Justin who broke in tonight?" he asked.

"I have no idea. He was wearing a mask, and I haven't seen Justin in years. He never came with Erin when she brought the kids to see me." She closed her eyes, as if picturing him. "The intruder was the right height, maybe five ten or eleven. He was wearing a bulky winter coat, but he seemed on the lean side. Not a particularly fast runner. If I hadn't slipped and landed in the barbed wire, I would have caught him."

"That's not enough of a description to know if it was him or not. Do you know if Justin still had a key to the house?" Matt asked. "If he did, he wouldn't have needed to break in."

She shook her head. "I don't know, but why would Justin need to get into Erin's house anyway?"

"He needed something that was here, and he couldn't call and ask for it. He's wanted. His face was all over the news today."

A knock sounded on the door. A deputy stood outside. Matt recognized Jim Rogers, who'd been with the sheriff's department for many years.

Rogers walked into the kitchen and stopped. He startled as his gaze swept over Bree and landed on Matt. "Flynn."

"Rogers," Matt returned the awkward greeting.

"You know each other?" Rogers gestured between Matt and Bree. "We do," Matt said.

Bree gave Matt a look and turned to Rogers. "Did you find tracks?"

"Yeah." Rogers cleared his throat. "He ran through the pasture. The footprints disappeared at the road on the other side. In addition to the tracks headed toward the road, there also were tracks leading this way. He probably left his vehicle back there and walked here across the field. I'll dust the door and kitchen drawer for prints before I go. You can stop by the station any time after tomorrow to pick up a copy of the police report."

Bree closed her eyes for a few seconds. "I don't remember if the intruder was wearing gloves."

"We'll dust anyway." Rogers hustled from the kitchen, returning to his vehicle for his fingerprinting kit. He pulled several prints from around the doorknob and a partial from the kitchen drawer. "I'll let you know if we get any matches."

He would run the prints through AFIS, the Automated Fingerprint Identification System, and look for matches in both criminal and crime scene databases. The prints he pulled probably belonged to family members, but it was always worth a try. Criminals could be unbelievably stupid.

After Rogers left, Bree checked on the kids, and Matt went to the garage for a piece of wood, which he nailed over the hole in the glass. They both returned to the kitchen.

"Both kids are sound asleep." Bree paced. "I guess the dog made them feel safe."

"Brody will hear anything unusual."

She studied him for a minute. "What's up between you and the deputy? I assume you used to work together."

"He shot me." Matt shocked himself with the blunt admission. "Him and another deputy. It was an accident. We were serving an arrest warrant on a drug dealer at a warehouse. The sheriff was supposed to send me and Brody in the south entrance, but he sent us to the north. We got caught in the crossfire between the dealers and the deputies. I don't blame Jim. It wasn't his fault, and he felt terrible afterward. But it does make things awkward between us."

"I'll bet," Bree said. "You don't sound very convincing when you say it was an accident."

"Remember the corrupt former sheriff I told you about?"

"The one who committed suicide?"

"That's him." Matt considered how much to tell her. "I saw the sheriff hit a suspect in the kidney with a baton, repeatedly. The guy was lying on the floor in handcuffs. He was no threat to anyone."

"Excessive force?"

"The sheriff had a temper." Matt nodded. "I should have reported him. It wasn't the first time. He was a real bastard. Thought he was above the law. No," Matt corrected. "He thought he *was* the law. But that's where it gets tricky with a sheriff. A police chief can be fired by the mayor or town council, but a sheriff is an elected official. He has to be charged with a crime and/or impeached."

"That's not an easy process."

"No. He was very popular at the time. There was no way I was going to talk the DA into charging him. The guy the sheriff beat up was too scared to testify. The sheriff was a powerful man who'd been in office for a long time. It would have been his word against mine."

Bree's eyes narrowed as she made connections. "You think the sheriff sent you in the wrong door intentionally."

"It has crossed my mind."

"Shit."

"Exactly," Matt agreed. "It was bad enough that I got shot. But Brody . . ." He paused. "I think Rogers felt worse about shooting the dog."

"Do you trust anyone in the sheriff's department?" Bree asked.

"I trust Marge," Matt said.

"Not Chief Deputy Harvey?"

"I don't know about Todd." Matt shook his head. "I hate to think he knew. He always seemed like a decent guy, but when I got out of the hospital, Todd and the other deputies treated me differently." As if he'd already been an outsider. Like the sheriff had already spun the story of the shooting in his own favor, and everyone had believed him. He'd been a very convincing man. He'd told big, brash lies with contagious confidence.

"Did Todd shoot you too?" Bree asked.

"No. The other guy left the department after the sheriff killed himself."

"So, maybe that guy knew."

"Maybe. There was an investigation after the shooting. Everyone gave their official statements and clammed up. The sheriff said I went in the wrong door. I didn't."

"His word against yours all over again."

"That's right." Matt flexed his hand. "The sheriff came to see me at home. He offered me a substantial settlement to let it go." Technically, the deal had come from the county, but the sheriff had had influence.

"And you took it."

"Only after he agreed to retire Brody and give him to me. His injury wasn't too serious, but there was no way I was letting him put his life on the line for that asshole again."

"Now I understand why it's awkward between you and the sheriff's department."

Matt's gaze dropped to a red smear on the floor. "Are you bleeding?"

"Maybe."

"Maybe?"

"I got caught in barbed wire." She waggled her fingers at him. Band-Aids covered two knuckles. She stooped to roll up the hem of her jeans.

"Sit here." Matt patted the granite island.

Bree hoisted herself up and swung her foot over the sink.

Matt rolled up her pant leg. "Your jeans are wet."

With a sigh, Bree told him the whole story of her discovering and then chasing the intruder. Not surprisingly, it was more complicated than her simply running off a burglar.

Matt's blood went cold. Armed cop or not, she could have been killed. "You should have locked the door and let him run. What if he'd been armed?"

Anger, and maybe a hint of embarrassment, flushed her cheeks. "I wanted to catch him. What if he was the man who killed my sister?"

Matt turned on the faucet. Did she not realize how important she was? Had her brain not computed the new responsibilities she'd assumed when her sister had died? Matt studied her for a few seconds. No, he decided. She hadn't processed her sister's death and all its consequences yet.

She was used to being alone, not having anyone dependent on her. How long would it take her to figure out that her life was completely different now?

"Those kids need you," he said simply.

She frowned, as if she hadn't thought that taking care of them meant taking care with herself. "I know, but he didn't attack me. He ran."

Not the point.

Matt rephrased his thoughts into language she'd understand. "Next time, promise you'll wait for backup, OK?"

"OK." She acknowledged his point with a nod, but he still felt as if she wasn't appreciating her new role in the kids' lives. Bree's brother, Adam, was not guardianship material. Too distracted. Too focused within his own world. The kids would always be an afterthought. It might not be intentional, but the kids would still suffer.

Not with Bree, though. She would put Luke and Kayla first.

Matt peeled off her bloody sock. He expected to find the two cuts on her ankle. The tattoo surprised him. It was a winding vine, done in shades of dark green and dotted with a few tiny blue flowers. The work was delicate. "Where's the first aid kit?"

She pointed to a door behind him. "In the pantry."

He found a small plastic box on a shelf and brought it to the island. "I can't believe you didn't feel these."

"It's been a rough night. I might be numb."

Matt cleaned the cuts with soap and water, closed them with butterfly strips, and covered them with Band-Aids. "This tattoo is beautiful work."

"Thanks." She studied it for a second.

Matt looked closer. Underneath the ink, two jagged lines of raised skin were barely visible. The tattoo artist had done an amazing job. "The tattoo covers a scar?"

"Yes." She paled, her brows dropping into a troubled line. "That's where I was bitten. It left an ugly mark. Before I got the tattoo, I never wore shorts or dresses."

Matt touched the scar. It was thin, but jagged in places. "How many stitches?"

She flinched at his touch and swung her legs off the counter. "I'd better check on the kids."

She moved to leave the kitchen, but he blocked her with a hand on each side of her body. "Does the fact that you called mean you're willing to work with me?"

She lifted one eyebrow. Her hazel eyes met his gaze without blinking. "I'm tired. I wanted another adult in the house to keep the kids safe tonight. I preferred someone solid who I was reasonably sure could handle himself. I thought of you."

"I'm flattered."

She tilted her head. Despite being more than a head shorter than him, she yielded no ground. "Does your helping me tonight come with strings attached?"

"Of course not." He took a step backward, regretting the dick move. What had made him think he could intimidate Bree into a loose partnership to investigate Erin's death and Justin's disappearance?

"Good." She ran a hand over her scalp, not to smooth her hair, but as if her head hurt.

Selfishly, beyond the investigation, Bree appealed to him. She was an attractive woman, but he knew plenty of those. He was old enough to want more than sex and a pretty face from a relationship. Something made her different. Complexity. Resilience. Fate had thrown marbles under her feet. She'd scrambled but kept her balance. Her straightforward attitude was refreshing too. He'd been an ass, and she'd called him on it immediately.

And because he'd been an ass—and he still wanted to work with her—he should be the first to offer information.

"When you called, you didn't disturb me. I wasn't home in bed." He explained about his visit with Justin's father and the information on a potential drug dealer.

"Maybe Justin owed his dealer money." She rubbed her eyes. "I hate to think he was using again, but it makes sense. If he wasn't, Erin would have taken him back. She wasn't good at ending relationships."

Something stirred in the front room, and Bree headed for the doorway. "Sounds like one of the kids is awake." Glancing back at him, she said in a low voice, "We'll continue this discussion tomorrow, when my brain is functioning. I'm going to try to get the kids to go to bed."

"You should get some sleep too."

"I'll try." She nodded. "There's a guest room."

"I can bunk on the couch." Matt wanted to stay closer to the doors, where he would hear an intruder. "Brody will keep guard."

"Thanks again." She left the room.

Matt filled a glass with water and drank it. In the morning, he'd follow up on Justin's drug dealer. Matt would love to give the chief deputy an alternate suspect.

He considered the camping gear. Why would Justin run and hide? Was he afraid of the man who had killed Erin? Or the police?

Or both?

CHAPTER ELEVEN

He sat back in his vehicle and stared at the small farm through the telephoto lens of his camera. The house was dark, and there was an extra vehicle parked out front. He took a picture of the big SUV. The lamppost in front of the house illuminated the license plate.

There'd been a news report on Erin's death and her family history. They'd shown pictures of the family, including a current photo of Erin's sister entering the sheriff's station that morning. The sister was a homicide detective from Philadelphia. She was going to be a problem. He could feel it. She was going to get in his way, just like Erin had.

But what could he do about her?

Fury roiled inside him, rising as rapidly as a flash flood. Erin had thought she was so smart. That she had his number. That she could interfere with his life. Well, she'd learned a hard lesson. The memory soothed him. He'd taken care of her. He would not allow anyone to fuck with him.

No one was taking what was his. Not the dead bitch. Not her sister.

He'd killed once, and he was more than willing to do it again, though the sister was a cop and would be harder to kill. He touched his pocket and felt the reassuring bulk of the gun. As he'd demonstrated Tuesday night, a bullet to the chest at close range took a person down fast. A gun truly was the great equalizer.

A curtain moved in an upstairs window—Erin's window—and a dark figure moved into view. Was the sister looking out? Could she sense him watching her?

He snapped a picture. She seemed to be looking right at him.

His breath locked in his chest. Though he was certain she couldn't see him, he slid farther down in his seat. He lowered the camera. Without the help of the telephoto lens, she was no longer visible.

His lungs loosened.

If he couldn't see her, then she couldn't see him.

Anger flashed again, heating him from the inside out. He shouldn't have to worry about this. Like Erin, the sister would bring on her own demise. A cop would never be able to mind her own business.

He needed to kill her, but he wasn't prepared to do it tonight. Killing a cop would take planning. The sister was armed, and she'd be wary, trained. He'd have to take her by surprise. He'd planned Erin's death, and it had gone off like clockwork. Well, almost like clockwork. But he would make use of the one deviation from the plan. He'd take the same amount of care with the sister's death.

He raised the camera again. The figure in the window had disappeared. Had she gone back to bed?

He'd watched Erin too. Her behavior had been pathetically routine, almost OCD. With thoughts of planning in his head, he picked up a notepad from the passenger seat and wrote down the time the figure had appeared in the window. If she didn't sleep well and was often up at night, he needed to know.

The house remained quiet for the next fifteen minutes. He started the engine and eased off the shoulder of the road.

The anger in him had diminished, but it never went away. It simmered in his chest like a pilot light waiting to ignite a larger flame.

The sister had better not interfere, because he would do whatever was necessary to keep what was his.

CHAPTER TWELVE

The house was silent Thursday morning as Bree worked her way through some sun salutations. She placed her head on her mat, lifted her hips, and slowly straightened her body until she was in a headstand. Yoga had taught her body and breath control, and the concentration required to not fall flat on her face cleared her head. She finished with a forearm stand and five breaths in the inverted V of downward dog. Then she showered, dressed, and crept down the stairs. The kids were both still sound asleep, but they hadn't gone to bed until three, and then only after Matt promised that Brody would be there all night.

From the bottom step, Bree could see Matt sleeping on the couch. On the floor at his side, Brody lay on a folded quilt Kayla had insisted he use as a bed. The dog's head was up, his big brown eyes focused on Bree. She paused, fear nudging her pulse.

She inhaled deep into her lungs and controlled her exhale. *The dog will not hurt you.*

That phrase was going to be her new mantra. She took a second slow breath and forced herself to walk past the living room, hating the relieved scurry in her step as she left the dog's sight.

In the kitchen, she brewed a pot of coffee. The sun streamed through the windows. Outside the sky was a brilliant winter blue. Bree checked the time. Nine o'clock. The horses needed to be fed. She shrugged into Luke's jacket and her sister's boots and opened the door. The cold hit her face like a wall of ice. She glanced at a thermometer mounted on the back porch. Nine degrees.

She stepped off the porch, patting the pockets of the coat and finding gloves. Sunlight gleamed on the frozen yard, blinding her. She shaded her eyes with her hand as she made her way into the barn. Three horses poked their heads over their stall doors. Kayla's chestnut pony, Pumpkin, occupied the first stall. He eyeballed Bree from under his bushy flaxen forelock. Luke's bay quarter horse, Riot, kicked his door. The last animal, a pretty paint Erin had named Cowboy, nickered softly for attention. The horses rustled their bedding. The air smelled of beasts, hay, and manure. Bree hadn't lived on a farm since she was eight, but the scents and sounds felt familiar in a way she couldn't deny, no matter how much she wanted to.

She used the plastic scoop to measure feed and gave each horse hay. Ice had formed in their water buckets overnight. Bree broke the ice with a hammer and refilled the buckets. The barn water supply was insulated and heated to prevent freezing. She slipped into each stall, straightened blankets, and checked each animal over in the daylight. They seemed fine.

Ironically, thousand-pound animals that could easily squash her didn't frighten her at all.

She patted them on the necks and went back to the house. Luke could muck the stalls later. She crossed the yard and opened the door to the kitchen. The smell of coffee was bliss, and the heat prickled on the frozen skin of her face.

Matt stood at the counter, pouring coffee into two mugs. Instinctively, Bree looked for the dog. Brody lay under the kitchen table, his face on his paws, his eyes on Matt. She couldn't prevent the quickening of her step as she passed him.

"Good morning," Matt said. He was rumpled and messy-haired, and his reddish-brown stubble seemed to have sprouted into a tight beard overnight.

No one should look that awake—or good—before coffee.

Clearly, she was caffeine deprived. She added sugar to her coffee and guzzled half the cup before returning his greeting. "Good morning."

"Do you have a plan for the day, and how can I help?" Even before coffee, his blue eyes were clear. Hers had been underscored with bags and dark circles. She'd slept poorly, waking in the darkness with a strange feeling that she was being watched. The break-in had left a mental mark.

"I have to call my boss. Clearly, I'm going to be here more than a couple of days. My friend should be here this morning with supplies from my apartment. I plan on making some calls and seeing how fast I can get an alarm installed."

"I know a guy. I'll get him out here today."

"Thank you." Bree sipped more coffee. The caffeine wasn't hitting her system fast enough. She finished the cup and poured another. Her stomach rumbled, and she went to the fridge and found yogurt. "More sugar than I'd like but it will do."

She offered one to Matt.

He declined. "I'm fine with coffee for now."

"Thank you for staying last night."

"You're welcome."

Bree looked at the dog. "I think Brody's presence made the kids feel more secure."

"Dogs are great for home security. Even the nice ones will usually tell you if someone is outside. The little ones bark like crazy."

Bree ate the yogurt and drained her second cup of coffee, her brain beginning to stir.

"I'm going to check on the kids. Be right back." She tiptoed upstairs and peered in on them. Kayla was sound asleep in Erin's bed, where she'd slept with Bree. In his own room, Luke looked unconscious, with his long arms and legs sprawled out. His feet hung over the edge of his twin bed. Bree returned to the kitchen and picked up her coffee. "Both are still out cold."

"They had a long, rough day yesterday."

"Yes." Sadness brought her exhaustion flooding back.

Matt ran a hand across the granite counter. "I have a question for you. How did your sister afford a place this nice on a hairstylist's salary?"

"She didn't."

Matt raised a brow.

"The farm belongs to Adam."

"Your brother?" Surprise lit Matt's face.

"I know. He looks like he's on the brink of homelessness." Bree tried to understand Adam, but the years of their childhood they'd spent apart had taken a toll on their relationship. "His paintings are hot commodities, but he doesn't care about money or buying things."

"Everyone cares about money."

"Nope. Not Adam. All he wants is to be left alone to paint. He drives the same old junker he bought in high school. He bought the place he's in years ago and hasn't put a nickel into it. All he sees is the natural light in his studio."

"He seems disinterested in you and the kids."

"He's interested, and he cares in his own way. If I called him right now and asked for ten thousand dollars, he'd transfer the money into my account before I could hang up the phone. He wouldn't even ask me what it was for." Bree rotated her shoulders and stretched her arms behind her back. "But he's always had an emotional disconnect. I don't know whether he was born that way or if it developed as a coping mechanism to our parents' deaths. He does the best he can to show us he loves us. But he is what he is. No one is perfect." Loving your family meant accepting them for what they were.

"He supported Erin financially."

"He wanted to put the farm in Erin's name, but I talked him out of it."

"Why? Was she bad with money?"

"No. She had bad taste in men." Before Bree could explain, Brody's head snapped up. He jumped to his feet and trotted toward the front of the house.

"Somebody's here." Matt followed the dog.

Bree brought up the rear. She looked out the living room window. A Dodge Durango was parked in the driveway. The rear hatch was open, and Dana was unloading a suitcase and a pet carrier. The sight of her nearly brought tears to Bree's eyes.

"That's my friend, Dana. She's also my partner."

Matt called Brody away from the door so Bree could go outside. Dana rolled the suitcase toward the porch. Bree greeted her on the bottom step with a hug. Dana patted her back. "I'm so sorry."

"Thanks." Misty-eyed, Bree released her.

Dana thrust the cat carrier at her. "You owe me. He howled for five hours."

"Thanks for bringing him. I'm probably going to be here for a couple of weeks. I don't want to leave him alone that long, and there's too much going on here for me to make the drive." Bree led her into the house and introduced her to Matt and Brody. Dana stroked the dog's head but gave Bree a questioning stare.

"Is there more in the car?" Matt asked.

"There is," Dana said.

"I'll get it." Matt went out the door, with the dog at his heels.

Dana pushed her sunglasses to the top of her head and watched him through the front window. Turning back, she gave Bree a Look. "Girl."

Bree rolled her eyes. "He's just a friend."

"Well, that's a damned shame."

"It's complicated."

"Uh-huh." Dana parked the suitcase next to the wall.

"He's my sister's ex's best friend."

"The same ex the local LEOs think killed her?"

"Yep."

"OK. That is complicated." Dana took off her coat. "He a cop?"

"He *was* a cop."

"So, he's going to stick his nose in the case. As are you."

"Yep."

"Do you think he's going to get in your way?" Dana asked.

Bree shook her head. "Actually, I think he's solid."

"Good." Dana peeled her bright blue hat off and tousled her hair. "You're doing all right with his dog?"

"I'm trying. He's a nice dog. The kids like him."

"Good for you." Dana stuffed her hat into the pocket of her jacket. "I brought everything on your list and threw in a few more things I thought you could use."

"I can't thank you enough for driving up here." Bree took her coat and hung it on the coat-tree.

"Of course I came." Dana looked offended. "We're partners."

"Well, thank you again. I have to call the captain and HR this morning and request emergency leave."

"Any ideas about what you're going to do long term?"

"No." Bree couldn't think about it. "I need to get through the next few days."

Matt brought two more suitcases and a box into the house. He set everything by the front door. Brody sniffed the cat carrier.

Bree eyed the amount of luggage and turned back to Dana. "Did you bring everything in my closet?"

"Just the winter stuff. The blue suitcase is mine."

"You're staying?" Shock washed over Bree.

"It sounded like you needed more than clothes, your cat, and your backup piece," Dana said. "I can stay as long as you like."

"What did you tell the captain?" Bree asked.

"I said bah-bye." Dana waved her fingers. "I shifted some PTO around. They were going to pay me for the days, but it's not a big deal. I'm still officially retiring on schedule. I'm just on vacation until then."

"I don't know what to say." Bree was overwhelmed.

"You don't have to say anything. You'd do the same for me." Dana shrugged. "Besides, you're a temporary reprieve from my cousin and that crappy night security job."

The cat let out a yowl from the carrier. Brody wagged his tail.

"How is your dog with cats?" Dana asked Matt.

"He likes them," Matt answered.

Bree opened the wire door. "This is Vader." The cat stalked from the carrier and sat, calmly contemplating the dog with bright yellow eyes. He lifted a coal-black paw and began washing his whiskers.

Brody whined and stuck his nose in the cat's face. With lightning speed, Vader smacked him solidly on the nose and went back to licking his paw and cleaning his whiskers as if nothing had happened.

The dog backed up three steps and looked up at Matt.

"Sorry, buddy," Matt said. "It's a cat. Nothing I can do."

"He can be a bully." Carrying the box of cat supplies, Bree led the way back to the kitchen. "Let's get you settled, Vader."

Matt leaned on the counter and crossed his arms. Dana set her purse, keys, and sunglasses on the island. Bree filled bowls of food and water. The cat leaped onto the kitchen island. He stared at Dana's face and lifted a paw over her sunglasses.

"Don't you do it." Dana shook a finger at him.

Maintaining eye contact, Vader knocked her sunglasses to the floor.

"Your cat's a jerk." Dana picked up her glasses, put them and her keys into her purse, and set them out of Vader's reach.

"Yeah, but he's my jerk," Bree said.

Dana helped herself to coffee. "Has anything happened since I talked to you last night?"

"No," Bree said.

"Good." Dana drank her coffee black. "I spent the entire drive thinking about the kids. Did Justin formally adopt them?"

"No, and with his addiction record, I doubt he could get custody now. The fact that Erin made him move out clearly indicated her feelings on the matter."

"Yes. So, where is their father?" Dana asked.

A chill ran through Bree's body. "I have no idea, and it scares the hell out of me. Luke is fifteen, almost sixteen. He'll have more to say in where he lives. But Kayla is only eight, and she has a biological father out there somewhere, though she's never met him."

"What's he like?" Matt asked, leaning on the counter.

"Good-looking. Smooth-talking. When he's actually employed, he's usually selling something. He's able to adapt his personality to the situation. He plays at being both a ladies' man and a man's man." Bree pictured his smug face. "Most people like him instantly."

"But not you," Matt said.

"No," Bree agreed. "The very first time I met him, he reminded me of my father." Jake Taggert had been a completely different person when other people were around than when he was alone with his immediate family. She'd seen a photo of him once with a smile on his face, and she'd barely recognized him. "Craig immediately set off my asshole alarm."

"Your sister seemed smart. How did he fool her?" Dana asked.

Bree's coffee soured in her mouth. "Craig Vance could sell sand to a desert. Erin's relationship with him was volatile. He got her pregnant with Luke when she was sixteen. Then he was in and out of her life for years. She could never count on him for financial or parental support. But every time he showed up on her doorstep, she took him back as if he had some kind of hold on her."

Dana drummed her fingers on the island. "When was the last time she saw him?"

Anger bubbled in Bree's throat. "When she told him she was pregnant with Kayla, he was pissed. He beat her up and went out to a bar."

Dana lowered her mug. "And you didn't kill him?"

"I wasn't here," Bree said, the guilt sliding over her like a scratchy old sweater. "Anyway, after he hit her while she was pregnant, Erin was finally done with him. While he was out drinking, she changed the locks, packed up his shit, and put it in the driveway. When he came home, she told him they were through. As far as I know, that's the last time she had contact with Craig."

"Good for her." Dana's eyes went fierce. "So, if he shows up, we shoot him on sight?"

Matt jerked a thumb at Dana. "I like her."

"Me too, but I don't think that's a viable plan." Bree paced. "I don't want to look for Craig, but I suppose it would be best to know where he is and what he's doing. I can't imagine he'd want the financial burden of two children he's actively avoided supporting for years."

"Right," Matt agreed. "But wouldn't the kids' natural father be their automatic new guardian? Won't the court try to find him or make you notify him?"

Bree shook her head. "He wasn't around when either of them was born, so he isn't listed on their birth certificates. Legally, the kids have no father. Even when he and Erin hooked up last time, he didn't legally acknowledge paternity of Luke. He didn't want the financial responsibility."

"You sister never pursued child support?" Matt asked.

"She was afraid he'd leave her if she pressed the issue," Bree admitted. Craig had definitely been Erin's weakness.

Matt frowned. "Is there any reason he could have killed Erin?"

"Not that I can think of." But the idea disturbed Bree.

Craig was selfish enough to be a killer, even if she couldn't think of a motive.

Matt looked skeptical of her answer too.

"I'll start inquiries this morning," Dana said. "Maybe you'll get lucky, and he died at some point over the years."

As cold as it sounded, Bree agreed with her.

"Brody and I are going to head home." Matt pushed off the counter. "He needs breakfast, and I need a shower. I'm going to talk to Justin's neighbors today, then maybe cruise some of the camping sites he likes. When I was at his house, I noted his gear was missing. I want to follow up on that other lead we talked about last night. I'll let you know if I learn anything interesting."

Bree nodded. "I have a ton of calls to make this morning. Then I thought I'd go over to the salon. Most of Erin's friends worked there. I can talk to her boss too."

"You're looking for a killer," Dana said. "I don't like the idea of either one of you finding one alone. I'd feel better if you watched each other's backs."

"Sure," Matt said with a small, slightly smug smile. "We could do that."

"Matt and I already decided to work together." Bree just hadn't told him yet. But what he'd said the night before had repeated in her thoughts over and over while she attempted to fall asleep.

Those kids need you.

He'd been right, and she'd been foolish to chase the intruder alone in the dark. She was used to being alone, to having no one except Vader dependent on her. But all that had changed with her sister's death. Bree had to be more careful.

"Good." Dana nodded. "Then that's settled."

Footsteps thundered on the steps. Luke and Kayla rushed into the kitchen.

"Dana!" Kayla ran to her.

Luke hung back a little, but Dana enveloped both kids in a huge hug. "I missed you two."

While Dana greeted the kids, Bree walked Matt to the door. "When do you want to meet?"

Matt checked the time on his phone. "How about I pick you up at noon?"

Bree nodded. "That'll give me time to make phone calls, but you don't need to pick me up. I can meet you."

"I'll pick you up." Matt and the dog left.

Bree frowned, irritated at his bossiness and also at the way her body relaxed as soon as the dog was gone. She still wasn't sure how she felt about Matt. He was sure that Justin was innocent, and Bree was not. Still, her instincts told her he was being straight with her. They had an additional suspect, but they didn't even have a full name for Nico, the drug dealer. Justin was still the prime suspect in Bree's mind, but thoughts of Craig left her distinctly . . .

Unsettled.

Chapter Thirteen

Matt sipped from his travel mug of coffee as Bree jogged from the house toward his SUV.

He'd spent the last few hours driving all over town and checking Justin's favorite camping spots. Matt had also called Justin's friends. No one had seen him.

"You didn't have to leave Brody at home," Bree said as she slid into the passenger seat, though she appeared relieved the dog was not with him.

"It's fine." Matt drove away from the house. "My sister promised to take him for a long walk this afternoon. She'll spoil him rotten. Where are we going first?"

"Halo Salon and Spa. I made an appointment to speak with the salon's owner, Jack Halo. I'd also like to talk to my sister's best friend, Stephanie Wallace, but she didn't answer her phone. Steph and Erin had stations next to each other for years. Halo changed ownership about a year ago. Erin was worried about her job for a while. She was relieved to have survived the transition."

"What are you doing about your job?"

"Between vacation and other accrued PTO, I can swing three or four weeks."

"Family and Medical Leave Act might apply to you too."

"The kids would have to be my legal wards for me to apply for that."

Matt knew she was going to raise those children, even if she wasn't ready to admit it yet. "Did you call the schools too?"

"Yes. The counselors both said to let the kids decide when they wanted to return to school. I was hoping for more concrete advice."

"At least they confirmed what you'd been thinking." Matt rubbed his jaw. He'd showered and shaved but still felt sluggish. "You should trust your instincts with the kids. You're good with them."

"I guess, but it feels like I'm treading water in the middle of the ocean with no land in sight. Sure, I know the mechanics, how to move my arms and legs to stay afloat. But how long could I keep it up before I sink?"

The amount of responsibility she was assuming must be suffocating.

"You OK?" he asked, his eyes probing hers.

Bree didn't answer. She looked as if she didn't know if she was ever going to be OK again.

"Erin loved her job. I tried to talk her into going to college, maybe becoming an accountant or something. But she loved doing something different every day. She enjoyed being creative and making women feel good about themselves. I probably should have appreciated her for what she was instead of always trying to change her."

Matt shrugged. "Sisters are supposed to be bossy. Mine is younger than me. She loves to tell me what to do."

Bree laughed, surprising him.

"Seriously, give yourself a break," Matt said. "You loved your sister. You cared enough to talk to her about her life and give her advice."

Bree nodded and sighed. "You know everything about my family. Tell me about yours."

"I have two siblings. My older brother is a retired MMA fighter. He just opened his own MMA studio. My little sister operates a dog rescue and runs the office of my brother's studio. Dad is a retired family doctor. Mom taught high school English."

"No deep, dark family secrets?"

"Afraid not," Matt said. "Nolan becoming a professional fighter was not a popular decision with my parents, but him going all black sheep is the only real family controversy."

"That must be nice."

"Here we are." Matt turned into the entrance of Halo Salon and Spa and parked. "Ready?"

"Yes." Bree reached for the door handle. They stepped out of the vehicle and crossed the lot. Matt opened the glass door for her, and Bree went inside. The lobby was open and modern, with a clear view of the main salon area. The space was designed with an open concept. Hairstyling stations were on the left side of the room. Behind them, shampoo sinks lined the rear wall. To the right were a cluster of manicure stations. Through a doorway, Matt could see chairs with footbaths in another room. In the back wall, there was a doorway on each side that led to the back of the building. In the front of the space, the reception counter divided the lobby from the salon. Shaped like a comma, it circled partially around an open spiral staircase.

They walked to the counter.

A middle-aged woman dressed in all black greeted them. Pink highlights shone in her blonde hair. "Can I help you?"

Bree gave her name and introduced Matt. "We're here to see Jack Halo. We have an appointment."

Matt wondered if that was his real name.

"Right this way." The woman emerged from behind the counter and led Bree and Matt up the spiral staircase to the second-floor landing. In front of the landing was a central hall lined with doorways. Additional hallways flanked the second story.

"What's up here?" Bree asked.

The women turned left and lowered her voice. "Private rooms for facials, massages, and waxing services, and administrative offices."

They passed a row of closed doors. The receptionist knocked lightly on a door, then opened it. Sticking her head inside, she said, "Jack, Ms. Taggert and Mr. Flynn are here."

She stepped aside, and Bree and Matt entered the room. A long table covered with drawings dominated the space.

A man of about fifty stood next to the table. He set down a pair of trendy red-framed glasses. His snug black T-shirt highlighted his paunch. He wore his silver-streaked hair slicked back and shiny. He sucked in his gut as he turned to greet them.

Bree offered him a hand. "Thank you for seeing us."

"Of course." He walked toward Bree, reaching for her with two grabby hands, his fingers curled into hooks. "I'm so sorry for your loss." He took both of her hands, pulled her closer, and kissed her cheek.

Though clearly not comfortable with the aggressive greeting, Bree accepted the kiss with grace.

"We're all heartbroken." Jack released Bree. "Erin was part of our extended Halo family."

"Thank you." Bree stepped back and introduced Matt as a friend.

They shook hands. Jack grabbed Matt's elbow and gripped his hand hard, like an alpha male wannabe. Matt was six inches taller and fifty pounds heavier. The thought of Jack being an alpha anything was laughable, but Matt let him have his illusion. Whatever made him talkative.

"I was hoping you'd answer a few questions for me," Bree said. "As you can imagine, this has all been such a shock. We're still not thinking straight."

"Of course." Jack wrapped an arm around her shoulders and steered her toward a chair, physically controlling her body and movement, as he'd done with Matt. "Please sit down."

Bree eased into the seat, and Jack went to a mini fridge. He pulled out a bottle of water.

She pointed toward the drawings on the table. "What are these?"

Jack twisted off the cap of the water bottle and offered it to her. "We're going to renovate the downstairs. These are some initial concepts I drew up."

Bree took the bottle. Matt scanned the drawings. Jack had talent. His plans were modern and sleek, with plenty of gray and white.

Instead of sitting at the table, Matt crossed his arms and leaned against the wall. Jack wanted to talk to Bree, so Matt would let her run the interview.

"Now, how can I help you?" Jack turned a chair to face Bree and sat.

"I'm trying to figure out what happened to my sister." Bree sipped the water.

Jack reached for Bree's hand and patted it. "What happened to Erin is horrible. I can't imagine. She was so . . . normal. Not the sort of person you expect to be murdered."

Bree blinked at the word *murdered*. With a quick shake of her head, she cleared her throat. "Erin worked for you for a long time."

"She's worked for the salon for ten years," Jack said. "But I only bought Halo last year."

"Her clients loved her."

"For the most part." Jack's voice went vague. "But she was acting different lately."

Bree waited for him to elaborate. Jack wanted to talk, but something was holding him back.

"Was her job performance affected?" Bree prompted.

"Erin was a model employee for the first eleven months she worked for me. Reliable. Never late. She only called out if one of the kids was sick." Jack enveloped Bree's hand between his own.

Bree raised a brow but didn't jerk away. "I'm sensing a *but*."

Jack looked away for a few seconds, his brows lowering. "She seemed distracted the last few weeks. She was late twice. She left her station to take personal phone calls, which is against company policy. I had to reprimand her." Annoyance creased his forehead. "Her ex came here, demanding to talk to her when she was in the middle of a blowout."

"Justin was here?" Bree clarified.

"Yes." Jack nodded. "They argued. He got loud and very emotional."

"Did you hear what they argued about?" Bree asked.

"No. At my suggestion, they took their conversation out into the parking lot." Jack released Bree's hand and sat back. "But she was out there for twenty minutes. Her client was very unhappy. I had to give her a free manicure and promise her a new stylist to keep her as a patron." He shook his head. "Erin and I had a long talk after that. I told her that it couldn't happen again, or she would lose her job."

Bree appeared momentarily speechless. In Matt's opinion, a visit from an agitated boyfriend seemed more like a situation for an employer to intervene and make sure his female employee was safe rather than reprimanded.

"Did she say anything about the argument?" Bree asked, and for the first time, it seemed she was struggling to keep her cool.

"No, and I didn't ask. I don't have time to be everyone's friend. I run a tight ship here." Jack flushed and picked a piece of lint from his T-shirt. "We have policies. I have over fifty employees. I can't make exceptions."

Can't? Or won't?

Bree's jaw grated, as if she was trying to control her temper. Her visible response was exactly why it was hard to investigate a case that hit too close to home. But the important thing was to get Jack talking, not win an argument with him, or make him see that he was a jerk.

"Of course." Matt stepped in. "It must be hard."

"These young people." Jack shook his head. "They have no work ethic. Give them an inch, and they take ten miles."

Anger sparked in Bree's eyes like a solar flare.

Matt cleared his throat. "Do you remember what day this happened?"

"Yes," Jack said. "The deputy asked the same question, so I looked it up for him. I filed a reprimand in Erin's personnel file last Friday." He opened a file on the table and showed it to Bree.

Bree gave him a small smile that looked more like she was baring her teeth. "Do you know when Erin left work on Tuesday?"

"The deputy asked that too." Jack nodded. "She worked from eight to four."

"Thank you so much for all your help," Matt lied. "We appreciate your cooperation."

"Of course," Jack said. "I hope they find out who did this to your sister."

"Thank you." Bree set the water bottle on the table. "I'd like to talk to some of the girls. I know Erin was close to a few of them."

"No. I'm sorry. You'll have to speak with them off premises," Jack said. "A sheriff's deputy was here this morning. He interviewed the staff and made them all cry. It was very disruptive." He spread his hands wide. "The salon is busy downstairs. I can't allow you to get the girls all upset again. I'm sure you understand."

Matt didn't, but there wasn't anything he or Bree could do about it. He was no longer in law enforcement, and this wasn't Bree's jurisdiction. No one *had* to talk to them.

Jack stood. "Let me get you the things in her locker. Wait here." He left the room.

Matt pushed off the wall. "I'm going to use the restroom. I'll meet you in the lobby." Since Jack had turned left, Matt went right. Fire code would require a staircase or two in addition to the spiral one behind the reception desk. At the end of the corridor, Matt spotted an EXIT sign mounted on the wall. He went through a steel door and down a set of concrete steps. On the first floor, he pushed through another steel door into a hallway that ran the length of the salon. He didn't run into anyone until he passed the restrooms.

Matt made his way to the reception desk to ask where he could find Stephanie Wallace, then he followed the receptionist's directions to a station on the other side of the room. Stephanie was a tiny brunette who tottered along in a pair of thigh-high, ankle-breaker boots. She was sweeping clipped hair from the black mat under her swivel chair.

"I'm a friend of Erin's sister," he explained. "We need to talk."

Her heavily made-up eyes welled with tears. She glanced back at the desk. "My boss . . ." She grabbed a business card from her station and wrote a phone number on it. "I'm off tomorrow morning. We can meet then. Text me." She turned around to greet her next client.

Matt slid the card into his pocket.

When he caught up with Bree in the lobby a few minutes later, she was carrying a black reusable shopping bag with the Halo Salon and Spa logo on the side. The expression behind her eyes suggested she'd like to chew Jack Halo's head right off his body.

Voices and blow-dryers echoed in the tiled space, and the air smelled heavily of perfumed products.

He leaned close to Bree's ear. "We'll talk to Steph tomorrow."

"Thank you," Bree said through tight lips.

Matt pushed through the glass doors and welcomed the nonperfumed air in his face.

Bree kept her emotions in check until she climbed into the SUV and closed the door. "My sister's ten-year career at the salon boiled down to the contents of one reusable nylon bag that he couldn't wait to get rid of."

"What an ass." Matt started the engine. "Good job not strangling him."

"Yes." She exhaled. "Now we know that Justin came here and argued with Erin."

Matt frowned but didn't comment, and he drove out of the parking lot.

"I don't want him to be guilty either," Bree said. "But you have to consider the possibility."

But he didn't have to like it. "Where are we going now?"

"I'd like to walk the crime scene and talk with Justin's neighbors. I called Todd Harvey this morning. He said Justin's house had been fully processed and released."

"Are you sure you want to see the scene?" Matt asked.

Her eyes said no as her voice said, "Yes. *Want* has nothing to do with it. I owe Erin." She leaned against the headrest. "If the chief deputy found a burner phone, would he tell you?"

"I don't know." Matt headed for Justin's place. "I think he would have asked me about it."

"Have you told him about the burner?"

"No," Matt admitted.

"Why not?"

"I'm not sure I fully trust Todd."

"Are you sure that's the reason? Or did you not tell him because it makes Justin look even guiltier?"

Matt didn't respond, but the answer was *maybe*.

Bree exhaled. "It could be an important lead, and we don't know what the sheriff's department has in terms of evidence at this point."

"You're right. I'll tell him. I want to touch base with him later today anyway."

But Matt was hoping by the end of today, he would also be able to give the chief deputy evidence that pointed at a different suspect. They drove the rest of the way in silence. Matt parked at the curb in front of the house. He got out of the SUV, reached into his pocket, and pulled out the key. Bree stood on the front walkway, staring up at the front door.

"Are you sure you want to go inside?" Matt asked.

Bree nodded. "But I'd like to walk the outside of the property first."

They walked around to the back of the house. Justin's yard didn't have a fence, and footprints obliterated the snow.

"Was the snow covered with tracks that night too?" she asked, scanning the yard.

"Yes. The storm was the week before, and there are a lot of kids in this neighborhood." Matt gestured toward the glass door. "The slider was open."

"Did Justin leave that way?"

"We don't know what happened here, including who was here when Erin was shot." Matt led the way back to the front stoop. He unlocked it, and they went inside. As they stood in the entryway, Matt sniffed. The house smelled normal, with no old blood scent.

Bree hesitated at the threshold. He didn't blame her. Her sister had died here.

"Why don't you search the kitchen and den, and I'll do the bedroom?" he suggested.

Bree paused, rubbing her solar plexus with one hand as if it burned. "I usually like to see the entire scene. As an investigator, there's a lot to be learned from getting the killer's perspective."

Is this something she needs to face to come to terms with her sister's death?

"I agree," he said. "I walked the crime scenes whenever I could, but the victim was never your sister. Do you *really* need to see that?"

"We'll stay together." Her fist was clenched against her gut, and Matt could feel the burning as if it were his own.

"Still don't trust me?" he asked.

"Not entirely." She led the way down the hall into the kitchen. "But that isn't the reason. You mentioned earlier that Justin's camping gear was gone. You've been in his house before. I haven't. Only you will spot other things that are missing."

Matt returned to her side. "That makes sense."

They walked through the kitchen, opening cabinets and drawers. Bree checked the refrigerator.

She touched the pizza box on the counter. "Erin loved pizza."

Her breath caught, and she took a deep breath before moving on.

Matt wandered into the den. "Justin's game system isn't here."

Bree walked over to stand next to him.

He pointed to a dust-free rectangle on the table under the TV. "Everything else seems the same in this room."

"Then let's tackle the bedroom." Bree turned toward the hallway and the scene of the crime.

CHAPTER FOURTEEN

Bree strode down the hall. If she hesitated even for a second, she'd lose her nerve. She stopped in the doorway to Justin's bedroom. A large square of the carpet had been cut out. Forensics had taken the blood-soaked piece with them. Dark red stained the raw plywood. Erin had bled so heavily that her blood had saturated the carpet and seeped through to the subfloor. Anger flared inside Bree, a rage so quick and sharp it burned. Her vision tunneled, the edges of her sight turning red.

She felt hands on her arms, steering her out of the room. The moment passed, her chest loosened, and the air rushed into her lungs. She tried to shake off Matt's hands. "I need to see."

"No, you don't." He gripped her biceps tighter as he marched her through the rest of the house and outside. She gulped cold air, snapping herself out of her anger.

Back at the SUV, she turned and leaned against the vehicle. She panted, her breaths fast and furious. "I *need* to know what happened." She wanted to imprint it on her mind so she would never forget.

"Why?" His question jarred her. "Why do you need to do this to yourself?"

Bree stared at the house. Images of her sister bleeding out on the beige carpet swept through her mind like a subway train. Unable to stop them, she let them pass through, shuddering when the barrage ended.

Why *did* she want to know? To see where her sister died. Why was it so important to her?

"Are you stoking some deep-seated need for revenge?" he asked.

"No. It's true I want justice for Erin, but I'm not a vigilante." Deep down, Bree knew even the desire for justice wasn't behind her need to experience her sister's death.

"There are crime scene photos to view. Why do you want to inflict this kind of unnecessary pain on yourself?" Matt's eyes lit with understanding. "That's it, isn't it? You want to punish yourself."

Bree turned away. His assessment rang all too true. She wanted to hurt. Pain felt good, like a release of sorts.

Matt leaned on the car next to her, his shoulder pressing lightly against hers. "Are you all right?"

Bree turned her face to the winter sun. The rays—or shame—heated her face. "I should know what was going on in Erin's head. My sister's life should not be a mystery to me."

"When she was in trouble, you were the person she reached out to. But someone killed her before you could help. That is not your fault. You dropped everything because you were worried about her."

She glanced at him. "Erin was murdered in that house, and I can't even woman up enough to walk the scene."

One of his eyebrows lifted. "In my eyes, you're pretty badass. But you're still human. Give yourself a break. This case is not like any other you've ever worked. There's no way to detach yourself from it. No way to see it objectively. That's why we're working together, remember?"

She swallowed, then nodded.

"Are you up to talking to the neighbors?"

"Yes." She needed action. Only Justin's block was long. "Let's split up. There are twenty houses on this street. I'll take that side."

"OK." Matt turned away and headed for the first house on the same side of the street as Justin's.

Bree jogged across the road. No one answered her knock at the first two houses she tried. She approached a white house directly across from Justin's house. She avoided a patch of ice on the front walk and rang the bell. Faded red paint peeled off the front door like sunburned skin. She heard footsteps behind the closed door, and a curtain shifted in the narrow window next to it.

A second later, the door opened. A young man stood in the opening, running a hand through his bedhead. "Can I help you?"

"Hi." Bree wished she had a badge to flash. "I'm investigating the murder that happened across the street Tuesday night. Can I ask you a few questions?"

His head drew backward a few inches, and he moved as if preparing to close the door. "Are you a cop?"

Then again, maybe she was better off not having a badge. She shook her head. "This isn't an official visit. The victim was my sister."

He relaxed. "Oh, man. That sucks."

"Were you home Tuesday evening?"

He nodded.

"My name is Bree."

"I'm Porter Ryan."

"Do you know Justin, Porter?" Bree pointed to Justin's house.

One shoulder shrugged. "Not by name, but, you know, I wave if I see him."

"Did you see any activity over there Tuesday evening?"

He shook his head. "I worked late. But I did notice something weird last night." His brow creased. "I saw a flashlight in the house."

"A flashlight?"

"Yeah. And it wasn't just for a couple of minutes. The light was there for, like, a half hour."

"What time did you see the light?" Bree wondered if the person with the flashlight was the same person she'd chased out of her sister's house.

"Between six and seven?" He didn't sound sure.

"Did you tell the sheriff's department?"

"No. A deputy came to talk to me late Tuesday night. That was the night before this happened."

"Would you be willing to give a statement about it?"

"Sure. Is it important?"

"Maybe." Bree raised a hand in a *Who knows?* gesture. She asked for his number, and he gave it to her. "I appreciate you talking to me."

"No problem. Sorry about your sister."

"Thanks." Bree turned away.

She wrote a note about what he'd said and continued down the street. She knocked on doors and interviewed more neighbors. No one else had anything interesting to add, though that didn't stop people from talking. It was late afternoon when she caught up with Matt at the end of the street. While they walked back to Justin's house, she told him about the flashlights Porter Ryan had seen.

"That is strange. If a deputy or CSI tech needed to go back into the house, they would have turned on the house lights. Only someone who didn't want to be seen would have used a flashlight. Could be the same intruder that broke into Erin's house."

"Right," Bree said. "How did you do?"

"Not as well as you. No one was home at a few houses. The woman next door thought she heard a car backfire somewhere around eight o'clock, give or take a half hour, something she said she already told the sheriff's department."

"What do we do now?" She stopped next to his SUV. "I'd like to know who was in the house and why."

"Me too." Matt stared at the house. "You up for a stakeout?"

"Yes."

"It's four o'clock. Porter said the lights didn't appear until six or seven. Let's grab food and come back." Matt walked around the front of his vehicle and opened the door.

Bree slid into the passenger seat. They drove to a deli, used the restrooms, and bought coffee and sandwiches. It was dark when Matt parked down the street from Justin's house. They ate while they watched the house.

He called his sister and asked her to feed Brody. Not wanting to need another bathroom break, Bree limited herself to a few sips of coffee. The quiet in the SUV felt comfortable as they watched and waited until lights flickered in Justin's front window.

"Go time." Matt set his coffee in the console cup holder.

She checked the time on her phone. "Six thirty."

"That's ballsy." Matt leaned across the seat and opened his glove compartment. He took out a big black Maglite, then found a smaller version in the console. "People are still coming home from work. Someone experienced in B and Es would wait until the neighborhood quieted down."

"Yes. My intruder waited until we were all asleep, but he knows no one is home here."

Since Matt wasn't armed, and a heavy metal flashlight was an excellent weapon, Bree took the small light.

They slid out of the SUV and jogged down the dark street.

"You have a key," Bree said. "You take the front door. He probably went in the back and left it unlocked." Bree angled toward the side yard.

"I don't like splitting up."

"I don't like that you're not armed." Bree drew her weapon. "You want my backup piece?"

"No."

She sighed. "We still need to cover both exits."

Grumbling, Matt headed for the front door. Bree crept to the slider. Putting her shoulder to the house, she peered around the doorframe. She saw no flashlight beam cutting through the darkness inside. Was he in the bedroom? Or had he heard them?

She could see straight down the hall. The front door opened, and Matt's big frame appeared. As he came toward her, Bree tried the slider and found it unlocked. She eased the door open and slipped inside. Neither of them used their flashlights.

Matt veered off toward the bedroom. Bree eyed the closed door of the walk-in kitchen pantry. She tiptoed to it and gently turned the knob. Empty. She moved toward the coat closet as Matt veered toward a closet in the den.

Bree reached for the doorknob. The door flew open. A hooded figure rushed from the closet and ran straight into her.

CHAPTER FIFTEEN

Bree landed flat on her back on the carpet. The impact sent the air whooshing from her lungs, and the person she'd collided with stumbled from the impact.

"Hey!" Matt lunged toward them.

The intruder regained his footing and leaped toward the sliding glass doors. As he jumped over Bree's body, she kicked out, sweeping his feet out from under him. The intruder face-planted on the carpet. Bree was on his back before Matt could cross the room. By the time he reached her, seconds later, she had one knee in the intruder's lower back and his arm chicken-winged behind him. His face was pressed into the carpet.

"Need help?" Matt asked over her shoulder.

"Nah." Gritting her teeth, Bree leaned forward. "I've got him."

He was not getting away.

Matt pulled out his phone and called the sheriff's department. He shoved his phone back into his pocket thirty seconds later. "A deputy is on his way."

"Ow. Ow. Stop," the intruder cried as she shifted her weight. "That hurts."

Ignoring his protests, Bree asked, "Are you armed?"

"No."

She began patting the outsides of his pockets. "Is there anything in your pockets that could cut me? Knives, needles, razor . . ."

"No," he said. "Wait. Keys. Do they count?" His voice was high-pitched, his words hurried.

Afraid.

Is this Erin's killer?

Rage and grief blinded Bree for a few seconds. She closed her eyes, took one deep breath, and opened them again. Training and experience took over, and she resumed searching him for weapons and drugs. She turned the pockets of his jeans inside out. She dropped a set of keys to the floor and tossed a wallet to Matt. The man was lying on top of his jacket pockets. "I'm going to release your arm. You aren't going to move."

"OK. OK." He froze as she slowly moved off his back.

"Roll over," she ordered. "Spread your arms out at your sides."

He did exactly as he was told. The hood dropped off his face. He was in his late twenties, yet acne still covered most of his skin. Thin, sparse facial hair dotted his jaw, looking more like dirt than a beard. The zipper of his jacket was open. Under it, he wore an oversized black T-shirt along with baggy jeans over a pudgy body.

Bree climbed to her feet. She rocked from her heels to her toes, unable to remain still with adrenaline rushing through her veins.

Matt opened the wallet. He plucked out the man's driver's license and compared the photo to his face. "His name is Trey White. He's twenty-seven. He lives over on Pine Road. That's only a few blocks from here."

"Why did you break in here today, Trey?" Bree searched his jacket pockets. "And why did you break into my sister's house last night?"

"What?" Trey asked.

A piece of fabric fell from his jacket pocket. A pair of black silk thong panties landed on the floor. Her stomach did a sick roll. Had the ME been wrong? Had Erin been raped? This guy could be a sexual deviant who'd returned to the scene of the crime to collect a trophy from his victim. She took a deep breath through her nose to quell the nausea. "Where did you get these?"

Trey's eyes opened wide. "A d-drawer in the bedroom."

"Are you a pervert, Trey?" Matt asked.

"I don't have to talk to you!" Trey's protest sounded weak.

"Maybe you saw her through the window and couldn't resist," Matt suggested. "It's understandable. She was a beautiful woman. Beautiful women are never interested in you, are they? Does that make you angry? Angry enough to kill her?"

Trey licked his lips. "No. You don't understand. I didn't hurt anyone. I would never . . ."

Matt gestured toward the panties.

"It's hard to explain." Trey groaned.

Bree rocked back on her heels. She moved her wool coat aside to reveal the gun at her hip. She couldn't whip out her badge, but she wasn't above bluffing. "Try us."

"Shit! Are you a cop?"

Trey didn't need to know Bree was a few hundred miles outside her jurisdiction. Instead of answering, she said, "The sheriff's department is on the way. This is their case."

Trey covered his eyes with a hand, and he began to cry.

This was not working. He was shutting down. Bree had to change tactics. They didn't need this guy to start screaming for a lawyer. If he was an experienced criminal, he would have already stopped cooperating. She wanted him to talk, and it didn't matter how she accomplished that. If acting like his buddy did the trick, so be it.

"Look, Trey." Bree shifted her tone from angry cop to big sister. "You've been here before."

He nodded. "I couldn't believe she was dead. I needed to sit in the last place she sat. To connect with her again." His gaze landed on the thong, and embarrassment flushed his cheeks. "I just wanted something of hers." Trey's gaze shifted from Matt to Bree. When neither responded, he continued. "To remember her."

"You knew her?" Matt asked.

Trey nodded with enthusiasm. "I work at the dollar store across from Halo." His gaze shifted to the panties and his flush faded to a sickly green color, as if he'd only just realized the full scope of what he'd done. "Erin came into the store, like, once a week. I always knew when one of her kids had a project. She was nice to me, not like most people."

Bree's adrenaline abandoned her. She went cold down to her bones. "You broke into this house and stole a pair of a woman's—a dead woman's—underwear because she was nice to you?"

He blinked away from her gaze. "When you put it like that, it sounds pretty bad."

"Is that what you were doing at her house last night?" Bree asked. "Trying to get a keepsake?"

Trey shook his head. "I don't know what you're talking about. I knew this place was empty, and it would be easy enough to pop the sliding door."

Matt leaned closer. "Do you do that often?"

"No, no. Geez, no," Trey stammered. "That's how I used to sneak back into my dad's house when I missed curfew when I was a kid. I'm not a criminal."

"Breaking and entering, burglary, and disturbing a crime scene are all illegal," Bree said.

The truth of that finally dawned in the guy's eyes. "I'm fucked."

"You are," Bree agreed. But she wasn't at all sure that he was the same man who'd broken into Erin's house the previous night.

A car door closed outside. Matt went to the door and let a deputy in.

"This is Trey White," Bree said. "He jumped out of a closet and tried to run away with these." She pointed at the panties. "I'll let him explain."

Trey stuttered through an explanation as the deputy handcuffed him, collected his personal effects, and bagged the underwear as evidence. The deputy said to Bree and Matt, "Chief Deputy Harvey wants to see you both in his office."

Bree nodded. "All right."

After the deputy took Trey away, Bree left Matt to lock the house. She stood on the sidewalk. The air had a frigid snap that bit into her lungs with every inhale, but the scent of smoke in the night was comforting. Someone close by had lit a fire tonight. Someone was living a normal life.

Matt joined her a minute later. He scanned her up and down. "Are you banged up?"

"No." A few bruises weren't worth mentioning. But weariness slid over her. Had she ever been this tired?

"Then let's go talk to Todd." He opened the vehicle door for her. Matt slid behind the wheel and pulled a bottle of water from a recess in the vehicle door. After twisting off the cap, he handed it to her and started the engine.

She sipped water as he drove to the sheriff's station. When they arrived, she was surprised to see the admin still behind the counter after business hours.

Marge escorted them to a conference room. "Todd will be here in a minute." She assessed Bree with one glance. "You look like hell." She turned to Matt. "Get her some tea with extra sugar from the break room."

"Tea would be much appreciated, but I don't use sugar," Bree said.

"You do today." Marge made a shooing gesture at Matt. "Get her some crackers from the vending machine too."

After he'd left the room, Marge lowered her voice. "You look like death. Go splash some cold water on your face."

Bree straightened her spine and walked to the restroom. Marge was right. Bree looked like a corpse. She followed Marge's orders and looked mostly alive when she was done.

Back in the conference room, Matt motioned to a Styrofoam cup of tea and a vending machine pack of crackers on the table.

"Do you always do what Marge says?" Bree sat down and sipped the tea.

"Yes." Shrugging, he drank from his own cup, which smelled like coffee. "She's worked in this department longer than anyone else. She knows everything about everyone."

"Good to know." Bree finished the crackers and tea, and her stomach settled. By the time the chief deputy walked into the room, she was functional.

Todd sat across from her. He took their statements, then pulled his notepad over a closed file. "Trey White is a tier-one sexual offender. He has a previous conviction for voyeurism and indecent exposure. He used to work at a department store. He drilled a hole in the wall, peeped in the ladies' dressing room, and masturbated while he watched."

"Trey is now a repeat offender." Matt scowled.

Todd tapped a finger on his closed notepad.

"Does he have an alibi for the last few nights?" Bree asked.

"Trey lives alone in the garage apartment of a private residence," Todd said. "No one sees him coming or going. But he says he was at work Tuesday night until nine. I sent a deputy to the dollar store to get a copy of their surveillance tapes. He just called. The store's security cameras aren't working, but the manager says Trey was scheduled to close Tuesday evening, and his time card was stamped in at three in the afternoon and out at nine thirty."

"Let me guess," Bree said. "He worked alone."

"Yes." Todd nodded. "And the last transaction on the register was rung up at six forty-four. Trey says he was stocking shelves. The store is never busy at night, so the lack of business wasn't unusual. The alarm was activated at nine eleven. My deputy is requesting tapes from the surrounding businesses. If he's telling the truth, he should show up on someone's surveillance feed going in or out of the store."

"Lacking an alibi isn't enough to make him the killer." Frustration burned in Bree's throat.

"It isn't," Todd agreed. "We'll also compare his DNA and fingerprints to samples pulled from the crime scene, and we're getting a search warrant for his apartment."

Something didn't feel right to Bree about Trey being Erin's killer. A work alibi was too easy to verify. If he hadn't been at work, he would have made up something harder to prove or disprove. "What will you do with him if his alibi checks out, Chief Deputy?" she asked.

"Call me Todd, and for now, he'll be charged with breaking and entering and burglary." The chief deputy leaned his elbows on the table and pinched the bridge of his nose. "He broke into a house and stole something very personal. His crime is disturbing, but he has no history of violence."

"He's still a sex offender," Matt said.

"True, and he's not going to get off easy. Burglary is a felony charge in New York State." Todd leaned back and scraped a hand across his scalp. "Trey doesn't have much money. With his prior convictions, he won't get released without bail, which we're hoping he won't be able to post." He shifted forward, landing on his elbows. "You should probably expect more weirdos to make appearances after that story on channel fifteen aired yesterday."

"What story?" Bree asked.

"I'm sorry," Todd said. "They rehashed your whole family history."

Bree used her phone to search for the channel's website. She hit "Play" on the video and turned up the volume.

"The Taggert family has a long history of violence and tragedy," the reporter began. Bree recognized the show she'd turned off when Kayla had been watching TV at Adam's house.

The journalist continued. "Erin Taggert, the sister of renowned artist Adam Taggert, was killed in the home of her estranged husband Tuesday night. In 1993, Erin and her siblings, Adam and Bree, survived the gruesome murder of their mother by their father. After shooting his wife, their father turned his gun on himself. All three children were home at the time of the murder-suicide. In an echo of that decades-old crime, Erin's estranged husband, Justin Moore, is currently wanted for his wife's murder. Is history repeating itself? Are these murders linked or simply a case of déjà vu?"

The reporter interviewed former neighbors and town residents. The video ended with a slideshow of family pictures. Bree's breath hitched at a snapshot of her and Erin and Adam shortly before their parents' deaths. She would have liked to have seen a normal family, but it wasn't there. Her eight-year-old eyes were haunted even before the killing. The violence had begun long before it imploded that January night.

She clicked "End." She'd heard enough.

Todd cleared his throat. "When we gave the media Justin's name as a person of interest, we posted a hotline number. We've had the usual fake confessions and false sightings, but calls to the hotline have increased tenfold since the program aired. People are calling about every white pickup truck they pass, and we've had thirty-seven sightings of Justin in the last twenty-four hours."

The exhaustion that sank into Bree's bones was more than physical. An hour ago, she'd thought she'd caught her sister's killer. Now everything felt wrong about Trey being guilty. She was back at square one.

"Do you have any new evidence in my sister's case?" she asked.

"Actually, I do." Todd shifted his weight forward again. "Justin's fingerprints were found in blood in several places inside his house."

Chapter Sixteen

Matt absorbed Todd's statement. "Justin was definitely in the house when Erin died."

"Yes." Todd clasped his hands in front of him.

Matt stood and paced the narrow space behind the conference table. "I still can't believe he would have shot her."

"Maybe it was an accident," Todd said. "Several of the men who worked at the auto shop stated that Justin was jumpy for the last few weeks. Maybe he took the gun because he thought he needed protection."

Matt shook his head. "If he and Erin just had sex, then she didn't surprise him. He knew she was there."

"True." Todd studied him for a few seconds, then did the same with Bree. "You're both connected to this case. I cannot allow you to contaminate the chain of evidence in any way."

Matt kept his mouth shut. He sensed a *but* the size of a Greyhound bus coming.

Todd nodded at him. "But I know Matt, and I've made a few inquiries about you." He inclined his head toward Bree. "You have multiple commendations, and I heard nothing but respect for you within the PPD." He breathed, long and deep. "You both have experience with homicide investigation. Your perspectives would be valuable. We can't work together in a formal sense, but I'd like to share information, under two conditions."

Matt stopped pacing. "Which are?"

"We keep our arrangement between us." Todd flushed. "No one here can know, except Marge. She knows everything anyway."

Matt read between the lines. Todd didn't trust all his own men.

"No worries," Matt said. "You don't have to explain the department's issues to *me*."

Bree nodded in agreement.

"And neither of you talks to the media." Todd glanced back and forth between them. "I'd like to control the information that goes public."

"OK." Matt dropped back into the chair next to Bree. "I hated being dragged into press conferences."

"It's fine with me too," Bree said to Todd. "What do you have besides the fingerprints?"

"This is what we know." Todd brought his file out from under his notepad and opened it. "Erin's fingerprints were found on the makeup and toiletry products in Justin's house, and the brands matched the products in her own bathroom. She definitely spent time at Justin's place. Most of the calls on her phone were to Justin and her kids, with a few to you and her friend from Halo, Stephanie Wallace." Todd looked at Bree. "But over the past three weeks, she received and placed seven calls to and from an unknown number. No texts. Calls only. Each call lasted eight to twenty-one minutes. This number appears to be associated with a prepaid phone. The carrier has no personal information on the user."

"Justin's dad said he had a burner phone," Matt said. "So far, we haven't been able to locate it."

Todd opened his notepad and wrote a note. "We don't know the number?"

"No." Matt tapped his fingers on the table. Justin had probably only used the burner for calling his drug dealer.

Todd lifted his pen. "Erin's bank statements show two cash withdrawals of three thousand dollars each over the past three weeks. Back in October, she withdrew an additional four thousand dollars. These withdrawals depleted her savings. Her income covered living expenses, and she was diligent about transferring some money into savings each month. But it took her a long time to accumulate that ten thousand dollars." Todd tapped the pen on the file. "The calls to the prepaid phone are clustered just prior to the withdrawals. It's possible she was giving someone money, either voluntarily or under duress."

"Can you get more information on this prepaid phone number?" Bree asked.

"I'm working on the warrant," Todd said. "That particular provider is not cooperative."

Every wireless company had different policies about releasing information to law enforcement.

"According to my nephew," Bree said, "October is around the time Erin bought a shotgun as well. Prior to that, she was very clear that she never wanted to own a firearm."

"Clearly, she felt threatened," Matt said.

"I understand the farm is owned by Adam Taggert?" Todd asked.

"Yes," Bree said. "Adam pays the insurance and taxes."

Todd squinted, his head tilting. "Would she have called you for money?"

"No." Bree shook her head. "Adam would write her a check with no questions asked. She would go to him if she needed cash."

Todd tapped his pen on his pad. "Why does your brother own the farm?"

Bree exhaled. "It seemed safer. Erin had a hard time saying no to the men in her life."

Todd scribbled on his notepad. "So, why did she call you on Tuesday evening if it wasn't for money?"

"I don't know, but she sounded scared." Bree's brows furrowed. "You heard the message."

"Maybe someone was blackmailing her," Todd said.

"Maybe." Bree lifted a shoulder. "Did you find anything interesting on Erin's laptop?"

"Nothing," Todd said. "Justin's was clean too, except he's been selling personal possessions online."

Matt leaned on the table. "What kind of personal possessions?"

Todd flipped several pages in his notepad. "Camping equipment. A game console. Some power tools."

Justin hadn't fled with his camping equipment.

Todd flattened his hand on the paper. "You realize this is the behavior of a drug addict looking for quick cash."

Matt said nothing, but the new information weighed on him. Every sign pointed to Justin using drugs again.

Todd rubbed his temple. "We tried to question his Narcotics Anonymous sponsor, but the man refused to talk to us."

"NA doesn't provide legal confidentiality," Bree pointed out. "He's not Justin's lawyer or doctor."

Todd rubbed the back of his neck. "We still can't force him to answer questions."

"You could subpoena him," she suggested.

Todd set down his pen. "And his lawyer would fight it, and in the end, we can't prove he knows anything key about Justin. The legal runaround isn't worth the time or effort unless we charge Justin with a crime, and we're sure the sponsor has important information."

"Do you have any theories about Tuesday night?" Matt asked.

"Maybe." Todd's forehead wrinkled. "We think Erin had a . . ." He hesitated, blushing. "Date with Justin."

"Sex and pizza," Bree filled in.

Todd nodded. "She showered and hung her towel in the bathroom. While she dressed, Justin took his turn in the shower."

Matt closed his eyes and pictured Justin's house. Erin had been fully dressed, including a knit hat. "That fits the timeline. Justin was supposed to go to the NA meeting with me."

"Maybe someone shot Erin while Justin was in the shower," Bree said.

"Yes." Matt opened his eyes. "Justin heard the shot, ran out of the bathroom, dropped the towel . . ." Matt's mental movie ended in a cliff-hanger. "Did he chase the killer? Did the killer force him to go with him? Did he run away?"

"If this theory is correct, then that's what we still need to find out." Todd stood. "We still have a neighbor we haven't been able to reach for an interview. Please let me know if you make any discoveries. I know you'll be investigating. If I were in either of your positions, I would."

Bree and Matt both shook his hand, and they left.

The moon shone from a star-dotted sky. In the SUV, Matt started the engine and turned on the steering wheel heater. The vehicle was freezing and his injured hand appreciated the warmth. "You didn't tell him about the kids' father."

"He didn't ask."

Matt lifted his brows. *Really?* "I told him about the burner phone."

She looked away, her mouth flattening into a stubborn, grim line. "Todd would go looking for Craig. When he found him, he'd make contact and tell Craig about Erin's death. I'd rather let Dana find him quietly and see what he's doing before putting him on notice."

"What if Craig killed your sister?"

"I can't think of why he would." Bree's eyes went dark. "But you'll have to trust me when I say the kids wouldn't be safe with him. He's a grifter. He would use them. That's what Craig does. He uses people."

Frustration welled up in Matt. He didn't want to damage his working relationship with Bree. He also didn't want to jeopardize the children's safety, but holding back information on potential suspects from Todd didn't sit right with him either.

"Promise me you won't tell Todd." Bree's voice tightened to a rasp.

"I can't do that." Matt couldn't let Justin take the blame for a crime he didn't commit.

"There is nothing to indicate Craig is in New York."

"Todd should know about him," Matt insisted.

Actually, Todd should have asked about the kids' father. Lack of experience or not, Todd should have thought about all the victim's exes.

"So, now you trust him?" Bree's eyes brightened with anger. If she could shoot daggers out of her eyes, he'd be in pieces.

Matt shrugged. "He didn't have to share today. He did anyway. It feels like he's being straight with us."

Bree clamped her mouth shut, and Matt knew she would lie to the pope to protect those kids. He admired the fierce nature of her loyalty, but not at Justin's expense.

"Think about it." He glanced at her. She looked spent, but she was also stubborn. "Where are we going now?"

"Home." Bree glanced at her phone. "I missed dinner, and I want to spend some time with the kids."

"The balance is going to be hard."

"No question."

Matt drove her back to the farm in silence.

He parked in the driveway and pulled the Halo Salon bag from behind the seat. "Here, you forgot this."

"Thanks." She reached for the door handle.

"Why don't you open it here?"

"Don't trust me?"

He gave her a look.

With a resigned sigh, she opened the bag on her lap and began removing items and placing them next to her on the seat: a black zip-up jacket, a black T-shirt, and a small makeup bag. "Erin was required to look perfect and made-up while working."

Matt picked up the jacket and checked the pockets. "Empty."

Bree opened the makeup bag and rummaged through it. "Mascara, concealer, lipstick." She froze.

"What is it?" Matt asked.

Bree opened the bag wider and tilted it so he could see inside. Nestled under the makeup products was a flip phone. It looked like a cheap model without internet connectivity.

"That's not her regular phone?" he asked.

"No. Erin has a normal smartphone."

"These cheap ones are usually burner phones."

"Yes." Bree handed him the bag. "Todd will be able to secure a warrant to get the records from the carrier."

"I'll drop it off at the sheriff's station."

"Maybe the phone will implicate someone else and clear Justin."

Matt could hope.

"Talk to you tomorrow." Bree slid out of the truck.

After she'd disappeared inside the house, Matt backed out of the driveway. Chances were high that the information on the phone would make Justin look guiltier. Todd was busy when Matt stopped at the sheriff's station. He left the burner phone with Marge and drove home.

Brody greeted him as if he'd been gone for a month. The dog sat and lifted a paw, and Matt scratched his chest. "Don't give me those big, sad eyes. I know Cady fed and walked you hours ago."

The house felt empty. Matt was used to living alone. Usually, he didn't feel lonely. But tonight, he was restless. Was it the case that had gotten under his skin?

Or Bree?

Whatever the reason, he wasn't ready to settle down for the evening. Brody barked at the door, and Matt looked out the window. His sister's van parked next to his SUV.

"Cady's back. Let's go see her." Matt opened the door, and Brody trotted outside. He sat next to her van until she stepped out and closed the door.

Cady leaned over to pet him. "You are such a gentleman." Brody's tail thumped on the driveway. "Let me get Ladybug." Cady let the black-and-white dog out of the cargo area.

The pointer mix jumped up and put her paws on Matt's thighs. He turned his body, forcing all four of her feet to the ground. "Sit."

Still wriggling, she planted her butt on the driveway.

"Good girl." He rubbed behind her ears. "How did she do?"

"Better. I gated her in the kitchen overnight. No accidents."

"That's progress." Matt straightened. Ladybug and Brody sniffed noses and wagged their tails.

"She doesn't bark. When she needs to go outside, she just stares at the door. If I'm not looking, I don't see her. I think if she was on a routine, she'd be fine." Cady smiled. "She is so sweet and calm."

"She would be a great kids' dog."

"I'll put her in the kennel and take a different dog home for the night." Cady tried to rotate the rescues through her home to spend supervised nights with her three dogs.

Matt watched Ladybug play bow in front of Brody. "I don't want to see her back in the kennel. I'll keep her in the house until you place her. Brody could use the company."

Cady walked over and kissed him on the cheek. "Thank you."

He grinned. "I want to see her placed in a home too. She's a terrific dog."

"I walked her before I put her in the car. She should be OK until bedtime." Cady handed him the leash and headed for the kennels.

Matt followed her. His phone went off just before they went inside. Todd. Matt stepped away from the barking to answer the call.

"Tell me how you found the burner," Todd said.

Matt explained that Bree had received Erin's personal possessions from the owner of Halo.

"You don't know where Erin got it?" Todd asked.

"No."

"OK. Thanks," Todd said.

Erin already had a cell phone. Why would she need a burner?

CHAPTER SEVENTEEN

The house smelled like garlic. Bree took a big whiff, and her stomach rumbled with hunger for the first time in days. In the kitchen, Dana was emptying the dishwasher. Luke and Kayla sat at the kitchen table. Kayla wrote in a spiral notebook. Luke typed on a laptop. Leave it to Dana to breathe some normal into the house.

The ordinariness of the scene tore at Bree's heart. Standing in the doorway, she let a wave of grief pass over her.

"Philadelphia was really the capital of the United States?" Luke asked.

"Yes." Dana removed a spoon from a drawer. "From 1790 until 1800, while the capital in DC was being built."

Bree stepped into the room. "What was for dinner?"

"Capellini." Dana opened the fridge and took out a huge container. "Don't worry. I made plenty."

"Did you make the sauce from scratch?" Bree filled the kettle and set it on the stove. In the pantry, she found a box of tea bags. It was too late for coffee.

"First of all, it's called gravy, and of course I made it from scratch." Dana sounded offended. "The kids and I went to the grocery store. Luke drove. Did you know he has his permit?"

"My driver's test is next month," Luke said.

She hadn't. Thank goodness Dana was paying attention to the details. Bree felt uncharacteristically scatterbrained.

Kayla looked up from her notepad. "We got cupcakes. Chocolate. We waited for you to eat them."

What time did Kayla go to bed? Bree glanced at the cow clock on the wall. Nine o'clock. It didn't matter tonight, she decided. Kayla would go to bed whenever she wanted.

"I love cupcakes." Bree walked to the table.

"You hafta eat your dinner first," Kayla said in a serious voice.

"Of course." Peering at Luke's laptop, Bree put a hand on his shoulder and squeezed. "Whatcha working on?"

"A history paper." He blinked up at her. "I want to go to school tomorrow."

"OK," Bree said.

Luke saved his document, closed the computer, and picked at the edge of a New York Rangers decal on the top. "It's gonna be weird."

"It will be at first." Twenty-seven years had passed, but Bree remembered the stares and whispers and isolation with startling clarity. She'd been in a room with thirty other kids, and yet she'd also been completely alone.

"I think the longer I wait, the weirder it'll be." Luke smoothed the decal back into place. "I want to get it over with."

Bree nodded. "If you want to come home at any time tomorrow, just call me or Dana."

"OK," he said.

Kayla closed her spiral notebook. "I'm gonna practice my violin. Am I going to my lesson tomorrow?"

Bree hesitated. She didn't know what tomorrow would bring. She wanted the kids to be her priority, but she also wanted to catch her sister's killer. Not a decision she'd ever thought she'd have to make.

"If you want to go," Dana said, "one of us will take you."

Seemingly satisfied, Kayla slid off her chair and left the room.

"I'm going to check the horses before I go to bed." Luke stood.

"I'll do it," Bree said. "I'll be up for a while anyway."

"OK." Luke went upstairs.

The sound of off-key notes drifted into the kitchen.

"How do you think they're coping?" Bree asked.

Dana scooped pasta onto a plate. "I think it will get harder after the funeral. Right now, they're still in shock."

"I need to talk to them about Erin's funeral. They should have a say in what happens."

"Did you?"

"No. My mother's funeral is a blur. Everyone in town came. Not sure whether they were supporting the family or gawking. There was no funeral for my father."

No one publicly mourned a killer.

Dana turned to her. "You know better than anyone what these kids are going through."

Bree nodded. "When do you think I should talk to them about the funeral arrangements?"

Dana put the plate in the microwave and pressed a button. "They've had a rough couple of days. I'd let them get a decent night's sleep. Tomorrow is soon enough. Where is Erin?"

Bree had arranged for a local funeral home to collect her sister's body. It would take the mortician a day or so to work his magic and make Erin presentable in case the kids wanted to say goodbye. Bree hadn't been given the option, and she'd resented that.

"I searched your sister's desk today," Dana said. "I found a copy of her will and her attorney's card. I left a message for the attorney."

"Did Erin name a guardian?" But Bree knew the answer even before she'd finished the question. Their parents were gone. Their grandparents were dead. The cousin who'd raised Bree had died as well. The Taggert siblings had only had each other.

And now there were two.

Dana met her eyes with a level gaze. "You are their legal guardian, but you already knew that. I'm sure Adam will help with the finances, but he's not capable of raising them."

Bree's thoughts scrambled. "My apartment is too small for three people."

"There are larger apartments in Philadelphia," Dana pointed out.

Bree glanced at the barn out back. "There's nowhere to keep horses in Philadelphia."

"I'm sure there are stables near Fairmount Park, but I imagine they're pricey."

The thought of dragging the kids from their home gave Bree indigestion, and she hadn't even eaten yet. "I can't do it. I can't take them away from here."

Dana didn't say a word as Bree processed the truth that should have been clear since the moment she'd learned her sister had died.

"I'm moving to Grey's Hollow." Bree watched a mental image of her career careening over a cliff.

"What will you do for a job?"

"I don't know. I guess I'll see if any of the local PDs are hiring. I don't really want to go back to patrol, but I might not have many options."

Or any options.

The kids had to come first. They'd just lost their mother. Bree would not yank them out of their lives. There was nothing she could do to lessen their grief, but she wouldn't add to their trauma. Which meant she was the one who would give up her life.

"Look on the bright side. You don't have a serious relationship to end."

"Last week, I didn't consider my single status a plus."

"See? Bright side." Dana checked the pasta. "Why did you break it off with that lawyer?"

"He was obsessed with his hair. He used more products than I do."

Dana laughed. "And the guy you dated before him—the arson investigator?"

"He had a creepy laugh." And the sex had been meh. "We didn't have any chemistry."

Dana took the plate from the microwave. "You have issues with commitment."

"You should talk, Ms. Two Ex-Husbands."

"At least I've made commitments." Dana opened a drawer and removed a fork.

Bree rolled her eyes. "My relationship status is hardly important right now. Can we get back to the problems at hand? Did you find anything that might indicate what kind of trouble my sister was in?"

"No," Dana said. "I found normal, boring personal papers: insurance policies, tax returns, etcetera. Her records are meticulous. She filed her appliance manuals alphabetically. She had a file for online accounts and passwords, so we can access all her phone and financial records. I'll start reviewing those tomorrow, as time permits. Then again, maybe there's nothing to find. Two sheriff's deputies already searched the whole house."

"You have no idea how thorough they were, and they didn't know my sister." Bree paced. "I feel like Erin would have left a record somewhere. She was organized. She kept records of everything. I'll search her room later tonight. That's where she would have stashed anything of a personal nature that she hadn't wanted the kids to see. Did you find Craig?"

Dana handed Bree the plate. "I found more than forty men named Craig Vance. You don't have his social security number, do you?"

Bree took her dinner to the table and sat. "Sorry, no."

"Then I'm slogging through the list, gathering data, knocking off anyone who isn't the right age, and calling those who might fit his general profile."

"What excuse are you using?" Bree asked.

"I claimed his uncle died and left him money."

"Good one. People cooperate if they think they'll get money."

"So far, I've narrowed it down to a dozen possibilities in the tristate region. If none of those pan out, I'll expand the search." Dana picked up some papers and brought them to the table. "In other news, Matt's friend came by and worked up a quote on a security system." She set the papers in front of Bree. "His plan seems thorough."

Bree flipped through the pages. "Windows and doors all covered, battery backup, central monitoring?"

"Yes, yes, and yes."

"Then it's a go."

"I'll call him in the morning and tell him yes," Dana said.

Bree heard more squeaky violin notes overhead. "How am I going to raise them? I've never *been* a parent or *had* a good parent."

"You love them, so you'll figure it out. You know what not to do." Dana glanced at the ceiling, where the painful sounds of an off-key note lingered. "Eat your dinner, then go help that child with her violin. I covered American history, but I don't know one music note from another."

Bree shoveled down her pasta, then climbed the steps and knocked on Kayla's doorframe. The second she went into the room, the little girl set her violin in its case and sat on the floor next to it. "I can't play today. My violin is too sad."

"It's OK." Bree lowered herself to the floor and crossed her legs. "You don't have to."

"Can you play this?" Kayla pointed toward the tune in her music book, "Twinkle Twinkle Little Star."

"Sure." Bree picked up the violin, tucked it under her chin, and played the simple melody.

"Play something else."

Bree lowered the violin. "Not today. It's been a long time. I'll have to remember some songs." The lie felt uncomfortable on her lips. But

Bree had mixed feelings about the violin. Her cousin, with no husband or children of her own, had pushed Bree hard to learn, saying it would boost her math abilities. Practice had been forced and not fun. But then, fun hadn't been part of Cousin Tara's vocabulary. Bree had attended top private schools, but her childhood had never been happy. The violin was caught up in those memories.

"Luke said he's going to school tomorrow. Do I have to?"

"Do you want to?" Bree set the violin down in its case.

Kayla shook her head. "I might cry. I don't want to cry in front of the other kids."

"It's OK if you cry. It's OK if you want to stay home too." Bree sidled closer, until their shoulders were touching. "I talked to your guidance counselor. She said when you go back to school, you can come to her office anytime during the day if you need some space."

"I don't want to go." Kayla's voice sounded thin and fragile enough to break.

"That's fine. Everybody's different. Don't feel like you have to do what Luke does."

Kayla nodded, then crawled into Bree's lap and cried softly. Bree held her until she stopped.

"Aunt Bree?"

"Yes."

"What will Mommy's funeral be like?"

"I thought you and Luke might want to help plan it. It can be whatever you both want."

The hell with convention and expectation.

Kayla nodded against her chest.

"Do you want to eat the cupcakes now?" Bree asked.

"Maybe." Kayla crawled off her lap. "Aunt Bree?"

"Yes?"

"What's gonna happen to me and Luke? Are we gonna have to move?"

"Would you like it better if I moved here?"

Kayla threw her arms around Bree. "Are you?"

"If that's what you want, yes." Bree hugged her back. *I'd do anything for you.*

They knocked on Luke's door, then all three of them went downstairs. As if by mutual agreement, dessert was quiet. When it was over, Kayla tugged on Dana's hand. "Will you watch a movie with me?"

"Of course." Dana followed her from the room.

Luke stood. "I have to study. Midterms are coming up."

"You'll let me know if it's too much?" Bree asked. "You teachers will give you more time. I talked to the counselor. She said for you not to worry."

Luke shook his head hard. "No. I don't want any special attention."

"All right," Bree said. "You can change your mind at any time."

A tear rolled down his cheek, and he turned away. He looked as if not crying was the most exhausting thing he'd ever done. He hurried from the room, probably seeking privacy before he broke down again.

How will he cope at school?

How much could or should she protect him?

Bree had never felt so useless. She cleared the table, taking comfort in the mindless chores. When she checked on Kayla and Dana, she found them sound asleep on the couch.

Suddenly exhausted, Bree double-checked the doors and windows, almost wishing Matt—and Brody—were in the house. She climbed the steps to her sister's room. The bed was in disarray. Bree hadn't made it that morning, but otherwise the room was tidy. Vader lay in the center of the pillow. Erin had kept important papers in her desk, but personal items would be in her bedroom, away from the kids.

Bree went to the closet and began searching. She checked every box, bag, and pocket but found nothing. The nightstand was full of paperbacks. Bree moved to the dresser. She went through every item of clothing, then removed each drawer to check underneath and behind. Nothing.

Maybe there wasn't anything to find.

At ten thirty, she went downstairs, dressed in a coat and boots, and trudged out to the barn to settle the horses for the night. The animals were quiet as she checked blankets and water buckets. Something scraped behind her, and a shadow fell over the aisle. Bree turned, expecting to see Dana or Luke in the doorway.

She froze when she recognized the man watching her.

"Hello, Bree," he said.

"Craig." Dread landed in Bree's gut like a punch. "What are you doing here?"

"Earlier today, someone called my secretary and said I might have inherited money from an uncle. Since I don't have any uncles, the call—and the personal nature of the questions the caller asked—felt suspicious to me."

Two kinds of people were the most suspicious: cops and guilty people.

"I did some digging around online and saw the news about Erin's death. Then it all made sense." He stepped into the light. He wore jeans and a blue parka. His blond hair shone in the barn light, but his gray-blue eyes were the same color—and about as warm—as a shark's. "Was it you who called?"

"No."

Craig's eyes glittered in the light. "Well, anyway. Here I am."

Bree left the paint's stall and locked it. "What do you want?"

"I don't know what you mean."

Bree stopped and waited.

A minute passed before he squirmed. "I came to see my children."

"What children are those?"

"Luke and Kayla." His face tightened.

"You know their names."

"Of course I know their names," he snapped.

"They don't know you." Bree kept her voice cool, which had always annoyed him.

"Don't get nasty—" He stopped himself. "I'm sorry. I know I haven't been a good father to the kids in the past, but I'm a new man. I've found God, and He has changed me. Erin's death is a sign from Him that this is the next step in the new path He has set out for me."

Bree could smell Craig's bullshit over the horse manure. "Why are you really here, Craig?"

"I want to see Luke and Kayla. I want to be their father."

"You're a stranger to both of them." As calm as her voice sounded, inside Bree was freaking out.

Craig's voice shifted into his *as smooth as twenty-year-old scotch* grifter tone. "I intend to rectify that situation."

Bree shook her head. "No. They're both upset. They don't need you to upend their lives."

"They're my children." He stepped toward her. "I came here tonight to give you fair warning."

"Warning?" Bree asked.

Craig flushed. "I intend to get custody of my children whether or not you make it easy on them."

"A good father puts his children's interests first, not his own," Bree pointed out.

He leaned close. "They are *my* children," he repeated. "Erin is dead. There's no court in the state that won't give me custody of those kids."

"Unless you're not fit to be a parent."

A muscle in the side of his neck twitched. He swallowed and smoothed his features. "I understand that you're angry and grieving. You must miss your sister, and to have her taken from you in such a violent fashion must have been even more shocking. I'll pray for you."

Bree said nothing.

"I'm a changed man. I'm an ordained minister now." He lifted his chin.

She suppressed a snort. Craig, a minister? "Where do you work?"

"A small church in Albany." Barely an hour away.

"Did you get that certificate online?" she asked.

"Either you allow me to see my children or I'll have my attorney arrange it." His evasion of her question was her answer.

"You'd better do that." Bree would not make it easy for him. Making him jump through legal hoops would give her time.

"Tonight's visit was a courtesy. I want the transition to be as smooth as possible for the kids. Apparently, you don't care about their well-being. You'll be hearing from my lawyer. If you change your mind and decide to be reasonable, here's my card." Pulling a business card from his pocket, he flipped it in the air. It spun and fluttered to the ground. Then he turned and left the barn.

Bree walked out into the cold and watched him trudge through the ice toward a sedan he'd parked halfway up the driveway. Craig had said he'd found God, but Bree knew the only thing he'd found was a way to separate a congregation from its collection money. She couldn't believe he wanted his children. He'd shown no interest in them for their entire lives. What was his endgame? What did he really want?

Whatever it was, Bree knew he was up to no good. She returned to the barn, picked up the card, and shoved it in her pocket.

The anger that rose in her chest was more than an hour of yoga could alleviate. She sent Matt a text. Is there a gun range nearby?

He answered: yes.

Can we go shooting tomorrow before we see Stephanie?

Sure.

Thanks. Bree slipped her phone back into her pocket. There was nothing like a visit from Craig to make her want to shoot something.

Bree closed the barn door and paused, her gaze sweeping the fields surrounding the house. The countryside was peaceful and quiet. It was also dark. There were no streetlights, no billboards, no headlights. Anyone could be out there. She could install an alarm system in the house, but there was nothing she could do about the sheer emptiness all around her.

CHAPTER EIGHTEEN

Matt drove toward the gun range. The morning sun glared on the hood of his SUV. He glanced at Bree in the passenger seat. "You don't look like you slept at all."

"I didn't." Bree stared out the window. "Erin's ex dropped by last night."

"Craig Vance?"

"Yes. He said he wants the kids." Bree's brows dropped into a troubled line as she described her conversation with Craig. "At one time, all she wanted was for him to want to be a husband and father. But that ended the night he beat her."

"Do you have any proof he's unfit?"

"No." She sighed. "I called a family law attorney this morning. Craig can file a paternity petition in family court, which will probably order a DNA test. Erin isn't here to object."

"He can get custody."

"Yes." Bree's voice was tight with bitterness. "If Luke objects, the kids would be separated, just like me and my siblings were."

"How *did* that happen?" Matt couldn't imagine having his parents and siblings all ripped away at the same time.

Bree hesitated. "Erin and Adam were raised by my grandparents. I was too difficult to manage. I acted out in school. I got into fights. I threw tantrums. What I remember most was an overwhelming sense of everything—my life—my emotions—being out of control. My grand-parents were elderly and not in the best health. They couldn't deal with me. A cousin in Philadelphia volunteered to take on the job."

"You were older and probably more traumatized."

"Not more traumatized, just differently traumatized," she said in a matter-of-fact voice. "Erin and Adam had their own problems. Adam has a hard time making emotional connections. You've seen that. Erin was the opposite. She had emotional dependency issues, and Craig manipulated her need to be loved."

"That's terrible." Matt respected her lack of self-pity.

Bree shrugged. "My cousin did the best she could. She made sure I received all the therapy I needed. I went to exclusive private schools. She gave me every advantage she thought was important, but she wasn't a warm person. She didn't realize how much I needed my bond with Erin and Adam. We understood each other in ways no one else pos-sibly could. After I moved to Philadelphia, we only saw each other on birthdays and major holidays. We should have been kept together. No Ivy League education could make up for our lack of connection."

"You must have missed them."

"Yeah." Her voice was wistful.

"You went to an Ivy League college?"

"Yes. Prelaw at Penn. My cousin was very disappointed in me when I applied to the police academy instead of law school."

"But you wanted to be a cop."

Bree was quiet for a minute. "I remember the night my parents died more clearly than I'd like. I remember huddling under the back porch. It was the sheriff who found us. I remember him pulling us out from under the porch, wrapping me in his coat, telling me I was safe." She paused. "It sounds hokey, but the way he treated us made a difference in my life, and I wanted to make a difference too. I don't think it takes a genius to figure out why I wanted to be a cop."

"It's not hokey at all." Matt respected her wanting to give back.

"Why did you become a deputy?" she asked.

"I wanted to help people, and I liked that every day was a new challenge."

"So, what will you do now?"

"That's a good question." For which Matt had no good answer. If he'd needed money, he probably would have figured it out by now. "I still want to train K-9s. I might start one of my sister's rescues with some basic training. She's too antsy and driven for most households."

"No long-term goals?"

"Not yet. I spent the first couple of years in denial that my law enforcement career was over." But now that he'd come to accept that fact, he did feel a little aimless.

"There's no chance you'll be able to go back?"

"No. I can't fire a weapon with my dominant hand, and I'm not even good enough with my left to qualify for concealed carry."

Former law enforcement officers could carry concealed as long as they demonstrated proficiency with their weapon.

"You could go into law enforcement administration," Bree suggested.

"A desk job? No, thanks. The routine would drive me crazy." He pulled into the driveway of the shooting range. He retrieved his gun and ammunition from the safe in the cargo area of the SUV and led the way into the indoor range, which had just opened.

"Hey, Matt." Carl waved from behind the counter. "You have the whole place to yourselves. Pick any stall you want."

"Thanks." Matt introduced Bree, paid the fee, and walked to the last partitioned stall. He set down his weapon. He was glad the place was empty. He didn't like to run into anyone he knew.

Bree set up in the next stall. They both donned ear protection.

Matt loaded his weapon. Just for the hell of it, he picked it up with his right hand first and pointed at the paper target twenty-five yards downrange. But he couldn't even squeeze the trigger.

Damn cold weather.

With a frustrated exhale, he gripped the gun in his left hand and aimed at the target. He fired six shots, lowered the gun, and pushed the button to reel in the target.

"Hey, you're getting better," Carl called out.

Matt wished Carl had something else to do.

But he was right. Five of Matt's shots had actually pierced the center mass of the man-shaped image printed on the paper. One shot hit the man-shape just outside of center mass, in the belly.

During the first year after the shooting, he'd had three surgeries on his hand. The following year had been full of rehab. He'd endured three physical therapy sessions a week. He'd stretched and strengthened through excruciating pain and progress that felt as slow as the movement of glaciers.

It hadn't been until the third year that he'd really faced facts. He would never regain full use of his right hand. He could manage most large motor functions. He could pick things up and put them down, so to speak, but his fine motor skills had reached their limit. Matt had spent a few months being depressed, then he'd started coming to the range and working on his left-hand accuracy. In the past six months, he'd made significant improvement.

He glanced at Bree in the next stall. She was shooting the absolute hell out of her target.

He sent his target downrange again, increasing the distance. As a deputy, he'd drilled in off-hand shooting at close range. He could hit his target with his pistol at close range, but his accuracy dropped off at longer distances. He fired nearly fifty bullets, inspecting and replacing the target as necessary.

Matt emptied his magazine, then reeled in the target for the last time. Most of his shots were within the outline. Some had missed the paper entirely, but he'd definitely improved.

Bree stepped to his side and removed her ear protection, letting the earmuffs hang around her neck. "That's decent shooting."

He pointed at her targets, which she had destroyed. "Not as decent as yours."

She shrugged. "I was the top marksman in my class at the academy. Most cops can't shoot like that."

"I used to."

She nodded at his target. "I think you could qualify."

"I don't trust my aim." Matt shook his head. "Anyway, it's time to meet with Stephanie."

He packed up his gear and walked out of the range without giving Bree a chance to respond. After locking his weapon in the safe in his SUV, Matt slid behind the wheel. Bree climbed in. He could feel her gaze on him as he drove. He'd been rude, but he didn't want to talk about his shooting. Could he meet the bare minimum standards? Maybe. But the fact remained that Matt wasn't comfortable with his now-limited ability, and he might never be.

The Wallaces lived on a country road about fifteen minutes outside of town. It wasn't a formal development, but mailboxes lined the road, each house sitting on what Matt estimated to be an acre.

Stephanie's house was a gray saltbox, with a flat facade and a centered front door painted red. Matt parked in front of the house, although the driveway continued around the house to a detached two-car garage. Behind the garage was another building. The truck in front of the garage bore the logo for Wallace Carpentry.

They walked up to the house and rang the bell.

A man in his late thirties opened the door. He wore jeans and a flannel shirt over a blue tee. "I'm Steph's husband, Zack. Steph's in the kitchen."

She was pulling a baking sheet out of the oven. Clearly dressed for work, she wore tall boots, black tights, and a short black dress. Tears were streaming down her face. Matt sniffed the air. French fries. Steph dumped the fries into a bowl, salted them, and carried them to the table.

"Please sit down," Zack said.

Matt and Bree chose chairs next to each other, facing Steph and her husband over the table.

Steph dropped into a chair. "Does anyone else want fries?"

Matt and Bree declined.

"Oh, my God. I can't believe she's gone," Steph cried. The words came out in between sobs and huge, heaving breaths.

"You're going to hyperventilate," Bree said. "Take slow breaths."

"You need to calm down, sweetie." Zack's voice was firm. "This isn't good for the baby."

"You're pregnant?" Matt asked.

"We just found out." Zack patted his wife's hand. "I told her she shouldn't talk to you. It was stressful enough when the police questioned her. She doesn't need this." Anger flashed in his eyes.

"I'm OK," Steph said. "Just a little morning sickness." She ate a fry, then reached for another.

Zack lifted her hand to his mouth and kissed it. "Those aren't good for the baby, and the grease will upset your stomach."

She frowned. "I need to eat before work, and I couldn't get anything down. This is the first thing that's appealed to me today."

"I'll get you some milk." Zack got up and headed for the fridge.

She smiled weakly. "He takes such good care of me." She blotted her teary eyes with a napkin. "I'm sorry. I just"—she hiccupped—"miss Erin."

"We understand," Bree said.

Steph reached across the table and clutched at Bree's forearms. "Do you know who killed her?"

"No," Bree said. "What was up with Erin the last few weeks?"

Zack set a glass of milk in front of Steph, but she didn't reach for it.

"I'm not sure." Steph ate another fry. "At first I thought it might have been the thing with Jack, but now I think it was more."

"What thing with Jack?" Matt asked.

"She didn't tell you?" Steph sniffed the milk. Her nose wrinkled in disgust.

"No." Bree shook her head.

Steph drank a sip of milk, then grimaced. "He's been hitting on her. She's been doing her best to not engage but also not be confrontational."

Zack's nostrils flared. "You need to quit that job. Jack is an asshole."

Matt agreed. "Erin could have sued him for sexual harassment."

"That sounds great until you try to prove it." Steph set down the glass and pushed it away. "In the real world, she would have been fired. It would have been her word against his. Jack would have told all the local salons that she was a problem employee. She wouldn't have been able to get a new job. This is a small town. She didn't have any other skills. Her career would have been over."

Matt swallowed a lump of anger. Was this the trouble Erin had called Bree about? Had she thought Bree, as a cop, would have been able to stop Jack or give her legal advice?

"Did you see Erin on Tuesday?" Bree asked.

"Yeah. We said goodbye when she left around four o'clock." A tear rolled down Steph's face. "That was the last time I spoke to her."

Bree touched her forearm. "Did Erin talk about anything unusual recently?"

"One day last week," Steph said. "I think it was Friday. Justin showed up at the salon. He was really upset. Erin tried to calm him down. Jack made them go out into the parking lot, and then he wrote her up for leaving her station. I think he wanted to use the reprimand as leverage to make her sleep with him."

"Has he done this before?" Bree asked.

Sexual predators were typically repeat offenders.

Steph lifted a palm. "I heard he's pressured other girls but not me. He knows Zack is very protective."

"Damned straight." Anger flushed Zack's face. He punched his palm. "He knows better."

"Do you know when Jack started hitting on Erin?" Matt asked.

"After she split up with Justin. He only targets girls without husbands or boyfriends." Steph bit into another fry.

"He doesn't want to piss off someone who can kick his ass," Zack grumbled. He pushed the glass of milk toward his wife.

Looking at it, Steph covered her mouth and bolted from the kitchen.

"Damn it," Zack said. "Her morning sickness is usually better by now."

A few seconds of silence ticked by.

"So, Zack, you're a carpenter?" Matt asked while they waited for Steph to return.

"Yeah," Zack said.

Matt remembered the truck parked outside. "You have your own company?"

"I do now." Zack frowned. "I used to work for a contractor, but he ran into some financial problems and had to let me go."

"That sucks," Matt said.

Zack lifted a shoulder. "Owning my own business has its ups and downs. I like being my own boss, but the hours are long."

Steph returned, her face pale. "I'm sorry."

Zack glanced at his wife. "You can't go to work until you keep some food down. You haven't gained any weight yet." His phone vibrated, and he picked it up. "It's a client. I have to answer this. Excuse me." He walked into the next room, closing the door behind him.

"I'm sorry if we've upset you," Bree said.

"It's OK." Steph waved a hand. "He worries too much. The doctor said it's perfectly normal to lose a couple of pounds in the early months." She stopped and sighed. "The pregnancy is really bad timing. We can't afford a baby right now. Zack already practically lives in his workshop, and when he comes inside, he has to shower right away because the smell of sawdust has been making me sick. Me getting pregnant has added a lot to his stress."

"You didn't get pregnant by yourself," Bree pointed out.

"I know." Steph's eyes were troubled. "That's what Erin said. She was such a good friend." She lowered her voice. "Zack and I went through a brief separation a couple of months ago. Erin was my rock. She was always there for me. I don't know how I would have gotten through it without her. She even let me stay at her house for a few weeks. She didn't judge me or tell me to go back to him like my mother did. Erin understood." Steph cradled her still-flat belly with one hand. "She was the *best* friend. I'll never have another like her."

"Did Erin talk about Justin at all while you were staying with her?" Bree asked.

Steph nodded. "We talked a lot about our marriages. They'd been separated a little longer, but the subject was still raw. I know she loved him. Making him move out was the hardest thing she'd ever done. She only did it for the kids, because of the drugs."

"Did she mention anything else that was on her mind?" Matt asked.

Steph frowned. "Yeah. She'd had some hang-up calls on her phone, and a few weeks ago, someone slit the tires of her car while she was at the salon."

Bree straightened. "Did they check the parking lot surveillance cameras?"

Steph shook her head. "Employees have to park way in the back. The cameras don't show that part of the lot."

"OK. If you think of anything else, please call me." Bree gave Steph her cell number.

"You already have my number," Matt said. "You can call either one of us."

They said goodbye and left the house. Back in the SUV, Matt reached for his vibrating phone. He glanced at the screen. Kevin. He held a finger to his lips.

Bree sat back and watched him.

"Yeah," Matt answered the call.

"I heard rumors about a white pickup truck," Kevin said. "What's that worth to you?"

"Fifty bucks," Matt said.

"The truck is at the old Fresh factory."

"I'll pay you the extra fifty when you set up the meeting with Nico." If Matt gave Kevin more money, the CI would disappear to party for another couple of days.

"You're an asshole." The call went dead.

Matt lowered the phone and stared at it. Could this be their first big break?

Bree straightened in the passenger seat. "What?"

"That was an old CI. I asked him to keep an ear out for news of Justin's whereabouts or Erin's vehicle. He says there's a white pickup at the old beverage factory."

"Good lead." Bree clicked her seat belt, then sat back.

Matt started the engine and put the SUV in drive. He pulled a TV-style U-turn on the main road, squealing tires and all. Then he punched the gas pedal. This was big. He could feel it.

Matt raced toward his house, taking the turns fast enough to make Bree reach for the armrest for balance.

"This isn't the way out of town," Bree said.

"I want to pick up Brody. Are you OK with that?" But her response would not have changed his course. He needed the dog.

"Sure," Bree said in a half-hearted tone.

"It's important. He'll sense people before we can see them." And if Justin was in the factory, Brody would find him faster.

"I know." Her voice sharpened. "I'll deal."

You'll have to, he thought with a small tinge of guilt.

At Matt's house, Bree waited in the SUV while he ran in for the dog. Brody jumped into the back seat and stared at Bree over the console.

She glanced over the seat. Stiffening, she slid a few inches toward the passenger door. "I feel like he wants to ride shotgun."

"He'll be fine. He rode in the back seat for his whole K-9 career." Matt drove away from the house.

The Fresh Beverage Company had gone out of business twenty years before. The old factory sat seven miles outside town, in the middle of nowhere. Snow-covered fields and woods lined the country road. The building was a hulking square of brick. The surrounding meadows were creeping into the parking lot, which showed more tire tracks than an abandoned building should.

"This building was a problem when I was a deputy. Homeless squatters, drug dealers, kids. If it was illegal, someone was doing it here." Matt stopped the truck and climbed out. After opening the rear door, Matt snapped the leash onto the dog's collar. Brody jumped down, his nose already working the air.

Bree kept her distance from Matt and the dog as they walked across the lot.

"The company that owns the property has given up on keeping people out." Matt led Brody toward the chain-link fence that surrounded the property. Across the building's face, broken windows gaped.

The gate listed on its hinges. Matt held it aside so Brody and Bree could enter the yard surrounding the building. They crossed the icy, cracked asphalt. Wind had blown sections of the blacktop clear. Snow drifted in other places. They stepped onto the concrete sidewalk. The front doors were solid steel and padlocked. They bypassed them to walk around to the back. Receiving and shipping docks lined the rear of the building. Several of the overhead doors were open.

Bree led the way to the first open bay.

Matt touched her arm, stopping her. "It's too quiet."

She raised a brow.

"I don't like it. There's always someone here." Matt glanced at Brody. The dog was calm and giving no signs he sensed other human beings.

"Maybe it's too frigging cold for vagrants to live here." Bree shivered. Her nose was red, and her breath fogged in front of her face. She pulled a hat and gloves from her pocket and tugged them on.

Matt went first, letting the dog lead. They walked into a large, high-ceilinged room with a concrete floor. Barrels were stacked against one wall. Trash, cardboard boxes, used needles, and what Matt suspected was human feces littered the floor. They crossed the concrete and approached another doorway.

Brody's head snapped up, his nose working. Brody had been a multiuse K-9. He was trained to sniff drugs and explosives. He'd also completed building searches and tracked suspects. The dog's intelligence and ability to adapt had always impressed Matt.

Bree frowned at Brody. "What is it?"

"Not sure." But it was definitely something. "He has something in his nose."

Metal clanged, the sound echoing through the open space.

The wind rattling something?

Brody stiffened. He whined and lunged at the leash. Signaling Bree to stand back, Matt braced himself. Brody's attention was fixed ahead, on the doorway and whatever lay beyond.

Chapter Nineteen

Bree pulled out her weapon and put her shoulder to the wall on one side of the doorway. Matt positioned himself on the other side. He held Brody back. The dog whined and shifted his weight back and forth. He wasn't growling. As much as Bree avoided getting close to K-9s, she knew individual dogs had their own alert cues.

"Threat?" she mouthed.

Matt shrugged and mouthed back, "Not sure."

Great.

Bree peered around the doorframe. A white F-150 SuperCab sat in the middle of another large, concrete-floored shipping bay.

Her heart double-tapped. Erin's truck. She didn't see anyone in the vehicle through the windshield. She scanned the rest of the room but saw nothing. Giving Brody some leash, Matt let the dog lead him through the opening.

Bree followed, sweeping the room from corner to corner with her weapon.

She moved forward, passing the dog and approaching the side of the vehicle. As she neared the driver's door, the dog barked once and lunged toward her. Bree startled and jumped sideways, away from the dog. Her heart continued to beat in double time.

Matt leaned back against the leash, but he was clearly having a hard time managing his dog.

Tension radiated through Bree.

The dog lunged again, and she jumped even higher.

"Can you control him?" she snapped.

"Yes. Sorry. He's never like this." Matt shortened the leash and issued a few sharp commands in German. The only visible reaction in the dog was a single flick of an ear. The truck commanded all his attention. His weight was squared on all four legs and shifted forward. Matt dragged him back a few feet, but he remained 100 percent focused on the pickup.

With one eye on the dog, Bree approached the vehicle. She pointed her weapon through the driver's window. "Come out of the truck with your hands up."

Nothing moved.

She rose onto her toes and scanned the interior of the vehicle, front and back. She expected to see a body inside, maybe Justin's, but the cab was empty. Looking closer, she noticed dark-red stains streaking the dashboard, steering wheel, and driver's seat.

"What do you see?" Matt asked.

"Blood."

Matt was at her side in two seconds. Brody stood on his hind legs, scratching at the truck's door, his nose working. He huffed. His mouth opened as if he were tasting the air. On instinct, Bree moved away from the dog.

"I'm sorry he's freaking out." Matt grabbed the dog's collar and pulled him back.

Bree moved to the other side of the vehicle. "Not your fault. I'm sorry I snapped before. I need to work through my fear of dogs."

With the truck between her and the dog, Bree took three deep breaths, concentrating on exhaling slowly to lower her heart rate. Her brain knew Brody was no threat to her, but her response was a reflex.

Matt made the dog sit. "You can't control it."

And that fact irritated Bree more than anything.

She studied the gray interior of the truck. "That's a lot of blood."

"There was a handprint smear on the frame of Justin's bedroom door," Matt said. "He could have touched Erin. Maybe he checked her pulse or tried to help her."

They were both quiet for a few seconds. According to the ME, she had been beyond help.

Bree peered through the narrow rear window. She spotted a stain on the bench seat. She eyed a clear handprint on the dashboard. "Todd should be able to pull fingerprints from that."

Matt stepped backward, his face grim. "I don't know what this means. Blood in the front and back seats? Was one person in the back seat while another drove? Or did the driver climb into the back to rest, and bleed, for a while?"

"Forensics will be able to tell us if there is one source of blood or two."

Matt was silent.

"There's a piece of paper on the passenger seat." Bree craned her neck but couldn't read the message from her angle. Blood spattered the paper.

Matt walked around to the passenger side of the vehicle. "I can't read it."

Bree backed away from the truck and pulled out her phone. "I have to call Todd. Forensics needs to work on this truck."

"I know." Matt shoved a hand through his hair.

A minute later, Bree lowered her phone. "Todd's on his way. ETA is ten minutes."

"I can't justify opening the truck door."

"No," Bree said. "We cannot contaminate the evidence."

She snapped pictures of the truck from as many angles as possible without touching it.

The inside of the factory felt colder than outside. The chill seemed to radiate from the concrete, through the soles of her sneakers, into the bones of her feet. Her toes felt like blocks of ice, and she bounced to get her blood moving.

Matt frowned at her feet. "Why don't you wear boots?"

Bree lifted a sneaker. "I can run faster in these."

"Do you own boots?"

"I do. They're safely stowed in my vehicle back at the farm." When she was on call, she kept boots and a change of clothes in her trunk, along with sanitizing wipes.

Matt shook his head. "You're going to freeze if we have to search the woods."

"Yes." Bree stamped her feet. "That will suck."

Their conversation was cut short by the sound of vehicles in the parking lot. Todd and two other deputies entered the shipping bay. Todd walked up to the truck and circled it, examining the exterior and what he could see of the interior. The two deputies cleared the building. When they returned, Todd ordered one deputy to dust the door handles for prints and the other to call for a tow truck.

Todd approached Matt and Bree. "What led you here?"

"I've had some feelers out with old CIs," Matt said. "One called me today to relay rumors about the location of a white pickup. Considering how many false sightings you've had, we wanted to make sure it was Erin's before we brought you in."

Todd returned to the truck. After the deputy pulled one partial print from the driver's door, Todd put on gloves and opened the door.

Bree walked closer. Matt held the dog back. The dog sniffed the air and whined. *Reacting to the scent of blood? Or does he smell Justin?*

Todd examined the inside of the door and driver's side of the interior. "The blood here is mostly smears. DNA testing will tell us if it belongs to Erin or Justin or some other person we haven't yet identified."

"What's the turnaround time for DNA testing in your lab?" Bree asked.

"Anywhere from two weeks to six months." Todd opened the rear door to view the narrow bench seat in the back of the vehicle. "There's a lot of blood on the seat." He crouched to look closer.

"And even more on the carpet." Bree pointed to a frozen puddle on the floor mat. "That's definitely too much blood volume for passive transfer. That was an actively bleeding wound."

Todd stood. He rounded the vehicle and opened the doors on the passenger side. Todd photographed the paper on the passenger seat, then picked it up by the corner. He tilted it to the light.

Shaky block print spelled out two words. Bree read them aloud over his shoulder. "I'm sorry."

Todd pursed his lips. "What does that mean? If Justin is suicidal, then he has a gun. He could have shot himself back at his own place or right here. Why leave the truck at all? It makes no sense."

Bree's bones shuddered. Just like her father. Was Erin's death a horrible case of déjà vu, like the news media had claimed? "If he's suicidal, then he isn't thinking straight."

Matt's mouth flattened. "We don't know when the truck was left here. We don't know Justin was driving it. We need to start searching."

Bree pulled up a map of the area on her phone. "There's nothing around here but woods and fields. Town is about seven miles away. Which way would he go?"

Justin could be lying out in the cold, dead or dying.

"I'll call the state police and see if they can loan us a K-9 team." Todd stepped away to use his radio.

"What if the driver wasn't Justin?" Matt suggested. "What if someone else drove while he was bleeding in the back seat? Justin could have been taken captive by whoever shot Erin."

"If Justin was kidnapped," Bree said, "then the real killer is either holding him somewhere or he dumped his body before he ditched the pickup here."

Matt pointed at the vehicle. "Then how did the killer get home from here? Not many people would want to walk seven miles in this cold."

Bree thought about the man she'd chased out of Erin's house. He hadn't been exceptionally fit. She spit out theories, ticking them off with her fingers. "He could have used an accomplice. He could have left a vehicle here beforehand. He could have walked a mile or so, then called a friend for a ride. A rideshare app is another possibility."

Todd turned back to them. "I can get a K-9 unit out here first thing tomorrow morning."

"That's too long," Matt said.

Todd gestured toward Brody. "That's the best I can do unless you want to let Brody give it a go."

Matt exhaled through his nose. "We'll try, but he's not wearing his working harness, and it's been years since he's done any trailing work. Can one of the deputies run out to my vehicle for something? Don't let Brody see it."

"Sure." Todd summoned a deputy, who jogged out of the shipping bay.

A few minutes later, the deputy returned and passed a ratty-looking stuffed animal from under his coat to Matt. He shoved it into his own pocket. Then he led the dog close to the driver's side of the pickup and pointed to the seat. Brody stood on his hind legs and inspected the fabric. Matt let him sniff his fill, then gave him a command. They walked in a circle around the truck. The dog sniffed the air and ground as he moved. Bree was no expert, but the dog seemed to know what he was doing.

They'd circled the vehicle three times, each circle slightly larger than the previous one, when the dog's posture changed. His ears pricked forward, his tail jutted straight out from his body, and his direction became purposeful.

"He has something," Matt said.

Brody beelined for the exit. In the doorway, he paused to sniff again, then resumed trailing. Bree and Todd followed. Brody made his way outside. In the parking lot, he appeared to lose the trail, walking in circles, sniffing the air.

"He isn't smelling the ground." Bree shoved her hands into her pockets.

"Wind dissipates scent particles." Matt gave the dog more leash. "There won't be a perfect track or cone of scent. He'll have to follow whatever scent particles he can find. Think of it like connecting the dots."

After a few moments of seemingly aimless wandering, Brody headed away from the exit and toward a strip of woods. The dog didn't travel in a straight, definite line the way he had done inside the building. Instead, he zigzagged.

At the edge of the parking lot, Matt called, "Keep an eye out for tracks in the snow."

Bree and Todd fanned out twenty feet on either side of the working dog. Bree stepped over the curb at the edge of the lot. The snow was ankle deep and began to soak into her sneakers immediately. Just ahead, she spotted an indentation in the snow. "Hold on!"

She trudged closer and looked down at a partial footprint. "I found a track." She visually tracked the line between the footprint and the parking lot and saw several faint indentations. "I see more prints. Someone walked this way." She bent over the closest track. Drifting snow had partially filled the print.

Todd walked over and crouched next to her. "The tread isn't clear, except for this edge right here."

Bree pointed to a few knobby-looking marks. "Probably a work boot of some type."

"That's not clear enough to determine which brand." Todd stood and squinted into the woods. "Let's see where he went."

Brody led the way. They found more boot prints along the trail the dog followed. Fifteen or twenty minutes later, the woods opened to another road. Bree crossed the street. No more tracks. "He must have walked along the road."

Brody began zigzagging again. His nose went into the air and sniffed. He turned north and serpentined back and forth along the shoulder of the road.

"There's a farm ahead." Todd pointed up the road. A half mile away, on the opposite side of the road, large outbuildings clustered around a white house.

"That's Empire Acre Farms," Todd said. "It's a big operation. It looks deserted now, but in the fall, they have Christmas trees, hay rides, and pumpkin picking."

A quarter mile short of the farm, Brody stopped. His tail dropped and his ears lowered to a relaxed position.

Matt led him in a circle. The dog sniffed but didn't alert again.

"This is the end of the trail," Matt said.

Brody sat in the road and whined.

"He sounds depressed," Bree said.

"He likes to find the person he's looking for." Matt turned to the dog, praising him in a high-pitched voice. He reached into his coat pocket and pulled out the toy the deputy had brought from his SUV. "You're such a good boy!"

The dog's tail wagged, and his ears came forward again as Matt squeaked the toy. "Do you want Mr. Hedgehog?"

Bree was impressed by his unabashed use of baby talk. "You brought a dog toy with you?"

"He loves this old thing. I carry it in the truck in case he gets bored, but it used to be his reward for working." Matt lobbed the hedgehog in a slow arc. Brody jumped for it, snatching it from the air. When his front paws hit the street, he shook the toy as if breaking its neck.

Bree shuddered and fought a flashback. Cold, damp air. The smell of wet dog. The rattle of a chain. Teeth sinking into her flesh. The shake. Todd's voice brought her out of it.

"You think he left from here in a vehicle?" Todd looked up and down the road.

"Probably." Matt rubbed behind Brody's ears.

"Could the snow have impacted the scent?" Bree asked.

"I doubt it in this case. If fresh snow falls on top of a trail, it can affect the scent. But this snow has been here for a week, and Brody didn't have any trouble following the trail to this point."

Todd scanned the road in both directions. "Maybe he had a ride waiting."

Bree didn't think so. "Dropping a car in the middle of nowhere or getting picked up requires another person. Even if that person isn't an accomplice, he or she would be a witness to our suspect being here. I doubt he walked. Town is seven miles away."

"And Brody would have continued to follow his scent." Matt stroked the dog's head.

Bree's gaze returned to the big farm up the road. "Or he used the Empire Acres Farm as a pickup point for the Uber or Lyft we talked about earlier. That way, there would be no record of a pickup at the factory where he left the truck."

"We have two most likely theories," Todd said. "He had a ride or car waiting, or he used a rideshare app."

Matt turned to Todd. "Can you get a warrant for rideshare company records?"

"Yes." Todd nodded. "Between the note and the blood, we can argue a severely injured person or potential suicide as an emergency situation."

They turned back and began walking. The wind was in Bree's face. Her nose was numb, and her feet were blocks of ice by the time they backtracked all the way to the factory. Inside, Todd snagged one of his deputies and set him on the task of applying for a warrant for the information from rideshare app companies.

In the factory parking lot, Todd walked to his vehicle. "I'll have the pickup towed to the municipal garage. A forensics tech can look at it there."

They stopped next to Todd's cruiser. The other deputies were still inside the factory with Erin's pickup truck.

"Have a minute, Todd?" Matt asked.

Todd's brows rose. "You have a lead?"

"A couple," Matt said. "First of all, did you hear rumors about Jack Halo sexually harassing his staff?"

"No." Todd's spine snapped straight. "And we interviewed everyone Erin worked with."

"He's intimidated his employees," Bree said. "They were probably not comfortable speaking freely with the deputies." When she wanted information about an employer, she interviewed employees off-site.

Todd reached into his pocket for a small notepad. He wrote down some information, then looked up. "You said you had a couple of leads."

"My sister's ex stopped by last night." Bree shivered as she told Todd about Craig's visit.

"I'll see what I can dig up on him." Todd wrote an additional note. "Can you think of any reason he'd want to harm your sister?"

"No," Bree said. "Craig cares about money. He always came back to Erin when he needed a place to live. I can't see how he would benefit from her death."

"The kids will receive social security survivor benefits," Todd said.

Bree hadn't thought of that. "Doesn't seem like that would be enough to commit murder."

Todd lifted a palm. "The teenager only has a few years left, but the little girl would collect until she's eighteen. That's ten years of monthly payments."

"Craig is always focused on money," Bree said. "He said he has a job, but maybe being a minister doesn't pay as much as he hoped."

"*I* have some news for *you*." Todd opened his vehicle door. "The search warrant for Trey White's place came through right before you called about the truck. I'll send deputies to execute the warrant first thing in the morning. We collected surveillance tapes from surrounding businesses, but none show the front of the store. His alibi is still unverified."

"Did you pull any information from the burner phone that was among Erin's belongings from Halo?" Matt asked.

Todd leaned on the inside of his vehicle door. "Both Erin's and Justin's fingerprints were on the phone. It was purchased at Eddy's Electronics four months ago. We're lucky that the store went digital with its surveillance videos last year. They keep security tapes for six months and were able to pull the video of a man purchasing the phone. He used cash, but the image is very clear. There's no question. It was Justin." Todd paused, his gaze drifting to the factory before he continued. "We already knew that Justin and Erin had an argument in the parking lot of Halo Salon last Friday. We had asked the salon owner to pull the security feeds from the parking lot cameras. In the video, Justin acted very agitated, and he definitely gave Erin a phone."

"What's on the phone?" Matt asked.

"Not much." Todd adjusted his hat. "According to the call log, approximately once a week, the burner received a text with no message except for a different phone number. If a call was made that week, that was the number used. Other than those number-only texts, the phone was used only to make calls. There were no other text messages."

Wireless providers kept records of text message content for a length of time. But there was no way to view the content of a verbal discussion. Justin hadn't wanted a record of his activity.

Todd continued. "Each of the numbers called by Justin's burner appear to belong to other burners."

Bree cut to the chase. "Drug dealers switch phones constantly to avoid being tracked or traced by law enforcement."

"Yes." Todd rested his hands on his duty belt. "We believe Justin used his burner phone to buy drugs."

"When was the last time he made a call?" Matt asked.

"Last Friday," Todd said.

"Shit." Matt pivoted in a frustrated one-eighty. Sitting at his feet, Brody looked up at him and whined. Matt's hand dropped to rest on the dog's head, but Bree wondered who was comforting whom.

Because Matt's friend had called his drug dealer four days before Erin had been killed.

Chapter Twenty

He paced, his anxiety churning.

The news played on the TV. The police had found Erin's pickup truck.

It doesn't matter.

He'd left no clues behind. He'd worn gloves. They would find nothing in the truck to tie her death to him. He was clear. Now he had to focus on what was important—to keep his eye on the prize.

After opening his laptop, he turned on his camera and transferred his recent photos to the computer. There she was. The telephoto lens allowed him to photograph her without her suspecting anything. She had no idea.

He opened his notepad and transferred her activities to the spreadsheet he'd created. He couldn't watch her 24/7. He'd done his best, but it wasn't good enough. There were too many gaps in her schedule, too much time unaccounted for. He needed to know where she was and who she was with at every moment of every day.

But he had other responsibilities. He couldn't devote all his time to watching her. He shouldn't have to, he thought with an immediate surge of anger that tunneled his vision and blurred his thoughts. He wanted to pummel his fists into something. He gulped air until the urge passed.

He grabbed his keys. He had an errand to run. He needed to be ready in case she betrayed him. A man couldn't be too prepared. Guns were useless without ammunition.

CHAPTER TWENTY-ONE

Back in his SUV, Matt directed the heat vents toward Bree. "What do we do now?"

Brody lay across the back seat, whining softly.

In the passenger seat, Bree shivered, her hands still shoved in her pockets. "We need to regroup."

"We need to find Justin." But Matt had no idea of where to look. His friend could be dying right this minute.

"I want to look at my sister's cell phone records. Let's go back to the house."

"OK." Matt drove out of the lot. In his head, he wanted to charge all over town, kicking in doors. But Bree was right. They needed to reorganize. Running around like idiots would waste time they didn't have.

"Dana found my sister's account numbers and passwords. We have access to all her online accounts."

"So does Todd." Though Matt didn't have confidence in Todd's ability to interpret the data.

"I want to see the information for myself. I never know what will jump out at me. Besides, I know Erin. I might see a pattern an outsider wouldn't recognize."

It was four o'clock by the time Matt parked in front of the farm. The sun sank low over the trees.

"Winter is depressing." Bree opened her door and slid from the SUV. "It'll be dark in a half hour."

They went into the house. Bree slipped off her sneakers. Her socks left wet footprints. Her feet must be freezing. In the entryway, Brody's nose shot into the air. Matt inhaled the scents of garlic and basil.

Bree hung their coats by the door. "Dana has taken charge of the kitchen. If I was cooking, we'd be rotating between Chinese takeout, pizza, and Cheerios."

They walked back to the kitchen. Dana and Kayla sat at the table, playing backgammon. Kayla jumped up and raced to greet Brody.

"Where's Luke?" Bree asked.

"In his room," Dana said.

Bree went to the oven, turned on the light, and peered through the door. "What's in there?"

"Lasagna." Dana got up, filled a bowl with water, and set it on the floor for the dog. "Coffee? It's fresh."

"Yes," Bree said. "I'm going to get dry socks. Excuse me for a minute." She ducked into the laundry room.

Matt accepted coffee. He wrapped his scarred hand around the mug to alleviate the cold ache. "My sister is always leaving vegetarian lasagna in my freezer."

Dana refilled her own cup. "Are you a vegetarian?"

"No," he said, mustering patience for the small talk. "But my sister never gives up trying to convert me. She runs an animal rescue."

"Good." Dana returned to her seat. "Because this is the extra-meat kind. I use ground beef in the filling, and I use pork bones to make the gravy. You'll stay for dinner."

It wasn't a question.

Kayla returned to her chair, and Brody stretched out on the floor at her feet. She pulled her bare feet from her slippers and brushed her toes through his fur. "Mommy rescued our horses."

Matt's heart squeezed at the wistful tone in the little girl's voice. "Did she?"

Kayla slid to the floor and pressed her face into Brody's fur.

"Erin bought them at the livestock auction," Bree said, walking in from the laundry room, her eyes misty. "They were headed for the kill buyer. She cared about soundness and temperament, not papers."

"My sister would agree," Matt said.

Kayla lifted her head and patted Brody's side before returning to her chair.

Bree picked up her coffee and leaned over Kayla's shoulder. "Do you know how to play?"

Kayla shook her head. "Dana is teaching me."

"She's a quick learner." Dana scooped the dice off the board.

"You can play next," Kayla said.

"I have a bit of work to do right now, but we can play later." Bree picked up her coffee and carried it toward the doorway. "We'll be in the office if you need us."

He followed her to the office. Bree closed the french doors and sat at the desk. Matt pulled a wooden chair next to hers and dropped into it. A laptop sat on the desk.

Bree booted it up. "This might take a few minutes. My computer is slow. I'm always too busy to update the software." She paused. "Erin's computer, the one the sheriff's department took, is a dinosaur. She bought Luke a new one for Christmas. She always put herself last."

"She was a good mom." Impatient to get back to the case, Matt tapped his fingers on the desk. "Is the blood in the back seat of the truck enough to convince you that Justin didn't kill Erin? That someone else shot her and likely him as well?"

"I wouldn't say convinced, but I'll accept it as a viable theory." Bree nodded. "Let's assume for the moment that Justin didn't kill my sister. Who are our other suspects?"

"Nico, Justin's drug dealer. I wanted to believe Justin was sober, but I was wrong." Before Erin's death, Matt hadn't suspected Justin was still using drugs. "He totally fooled me."

"What was Nico's motivation?" Bree pulled a piece of paper from a printer on a shelf behind her. "I wish I had a murder board to track clues and suspects, but a list will have to suffice."

"Money, maybe reputation. Drug dealers can't let clients get away with nonpayment."

"OK. We don't know enough about Nico to consider opportunity yet." Bree wrote his name and a dollar sign. "Who else?"

"Jack Halo."

Bree paused, her lips flattening. "Maybe Erin had some sort of proof that he was sexually harassing his employees."

"That would do it," Matt agreed. "Financial damages awarded in a civil trial can be unpredictable."

"He wouldn't want his dirty deeds made public, especially since his business catered largely to women."

"Alleged dirty deeds," Matt said.

Anger flushed Bree's cheeks pink. "My sister wasn't a liar, nor was she overly sensitive. If she told Steph that Jack was harassing her, it must have been pretty bad."

Matt raised his hands, palms toward her. "I'm sorry. I meant we have no proof. Hearsay doesn't count."

"If Erin was a threat to Jack Halo, she must have had some sort of evidence. Somewhere."

"Right," Matt said. "In that case, he'd settle, which would cost him."

Bree skipped down the page and wrote his name and the word *harassment*. "We need to ask Todd if Jack has an alibi for Erin's murder."

"Yes," Matt said. "Who's next?"

"The kids' father, Craig Vance." Bree started a column. "Maybe he's after the social security, or—more likely—he thinks my sister had money put away for the kids. Craig's motive will be money."

Matt pointed to the computer. "Open a browser. Let's see how much the average survivor collects as a benefit."

"The average monthly benefit is eight hundred dollars." Bree sat back. "I still doubt anyone would kill over that much money." She sounded skeptical.

"I guess that depends on your financial situation. Ten years of monthly payments . . ." Matt closed his eyes for a few seconds. "Let's look at those calls your sister received and the cash withdrawals."

Bree logged into her sister's accounts and printed her bank account and call records for the past four months. Then they laid the reports side by side with the bank statements in front of Matt.

He took a highlighter from a pencil cup and marked the withdrawals. "There really aren't any other large movements of money except for the three cash withdrawals."

"Erin was paid an hourly rate by the salon plus tips. She had an established client base, and did well, but she wouldn't have been able to keep this farm if Adam didn't cover the mortgage, taxes, and insurance. Most of her income went to living expenses."

Matt gave Bree the dates, and she pulled out the corresponding pages of the call logs.

"There are several calls from this number in the days just before the withdrawal." Bree used the highlighter to mark the calls.

Matt tapped on the highlighted number. "Could this be Craig's burner phone? Could he have been blackmailing your sister?"

"Now that sounds completely plausible." Bree tapped a forefinger on the desk. "Todd needed a warrant for the wireless provider. It'll probably take a few days to get the records."

Matt pulled out his phone and dialed the number. No one answered, and the voice mail invitation was computer generated. He didn't leave a message. "Try reverse lookup."

The only information was the wireless provider name.

"Let me make a call. I know a former local cop who's now a PI. He has access to additional search engines." Matt called Lance Kruger, who called back in ten minutes. Matt thanked him, then relayed the info to Bree. "There's no personal information available, but the number was activated in Albany, New York."

Bree froze. "Craig lives in Albany." She pushed her chair back and got up to pace the small office. "We need to know what he's up to."

"Can we talk to his employer?"

She pivoted in a frustrated, tense movement. "We have no official status on this case."

"Todd does," Matt said.

"He'd either send a deputy or ask a local cop." Bree shook her head. "We're going to have to lie to get the information we need. And we need Craig to be out of the way."

"Do you have a way to contact him?"

"Yes. He gave me a number."

"Set up a meeting with him to discuss his intentions."

Bree spun on her heel. "I don't—"

"While you occupy him, I'll GPS his vehicle."

A sly smile spread across her face. "I like it."

"Thought you would." Matt pulled a piece of paper from the printer.

"It's not legal."

"No plan is perfect." Matt was willing to take risks to find Justin. "I won't leave prints on the unit." He began listing their plans. "Once we know he's away from his place of employment, we'll decide on a good lie for his employer."

"He's the minister of a church," Bree said dryly.

Matt snorted. "If we survive the lightning strike, we might come away with some useful information."

"GPS data on Craig could prove to be interesting." Bree resumed her pacing. "Other suspects?"

"Trey White?" Matt asked. "He was fixated on Erin enough to break into Justin's house multiple times and steal her underwear. Todd was unable to verify his alibi at the dollar store."

"We need more than lack of an alibi. I wish we could search his residence."

Matt shrugged. "He lives alone, and he's in jail. Who says we can't?"

"The law."

"We won't take anything." Matt didn't want to wait, and he was afraid the deputies would miss something. Justin's life could hang in the balance of this investigation.

"It's still illegal."

"Only if we get caught," Matt said. "It'll be dark soon. Tonight is our last chance. The sheriff's department will execute their search warrant in the morning." Matt wanted to do whatever he could to find Justin now. He could be dying at that very moment.

"We should let the deputies handle it."

"Todd isn't going to perform the search himself. Who knows who he'll send?"

Disapproval narrowed her eyes. "I can't believe I'm considering this." Bree chewed on her lip. "We'd have to wait until later tonight, after the kids go to bed."

"Of course," Matt said as if it was obvious.

"We have four suspects and a plan to investigate three of them."

Matt's phone vibrated. He glanced at the screen. "It's my CI."

He answered, "Yeah."

"Midnight tonight. The usual place. Bring my money." Kevin ended the call without waiting for a response.

Matt set his phone on the desk. "And that rounds out our list. Looks like I'm meeting Nico."

Bree stopped pacing. "No. *We're* meeting Nico."

CHAPTER TWENTY-TWO

Bree dialed the number on the business card Craig had given her. With one eye on Matt, she leaned back in the chair and flicked the card as the line rang. Craig's title was listed as *Pastor, Grace Community Church*.

When Craig answered, he was breathless. "Yes."

"I want to meet."

"Why?" He sounded suspicious.

"To discuss the situation."

Three heartbeats of silence passed. "Praise the Lord. I knew He would intervene and influence your decision." Despite his religious words, his tone was smug. He was gloating. He thought he had her backed into a corner.

Bree gritted her teeth and kept her voice level. "I just want what is best for the kids."

"*My* children are my priority as well."

"Are you free tomorrow morning?"

"I have a youth group commitment in the afternoon. It would have to be early."

"No problem," Bree said. "I can come there. I have the church's address."

"No." His answer came just a beat too quickly. He didn't want her near his church. Telling. "I'll meet you halfway." He gave her the location of a restaurant in Saratoga Springs. "Ten thirty."

The line went dead.

Bree stabbed the "End" button on her phone anyway. "He's such an ass."

"But he agreed to meet you?" Matt asked.

"Yes." She shoved her phone into her jeans pocket and summarized the call.

Dana knocked on the french door, then opened it. "Dinner's ready."

Bree took their notes off the desk, folded the papers, and stuck them in her purse before locking the rest of the papers in the bottom drawer. Then they went back to the kitchen and made small talk while they ate Dana's lasagna.

"Is Mommy in heaven?" Kayla asked.

"Yes," Bree said. If there was a heaven, Erin was definitely in it.

"But you said we're gonna have a funeral." Kayla's brow creased.

Bree searched for a simple explanation.

Luke jumped in. "Mom's body is still here on earth, but her soul went to heaven."

Kayla turned to her brother. "What's a soul?"

"The part of Mom that made her Mom." Luke's answer seemed to satisfy Kayla.

"Do you want to have a funeral for your mom?" Bree asked.

"We should, right?" Luke tilted his head. "I mean, lots of people loved Mom. Everybody should get to say goodbye to her."

Bree nodded. "Do you want to say goodbye?"

Both kids nodded.

Luke stared down at his hands. "Can I see her?"

"Yes," Bree said. "If you want, but you don't have to. Don't feel pressured either way. You do what you think you need."

He lifted his gaze. "I want to, but not in front of everyone."

"You want a private viewing and a public service?"

"I think so." His eyes went moist and he swiped a finger under one.

"Kayla, what do you want?" Bree asked.

"What Luke says." Kayla's voice was small and thin.

Bree didn't push. She could start making plans, and honestly, her sister's funeral was the last thing she wanted to think about. Even though she'd seen Erin, she was still partially in denial. When the funeral was over, she'd have to accept the fact that her sister was gone forever.

Brody set his giant head on Luke's leg and whined, giving the boy a pleading look and breaking the tension in the room.

"I'd better feed him." Matt went to the SUV for his kibble. When he'd set a bowl in front of the dog, Brody gave a disappointed sigh and half-heartedly ate a few nuggets.

"Poor Brody." Kayla cleared the table. "He wants lasagna."

Kayla slipped the dog a noodle, and Matt pretended not to see.

"Is it all right if I leave Brody here overnight?" Matt asked.

"Happy to have him," Dana said.

"I could dog-sit!" Kayla threw her arms around the dog's neck. "He could sleep with me and everything."

Bree made coffee and played a game with the kids before bedtime. By nine o'clock, Luke went to his room to read, and Bree tucked Kayla in. Brody walked into the room and jumped onto the bed. Bree moved a few steps away, but Kayla shared her pillow, throwing one arm over the dog's neck.

Matt poked his head in the doorway. "Is that all right?"

"You tell me." Bree swallowed her anxiety.

It's OK. Daddy's dogs were never like Brody.

Matt seemed to read her mind. "She's safer with Brody than without him."

"OK then." Bree turned out the light.

"Aren't you going to kiss me good night?" Kayla asked.

"Sure." Bree returned to the bedside. She wiped her sweaty palms on her jeans. It took her a few seconds to muster the courage to lean closer to the dog. Her face was inches from Brody's. She kissed Kayla and straightened, quickly moving backward a few steps.

"Good night, Kayla. Love you," Bree said.

"Love you back, Aunt Bree."

Bree's knees shook as she left the room.

"I'd call that progress." Matt led the way downstairs.

Bree called it indigestion. She stopped in the kitchen for an antacid. "You're sure she's safe with him?"

"Absolutely. He'd give his life to protect her."

"I'm trusting you." She met his gaze.

"I know."

Bree filled Dana in on their plans, grabbed her purse, and checked her weapons. "The dog is in bed with Kayla."

"OK. I'll check on them in a bit. You be careful." Dana looked worried.

"We will," Matt assured her.

At the front door, Bree put on her coat and added a knit cap, gloves, and a scarf. She fetched her boots and body armor from her trunk. She put on the boots and carried the Kevlar vest to Matt's SUV.

Trey White lived on Pine Road, four blocks from Justin's house. Matt slowed the vehicle as they passed the address.

The house was a big brick Colonial. Behind the house, Bree spotted a detached garage with a second-story addition. A light above the upstairs door illuminated a set of wooden steps. "Looks like the entrance to Trey's apartment is on this side." Tall evergreen hedges lined the sides of the property. "Plenty of shadows between the street and the garage, but we'll be exposed on the stairs." In the main house, an upstairs window glowed with light.

"We'll have to wait until the homeowner goes to sleep." Matt drove past and pulled to the curb in front of an empty lot at the other end of the street. They could still see the house.

Bree tugged gloves onto her cold hands. Ten minutes later, the second-story window went dark. She checked her watch. "We'll give the homeowner thirty minutes to fall asleep?"

"OK," Matt said. "Shouldn't take us long to search the place. It's small." Matt opened his glove compartment and pulled out a mini tool kit.

"How good are you at picking locks?" she asked, thinking of their exposure at the top of the steps. "We'll have to get in fast."

He flexed his gloved hand. "It's not one of my better skills. Takes dexterity."

Bree took the tool kit from him and set it on her thigh. "When I was in high school, my cousin used to lock the door at midnight. She thought that would teach me to be home on time. Instead, I just learned to pick the locks."

Matt grinned. "I'm relieved."

"At what?"

"That you're not perfect." He turned off the engine.

"Perfect? I'm terrified of your well-behaved dog." The mental image of the big dog's head so close to Kayla brought back a memory she'd long suppressed. Her shoulder ached, and humiliation flooded her. If she hadn't been shocked and vulnerable after her sister's death, would she have shared so much personal information with him?

She glanced at him. He was easy to talk to, and she wasn't sure how she felt about that. How could being overly comfortable with someone make her uneasy?

Matt was studying her. "You seem to be doing better, though."

"I'm trying. I hate being afraid of dogs. Every time I have to work with a K-9 team, trying to act normal is a nightmare." Controlling her anxiety around canines consumed mental and emotional energy that took away from her investigation. It was exhausting, distracting, and irrational.

"No one knows?" He sounded surprised.

"Just Dana. She runs interference when she can." Bree rubbed her gloved hands together. With the engine off, the vehicle was cooling quickly. "It's not the kind of thing you want circulating around the department. Can you imagine the flak I'd take?"

Normally, Bree could handle the metaphorical ball-busting that came with the job. But when it came to this one thing, this particular terror, she was too sensitive. Then there were the few throwback macho types who didn't believe women belonged in law enforcement and who would latch on to any reason to discredit or disarm her.

"Cops can be brutal."

"I guess you'd know all about that."

"Yeah."

Bree studied the dark street through the windshield. "I was five. My father had at least a dozen dogs. I don't know what breed they were, but they were *not* pets. He called them hunting dogs, but that was bullshit. Looking back on my memories, I suspect he had fighting dogs. They were tied up at the rear of our property, and I was told not to go near them."

The last thirty years evaporated, and she could hear the barking and panting as if she were back at the farm. "It was cold that day too, icy like the past couple of weeks have been." Her hands trembled and she stuffed them into her pockets.

As the memory played out, she smelled the dog runs and felt the chill of her soaking-wet knit mittens. "It had snowed the night before, just an inch or two, but I was determined to build a snowman. I was gathering snow from all over the yard and not paying attention to where I was. I ventured too close to the dogs' area. One of them broke its chain and charged me. I knew better than to run. A running, crying child can trigger the prey instinct in certain dogs, like this one. But I couldn't stop myself. I was terrified." She breathed. "It caught me." She made a snapping motion with her right hand around her left shoulder. "And gave me a good neck-breaking shake."

Like Brody had done with the hedgehog toy.

Bree could feel Matt's gaze riveted on her profile. But he didn't say a word, and he didn't move. Inside the SUV was as utterly still as the dark street in front of her. Her gaze turned further inward, another jolt of phantom pain searing her shoulder.

She continued. "I don't blame the dog. I'm sure my father was as abusive to his animals as he was to his family. He would have wanted the most aggressive dogs in the county. He would have considered it a point of pride. I remember once he told me it was best not to feed them much. Hungry dogs responded better to training. His were always on edge. If they caught a squirrel or rabbit, they ripped it to shreds in seconds. He liked that he was the only one who could handle them. It played to his ego."

A shudder rippled through her. Despite the decades that had passed, she could feel the tearing of her flesh, the cold air on her exposed skin, and the warm blood running down her torso and arm.

"I thought it was going to rip my arm off, but the dog dragged me back to its kennel. I kicked and fought. It lost its hold for a few seconds and dropped me. I tried to crawl away." Bree's lungs tightened, and her next breath wheezed. "But it got me by the ankle. I must have been screaming bloody murder the whole time, because suddenly the dog released me." She stopped. Under her coat, sweat soaked her sweater. Her heart banged against her ribs. "The attack probably lasted only a minute or so." But it had felt like an eternity.

She paused, breathing, remembering. "My mother took me to the ER. I was there all night. After I came home, my father took me back to the kennels. He said I needed to learn a lesson about responsibility, that actions and disobedience had consequences." Bree's stomach turned as the mental video played. Her very detailed story ended abruptly with one last image. Her father raised the shotgun and commanded her to watch. The shot boomed through the woods, and the big beast dropped to the icy ground, half of its head blown off, blood and bone and brain matter spattering the snow. Bree's stomach heaved. Thirty years later, her body vividly remembered vomiting. "He shot the dog in front of me and told me it was my fault."

"That's horrible."

Bree turned away, her face heating again. Dana didn't even know the whole story, only a three-sentence summary. She glanced at him. A short, false note of laughter bubbled out of her. "That was probably TMI."

"I'm glad you told me."

"It's not like me to overshare."

"I told you about my shooting."

She lifted one eyebrow. "Then we're even."

"You didn't owe me anything."

Then why had she told him?

"I'm sorry if I've been pushy about the dog." Matt frowned. "You told me you were afraid, but I had no idea how traumatic your experience was."

"I don't expect to be coddled. K-9s are useful tools, and Brody has been very helpful. My fears are mine to handle."

"We both know it's not that easy. Plus, shepherds are big, scary-looking dogs." Matt's brows knitted. "What you need is a gateway dog."

"A gateway dog?"

"Yeah. Spending time around a calm and less threatening dog might help desensitize you to them."

The idea of spending time with any dog did not appeal, and she didn't want to talk about it anymore. Bree checked the time and pointed to the house. "I haven't seen any movement in a half hour."

"Yeah. Let's do this." Matt turned off the dome light, and they slipped out of the SUV.

Bree started down the street, glad to be moving rather than thinking. "We're just a normal couple out for a walk." Matt took her hand.

Bree stared down at their joined gloves. The contact was . . . distracting. She tried to pull her hand away, but he held on. When she looked at him, the corner of his mouth was turned up and his eyes were laughing.

She rolled her eyes. "I'm going to sprain an eyeball hanging around with you."

They neared the brick house, and he tugged her behind the hedge. They crept in its shadow past the house until they were parallel to the detached garage. Bree pulled her hand from Matt's and signaled for him to stay put. She jogged up the wooden staircase. Taking two slim tools from the kit, she inserted them into the doorknob. She felt for the pins and popped the lock. She opened the door. Matt came up the stairs and slipped inside behind her. He closed the door.

Blinds covered the windows, blocking out the moonlight and leaving the apartment pitch-black. Bree used the flashlight app on her phone to illuminate the room. The apartment was a studio with a kitchenette occupying one corner and a small bath tucked into the other. A bed and a sitting area took up the rest of the space.

Matt headed for the kitchen area. He opened a drawer and shone a penlight into it. Bree went into the tiny bath. A pedestal sink, a toilet, and a shower the size of a phone booth were crammed into the space. She opened the medicine cabinet. The bottom shelf held a few hygiene and grooming products. Prescription bottles were lined up across the top shelf. She photographed the labels with her cell phone.

She exited the bathroom. Matt was standing next to the bed, shining his light into the top drawer of the nightstand.

"Find anything?" she asked in a low voice.

"A pricey 35mm camera with a telephoto lens."

"Being a voyeur is expensive."

Matt snapped a picture. "And porn. Lots of porn."

She moved to the living area. A ratty leather couch faced an entertainment center. The TV was a forty-inch flat-screen. A game console and controller sat next to it. "He spent all his money on the TV and gaming system."

She opened the top drawer under the TV. It was full of video games and DVDs. She put her phone inside the drawer to contain the light. Turning her head, she read a title, *Game of Boners*. She snorted. Points for creativity. "Porn here too."

She took a picture and moved on to the bottom drawer. There was only one item inside, a photo album, snapshot size. She opened it and gasped. Her sister's face stared back at her.

"What is it?" Matt asked over her shoulder. "Oh."

Bree turned the pages. In one, her sister was getting out of her truck in the salon parking lot. The next showed her sister leaving the salon. Bree recorded each picture with her cell phone camera. "They're all like this."

"She didn't know she was being photographed."

"No." The hairs on Bree's arms rose. "He was watching her."

"Stalking her," Matt corrected. "For how long?"

"Months, at minimum." Bree pointed to an image of Erin in a skirt and short-sleeved shirt. "Erin isn't wearing a jacket. This must be summer."

"Some of these pictures were taken from the dollar store with a telephoto lens."

"Not this one." Bree stopped on a photo of Erin walking up Justin's driveway. She tucked her phone back into her pocket. "I'd say we've established solid motivation."

Matt gestured to the picture of Erin in front of Justin's house. "There's snow on the ground. This photo is recent. We have more than motivation. This is the crime scene. We have proof Trey was at Justin's house in the last week. He was fixated on Erin, and he knew about her continuing relationship with Justin. He was jealous."

"Maybe jealous enough to kill her," Bree said. "The photos aren't date-stamped. We still need physical evidence that puts Trey *in* Justin's house the night of the murder."

"Give it time. The forensics reports aren't in yet."

"True."

Something thumped outside. Bree froze. Matt did the same, then turned off his light. Another thump lifted the hairs on the back of her neck.

Why had she let him talk her into breaking and entering? Because he cared about his friend, and she respected loyalty. She'd also ignored the risks because she was obsessed with solving her sister's murder. But that wouldn't help her if they got caught. Her getting arrested would be fuel for Craig in a potential custody battle.

CHAPTER
TWENTY-THREE

Matt eased the drawer closed and moved next to the window. He peered through the skinny gap between the frame and the blind. Outside, a man walked toward the garage from the house. Matt pointed to the window and mouthed, "Homeowner."

Bree nodded, her face grim. If Matt got caught in Trey's apartment, he'd get a slap on the wrist, and maybe have to pay a fine. As a police officer, Bree had much more to lose.

The homeowner walked closer. Matt scanned the apartment. Was there anywhere to hide? Bree pointed toward the bathroom. It was the only space large enough to conceal them. He turned back to the window. Outside, the man was almost to the garage. Matt held his breath and leaned away from the glass.

But the man didn't approach the stairs. He opened the overhead garage door and went inside. Matt glanced behind him. Was there a second entrance to the apartment? He didn't see an additional doorway.

A few seconds later, a car door closed beneath them. Then an engine started. A Toyota Camry backed out of the garage, down the driveway, and into the street.

Matt exhaled. "It's clear."

With a tight nod, Bree headed for the door. "Let's get out of here."

They left the apartment exactly as they'd found it. Bree locked the door on their way out. They crept down the stairs and into the shadow of the hedge. Crouching, they jogged all the way back to Matt's Suburban.

He started the engine. "I'm sorry I talked you into breaking the law. You could lose your job."

Bree faced him from the passenger seat. "I don't blame you. I'm an adult. I made my decision. That's not the issue. I might not be going back to the PPD anyway. Before Craig showed up, I'd decided to move here to raise the kids. That's what Erin wanted. But if he wins . . . Hell, I don't know what I'll do. Part of me says I should stick close to them no matter what. But Craig hates me. If he successfully sues for custody, he won't let me near them. But if there's a custody suit, a B and E won't help my case. As much as I want to solve my sister's murder, I can't afford to do anything like that again. I can't let Erin's case make me lose sight of what's important."

"If he sues for custody, you'll fight him in court?"

"I don't know." Bree stopped and reached for the door handle. "It depends on what the kids want and what my chances are. The last thing I want to do is hurt them. We'll see what the lawyer says when she has all the information."

So many factors to weigh in every decision. So much at stake for two grieving children. Bree's responsibilities went way beyond her needing to remain alive.

"Do you want me to take you home before I meet with Nico?"

"No. You can't go alone. You need backup. At least Nico isn't a hidden threat. We know what we're getting into."

Not entirely. How can I shift some of the risk away from Bree tonight?

"How are you with a long gun?" he asked.

"I'm good." Confidence with no bravado rang in her voice.

"Then you'll cover me."

From as far away as possible.

Matt stopped at his house and picked up his rifle. Then he drove to the same warehouse complex where he'd met Kevin earlier in the week. He turned into the parking lot. It looked much the same, except a few more tire tracks crossed the snowy asphalt. "We have thirty minutes. You need to get into position."

Bree donned her body armor and shrugged her wool coat over it. She gave him some side-eye. "You should be wearing a vest too."

"I'm not a cop anymore."

"You still bleed."

"I have no reason to own body armor." Matt stepped out of the SUV.

Bree met him behind the vehicle. "We're in the parking lot of a vacant warehouse meeting your old confidential informant and a drug dealer. I think that's a damned good reason."

"Good thing I have you for backup."

"You'll take this." Bree removed a backup piece from her ankle holster.

"No."

"Damn it. What if something happens and you need to back *me* up?" She leaned into his SUV and put the gun in the console. "I know you shoot better than you think."

"Fine." Matt retrieved his rifle from the cargo area of his SUV and handed it to her. "Sorry. It's not an AR."

"I can do old school." She took it and sighted down the barrel, then switched on the laser sight. A green dot appeared on the building fifty feet away.

After scanning the lot, she nodded toward the abandoned warehouse in the rear of the complex. Most of the windows were broken. "I'll find a concealed spot." She balanced the rifle in the crook of her arm. "I'll be watching." She turned, jogged across the snow, and disappeared into the shadow of the building.

Matt climbed back into his truck to wait. He missed Brody, but he didn't want to risk the dog getting shot or distracting Bree. Kevin wouldn't fall for the same trick again. He'd come prepared to deal with the dog.

Matt reached into the glove compartment for his camera. He ignored the gun.

Waiting sucked. He started the truck every ten minutes to blast the heat, but his hand began to cramp. He checked his watch. Fifteen minutes before his scheduled meeting time, headlights appeared on the main road. Matt looked through his camera and focused on the entrance to the parking lot. It was too dark to see the license plate, but the vehicle was Kevin's pickup truck.

The pickup turned into the lot and stopped a few feet short of the pool of light cast by the streetlamp. The door of the pickup creaked open, and Kevin climbed out. Matt stepped out of his Suburban. They met in the middle, under the streetlamp.

"Where's my money?" Kevin asked.

"Nice to see you too."

"Fuck you. We had a deal."

"OK. OK. Relax." Matt reached into his jeans pocket in a slow, deliberate motion. He pulled out the folded bills and offered them to Kevin.

Kevin wore a knit hat low on his brow. Under it, his eyes avoided contact with Matt's as he snatched the money.

The skin between Matt's shoulder blades itched. "What's going on, Kevin?"

"I'm sorry, man. I tried to warn you." Kevin lifted his eyes. A grim frown split his gaunt face.

Tires grated on snow. Matt's head whipped toward the sound. A vehicle was pulling off the main road. Its headlights flipped on.

Kevin stepped back, raising his hands. "Nothing I could do, man. Nico doesn't like people asking questions about him."

The new vehicle was a black Ford Explorer. As it drove closer, the overhead light reflected on the windshield, creating a mirror effect. Matt's heart thudded. The light shifted and he could see a vague shape behind the wheel, but he couldn't tell how many people were inside. Mud partially obscured the license plate, but Matt could see the first three letters.

Kevin jumped into his pickup truck and fishtailed out of the lot.

Despite the freezing wind, cold sweat broke out on Matt's back as he waited. Thirty seconds later, the driver's door of the Explorer opened, and a man climbed out. Lean and wiry, he studied Matt for two breaths before approaching. The dealer wore a black knit hat and a heavy coat that concealed any weapons he might be carrying, and Matt was sure he was carrying multiple weapons. He stopped a few feet away. His face was narrow, his eyes colder than the wind blowing across the surrounding fields.

"Are you Nico?" Matt asked.

Though he didn't admit to anything, the man's eyes flickered with recognition of the name. "What do you want?"

"I want to buy some oxy."

A scar that bisected Nico's eyebrow shifted as he squinted. "Don't fuck with me. I want to know what is going on right now."

"I need information," Matt said.

Nico didn't move. "Are you a cop?"

"No," Matt said. "In fact, I'm trying to find my friend before the cops do." He pulled out a picture of Justin. "I know he was an *acquaintance* of yours."

Nico ignored the photo. "Don't know him."

"I'll pay you for the information," Matt said.

Cold anger flared in Nico's eyes. "I don't sell *information*." He reached into his pocket and whipped out a switchblade. "How can I make it clear that I am not interested?"

Sweat broke under Matt's arms, and he wished he had Bree's gun in his pocket. But no, he'd been stubborn. Nico opened the knife with one smooth flick of his wrist.

A small green dot appeared in the center of Nico's chest.

"I wouldn't do that if I were you." Matt nodded toward the light.

Nico froze. His gaze dropped to the laser dot. The light slowly drifted up from the center of his chest to his face. His hand opened, and he dropped the knife in the snow.

Matt held the photo up in front of Nico's face. "I just want to find him. That's all."

Nico focused on the picture. "I know him. That's the guy the cops want for killing his wife."

"But you know him from before."

"Yes."

Matt lowered the photo. "Did you kill her?"

Nico's gaze followed the green light as it wandered back down the centerline of his body to stop on his groin. Beads of sweat broke out on his forehead. "Kill who?"

"Justin's wife."

"Why would I kill her?" Nico dodged the question.

"Because Justin owes you money," Matt suggested.

Nico shrugged. "He doesn't. I don't extend credit. This is a cash-only business. And even if he did, killing a client would not result in collecting payment. A good beating, on the other hand, can be an excellent motivator. Hypothetically speaking."

"When was the last time you saw Justin?" Matt asked.

"I seen him about a week ago," Nico said. The green dot on his groin still held his attention. "Last Friday he called me in the morning, but he didn't have enough money for what he wanted. He only had enough to score some H—again, hypothetically speaking."

Shock paralyzed Matt for a minute. *H* was heroin, and plenty of people who became addicted to oxycodone eventually ended up on heroin because it was a cheaper alternative. But he'd never thought Justin would become a heroin addict.

"Did he buy heroin?" Matt wished he could arrest Nico.

Or shoot him.

How many people does he supply with that poison every day? He should be in prison.

"He declined," Nico said. "But I expected him to call saying he changed his mind. That's what usually happens." He raised both his hands. "Look, man. That's all I know."

"Do you have an alibi for Tuesday evening?"

"I was at my grandmother's viewing. There are fifty people who will vouch for me, including the funeral director." Nico glanced at the green dot. "Murphy's Funeral Home in Scarlet Falls."

"I'm sorry for your loss." Even drug dealers had grandmothers, Matt supposed.

"Yaya was ninety-two and died in her sleep. We should all be so lucky." But moisture in Nico's eyes belied his nonchalant attitude.

Matt tossed a hundred bucks onto the snow next to the switchblade, then he stepped backward and gestured toward the ground.

Nico scooped up the cash and his knife. "Don't call me again. I won't be surprised a second time." Then Nico backpedaled to his vehicle and sped away.

Matt watched the taillights fade into the darkness.

A few minutes later, Bree appeared at his side, rifle in hand, and they headed for the SUV. Their breath puffed out in front of them. Her cheeks were bright from the cold.

Inside the vehicle, Matt returned her gun, started the engine, and pulled his phone from his pocket. "I recorded the conversation, just in case I might need it later."

She slid her compact 9mm back into its ankle holster.

He played the recording for Bree as he drove out of the lot. "Three letters and the make and model should be enough to ID Nico through his vehicle registration."

"Then we can verify his alibi."

"Yes," he said.

"I'll email the funeral home in the morning. It's the same one I'm using for my sister. I'll arrange a meeting with the director."

"I can take care of the alibi if you want to focus on your sister's funeral."

"No, actually it seems right to work on finding her killer at the same time."

"Whatever you want."

Bree spread her hands in front of the heat vents. "Justin wanted to buy oxy last Friday morning, but his dealer only offered him heroin. Friday is also the day he showed up at the salon, upset, and demanded to see Erin."

"I know Justin." Matt leaned back in his seat. "I think he was freaked out by the thought of moving to heroin. He could blame popping pills on his injury from the car accident and his chronic pain, but shooting up heroin? Pills say substance abuse. Heroin says junkie."

"Then why did he go to Erin? Why not you?"

Matt grimaced. "I would have insisted he go back to rehab."

"That would have been the right move." Bree removed her coat and vest, then put the coat back on. She tossed the body armor into the back seat. "Why did he give Erin his burner phone?"

"Maybe that was his way of cutting ties with Nico and making sure he didn't buy heroin."

"He could have destroyed the phone," Bree said.

"Maybe he just couldn't."

Bree sat up straighter. "What if that was her idea? Maybe that's how she calmed him down enough for him to go home alone."

"She took away his ability to change his mind so he couldn't call Nico and buy heroin."

"But did she know how low he was sinking before Friday?"

"I don't know. Maybe. He had become very good at concealing his habit." Matt wrapped his fingers around the heated steering wheel. The ache in his hand began to subside.

"In a way, I understand his freak-out. He was out of control and terrified by the temptation to try heroin."

"Justin and I were injured at around the same time. We were both prescribed oxycodone. We both have residual pain. Why did he become addicted and not me? It never even occurred to me to seek more drugs after my bottle ran out."

"I've read studies that show the tendency toward addiction is hereditary. My father was a drunk, his father was a drunk, and so on. It's why I never have more than a single drink, and it's the reason I turned down painkillers when I threw out my back tackling a suspect a few years ago. Drug and alcohol addiction scare me almost as much as dogs. I have too many fears."

"You aren't afraid to chase potentially armed criminals," Matt pointed out.

"It's the loss of self-control that I fear. Alcohol brought out the violence in my father's nature. Sober, he was just mean. Drunk, he was terrifying." Bree rubbed the armrest. "Addiction destroyed my family."

Matt wondered if it had also killed her sister.

CHAPTER TWENTY-FOUR

Bree rose before the sun and went through her morning yoga routine. She would have loved to go for a run but was wimpy about the cold this early in the morning. After she'd showered and dressed, she tiptoed into Luke's bedroom and shut off his alarm. Normally, he got up to feed the horses, but there was no reason they both needed to be up this early. His light had still been on when she'd returned home past midnight. She wasn't sleeping well and suspected neither was he. He was snoring when she left his room and pulled the door almost closed.

Kayla's door squeaked and moved. Brody's nose appeared in the opening as he nudged the door open. Bree moved to the other side of the hall. Her pulse accelerated and sweat broke out on her palms.

She breathed, frustrated. She knew the dog wouldn't hurt her but couldn't control her automatic response.

He probably had to go outside. His leash was downstairs. Could she walk him? Could she get close enough to snap it onto his collar?

The guest room door opened, and Dana came out of the room. She wore jeans and a bright cobalt sweater. Her lipstick matched a pair of raspberry-colored reading glasses that hung in the crew neck of her sweater.

"How do you look like that already?" Bree asked.

"Here's a pro tip from someone who's been dragged out of bed at all hours for the past thirty years. A little lipstick makes you look like you have your shit together even when you're so tired you can barely spell your own name."

"I'll remember that."

Dana gestured toward the dog. "I'll take him out."

Bree hung back, berating herself for being such a coward, until Dana and the dog disappeared down the stairs. Bree went down to the kitchen and started a pot of coffee. After stepping into boots and donning a coat and gloves, she went outside. The sun was shining, and the air didn't feel as cold on her face.

Brody was sniffing his way across the melting snow, with Dana in tow. Bree passed them and went into the barn to feed the horses. She performed the morning barn chores with a rhythm that seemed familiar, almost comforting. When she returned to the kitchen, Dana was pouring coffee. Brody crunched kibble. Vader sat on the island and meowed for his breakfast. Bree filled his bowl and scratched behind his ears. He purred while he ate.

"I know Brody is large and intimidating, but he's a really nice dog." Dana handed her a mug of coffee.

Bree sipped. "I feel like an idiot, but I've been avoiding dogs all my life. When I look at Brody, I see a K-9 chasing and bringing down a suspect. Matt says I need to spend time with a less intimidating dog."

"That's a good idea."

"Maybe something really small and old with no teeth."

Dana laughed. "What's on your agenda for today?"

"Nothing pleasant. Starting with a visit to the funeral home and moving on to a meeting with Craig." Bree updated Dana on the previous night's activities.

"I'm sorry. That's going to suck."

"Yes. There's so much up in the air right now, Erin's death still feels surreal." But Bree wasn't looking forward to the funeral's aftermath and the crash of reality. "Even if I get through her funeral and find her killer, how am I going to keep Craig from taking the kids?"

"If anyone can, it's you." Dana patted her shoulder. "Let me make you some breakfast."

"You don't have to cook for me."

"I love to cook, and I'm retired. I can do whatever I want now," she said in a *don't mess with me* tone.

Bree raised both hands in surrender. "All right."

"I found a waffle maker yesterday." Dana bustled around the kitchen. Twenty minutes later, the kitchen smelled like waffles and bacon. The kids drifted down the steps.

"Do I smell bacon?" Luke rubbed a bleary eye.

Kayla bounced into the kitchen, her face bright with the first real smile she'd worn in days. "Yay! Waffles."

Luke poured himself a glass of milk and settled at the table. Before Bree finished her first waffle, he'd plowed through two helpings, including a half pound of bacon.

Dana poured more milk into his glass and shook the carton, which sounded nearly empty. "I'll buy more milk today. Any other requests from the store?"

"What are you making for dinner?" Luke reached for another waffle.

"How do you feel about chicken parm and homemade focaccia?" Dana started a grocery list.

Kayla dredged a piece of waffle in syrup. "What's focaccia?" She carefully enunciated each syllable.

"A flatbread made with herbs," Dana said. "I'll make double and we can have homemade pizza tomorrow."

"Can I help make it?" Kayla popped the food into her mouth.

"Of course!" Dana wrote on her list. "I was counting on it."

Watching the exchange between Dana and the kids, Bree swallowed a rush of panic. Dana was just here temporarily. She had her own life back in Philly. If Bree succeeded in keeping the kids, how would she manage all this on her own *and* find work? Just dealing with two grief-stricken children seemed like a full-time job. Were the kids better off with Craig? Had he really changed?

Her instincts said no. But maybe she simply didn't want to let the kids go. They were her only link to her sister. Was her desire to keep them selfish?

Brody went to the kitchen door and barked once. A minute later, Matt appeared on the porch. Dana opened the door for him.

"I thought you'd be back here," Matt said.

"Waffles, coffee, bacon?" Dana asked.

"No, thanks. I already ate."

Bree carried her dirty dishes to the sink. "I'll get my coat."

"You're leaving? But it's Saturday," Kayla protested.

"I'm sorry." Bree touched her head. "I have to go to the funeral home to tell them what we want to do. I'll try to be quick so we can spend the afternoon together."

The little girl nodded, but her smile had faded. Guilt pinged in Bree's chest as she and Matt left the house.

She paused next to her car. "How do single and working moms cope?"

"I guess they just do their best." Matt jingled his keys. "I called Todd this morning. He was able to trace Nico through his partial license plate. His full name is Nicolas Kosta. He has one prior conviction for felony possession of narcotics with intent to sell, for which he served eighteen months. He was released three years ago with no subsequent arrests."

"Is Todd going to pick him up?"

"No." Matt frowned. "We have no proof he's dealing. He was careful with his word choices. I suspect his alibi will pan out. I checked the obits. A viewing and memorial service for Helena Kosta, age ninety-two, was held at Murphy's on Tuesday evening from seven to nine."

"Nico's alibi is probably legitimate." Bree opened her car door. "I'd hoped he lied last night."

"Me too."

Not wanting to arrive at the meeting with Craig together, they drove their individual vehicles. Matt followed her to the funeral home. Outside, Bree paused on the sidewalk. The sun's rays were warm on her face.

"Are you ready?" Matt asked.

Bree tried to take a deep breath, but grief tightened her chest. "No. But no amount of time will change that."

They went inside. The air smelled thickly of flowers. Two fresh purple-and-white sprays stood on a sideboard in the lobby.

"Ms. Taggert?" A man in a dark suit walked in.

Bree nodded and introduced Matt as a friend.

The director ushered them into a conference room. "I'm sorry for your loss."

"Thank you." Bree managed to keep her act together as they scheduled the service for Tuesday. She didn't break until they discussed the children's requests.

The director handed her a box of tissues. "It's particularly sad when a loved one passes at such a young age."

Bree plucked a tissue from the box and dried her eyes. Her throat was tight and raw.

Matt reached for her hand, gave it a squeeze, and took over the conversation. "You come highly recommended from a family who held a viewing here last Tuesday night."

"Ah, yes. Mrs. Kosta." The director folded his hands on the table. "It was a beautiful service."

"Her grandson recommended you," Matt said.

The director nodded solemnly. "Nicolas made sure his grandmother's service honored her life."

"He was here for the whole service?" Matt asked.

"Why, yes. He never left his mother's side." A wary look crossed the director's face. "Why do you ask?"

Bree cleared her throat. "Shall I write you a check?"

The funeral director immediately forgot his suspicions and gave her the amount of the required deposit.

Matt and Bree went out to the parking lot. Ten minutes later, they were headed south on I-87. Matt sped ahead. Bree maintained the speed limit. She didn't want to arrive too close together. She took the Saratoga Springs exit and drove a mile to the restaurant. She spotted Matt's SUV and parked two rows away. He was drinking coffee at the bar when she entered the tavern. The decor was stereotypical Irish bar, with dark wood and green-and-white linens.

Bree scanned the restaurant but did not see Craig. Tall-sided booths filled the area near the bar. Standard tables and chairs were evenly spaced throughout the main dining room. About a third of the tables were occupied. Bree let the hostess lead her to a table, then she chose a seat facing the door and ordered coffee.

Craig strolled into the restaurant ten minutes late. He shot a charming smile to the hostess. She flushed and stammered as she led him to the table.

Bree did not roll her eyes, but she wanted to.

"Coffee?" the hostess offered.

"Yes, please." He sat down, shook out his napkin, and draped it across his lap. He met Bree's gaze over the table. "I'm glad you asked to meet. This will be much easier on the kids if we behave civilly."

"I'm all about doing what's best for the kids." Out of the corner of her eye, Bree watched Matt leave the bar and walk out of the restaurant.

Craig opened his menu. The waiter brought his coffee. "Are you ready to order?"

"I'll stick with coffee," she said. His smug face had ruined her appetite.

The waiter took his order for a ham-and-cheese omelet and left. After they were alone, Bree asked, "How did you become a minister?"

"It wasn't something I ever intended to do." Craig rested his elbows on the table and steepled his fingers. "I was called to it."

"How did that happen?"

"I was sailing on a lake a few years ago. I'm not the best sailor. A gust of wind hit the sails and capsized the boat. I hit my head, and the water was cold. I was disoriented and could barely keep my head above the water. I was out of it, holding on to the hull, shivering, when I heard a voice telling me to turn around. I did, and I saw a life preserver floating a few feet away. Another boat came along a few minutes later. The man driving it told me he hadn't planned to take his boat out that day, but he woke up *needing* to do it. The next day, I heard the same voice telling me I had to go to church. I sat in the pew and this feeling of calm came over me." He paused to sip his coffee. "My life has never been the same."

"That's amazing." Bree poured herself more coffee. "I didn't know you sailed."

His eyes narrowed. "It's not hard." He smoothed his face into its previous amicable expression. "I was working at a lake resort."

"Where are you living?"

"The church provides me with a small house. There are three bedrooms, so there's room for Kayla and Luke."

"What if they don't want to move?"

His mouth pursed. "They're children. Major decisions are best left to the adults in their lives. Children need plenty of guidance. They'll benefit greatly from joining the church. They don't attend now, correct?"

"You should probably ask them," Bree said, careful to keep her voice neutral. Craig was playing a game of who could hold their fake sincerity the longest. Once, while interviewing a suspect, Bree had pretended to have a husband and three kids to get a man to confess to killing his wife and children. The interrogation had lasted twelve hours. She was as good at lying as Craig. "Have you checked into the school system?"

His eye twitched. "The schools are excellent."

Liar. The thought of checking out the schools never occurred to him.

"How are you going to ask the kids to live with you?" Bree asked.

The waiter brought his breakfast, and Craig broke his omelet with his fork. "I won't be asking. I'll be telling them where they're going. I'm sure they'll be upset at first. I recognize that we don't know each other very well."

"You're a complete stranger to Kayla."

"Yes." He set down his fork. "I take full responsibility for that, but I'm a changed man."

"You'll be taking them away from everything they know and the only home they remember."

"It will be hard at first, but they'll adjust."

"Where will you keep their horses?"

Craig coughed. He drank some coffee and thumped the center of his chest with one fist. "Excuse me. That went down the wrong pipe."

He hadn't considered the kids' animals any more than he'd thought about schools.

Bree waited while he signaled for the waiter and asked for water. He was stalling for time, trying to think of an answer to her question.

He wiped his mouth with his napkin. "I'm afraid being a minister doesn't pay enough to keep horses. We'll have to sell them."

"That would devastate the kids. They've already lost their mother."

"It is unfortunate, but I simply can't afford it." Craig's tone sharpened. "If you want to cover the board, they could keep them."

"Cops don't make that much money either." Over his shoulder, Bree saw Matt walk through the doors and return to his seat at the bar.

"Then how were you planning to handle the horses?" he asked in a smug voice.

"I'm prepared to give up my entire life and move to Grey's Hollow for those kids."

"I can't do that." Irritation flashed in his eyes. "They'll get over it. People are more important than animals."

Bree wanted to smack him but settled for a sad smile. "I'd hate to see their hearts broken again."

Craig looked up. Anger flushed his face. "It can't be helped."

Bree finished her coffee and pushed the cup away. She was so done with this conversation. "Have you hired a lawyer?"

"No. I assumed I wouldn't need one since you called for this meeting."

"The only thing this meeting has done is convince me you are not fit to be a parent. You are too selfish. You'll never put those kids before your own needs."

His face reddened, and his voice rose. "I don't know what you're up to—"

"Now. Now." Bree held up a hand to silence him. "What would your congregation think of their pastor losing his temper?"

Other diners were staring as she tossed some cash and her napkin on the table and walked away. But she took no satisfaction from leaving him fuming. He would be a terrible parent. But he wanted those kids. *How far would he go to get them?*

CHAPTER TWENTY-FIVE

Matt parked in the lot of Grace Community Church. He checked the GPS on the app on his phone, which was tracking Craig's car. "Craig stopped at the YMCA."

"He said he had a youth group commitment this afternoon," Bree said. "Hopefully, he'll be gone for a while. We shouldn't need more than an hour."

Matt lifted his phone. "I'll know if he leaves the YMCA."

They'd given Craig a fifteen-minute start. Then they'd left Bree's car at the restaurant and headed south on I-87. Matt had called ahead and made an appointment with the church secretary.

"We're Mr. and Mrs. Flynn. I'm Matt, and you're Barbara, and we're looking for a new church." Matt handed her a wedding ring.

Bree slipped it onto her finger. "You thought of everything."

"I try."

"Should I ask where it came from?"

"My sister loaned it to me. She's divorced. She said I could melt it down for scrap metal." Matt stepped out of the SUV.

Bree met him on the sidewalk. "Ouch."

"Yeah."

Bree stared up at the cross mounted on the front of the building. "Lying in a church feels so very wrong, but I have no doubt that Craig is scamming them in some way. Maybe we can figure out his game and prevent him from sucking the coffers dry."

The church looked like a New England meetinghouse, a white clapboard square with a centered steeple. They went inside. The lobby smelled of lemon furniture polish and musty books. They followed a sign down a hallway to the church office in the back of the building.

A mature woman typed on an ancient computer. Matt could hear it chugging and groaning from across the room. A nameplate on her desk read MRS. PETERSON.

Matt knocked on the doorframe. "Mrs. Peterson?"

She blinked at them over her glasses. "Yes, may I help you?"

"We're the Flynns." Matt stepped aside so Bree could enter the office first.

Mrs. Peterson stood and rounded the desk to meet them. "It's a pleasure to meet you."

They shook hands.

"Would you like to ask questions first or see the church?" Mrs. Peterson asked.

"Can we do both?" Bree smiled. "Then we won't take up too much of your time."

"Certainly!" Mrs. Peterson beamed. She led the way out of the office into a large open space. "This is our community room. This is where we host coffee hour between services on Sunday. During the week, the space is used for everything from Bible study to youth group meetings." She opened a swinging door. "We have a full kitchen."

They continued to the main hallway. Mrs. Peterson opened a set of double doors. "This is our sanctuary." Her voice rang with pride.

Matt counted the white-and-dark-wood pews and did a quick calculation. The church could seat three hundred people. The congregation might not be the largest in town, but they had money.

Bree pointed to the pulpit. "Tell me about your minister."

"Reverend Vance is wonderful." Mrs. Peterson clapped her hands together prayer-style. "You will love him. Everyone does."

"Has he been with the church for a long time?" Matt asked.

"No. Reverend Vance just joined us last October. We lost our previous minister over the summer. Poor Reverend Hollis had a stroke. It was very sudden. He'd led our congregation for twenty-two years. We have an assistant pastor fresh out of the seminary, but he doesn't have enough life experience to lead the church." Mrs. Peterson led them out of the sanctuary and back to the main office. "We were without a minister for some time. We turned down several applicants who didn't meet our criteria."

"Does Reverend Vance have a family?"

"Yes." Her lips pursed. "He has two children. He was not married to their mother, and she refused to let him see the children. The reverend acknowledges she had reason." She stopped outside her office door. "Please don't think I'm gossiping about our reverend's personal life. He stood on our pulpit and told the entire congregation about his previous life as a sinner and how the Lord's calling transformed him."

"How inspiring." Bree's voice lacked conviction.

"It was an amazing testimonial." Mrs. Peterson rubbed her arms. "I got goose bumps listening to him."

"Where did he go to seminary school?" Matt asked.

Mrs. Peterson's face puckered as if Matt's question were a bad smell. "He went to an online college."

Matt raised his brows.

"Not everyone can afford to attend college. We shouldn't discriminate," Mrs. Peterson said in a lecture tone. "You really have to listen to him preach to understand why we hired him. His testimonial is the sincerest I've ever heard. His honesty and transparency help him relate to our members. I think it's one of the reasons people feel comfortable talking to him about their transgressions. He's been so open about his own imperfections and journey."

They returned to the church office and stopped just inside the door.

"Do you have more questions?" Mrs. Peterson crossed the room and lifted a pamphlet from a sideboard. She offered it to Matt. "Our services and Bible study programs are listed here. The ladies get together on Tuesday afternoons for a potluck lunch. The men meet on Wednesday evenings."

"Thank you." Matt accepted the brochure. "We would love to meet Reverend Vance."

"You could come to a service tomorrow," Mrs. Peterson said.

"That would be perfect, but unfortunately, we have a family commitment." Matt tried to sound disappointed.

"Let me check his schedule." Mrs. Petersen returned to her desk and opened a planner. "The reverend is busy with a fund-raiser for our youth group today. He's helping the kids raise money for their mission trip to rebuild a flooded community in South Carolina. Tomorrow is Sunday. He'll be here all day, of course."

"It doesn't sound like the reverend has much time off," Bree said. "Doesn't he ever get to go home?"

"Well, he lives in the apartment over the church garage, so technically, he's always here." Mrs. Peterson laughed. "Monday is blocked out, and he has Tuesdays off. How about Wednesday? He does hospital visits in the morning, but he keeps office hours from noon to five. You are welcome to stop by then. No appointment needed."

"That's perfect." Matt reached across the desk and shook her hand. "Thank you so much for all your help today. The church is lovely."

"I hope we see you again soon." Mrs. Peterson turned to her computer.

Bree was out the door first. Matt followed her hurried steps out into the parking lot. She strode into the wind, her strides purposeful, her shoulders back. They stopped next to his SUV.

"We didn't get struck by lightning," he said. "I call that a win."

"If Craig hasn't been struck, we're clear." Bree propped her hands on her hips, showing the butt of her weapon. "I can't figure out what he's up to."

"You wore a gun in church?"

"Yep. Both of them," she said. "They're the perfect accessory. Go with everything."

Matt shook his head. "Mrs. Peterson seems happy with Craig."

"Yes. He can be very charming." Bree frowned, her brows knitting. "If that was any other person, I'd be tempted to believe he'd changed."

"But not Craig?"

"No."

"Are you sure you're not biased? People *can* change." Though in Matt's experience, it didn't happen often.

"I'm positive. He says all the right words, but he slips when he loses his temper, and I see the real Craig." Bree glanced over her shoulder at the church. "This is an act, and it's easy for Craig to play his part here. No one here challenges him or makes him angry." She went to the passenger door. "Something that Mrs. Peterson said is bugging me, but I don't know what." She stepped into the vehicle.

"Didn't he tell you he lived in a three-bedroom house?"

"Yes, and clearly he lied about that. But that's not it." Bree's forehead creased.

Matt checked his phone. "Todd left a message." He listed to the recording. "They searched Trey White's apartment. He wants us to come down to the station to talk about what they found."

Bree snorted. "Now to pretend we don't already know."

"Yep." Matt swung the SUV around and headed back to I-87. He drove to the restaurant. They picked up Bree's car, and he followed her to the sheriff's station.

They walked inside, and Marge led them back to the conference room. "Todd will be with you in a minute."

Todd came in and closed the door behind him. He set a laptop and a folder on the table. "So, we searched Trey's apartment this morning and found something very disturbing." He opened the folder and removed two photos. "These are just two examples. There were more."

Bree pulled the photos in front of her and studied them. "He took these without Erin knowing."

"Yes." Todd tapped the second photo. "This one is Erin in front of Justin's house. Trey knew about her relationship with Justin and where Justin lived. Since there's snow on the ground, we think this picture was taken during the week before she died."

Bree slid the photos to Matt.

"Trey was stalking Erin?" Matt asked.

"Yes." Todd opened the laptop. "I went to the jail this morning and questioned him about it. I have a copy of the interview. I thought you might want to see it." He turned the computer to face Bree and Matt and then pressed "Play."

A video on the screen began to roll. Trey and his lawyer sat on one side of the table. Trey was handcuffed to a ring set into the metal table. Across from them, Todd recited the names of the three people in the room for the record. Then he read Trey his Miranda rights, and Trey signed a form acknowledging he understood those rights.

With the opening legalities out of the way, Todd pulled a photo album from an accordion file on the table. Matt recognized the album he and Bree had seen the previous night at Trey's apartment.

Todd spun it around and opened it, so that Trey could see the pictures. "We found these in your apartment, Trey."

Tears brimmed from Trey's eyes and ran down his face. "She was so fucking beautiful."

"Did you take these photos?" Todd asked.

Trey leaned forward and wiped his face on the sleeve of his orange shirt. He was quiet for a minute, staring at the first picture. "Yeah."

"Why?" Todd turned the page.

Trey's eyes were riveted on the next picture. "I loved her."

"So, you followed her around town?"

"Yeah." Trey sighed, a long sound full of desolation. "A woman like her would never go out with a dude like me, but I wanted to be close to her."

Todd turned to the next page. Trey leaned forward.

Matt was impressed. So far, Todd was engaging the suspect.

Todd rested his forearms on the table. "What else did you do besides follow her and take her picture without her knowledge or consent?"

Trey flinched and shifted back. "What do you mean?"

"Well, you violated her privacy, and you have a record of being a Peeping Tom. What else did you do to Erin?"

"Nothing!" Trey's face paled.

Easy. You're losing him, Matt thought. An interviewer had to know when to pressure a suspect and when to ease off.

Todd turned to the photo of Erin in front of Justin's house. "Do you know who lives here?"

Trey's shoulders slumped. "Her boyfriend."

"Did you know him?" Todd asked.

Trey shook his head.

Todd leaned over his hands, getting into Trey's space. "Did you ever see them together?"

Trey looked away from the picture. "Maybe."

"When and where?" Todd asked.

Trey's shoulders hitched. "They had a fight in front of the salon where she worked."

"Did you hear their fight?"

"No. I was across the parking lot, in the store." Trey's fingers closed into fists. "But he was yelling at her, and she was upset." He looked up, his eyes bright. "He had no right to treat her like that."

"You didn't know that he was her husband?"

Trey's eyes darted to Todd's. That had surprised him. "No."

"Yes. They were separated but trying to work it out."

"He didn't deserve her." Trey frowned at the photo, the muscles in his face tight.

"When did you take this picture?" Todd pointed to it.

"Last Friday night. I was worried about her. I thought he might come back when she got off work, so I followed her." Trey's eyes snapped up. "Just to make sure she got home safe."

"But she didn't go home."

Trey's gaze stayed on the image of Erin in front of Justin's house. "No. She went to his place." His voice deepened, and Matt heard a hint of a new emotion, something deeper than anger. Jealousy? Betrayal? Maybe both.

"Why do you think she did that?" Todd prompted.

"She had sex with him." Trey's voice went cold.

"How do you know?"

"I saw them through the window." Trey sounded robotic now. His attention wasn't on Todd, but within himself. Was he seeing Erin and Justin all over again in his mind?

Matt's gaze shifted to the lawyer, who did *nothing* to stop his client from confessing to a crime.

"Which window?" Todd asked.

"It's around the side of the house," Trey said in that same detached tone.

"What exactly did you see?"

Trey flushed, embarrassment bringing him back to the present. "Them. Having sex. In his bed." He turned away from the photo album as if he couldn't bear to look at it any longer.

"What did you do then?"

"I went home." Trey shifted back.

"What did you do at home?"

Trey's gaze dropped to his hands, still clenched in fists on the table. Beads of sweat broke out on his upper lip. "Nothing."

He was lying. Matt would bet a hundred bucks Trey went home to masturbate, if he didn't do it while he was sitting in front of the house. Voyeurs got off on peeping. It was their thing. Matt would have pounced on that.

But Todd didn't press. "When did you see Erin again?"

"Tuesday." Trey's eyes lifted again.

Back to the truth, Matt thought.

"I saw her leaving the salon. I waved. She waved back." Anguish twisted his features. "I'll never see her again."

Todd flattened his hands on the table. "Did you kill her?"

"No!" Trey jerked straight.

"You didn't follow her? You weren't angry that she was having sex with someone not worthy of her?"

"No! Yes! Wait." Trey's breathing sped up.

The lawyer finally intervened. "One question at a time, please."

Trey took a deep breath, trying to compose himself. "I didn't follow her. I worked until closing. She left the salon around four, I think. That's when her shift usually ended." He exhaled hard through his nose, his nostrils flaring. "But yeah, I was angry that she would waste her time with a man like him. She deserved so much more."

"She deserved you, right?" Todd asked.

Trey shook his head, the motion slow and purposeful and full of denial. "No."

Todd pressed his point. "Are you sure you didn't leave work for a while Tuesday evening? It wouldn't have taken long. The store was empty. The surveillance cameras didn't work. No one would know. You could have driven to her husband's house and shot her."

"No," Trey insisted. "I would never have hurt Erin."

"But you would have shot her husband."

"I didn't say that!" Trey's face was bright red.

The lawyer put a hand on Trey's arm. "Do you have a question, Chief Deputy? Or are you just going to keep theorizing?"

Todd shifted his weight back. "Was it an accident, Trey? Did you go there to shoot Erin's husband? Did she surprise you or get in the way?"

"No!" Trey yelled. "Stop! I didn't shoot anybody. I don't even have a gun." He bent forward and rested his forehead on the table.

Todd tapped a finger on his file. He clearly didn't know what to do with the interview now. But then, Trey was done. He'd shut down. The interview ended.

Todd closed the computer. "He wouldn't answer any more questions, but as you can see, he's a definite suspect. He was stalking Erin. He was angry that she was sleeping with Justin. Maybe he went into the house to shoot Justin and Erin got in the way."

"It's possible," Bree said, but her voice was hesitant.

Todd frowned. "Matt, what do you think?"

"I don't know," Matt said. "There were a few times he was definitely lying, but he never wavered on where he was and what he was doing Tuesday night."

"Where do you stand on forensics reports and DNA tests from Justin's house?" Bree asked.

"DNA won't be in for weeks," Todd said. "But I should have more from forensics soon."

She frowned. "Some physical evidence proving Trey was inside Justin's house might help you break him if he's guilty."

Todd nodded. "But he did confess to peeping through their window."

"That's not enough," Bree said.

"No," Todd agreed. "I have other news. The blood on the dashboard of Erin's truck was her type, O positive. The blood in the back seat matches Justin's type, A positive. These tests aren't conclusive like

DNA. We can't say for certain that the blood is theirs, but we know it came from two different people."

"And this information suggests that Justin is hurt." Matt's gut soured at the thought of his friend injured and bleeding.

"Yes," Todd continued. "Also, I talked to Jack Halo. He denied harassing any of his staff and was offended at the suggestions. But he provided an alibi for Tuesday evening. He was in his office. The receptionist confirmed that he didn't leave until the salon closed at nine."

Bree frowned. "Did anyone see him between seven thirty and eight thirty?"

Todd shook his head. "He said he was alone working on renovation designs."

Matt thought about the layout of the salon. "Does the salon have cameras covering the back of the building?"

"Yes, the cameras face the exits on the outside," Todd said. "But they're only activated when the alarm system is set for the night. They're not turned on during salon operating hours."

"The salon has a staircase on either side of the building, at the back. Jack could have left through one of those doors and returned without the receptionist seeing him."

"Wouldn't that be risky?" Todd asked. "The salon was full of people every time I've been there."

"Maybe risky, but possible," Matt said. "When we talked to Jack, I took the side stairs without running into a single person, and the salon was busy."

"Have either of you found anything?" Todd asked, his eyes shifting back and forth between Bree and Matt.

"We've been digging into Craig Vance's background, but we haven't found anything incriminating," Matt said vaguely. "We'll let you know if something pans out."

He had nothing else to add. He and Bree had met with a drug dealer, illegally searched Trey's apartment, and planted an illegal GPS device on Craig's car. All things Todd didn't need to know about unless those activities yielded a significant break in the case.

"I've been reviewing my sister's papers and planning her funeral," Bree said.

Todd said, "I'll let you know if anything interesting comes in from forensics."

"Thank you." Bree stood. "I appreciate you keeping us updated on the investigation."

Matt and Bree left the station.

Outside, Bree turned her face to the sun. "Trey *could* be a very good liar, delusional, innocent, or any combination. He definitely has some sort of mental illness."

"Yep." Matt stopped next to his vehicle. "I'm glad we searched his place. Todd didn't mention all the pornography or the camera."

"Or the summertime photos of my sister," Bree added. "Does he realize the importance of those items?"

"He must, but it's not like we can ask."

"No."

"Where do you want to go now?" he asked.

"Back to the house. I want to review my notes. I'm missing something." She rested a hand on the top of her car door.

"Would you copy me on your notes?" The one thing Matt had not missed about leaving the force was no longer needing to write up reports. He was sure Bree's would be thorough.

"Yes. They're all on my laptop. I'll send you a copy today," Bree said. "I need to spend the rest of the day with the kids. We need to pick out pictures of Erin for the memorial service."

"Yeah. You should do that as a family," Matt said. "I have brunch with my parents tomorrow morning. It's a regular Sunday thing. You, Dana, and the kids are welcome to join us. My mom and dad love to entertain. There's always tons of food."

Bree shook her head. "I need to write Erin's eulogy too, and plan the rest of the service. Unless something comes up, I'll probably need tomorrow for the family as well."

Matt understood, but he would be looking for Justin. Justin had driven Erin's truck after she'd died. He'd literally had her blood on his hands. But he'd also bled all over the rear seat. He was injured and had lost a significant amount of blood.

Matt had to find him—and fast.

Chapter
Twenty-Six

Late that afternoon, Bree leaned back on the sofa and stared at the photo collage. "Is that enough pictures?"

Nodding, Kayla looked away from the poster board and wiped a hand under her nose.

"It's good," Luke said in a heavy voice. "I'm going to my room."

Luke's eyes were red-rimmed, and both kids looked as exhausted as Bree felt. Luke disappeared up the stairs.

"Can I go help Dana with the bread now?" Kayla sat cross-legged on the floor at Bree's feet.

"I'm sure she'd love that." Bree's brain hurt, and her eyes were sore. They'd spent the last three hours going through pictures of Erin and the kids.

And crying.

There'd been plenty of tears all around. Sadness weighted Bree's chest like a lead pullover. She needed to write a eulogy but couldn't get past three words without choking up. She tried to get Adam to come over and help, but he refused. He said he trusted them, and he was working on a project—something special he wanted to finish before the funeral. Bree had given up. If she managed to drag him out of his studio, he'd be too distracted to participate anyway.

Kayla stood and looked back at the collage, her eyes full of tears and sorrow. "Can we keep it after?"

"If that's what you want." Bree got up to stand next to her. She wrapped an arm around the little girl. "We'll bring it back here."

"Good." She sniffed. "I don't want to forget what Mommy looks like."

Bree sucked in a hard breath. Her heart aching, she crouched down to the child's level and took her gently by the shoulders. "We will never forget your mommy. I promise."

With a quick nod, Kayla ducked out from under Bree's arm and ran to the kitchen. The afternoon had been hard. They all needed a break. But building the collage had been cathartic. Bree turned to scan the photos. So many good moments captured. Should she be focused on those instead of searching for Erin's killer?

She couldn't.

She'd promised to take care of her little sister, and she'd failed. The least she could do was give her justice. After her killer was caught, Bree could move on.

She walked to the office and sat in her sister's chair. During the tour of the church with Mrs. Peterson, Bree had felt like she'd missed something, but she couldn't pin it down. Given time, her brain would sort it out. Sometimes her best solutions came to her while she wasn't thinking about the problem. She opened her laptop and typed up her notes from the interview. Then she unlocked the bottom drawer of the desk and pulled out Erin's call logs and financial statements and began to review them. An hour later, her head ached, and she was still clueless.

She pulled the phone log back to the front of the pile. Did Erin receive a call from the prepaid cell the day she died? Bree skimmed the numbers with her finger. But it wasn't the prepaid number that stopped her. She didn't see any calls to or from that cell on that day.

Erin had received a call at six o'clock that evening. The number looked familiar. Bree checked the list of Erin's known contacts. The call had been from Steph. Bree flipped back to her notes on their interview with Erin's best friend. Steph had said she last talked to Erin when she left work around four, but that couldn't be true.

Bree called Steph's number, but the call went to voice mail, and she left a message.

Maybe there was a simple explanation, something so trivial she'd forgotten. But that didn't feel right. Nothing was trivial on the day someone was murdered.

Did Steph lie?

She was Erin's best friend. They'd worked together for years. Steph had been crying and nauseated when Bree and Matt had questioned her, and her husband had been with her. Maybe all those factors had thrown her off.

Bree drummed her fingers on the blotter.

Steph had no reason to lie to Bree.

Enough. Your brain is mush.

The afternoon funeral planning had drained her. She returned the papers to the drawer, locked it, and followed the smells of food to the kitchen, where dinner was ready.

Dana's chicken parm and focaccia bread was a huge hit. Luke ate two helpings in fifteen minutes. After dinner, they watched a family movie. Then Bree put Kayla to bed. She locked her guns in her biometric handgun safe, with a fingerprint reader for quick access. She slid it under the bed next to Erin's rifle safe. But if she was going to stay here, she'd have to find a more convenient location. She opened the drawer of the nightstand. Her safe would fit, but she'd have to clear out her sister's books.

She glanced around the rest of the room. Regardless of whether she moved in here with the kids or they went to live with Craig, Erin's belongings would need to be sorted. Kayla and Luke would want some of their mom's things, and so would Bree. Maybe she could donate the rest.

The thought depressed her. Exhausted, Bree took a long, hot shower and dressed in flannel pajamas and a sweatshirt. Vader appeared out of nowhere, kneaded himself into a comfortable spot in the exact center of the bed, and stretched out. Bree lay down next to him and stroked his side. He purred. She petted him again, then a third time. He curled around her arm and bit her.

"I know," she said to the cat. "I'm only allowed to pet your belly twice. I don't know what I was thinking."

She pulled her arm away and examined the skin. He'd left a welt but hadn't broken the skin. He flipped over and pretended to ignore her, but his tail flipped on the bed and one ear twitched every time she moved.

She glanced at her phone. Nine o'clock. Time for barn check. She trudged downstairs.

Dana was in the kitchen, reading a book and sipping a glass of red wine. "Do you want some?"

"No, thanks. I just came down to do barn check before I fall asleep." Bree stepped her bare feet into a pair of boots, grabbed a coat, and went outside. The day had been warmer, and the snow had begun to melt, leaving the grass spongy. If the thaw continued, the horses could be turned out into the pasture. Bree made a mental note to fix the fence she'd landed on when chasing the intruder a few nights back.

She checked blankets and water buckets. Riot pawed at his straw. She stopped and rubbed his forehead, but instead of relaxing, the horse bobbed his head. "What's wrong, boy? I know you've been cooped up, but it's been too icy to let you out. You don't want to break a leg. Another day or two above freezing and the pasture will be safe."

The horse kicked his door.

A boot scraped, and Bree whirled around.

Craig walked into the barn and stopped just inside the door. He pulled his hands from the pockets of his blue parka. "What were you doing at the church today?"

"Excuse me?" Bree squared up to face him fully. "This is private property. You have no right to waltz in whenever you want."

He'd already ambushed her once here. She should have been warier.

"I'll do what I like." He stepped into the light. His handsome face was hard, his eyes as cold as the snow outside. "I asked you a question."

"You did." Bree studied him. His temper was heating up. Her and Matt's visit to the church had threatened him.

"I know you were there."

She tilted her head.

"Mrs. Peterson gave me a detailed description. It was you."

Bree didn't deny it. "The church is a public building. Anyone can go inside."

He stepped closer. "You listen to me. Stay away from Grace Community."

"Why?" Bree leaned toward him. "What are you afraid of?"

"Nothing!" he snapped. "But I know you. You never liked me. You'll do anything to keep me from having a good life."

"Craig, I couldn't care less about you." Bree sized him up. He still had no control over his temper. Could he be goaded into saying more than he wanted? "You said the church provided you with a three-bedroom house, but you live in an apartment over the church's garage. You realize each of the kids needs their own room, right?"

"That's because I'm a bachelor. They provide housing according to need. As soon as I get custody, I'll get an increased housing allowance and a larger residence." Craig's straight white teeth flashed as he nearly snarled. "I swear. If you screw up my job, you'll never see Luke or Kayla again."

Bree threw him a curveball. "Did you kill Erin?"

"W-what?" he stammered.

"You heard me." Bree closed the gap between them. "Did you kill Erin?"

"No." His head drew back. "What would make you think that?"

"Because I know you."

He lifted his chin, taking fake offense. "I'm not the same man I was back then."

"You came here to threaten me, so I'd say you're exactly the same."

Red flushed his cheeks. He raised a hand and stabbed a finger at her face. "Stay away from the church."

"Or what?"

"You'll be sorry."

"Are you threatening me again?" Bree asked. She wished she had her cell phone so she could record this conversation, but she'd left it in the house.

"Yes." Craig scanned her from head to toe. Her coat was open, and she was wearing her pajamas. He stepped closer, until she could smell the stale coffee on his breath. "You're not wearing your weapon."

"Do I need a weapon?" Bree asked.

"Maybe you should learn to be nice. Aren't you afraid of being alone with a man you've antagonized?"

"You?" Bree snorted. "Nope."

He frowned, his gaze—and confidence—wavering. He gritted his teeth, visibly firming his resolve. "Maybe you should be."

Bree would have no trouble introducing Craig to the ground, but maybe it would be even better to let him hit her. Then she could file a complaint and have him charged with assault. "Are you going to hit me like you hit Erin?"

His lip curled. Bree expected him to deny it, but he didn't.

"You know what I like best about my job?" he asked. "I get to tell women they are required to obey their husbands. Good wives know their place."

"How did that work with Erin? Oh, wait. You were never married."

"You need someone to teach you respect."

Fresh anger narrowed his eyes. His hand at his side curled into a fist, and his weight shifted. The movement was subtle, but Bree had been reading suspects' body language for thirteen years. She was 90 percent certain Craig was going to take a swing at her.

Bree transferred her weight to the balls of her feet.

"Hey, pretty boy," Dana called from the doorway. "Were you invited here?"

Craig spun around. "Who are you?"

"Someone who isn't going to take your crap," Dana answered. "Not that Bree would either."

Bree's feelings at Dana's interruption were mixed. On one hand, Dana might have heard some of their conversation and could possibly testify that he'd threatened Bree. On the other, Craig wouldn't hit Bree with a witness present.

Craig took a step toward Dana. "Look, bitch. We're in the middle of a private conversation."

Overconfident much? Dana had been a street cop and a detective for decades. She'd worked her way up in the department before it was normal to see a woman rising in the ranks. Bree and her generation owed their smoother career paths to women like Dana. She could certainly handle the likes of Craig.

"Such language for a minister." Dana pulled her Glock from its holster and pointed it at Craig's face. "Leave. Now. You are trespassing. I'd hate to mess up all that pretty hair with a great big hole."

Looking down the barrel of the gun, Craig's face went white. He backed up, raising his hands. "You can't shoot me."

"You already threatened Bree. You're on private property. If I feel threatened, I am within my rights to defend myself."

"That would never hold up in court." Craig took a step back. "It would be your word against mine, and I'm a minister."

"That's funny. You think you'd be alive to go to court." Dana sighed. "If I shoot you, the only person you'll be giving testimony to is St. Peter at the pearly gates. And I don't think *he's* going to fall for your bullshit."

She moved sideways and inclined her head toward the exit. "Don't let the door hit you in the ass on the way out."

"This is outrageous," Craig huffed. He sidled sideways, not turning his back on them, until he was outside. Then Bree heard his steps quicken until he was running. She moved to the door and watched him. Like on his previous visit, his car was parked halfway down the driveway. She didn't take her eyes off his vehicle until the taillights disappeared down the dark road. "I want to add motion detectors on the driveway and security in the barn to the new alarm system."

"I'll call the alarm company tomorrow. Are you OK?" Dana asked. "I know you could have kicked his ass, but you shouldn't have to. You have enough on your plate."

"Actually, I was going to let him hit me and file assault charges." Bree shrugged. "But I'm glad you stepped in. I don't know how that would have played out in a custody battle. It would have been his word against mine, and he can be very convincing."

Dana holstered her weapon and slung an arm around Bree's shoulders. "In any case, I'm glad I saw him from the kitchen window and saved you a black eye."

"Nah, he would have hit me somewhere it wouldn't leave a mark. Did you really hear him threaten me?"

"I heard him say you'd be sorry and that someone needed to teach you respect," Dana said.

"But not the part where he said if I showed up at the church, I'd never see the kids again?"

"No, sorry."

They closed up the barn. As they walked up the back lawn, Bree summed up her conversation with Craig. "Could Craig's motivation to take the kids be the increased housing allowance he'd get? If you add that to the social security survivor's benefit he'd receive, those kids could increase his income considerably."

"I don't think ministers make big bucks, unless they're the owners of a megachurch," Dana said. "They're not supposed to be in the business for the money. But, yes, I think that could be adequate motivation."

In the kitchen, Bree shed her boots and coat. "A theory isn't proof, and it's all I have."

Dana toed off her shoes.

No longer ready for sleep, Bree paced.

Dana picked up her wineglass and set it in the sink. "I'll make tea."

"I'm getting my notes." Bree went to the office, unlocked the drawer, and grabbed her files. Back at the kitchen table, she began sorting her notes. "I need to review everything. I'm missing something."

"We'll do it together. Pass some to me." Dana brought two cups of tea to the table, slid into a chair, and made a *gimme* gesture. "Maybe you need fresh eyes."

Bree had written up careful notes on each interview and encounter—except the blatantly illegal ones. Dana reviewed each page and asked questions.

"Someone was blackmailing Erin," Bree said.

"I agree." Dana rubbed her eyes. "Let's look at these dates on a calendar. Maybe we'll see a pattern if we reorganize the data in a different way."

"I have an idea." Bree went to the office and grabbed the desk-size calendar blotter. Dana had written the calls and transactions in their own side-by-side lists. Bree transferred the data to the physical calendar, and it clicked into place—the idea Mrs. Peterson had jogged and Bree hadn't been able to single out.

"That's it. Erin was killed last Tuesday." Bree flipped the calendar pages to October. "Erin received a call from the prepaid phone this Tuesday morning." She tapped the day on the calendar. "That same afternoon, she withdrew four thousand dollars from her bank account."

Bree checked the next two, more recent, withdrawals. "The next two large withdrawals also took place on Tuesdays. I haven't written up my notes from the interview with the church secretary yet, but guess whose day off is Tuesday."

Dana sat back. "Craig?"

"Bingo."

They'd been focused on the withdrawals' relationship to the prepaid cell calls, and they'd missed a simpler pattern.

Dana sighed. "Everything you have is circumstantial."

"Cases have been won on circumstantial evidence."

Dana lifted her brows. "Only with overwhelming amounts of it."

"It's better than nothing, which is what I had before." Bree spotted a message on her phone. "Matt left a message while I was out in the barn." She pressed "Play."

His voice came out of the speaker on her phone. "Craig is at your place. I'm on my way."

Bree called him back. "You don't need to come over. He's gone."

"Is everything all right?" Matt sounded almost disappointed.

She could hear a vehicle engine in the background. "Yes. Dana and I handled him."

"What happened?"

"He threw a hissy fit," Bree said. "He knew you and I were at the church, and he wasn't happy about it." She told him about the Tuesday cash withdrawal connection. "Todd should bring Craig in for questioning."

"Definitely." Matt whistled. "That's going to set off his temper."

"That's the plan."

CHAPTER TWENTY-SEVEN

The next morning, Bree walked out of Cowboy's stall and tossed the currycomb into the bucket of grooming tools.

"Pumpkin is bored." Standing on a step stool, Kayla brushed her pony's back. Pumpkin stood in cross ties in the aisle. The pony's head hung low, and one rear hoof was cocked on its toe. Pumpkin was dozing.

"Are you sure it's Pumpkin who's bored?" Bree sat on a bale of straw and picked up the stainless steel mug she'd left on the ledge.

Kayla swept the brush along the pony's fat side. A cloud of dust billowed. "I haven't been able to ride him all week." She hopped off the stool and moved it out of the way to work on the pony's legs. But Pumpkin was wearing his thick and shaggy winter coat. He looked like a bear. Nothing short of a thorough bath was going to get him really clean, and a bath wasn't happening any time soon, not that the pony seemed to care.

"I'm hoping they can go out in the pasture today." Bree walked to the doorway. "I'll go check for ice."

Most of the snow had melted. The area around the gate was muddy, but the grass was merely soggy. Bree ducked back into the barn. Finishing the last of her coffee, she left the mug on the ledge.

"I'm going to fix a section of broken fencing. Then we can turn them out for a few hours."

"Can I ride?"

"Sure."

"Yay." Kayla patted her pony and went into the tack room.

Bree had left a message for Todd about Craig's visit the previous night. But the chief deputy hadn't called back yet. Bree had called the station. The deputy who had answered the phone said Todd wasn't in. Steph hadn't returned Bree's call either. Until someone got back to her, Bree was out of leads.

Today was Sunday. She would spend the day at home, hanging out with the kids and writing her sister's eulogy. Tomorrow, she'd start fresh.

Tomorrow, her sister would be dead for six days.

She let the wave of grief roll over her. Then she left the barn and headed to the garage. She found a small roll of wire, a toolbox, and leather gloves. The grass squished under her boots as she trudged out to the broken section of fence. She removed the broken wire, examined the adjacent fencing, and fastened a new piece of wire as best as she could. She was no handyman, but it held when she pulled on it.

She returned the supplies to the garage. Sticking her head in the kitchen door, she called for Luke. He appeared a second later.

"Kayla is going to ride Pumpkin. Does she need the saddle and bridle checked?" Bree hadn't saddled a pony since she was a child, and she didn't know the correct parent protocol. Pumpkin was bombproof, but instinct told Bree it was better to be overprotective.

"Mom usually helps her. I'll show you." Luke grabbed a jacket and boots. They walked across the yard side by side. Kayla led Pumpkin out of the barn. The fat pony wore an English saddle and bridle. Kayla wore a hard hat.

Luke checked the bridle buckles and tightened the girth. Kayla scrambled aboard. She walked the pony around the barnyard once, then steered him toward an empty patch of meadow that ran alongside the pasture. Mud sucked at the pony's hooves as he broke into a slow jog. Kayla posted with his gait. Healthy color flushed her cheeks as she trotted the pony around the meadow.

Bree leaned on a tree. Her heart cracked as she thought of the pony being sold. If Craig took the kids, Bree would have to find a way to keep the horses. She would not let the kids suffer one more loss.

Luke faced her. "I saw Craig leaving the barn last night."

Ugh.

Bree nodded. "I was trying to decide how to tell you he was here." She nodded at Kayla. "Does she even know who he is?"

"No." Luke shoved his bare hands into the pockets of his jacket. "I barely recognized him. Why was he here?"

Bree inhaled. "He wants custody of you and Kayla."

"What!" Luke's eyes opened wide. "Why?"

Bree searched for words and decided honesty would be best. "I don't know why. I'm sorry I didn't tell you right away. I don't know what to make of him."

Anger brightened Luke's eyes. "Are you going to let him take us?"

"What do you want me to do?"

He crossed his arms over his chest. "I'm not going with him."

"You want me to fight him for custody?" Bree clarified. "I am more than willing. I'm prepared to move up here. But I don't want to make life worse for you or Kayla."

"I heard Dana tell you that Mom wanted you to be our guardian."

"She did. But Craig is your biological father. I'm honestly not sure how a judge would rule."

"They can't make me live with him." Luke's eyes went moist.

"I'm going to be totally honest with you. You're almost sixteen. The court would likely consider your wishes."

"What about Kayla?" Luke's eyes darted to his sister, trotting in a big circle on her pony.

"She's young. The decision would be made for her."

Luke gnawed on his lip.

"What do you remember about the time he lived here with you and your mom?" Bree phrased her question carefully. She wanted Luke's impressions. She didn't want to put ideas into his head.

"I remember him yelling a lot. He was mean to Mom, and he scared me." Luke's jaw went tight. "He wouldn't scare me now. If I was older and bigger back then, I wouldn't have let him treat Mom that way."

"You were eight." Bree nodded toward Kayla and Pumpkin. "No bigger than your sister is now. You were not to blame for anything that happened."

Craig was at fault for being an asshole. But Erin was also to blame. She'd put up with Craig's emotional abuse and obvious mooching until he'd physically abused her. Bree couldn't remember how many times Erin had taken him back after he'd left her.

"I wouldn't let Kayla go alone," Luke said.

"You're a good brother."

"Where would he take us?" Luke asked without taking his gaze from his sister.

"He lives in Albany. He's a minister now."

Luke glanced at her. "Seriously?"

"He says he's changed," Bree said in a neutral voice. She would never say anything bad about him to the kids. He could win. They could have to live with him. Bree would not make the situation worse for them.

Luke shook his head hard. "Nope. I don't believe him. He lied to Mom and me all the time."

"If you want me to, I will get the best lawyer and fight him as hard as I can."

"That's what I want."

"All right, then," Bree said. "I have to tell Kayla. I don't want her to find out from anyone else."

He nodded. "You should wait until after Mom's funeral. Kayla's kind of strung out right now."

"Maybe you're right. And when I do tell her, I'd like you to be there. I don't want to scare her about him, though. OK?"

"OK," he agreed. "But I won't lie to her."

"Fair enough," Bree said.

Luke had overheard her conversation with Dana. Had he eavesdropped on other discussions?

"Can I ask you a few questions about your mom's friend Steph?" Bree asked.

"Sure."

"She stayed with you guys recently."

"Uh-huh. It was after Justin moved out. Mom and Steph spent most of the time sitting in the kitchen and talking."

"What did they talk about?"

"Steph's marriage. She cried a lot."

"Did they ever argue?"

"Yep. They had a pretty big fight when Steph moved back in with Zack. Mom didn't want her to get back together with him. She didn't like him much."

"What did Steph say?" Bree asked.

"She said Mom was just hating on men since she'd split up with Justin."

Erin had been angry and resentful when Justin had been arrested for the second time.

"They made up, though," Luke said. "Mom apologized, and they were still friends." He cocked his head. "But they didn't seem as close afterward. They didn't talk or text as much. Before Steph moved back home, she and Mom used to go out every other Friday night. Nothing big. Just a movie or dinner."

"Girls' night."

"Yeah." He nodded. "But they stopped doing that."

"They made up, but their relationship suffered for it."

"Yeah. Things always seemed awkward between them afterward."

Yet, Steph had said Erin was her best friend. *Did she lie about that too? Did something else happen between Erin and Steph?*

"Do you know why Steph and Zack broke up?" Bree asked.

"Zack came here one day, and they talked on the porch. All the windows were open. I heard the whole thing. Zack said Steph cheated on him." He lifted a shoulder. "She denied it, but he seemed pretty sure, at least at first."

"What happened?"

"She convinced him he was wrong. Told him she loved him. All that." Embarrassment flushed Luke's cheeks.

Kayla trotted back and stopped the pony in front of Bree and Luke.

"Are you finished?" Bree asked.

"Yep." Kayla slid down off her pony and led him toward the barn.

For the next half hour, Luke refreshed Bree's knowledge of tack and horse care.

"I'll have to practice," she said.

Luke gestured toward the paint. "You can ride Mom's horse, Cowboy. He's a great trail horse. Never spooks or anything, and he'll need exercise."

"I will." The thought perked Bree up. Some of her only good memories from her childhood involved her old pony. He'd been sold after her parents' deaths. Bree had been heartbroken all over again.

She would definitely find a way to keep these horses no matter what happened, even if she had to beg Adam for money.

They turned the horses out into the pasture. Riot bucked and raced away, mud flying from his hooves. Pumpkin and Cowboy were more interested in grazing.

"Riot looks full of it." Bree shielded her eyes from the sun and watched Luke's quarter horse prance the fence line.

"Oh, yeah," Luke said. "I'll ride him after he burns off some of that energy."

They went inside and stripped off their outerwear. The kids washed their hands, and Kayla told Dana all about her ride while Dana made sandwiches.

"I'm going to shower." Bree had forgotten how dirty barn work was. Her jeans were caked with mud. Even her hair smelled like horses.

She went upstairs and closed the bedroom door. In the bathroom, she began stripping down and piling her clothes on the tile floor. They would stink up the hamper and needed to go directly into the washer.

Bree peeled off her socks and pulled the Band-Aids off her ankle. The barbed wire cuts had scabbed over. She traced the vine tattoo around her ankle and the raised scar beneath it. Looking up, she turned around to see the tattoo on the back of her shoulder in the mirror. The scar on her ankle had been two thin lines where the dog's canines had grabbed and torn her skin. But her shoulder was covered with a web of irregular lines. He'd had a much better grip on her there, and his teeth had sunk deeper into her flesh.

The vines mimicked the design on her ankle, dark green with a few tiny blue flowers. They started at her collarbone and meandered over her shoulder. On her back, intricate vines curled from the base of her neck to the bottom of her shoulder blade. In the center, over the deepest part of the scar, the artist had inked a dragonfly the size of a fist. Shades of brilliant blue and pale green were almost iridescent.

It had taken six months to complete. She remembered the day it had been finished, when the reminder of her childhood tragedy had been completely covered, like a mural painted over graffiti.

She'd taken an ugly reminder of her past and turned it into something beautiful. She'd felt like she finally owned her past.

But now, her sister's death brought every ugly detail back. Her parents' volatile relationship. Her father's final and ultimate betrayal.

He'd had the last word. But Erin's marriage hadn't been like that. Justin had never been violent.

But someone had killed her sister.

Had Bree been completely wrong about Steph? Had she fooled Bree with her bestie act? Bree's father had been a chameleon, able to change his personality to suit his social surroundings. Could Steph also have that ability? Was she manipulative?

Bree rubbed her temples with her forefinger and thumb. The idea forming in her head was creating an ache behind her eyes. She didn't want to think about Steph lying to Erin, to her husband, and to Bree.

The intruder Bree had chased out of Erin's house had been male. Maybe he wasn't the same person who'd killed Erin.

The fact remained that Steph had told Bree she'd last seen Erin as Erin had left work at four o'clock on Tuesday. Yet, she'd called Erin at six. Had she forgotten, or had she lied to Bree?

Bree turned on the shower and dialed the temperature to hot. She stepped under the spray and let the water run over her, washing the dirt away.

Erin and Steph *had* been best friends at one time. They'd confided in each other. Maybe Erin had known something about Steph. A deep, dark secret Steph wanted to keep. If Steph *had* cheated on her husband, Erin could have been the only person who knew the truth. Maybe Steph's marriage depended on Erin's silence.

When Bree was clean, she turned off the water and dried off. She wrapped the towel around her body, tucking the end over her breasts, and stepped out of the shower. She reached for her phone.

Bree needed to interview her, without her husband. There was no way that Steph would admit having an affair with Zack at her side. But how could she get her alone?

Then Bree had an idea. The salon was open from noon to five on Sundays. She called Halo.

"Halo Salon and Spa. May I help you?" the receptionist said.

"I'd like to make an appointment for a haircut with Stephanie Wallace."

"When do you want to come in?"

"As soon as possible," Bree said.

"Steph is off today. Let me look at tomorrow. You're in luck. She had a cancellation at four o'clock. Would that work for you?"

"That's perfect," Bree said.

She'd just guaranteed an hour with Steph. A busy salon wasn't the best option for an interview, but at least Zack wouldn't be there, and Steph would be unable to avoid Bree's questions.

Bree used a hand towel to wipe the steam from the mirror. Her reflection was blurry, but she could see the bags under her eyes very clearly. Her eyes were slightly bloodshot and red around the edges. Grief left marks.

Craig could have killed Erin, or he could simply be taking advantage of the opportunity her death presented. As much as Bree didn't want to admit it, Steph was now on her suspect list.

After all, killing someone was the only way to make sure they took a secret to their grave.

Chapter Twenty-Eight

Monday morning, the sun peered through the blinds in Matt's kitchen. He drank coffee and scrolled through the testimonials on a religious website. The day before, he'd had brunch at his parents' house, worked with his sister's rescue dogs, and then spent the rest of the day reviewing Bree's detailed notes.

He'd been researching Craig and his church online. He clicked on "About Us" in the menu and Craig's bio, which included both his education and a summary of his testimonial. Then Matt wondered how hard it was to become a minister.

He drank more coffee and began researching the online college where Craig had received his ministry certificate. The program looked light, but he didn't see anything that suggested the institution was illegitimate. Still, Craig didn't seem to have the experience Matt would have expected. The church secretary had insisted that Craig's testimonial had been the key.

Matt googled *Christian Testimonials* and received pages and pages of websites devoted to them. There were too many to read each one. He went back to the search engine and added key words from Craig's story.

Boom.

The first search result was a testimonial dated ten years before.

> I took my sailboat out on the lake. It was a beautiful fall day. The sun was out, and the leaves were turning. But a sudden gust of wind hit the sails and capsized the boat. As the boat went over, the boom swung around and hit me on the head. I got dumped into the lake. The water was freezing, I was confused, and my vision was blurry. I couldn't swim. I was barely able to hold on to the hull when I heard a voice telling me to turn around. There was a life preserver floating a few feet away. A few minutes later, a small boat came along. The man told me he woke up needing to take his boat out on the lake. The next day, when I woke up, I heard the same voice that directed me to the life preserver telling me to go to church. As soon as I entered the sanctuary, I was floored by a feeling of peace. My life has never been the same.

He switched computer windows and returned to Craig's story.

It was nearly identical. But the story from ten years before had been written by a man named Brandon Smith. Ten years ago, when he'd posted his testimonial online, Brandon had been a fifty-year-old reformed alcoholic living in Idaho.

Craig had stolen his testimonial, almost word for word.

"What a scumbag," Matt said to Brody.

The dog barely flicked an ear.

Matt picked up his phone and called Bree. When she answered the phone, he said, "Craig plagiarized his testimonial." He read the online story to her.

"That is not a surprise." Bree snorted. "The temper tantrum he threw here Saturday night told me he was very nervous about us talking to anyone at the church. He's getting by on his charisma, but the church isn't going to overlook lying."

"How was your Sunday?" he asked.

"I added Steph to the suspect list." Bree explained her reasoning behind her theory that Erin might have been the only person who knew that Steph had cheated on her husband. "Steph neglected to tell me she called Erin shortly before she died. Nor did she mention they had a major argument. Luke says Erin and Steph didn't talk to each other nearly as much after that. I left a message for Steph, but she hasn't called me back."

"Either she's avoiding you or she's sick."

"She's scheduled to work later today."

"Maybe she exaggerated her morning sickness," Matt said.

"That's what I was thinking. It's also ironic that she got pregnant almost immediately after getting back together with her husband."

"He was very attentive when we met with them."

"Maybe she did it to ensure he wouldn't break up with her," Bree said. "I made an appointment for a haircut with her at the salon. I used Dana's name. Steph won't know it's me until I show up."

"I doubt she'll answer any questions in a very public place."

"But I will surely catch her off guard," Bree said.

"I'll be in the parking lot, just in case anything goes wrong. The gun that killed your sister is still missing."

"I'm the one who's armed," she pointed out. "Speaking of suspects, Dana got a return call from my sister's attorney this morning. It turns out that Erin had a small life insurance policy."

"How small?"

"Fifty thousand. The kids are the beneficiaries, but the money would be managed by their guardian until they turn eighteen. She took it out shortly before she got pregnant with Kayla. Craig was living with her at the time."

"So, he could know about it."

"Yep," Bree agreed. "What's up with Craig's GPS?"

"He spent all day yesterday at the church, which is what we expected. Hold on. Let me see if he's moved this morning." Matt transferred her call to speaker and opened the app on his phone. "He's in Saratoga Springs."

Matt zoomed in on his location. "He's at the Springs Casino." He was only mildly surprised.

Bree began to laugh. "Gambling? It can't be that simple."

"There's only one way to find out."

"We're going to the Springs Casino?"

"Yep. I'll pick you up in fifteen minutes."

An hour later, Matt pulled into the parking lot of the casino. The lot was half-full.

In the passenger seat, Bree pointed through the windshield. "There's Craig's car."

Matt parked two rows behind and facing it.

"What's the plan?" Bree asked.

"You stay out of sight," Matt said. "He'll spot you in a second. I'll go inside and see if I can find him. You let me know if he leaves the building."

"I don't love it, but OK." She hunkered down in the seat.

Matt slid out of the SUV and went inside. He toured the casino but didn't spot Craig on the gaming floor. He went down a wide staircase to the lower clubhouse, where simulcast racing was broadcast on rows of monitors. People read and made notes in their racing forms. Gamblers lined up at windows placing bets, including Craig, who was next up at the window.

Matt checked the time. The simulcast of horse racing began at noon. He grabbed a racing form. Leaning against the wall, he pulled out his phone and pretended to be sending a message. Instead, he videoed Craig placing bets.

Craig left the window and found a place in front of a monitor.

His posture was tense. He tucked the folded racing form under one arm and crossed his arms. On the screen, the horses burst from the gate. The animals raced through the first turn and down the backstretch as a unit, until three animals broke out of the pack at the top of the homestretch. Craig's hand closed into a fist. Halfway to the finish line, one horse dropped off, spent. Craig's hands flew in the air, the heels hitting his forehead, his features locked in a shocked grimace.

He'd lost.

The next race began. Seconds after the bell rang and the horses charged from the gate, Craig's shoulders slumped, and Matt had to conclude that the horse he'd bet on was at the back of the pack. The third race didn't go well for him either.

Matt texted Bree: Betting on the horses and sux at it.

Bree sent him back a thumbs-up emoji.

Craig placed a few more bets and seemed to win one. Overall, though, Craig was going home a loser. He headed for the exit, his posture defeated.

Matt texted: He's coming out.

Bree's response came back immediately: OK.

Craig left the building. He headed across the parking lot, his head bent over his phone. Two rows from his car, he looked up, saw Bree, and stumbled.

She was leaning on his vehicle. "Hello, Craig."

"What are you doing here?" Craig recovered his stride, but he was sweating, despite the temperature hovering around forty degrees. Her presence at the casino had shaken him.

Matt circled around so he could see them both in profile and hear their conversation, but he hung back about ten feet. Craig didn't seem to notice him. He was too focused on Bree.

She lifted her cell phone and snapped a picture of Craig. "Great shot with the casino sign in the background."

Craig lunged for the phone.

She sidestepped, keeping the phone out of his reach. She extended one finger at him. "Do not put your hands on me. You won't like what happens."

He stared at the phone, his eyes narrowing. A vein in his neck throbbed. "That's an invasion of my privacy!"

"Legally, there is no expectation of privacy in a public space," Bree said. "There are cameras all around us. That casino is full of them. You're being filmed every time you walk into any public space. How do you think your congregation will feel about their minister gambling?"

Craig said nothing. His jaw sawed back and forth. His body wasn't moving, but inside, he was clearly freaking out. "Who says *I* was gambling? Maybe I was here to help a lost soul."

"Remember those cameras I mentioned before?"

"This isn't your jurisdiction. You have no authority here. Casino security would never give you copies of their surveillance videos."

"But they'd give them to the Randolph County Sheriff's Department after I have a long talk with them."

Matt could see Craig searching for a spin.

Matt walked past him and stood with Bree. "I have a great video of you placing bets at the window."

"Who are you?" Craig asked.

"A friend of the family," Matt said. "But that's not important."

"So, let's talk," Bree began.

Craig's gaze shifted back to her. "What do you want?"

"Did you kill Erin?" Bree asked.

"No!" His head reared back. "Why would I do that?"

"You have a gambling problem." Bree raised a finger with each point. "Ministers don't make much money. The two kids would come with survivor's benefits. The church will give you a higher allowance. So, in short, money."

Craig narrowed his eyes. "That's the most ridiculous thing I've ever heard." But his voice lacked fire, and his expression was tight, as something she'd said hit too close to the truth.

"Is it?" Bree asked.

Craig took a step back and composed himself. His features transformed, the anger draining off, but underneath his new, calm demeanor, Matt could see a calculating mind. Craig was a gambler. Was he bluffing?

"I have a video of you placing bets at the casino," Matt said.

Craig shrugged. "So, I was weak. Men sin. It's part of being human. I'll repent. Forgiveness is there for all who seek it. I'll turn this whole experience into a sermon."

Matt had no doubt Craig could spin it well. He wasn't bluffing. He knew just how far he could ride his charisma.

He jabbed a finger at Bree. "Don't come at me with false accusations again. You'll be hearing from my attorney about the custody suit." He lowered his hand. His gray-blue eyes were as cold as a glacier. "Those are my children. They will be coming to live with me, and there isn't anything you can do about it."

Craig turned, walked to his car, and drove away.

Matt watched the car disappear onto the main road. "I thought he might cave when we caught him gambling, but I underestimated his ego."

"It is massive," Bree agreed.

"Look on the bright side," Matt said. "We know Craig has a gambling problem. He's probably in debt. We can take what we have to Todd. This should be enough to bring Craig in for questioning."

"We still have no proof that Craig and Erin had any recent contact. Todd has been focused on people in Erin's current life, not someone she supposedly hadn't seen in years." Bree turned to the passenger door of the SUV. "Unfortunately, now we've shown Craig our cards. We won't surprise him again. He'll be ready for us."

CHAPTER TWENTY-NINE

He pulled the Sig Sauer P226 from his pocket and rubbed the barrel. He'd brought his own Ruger 9mm to Justin's house that night, but when he'd seen the Sig sitting out in the open, he'd used that gun instead. It was a beautiful gun, a classic. He'd left it on the floor next to the body, hoping Justin would be blamed for Erin's death. Unfortunately, Justin had picked it up and chased after him.

A decision Justin had quickly regretted. Justin was out of action now, but that bitch was a problem. She could ruin everything.

He opened his notepad and reviewed his notes. He'd been watching everyone, and his plan was falling into place. Erin's life insurance would be the key.

It was all about the money.

He turned to his laptop and scrolled through the photos. She wasn't falling into line. She thought she could defy him—betray him, even.

The fury that swirled inside him felt so familiar it was comforting. It was with him almost all the time now, like a friend he knew was trouble but liked hanging out with anyway.

He opened the reusable nylon shopping bag from Bill's Sporting Goods and began to unload it. He lined up the boxes of bullets next to the hunting vest he'd purchased earlier in the day. He filled the pockets with ammunition and laid out his weapons—the Sig he'd taken from Justin's house and his own Ruger. He loaded both guns and the Ruger's extra magazine. Then he filled the vest pockets with bullets.

A man should get what he deserved, what he'd earned. And if anything—or anyone—tried to stop him . . .

Then she should die.

CHAPTER THIRTY

"You didn't have to drive me," Bree said from the passenger seat of Matt's SUV.

From behind the wheel, Matt glanced at her. "We promised Dana neither of us would go off on our own, right?"

"Steph isn't going to shoot me in the middle of a busy salon," Bree said.

"Jack is in there too. I know he has an alibi, but it's weak in my opinion."

"True." Bree studied the front of the salon. "I'm just going to ask her questions. I do this every day. Have some faith."

He nodded. "Still, we agreed to provide cover for each other. So, I'm sitting out here. Text me if anything goes sideways."

"In that case." Bree removed her baby Glock from her ankle holster and put it in his glove compartment. "For emergency use."

He nodded once but didn't look happy.

Bree glanced around the lot. Matt had parked in the rear, in the shade of a mature oak tree, and backed into the space. From here, he had a clear view of the salon, including a straight line of sight into the plate glass windows in the front of the building.

She grabbed her purse and slid out of the car. She looped the cross-body strap over her head and shoulder as she crossed the lot. Inside, four receptionists hustled to check in a short line of clients. When it was her turn, Bree gave Dana's name, which she'd borrowed to make the appointment.

A slim young woman dressed in all black led Bree back to the shampoo area and gave her a cape. Bree leaned back and tried to enjoy the shampoo and head massage, but her mind couldn't let go of the incident with Craig. The only ring of truth she'd heard in their entire conversation outside the casino was when he'd denied shooting her sister. Assuming for two seconds that Craig wasn't Erin's killer, how was Bree going to protect the kids from him?

Luke had made it very clear he wanted no part of Craig. How much influence would the boy's distant memories have with a judge?

If she couldn't prove Craig was grossly unfit, he would probably be granted custody. He was an upstanding citizen, employed as a minister, no less. Bree was sure he could parade a long line of church employees and congregants into court as character witnesses. Nothing short of a felony would sway a judge under those circumstances.

The shampoo girl escorted Bree to Steph's station. Bree settled in the chair and hung her purse on a tiny hook under the counter. The salon was busy and loud. Voices and the whine of blow-dryers echoed in the high-ceilinged, tiled space.

Steph buzzed around the corner in black suede booties, black tights, and a snug black knit dress. Her eyes were red-rimmed and puffy, her face pale enough to make her red lipstick seem garish. When her gaze landed on Bree, Steph froze, and what little color was in her cheeks drained away.

Bree had come in hoping to catch Steph in a lie, but seeing her, worry overrode her plan. Steph looked terrible. Was guilt eating her alive? Or was it something else?

Steph would be the worst poker player ever. A quick play of emotions crossed her face: shock, a flash of hope.

Then fear.

An uneasy feeling stirred in Bree's belly. She had gotten something wrong. What had she missed?

"Bree!" Steph walked toward her, hands outstretched. "I didn't know you were my client. Your name isn't on my list."

"Sorry about the mix-up. My friend made the appointment." Bree stood to greet her.

Steph gave her a quick, one-armed hug. "It's no problem." But her voice shook.

"I could get someone else if you don't want to cut my hair," Bree offered.

"Why would I not want to cut your hair?" Steph patted the back of the chair, and Bree sat.

Each salon station consisted of a chair, a dark gray counter, and a mirror. Underneath each counter was a vertical column of drawers. Steph opened a drawer and pulled out a comb.

"I wanted to see you again, and I need a trim."

"Well, I'm glad you came in. Erin would be upset if you showed up at her funeral with less than fabulous hair." Steph combed Bree's wet hair straight. "Just a trim then?"

"Yes, please." Bree kept her hair in a basic shoulder-length cut that could easily be contained in a ponytail or bun. She received too many middle-of-the-night callouts for anything fancier that required actual work.

"Of course." Steph opened another drawer and chose a pair of scissors with hands that trembled just enough to make Bree swallow.

Whose idea had it been to question a potentially unstable woman while she was holding sharp scissors so close to Bree's throat?

"How are you feeling?" Bree asked.

Steph's mouth flattened. "OK. The morning sickness is getting better."

Then why does she look like death barely warmed over?

"Zack seems really excited, but then he isn't the one throwing up every morning," Bree said in a light tone.

At the mention of Zack's name, Steph tensed. She nicked her finger with her scissors. Blood welled from the cut.

"Are you OK?"

"I'm fine. It's just a scratch." Steph smiled, but her expression was still strained. She set down her scissors, opened a drawer, and retrieved a Band-Aid.

"Are you upset about tomorrow?" In the mirror, Bree watched her wrap the bandage around her finger.

Steph sniffed and wiped a tear from her face. "Yes and no. I mean, it's gonna suck, but I feel like it'll help too, you know? Like sharing our love for Erin and the good memories will help us heal. Maybe all that love will bring her spirit around too."

Bree reached up and touched Steph's arm. "That's a lovely thought. Thank you."

"Do you feel her around you?" Steph tossed the Band-Aid wrapper in the trash and went to work. She combed Bree's hair and snipped the ends, her scissors moving with skill and practice. Now that she was working, Steph's movements smoothed out, but every time she paused, Bree could see that the tips of her fingers still trembled.

"Sometimes, when I'm in the house with all of her things, I do," Bree said. "The cows."

A short bark of laughter erupted from Steph. She covered her mouth. "She did love cows. She wanted to buy a real one last year, but Luke talked her out of it."

"Good thing he's a sensible kid." Bree smiled. She wasn't getting any dishonest vibes from Steph, just bittersweet sadness and a vague nervousness that Bree couldn't pinpoint.

"I just want to get tomorrow over with," Bree said, the honesty in her statement tightening her chest. "I'm worried about the kids. Planning the service has been hard on them, but like you said before, maybe it's also cathartic. There's no way around grieving. No matter how hard it is, we all have to wade right through it."

"Those poor babies." Steph choked up for a few seconds. Then she combed through Bree's hair again, checking for evenness, snipping where the line of her cut wasn't perfectly straight.

"Are *you* excited about the baby?" Bree asked.

"Who wouldn't be?" Steph forced a smile. "It was a surprise, though. We didn't plan it. But I guess these things happen. It would be my luck to be part of the one percent who gets pregnant on birth control, right?"

"Someone has to be the one in a hundred."

"Yeah."

Steph's tone and demeanor set off more alarms in Bree's head. Something wasn't right, which reminded her of the call she'd come here to ask about. Steph's odd behavior had thrown Bree off her game.

"I was thinking about my whole last conversation with Erin," Bree said. "We didn't talk about anything important. I don't remember if I told her I loved her. If I had known it would be the last time I got to speak with her, there are so many things I would have said."

Steph's eyes welled up. "Me too. I didn't even say goodbye. I was with a client, and she was rushing out the door."

"You didn't talk to her after work?"

Steph shook her head. "I went home and took a long, hot shower. I did a smoothing treatment that afternoon, and the fumes made me super sick. I wanted the smell off me."

"Are you sure? I saw a call from your phone to Erin's at six that evening."

Steph set down the scissors. "That's not right. I remember Tuesday very clearly. I nearly threw up on my client."

"That would not have been good."

"Not at all." Steph glanced around, then reached into her pocket for her phone. "We're not allowed to have our phones out while we're working, but I don't see Jack. I'll show you." She scrolled on her phone. Her face creased, her brows lowering in confusion. "I don't understand. There's a call here." She lowered the phone so Bree could see it and pointed to Erin's number. "I know I didn't make this call."

Lying was stressful, and most people exhibited nervous tells. But Steph's denial sounded legitimate.

"Who had access to your phone while you were showering?" Bree asked. But she already knew. Cold slid over her.

"The only person who was home was—" Steph sucked in a breath. She covered her mouth with a hand. "Oh, my God."

Steph dropped the hairbrush. She put a hand on the counter, leaned on it, and started hyperventilating.

Bree jumped to her feet and supported her other arm. "It's all right."

"It's not all right." Steph gasped.

"Take a deep breath and let it out slowly," Bree said.

"You don't understand." Steph shook her head. But she wasn't crying. Instead, she looked horrified.

"But I do," Bree said, cold sliding over her. Justin wasn't the man who was a personality chameleon like her father had been. It was Zack. Bree should have seen it.

Steph's phone rang in her hand. She jumped, almost dropping it. "It's him."

"Don't answer it."

"I have to. He freaks out if I don't." Steph touched her cheek.

Looking closer, Bree could see the faint color of a bruise bleeding through Steph's makeup. Anger surged. Bree hadn't been here when Craig had beaten her sister, but she was here now. And she would not let Zack hurt Steph again.

The phone rang twice more. Steph's finger hovered over the device, fear hovering in her eyes. "He's going to be mad."

"Does he hit you?" Bree asked.

Steph's gaze drifted to the floor. "Yes."

The phone rang again.

"Don't go home to him," Bree said. "You deserve better."

"That's what Erin said." Steph sniffed. "She didn't want me to go back to him, and he hadn't even hit me then. She said he would. She just knew."

The phone stopped ringing. Steph's hands trembled harder. "You don't know what he's been like lately. Me being pregnant set him off. He's become possessive—no, obsessive. He doesn't like to let me out of his sight. He calls me every hour or two and insists I answer. He tracks my diet and exercise. He checks my phone and online activity." She swallowed. "I don't want to go home. I can't live with him—with the fear—any longer. I packed a few things in a bag this morning. I'm not going home. I'm leaving him."

"Where will you go?"

"I don't know. A hotel, I guess. I have cash." Steph's phone vibrated. "He's texting. He says, 'Call me right now.'"

"Ignore him."

"I can't. I have to talk to him, or he'll know something's up. He'll know I'm leaving him. He has a gun." The little color in Steph's face drained away.

Bree took Steph by the shoulders. "Why would he have called Erin Tuesday night?"

"I don't know."

Bree didn't like the hunch swirling in her gut. "Would Zack have any reason to kill Erin?"

Panic scurried in Steph's eyes. "No. He couldn't have."

She didn't say *wouldn't have.*

The phone rang again.

Steph answered, her voice artificially high. "Hey, babe."

"You didn't answer my call." Zack's voice was loud enough for Bree to hear him. "I told you what would happen if you ignored me."

"I'm sorry. I just saw your call. I was in the bathroom. You know I have to pee all the time these days." Steph spoke too fast, her words stumbling over each other.

"That's bullshit." His tone was angry-cold. "Who are you with?"

"A client."

"Who?"

Steph's eyes went helplessly wide, and she looked as if she was going to break down. "No one you know."

"You're lying. Who. Are. You. *With?*" Zack screamed the last word.

Bree wanted to rip the phone away and yell back at the bastard.

"Her name is Dana." Tears poured from Steph's eyes. "You don't know her."

"I know you're lying. I saw Erin's sister go into the salon, and I know you packed some of your stuff this morning. I told you I'd never let you go." The line went dead.

Steph stared at the phone. She lifted her gaze to Bree's. The shaking started in her hands and spread through her body until she could barely stand. Her already-pale face turned the color of old snow. Her knees buckled.

Bree ripped off the plastic cape and steered Steph into the chair. "Take a deep breath and hold it. That's it. Now exhale, nice and slow."

She coached her through a few more breaths, not speaking again until she was sure Steph wasn't going to hyperventilate or faint.

"It's going to be all right," Bree said.

"It isn't. It really isn't. You don't know him." Steph leaned forward, her hands curled protectively around her belly, shaking her head over and over.

"It doesn't matter." Bree crouched to her level. "Look at me."

Steph lifted her eyes.

Bree said, "I'm going to protect you—"

Steph's phone beeped three times in rapid succession. They both looked at the screen. Three messages from Zack appeared.

I warned you.
all your fault.
U R dead.

CHAPTER THIRTY-ONE

Matt jerked straight. Through the windshield he watched a car pull up to the curb in front of the salon. Zack Wallace stepped out of the driver's side. Dressed in jeans, a red-and-black flannel shirt, and a hunting vest, he stood next to his car for a few seconds, staring at the salon. Then he closed the door and walked around the front of his vehicle. His gait was shaky, and he was so focused on the building that he stumbled over the curb.

His presence shouldn't have raised any flags. Zack's wife worked inside. He could be stopping for any reason. She could have called him. She could have left something at home that she needed. Maybe he just wanted to see her for another reason.

But Zack's posture, his stiffness, sent Matt's balls crawling into his body. Instinct pulled him out of his SUV.

As Zack turned to open the door to the salon, Matt spotted two guns tucked into the waistband of his pants.

Matt reached back inside his vehicle and collected Bree's handgun from the glove compartment. Running toward the building, he pulled out his phone and pressed buttons. He sent Bree a quick text—Zack coming in armed—then called 911.

"What is your emergency?" the dispatcher asked.

"An armed man just walked into Halo Salon and Spa." Matt jogged toward the door as he gave the address and Zack's description.

"Have any shots been fired?" the dispatcher asked.

Matt hit the cement just shy of the door. The *pop pop pop* of gunshots sounded from inside the building, followed by screaming. Fear gripped his belly and squeezed hard.

He breathed. "Three shots have been fired. The shooter has at least two weapons. Handguns."

"Officers are en route. ETA three minutes. Are there any injuries?"

"I don't know. I'm outside the building." Matt checked the magazine on Bree's pistol. The subcompact Glock 26 held ten rounds in the magazine plus one in the chamber. The gun was fully loaded, which gave him eleven shots. Bree, wherever she was, carried a Glock 19. Standard magazine capacity was fifteen rounds.

Who knew how many bullets Zack had brought? His hunting vest was designed to carry extra ammunition. Matt and Bree could be outgunned. Every shot had to count, which meant Matt would have to get close.

"I'm going in. Advise responding officers that a former deputy is on site and armed." Matt gave a description of his own clothing. "And that an off-duty detective is currently inside the building, also armed." He added a description of Bree. "I'll update when possible."

Matt ended the call before he was told to remain outside and wait for law enforcement. He lowered his phone. Bree had not responded to his text. Most active shooter incidents were over in four minutes. Every second that passed could result in another innocent victim. There was no way Matt was waiting, letting people get shot when he could potentially intervene.

Even if he could be shot, by Zack or friendly fire.

His hand ached as he remembered the bullet piercing it. He made a fist and released it. His heart shifted into high gear as he approached the building.

He cupped a hand over his eyes and peered through the glass. Zack wasn't in sight. Matt tried the door, but it was locked. People were on the floor in the lobby, huddling together and crying. Matt knocked on the door, but no one could hear him over the screaming.

He ran around the corner of the building and along the side wall toward the employee entrance. He hoped the door wasn't locked from the inside. The door flew open, and a woman burst out, her eyes wide with panic. Matt caught the door before it closed and quietly slipped inside. Cracking the interior door, he paused for three breaths to listen.

Two more gunshots sounded from inside. People screamed. A man shouted, "Get down! On the floor. Do it now!" He yelled something else, but Matt couldn't make out the words.

Matt went into the hallway. A woman ran, sobbing, toward him. He grabbed her by the arm and pushed her toward the exit. As she ran to safety, he walked toward the gunfire.

Two out, but how many people are inside?

Matt's pulse scrambled as he moved down the hall. He passed the room with the big chairs and footbaths. Three women crouched behind a partial wall. One screamed as she caught sight of Matt with his pistol. He put a finger on his lips and pointed them toward the side exit, but he couldn't stop to make sure they got out. Realizing he wasn't the shooter, the women ran down the hall toward the door where Matt had come in. Two of them were barefoot.

More screaming. Two more gunshots from the main salon area.

"Do it!" the man yelled.

A woman sobbed, "No. No. No. Please."

Two more shots rang out.

"Oh, my God. Oh, my God. Ohmygod," a woman cried.

Matt smelled smoke. The fire alarm went off, screeching like a billion cicadas playing through concert speakers. At the end of the hallway, Matt paused, but there was no way to hear the shooter now. The fire alarms blocked out all other sounds. In the main salon and nail area, the fire sprinklers turned on. After an initial sputter, water rained down.

He peered around the corner. Smoke hovered over the nail stations, above a pile of smoldering debris, the fire the sprinklers had extinguished. His gaze swept over a dozen women crouching on the floor behind the shampoo sinks. Matt could only see 80 percent of the main room. The tall mirrors facing each chair blocked his view. But if Zack was behind one of the stations, the women would be focused on him. Instead, they were hiding under counters and behind wheeled carts—as if that would help them. Above their heads, water poured down, landing on live electrical appliances. Electrical cords trailed into the puddling water. He hoped a breaker tripped before someone was electrocuted.

He looked for Bree. She'd been scheduled for a haircut and should have been at Steph's station in the rear of the salon area. But he didn't see her, nor did he see Steph.

Matt reviewed the floor plan of the salon in his head. He'd been inside the building only once, when he and Bree had interviewed Jack Halo. Most of the first floor was comprised of the hairstyling section. To the left, about twenty stations were lined up in front of a row of sinks. The fingernail area was off to the right, along with the semiprivate room for doing toenails that he'd already passed.

In the back of the salon were private rooms for other treatments. Upstairs held office space and more private rooms. In addition to the spiral staircase, stairwells flanked the building on each side at the rear corners.

Crouching, Matt eased around the corner and crept along the wall until he could see the lobby. Salon employees were dressed in all black. Behind the reception desk, one female employee lay on her back, bleeding heavily from an abdominal wound. Matt recognized her as the receptionist who had greeted him and Bree when they'd interviewed

Jack. Another employee knelt next to her, trying to staunch her wound with a folded towel.

A few feet away, a female client sprawled on the floor, arms and legs akimbo. Matt didn't need to check her pulse to know she was dead. Red bloomed across her white sweater. Her eyes stared right at Matt, but she didn't see him. A young man in a black logo T-shirt and black skinny jeans held her hand. His own hands were covered in blood, as if he'd tried to stop the bleeding. Around him, the accumulating water turned pink as it mixed with the blood.

Matt wanted to stop and help. He'd been trained in advanced first aid, but he needed to keep going. He needed to find Zack and stop him before more people were hurt or killed.

And he needed to find Bree. Where was she?

His gaze snapped back to the woman with the belly wound. *She was going to bleed to death too, if she didn't get medical help quickly.*

Damn it.

The woman staunching her wound wasn't big enough to carry her outside, but she and the man crying over the dead woman could do it together. Matt eyed the glass door on the other side of the lobby. The key was still in the lock.

If Matt could help them get her to the door, they could drag her outside. If the salon employees weren't in shock, they would have thought of it already. But people didn't always react logically in these types of situations. People hid right next to exits. They froze from fright.

He squinted through the glass. Two sheriff's department vehicles were parked fifty feet in front of the salon. He couldn't see if the deputies were in their vehicles, but someone must be watching the front door. At the back of the parking lot across the street, Matt could see swirling lights reflecting on glass. First responders would set up a command center somewhere nearby but out of the gunman's line of sight.

He started texting Todd details.

Matt: I'm inside the salon. The shooter is Zack Wallace.

Todd responded in seconds. where is he?

Matt: don't know. wounded woman near front entrance. bringing her out. don't shoot us.

Todd: OK. entry teams organizing now.

Then Matt sent one more quick text, to Bree, because she hadn't responded to his earlier message. whr r u?

Matt analyzed the lobby. The open spiral staircase created a tactical nightmare. If Zack was on the second floor, he could pick off anyone who tried to go up the steps or cross the lobby.

Including Matt.

Boom!

Matt dropped flat to the floor and covered his head with his arms.

The noise had come from the main salon area and had sounded like a shotgun blast, but Matt hadn't seen a shotgun on Zack. Nor had he been wearing anything long enough to conceal one.

With one eye on the open area above the spiral staircase, Matt ran in a crouch across the lobby. He touched the male employee on the shoulder and pointed to the wounded woman. The man blinked at him, then scrambled to his feet.

Matt paused next to the wounded woman.

No time for first aid. Just get her out.

Hooking his hand around one of her arms, he began dragging her across the tile. The woman who'd been trying to stop the bleeding ran for the door, unlocked it, and opened it. The man grabbed the victim's other arm and helped Matt.

At the door, Matt nodded for the woman to take his place. She stepped in and helped the man drag the bleeding woman through the doorway and out onto the concrete toward the sheriff's department vehicles.

Shots erupted from deeper in the building.

Dread balled up in Matt's chest. How many people had been shot so far?

He turned and ran back through the lobby, getting away from the spiral staircase opening as quickly as possible. Zack was not in the main rooms. He was either in the back of the first floor or upstairs. Matt raced for the side staircase.

Toward the gunfire.

Chapter Thirty-Two

Water from the sprinklers poured down Bree's face. The alarm was deafening and filled her head like massive congestion. She pushed Steph and the other women, a mix of employees and clients, out of the main salon and into the hall. At the end of the corridor, an Exit sign glowed in the dimness. A dozen doorways lined the passage.

"He wants me," Steph cried into Bree's ear over the screech of the alarm. "I don't want anyone to die because of me."

Steph would be Zack's primary target. The first gunshots had sounded two minutes after he'd texted. Zack must have been close by, maybe watching the building, ready to strike, his rage already triggered, when he'd called. After the first burst of gunfire, Bree had collected the women around her and moved them toward the back hall—away from the shots. She hadn't seen Zack yet, only heard him shooting. But one glance toward the lobby had been enough to know he'd hit at least two people with his initial shots.

Bree's mind was on two things: Where was Zack now? And what had he set on fire? She scanned the room. Smoke and the noxious fumes of burned plastic and toxic chemicals fouled her nose. They passed a treatment room. Bree glanced through the doorway. Her gaze swept over the furniture. The treatment table was made of wood, with fat, square legs and drawers underneath a padded top. It looked heavy. The women could barricade themselves inside a room if necessary. Bullets would cut right through the wallboard and hollow door, but at least they wouldn't be visible targets.

Bree leaned close to Steph's ear and shouted, "Head for the exit. If he cuts you off and you can't get out, barricade yourselves in a room."

Gun in hand, Bree headed in the opposite direction—toward the last gunshots she'd heard.

"But—" Steph protested.

Bree pointed at her. "Do it."

The fewer people inside the building, the better. They couldn't help, and their presence would give Zack leverage. He could take hostages, and he'd already shown he was in a killing mood.

Bree glanced back. Steph stared, her hands clenched at her sides as the other women began pulling her toward the exit. Bree turned away before Steph could argue. The salon had been busy. There were more women still in the building, no doubt hiding. Bree needed to find and stop Zack.

As she moved down the hall, the lights flickered, and the power went out. The hallway went dark. The corridor was an interior one, with no windows. Bree could barely see. The sprinklers hadn't been triggered in this part of the building, but water ran from the main salon into the hall. She slid on the slippery tile and went down on one knee. She dropped her gun, and it slid a few feet away.

No.

She put a hand to the wall, her pulse scrambling as she regained her footing and picked up her weapon. The piercing alarm ripped at her jagged nerves and amplified the sense of complete chaos.

Where is Zack?

And where was law enforcement? She checked her phone, lowering the brightness to the bare minimum to reduce the chance that the light would make her more visible. She'd received Matt's text six minutes before. Surely, he—and others—had called 911. The sheriff's department would be the first responders, followed by cars from surrounding communities and state police. Law enforcement should be outside the building, organizing their entry. Would they wait to set up a command center, call in a nearby SWAT unit? More current protocols in active shooter situations recommended immediate entry for first responders to confront and stop the shooter and minimize casualties. But Bree didn't know this sheriff's department's policies. They were running on half staff. Had they received recent training? Were they operating on alternative protocols?

She pulled out her phone to send Matt a text. She had multiple messages from him telling her that Zack was entering the building armed and asking where she was. She hadn't heard her phone ring or felt it vibrate because of the general chaos.

She responded: I'm in the 1st floor hall. Cops?

Just because she hadn't heard or seen officers didn't mean first responders weren't already in the building. She would not hear sirens over the fire alarm. She could barely hear her own thoughts. She needed to be on the lookout for law enforcement as much as Zack. She was armed and not in a uniform. They could shoot her by accident. Did they know she was inside the building?

Shit.

She sent Todd a text letting him know she was inside the building and armed.

Todd responded: Teams getting into place.

The sheriff's department was coming. Hallelujah. But once they were inside the building, the squealing alarm would render police radios useless. Communication would be difficult. Bree couldn't count on police response. On the bright side, Zack would not hear her sloshing through the half inch of water on the tile. But she wouldn't be able to hear him either. They could surprise each other at any moment.

Just in case the alarms shut off, she turned her phone to silent before sticking it back in her pocket. Then she crept down the dim corridor into the main salon. The sprinklers continued to run, soaking everything, including Bree as she moved into the big room.

Boom!

She jumped. That was the second loud blast she'd heard.

What was it?

Explosion? Shotgun?

Bree's heartbeat echoed in her ears. Her body dumped a fresh load of adrenaline into her bloodstream. Her pupils dilated, improving her sight in the dimness, but also narrowing her field of vision. She fought the tunnel vision with a deep breath, holding the air in her lungs for three heartbeats before slowly letting it out.

Another *boom* echoed. It seemed to come from the direction of the nail area. Had Zack circled back? She turned. Leading with her weapon, she moved toward the sound.

Though it was dark outside, windows in the main room let in light from the parking lot. The room was brighter than the hallways had been.

Shaking water from her eyes, Bree scanned the space. Nothing moved. Anyone who was left was either dead, wounded, or hiding. She hoped most had escaped like Steph. Bree passed the pedicure room. Empty. She swept her gun through the manicure area. A large pile of wet debris on the floor smoldered. Who had set a fire?

The fire alarm shut off abruptly, leaving Bree's ears ringing, but water still poured from the sprinklers. Something cracked overhead. Bree looked up, instinctively shielding her face. A ceiling tile, heavy and saturated with water, dropped to the floor with a *boom*.

The sound hadn't been a shotgun.

She kept moving into the large main room, aware of the slosh of her sneakers in the water. Crouching, she slipped past hair stations. A scream echoed in the large, open space.

Bree moved toward it.

She stopped just short of the lobby. The scream had come from the opening of the spiral staircase.

Zack was upstairs.

Something moved on the other side of the room. Matt. Her gaze met his. She pointed to her own chest and then at the spiral stairs. Then she pointed to Matt and made what she hoped was a climbing-stairs motion with her fingers. Then she pointed to the south corner of the building. If she could go up the spiral steps, and Matt used one of the side staircases, they could box Zack in.

Matt shook his head and started toward her, tapping his own chest. He knew the spiral stairs had no cover, and *he* wanted to be the one to go up them. Bree pointed harder toward the southern corner. She appreciated the chivalry, but they didn't have time for it.

"No." The voice of a begging woman floated down the spiral staircase. "No. Please. I have children."

A single gunshot. A scream. Then crying, quieter, desperate.

Bree and Matt locked gazes again. She jabbed her finger toward the side staircase. Grimacing, he nodded, spun, and ran toward the hall. He moved fast, and the building wasn't large. It would only take him a minute or so to get into position. Now she had to do the same.

Bree's heart hammered and her stomach knotted as she moved toward the staircase. She paused at the bottom, pointing her gun up the center of the curving steps.

She couldn't see Zack, and she'd be vulnerable on the stairs. There was no getting around it. Bree put her foot on the first tread and started up the steps. She wound around, stopping as her head became level with the second-floor landing.

"There you are," Zack said.

Bree froze. Had he seen her?

"Please stop." A woman's voice cracked in fear.

Bree exhaled. Zack was talking to someone else.

She peered over the top tread. The woman wearing a black spa robe stood on the second-floor landing. She was turned three-quarters away from Bree. Next to her, a female employee sobbed on the floor. Her hands clutched at her thigh. Blood seeped around her hands.

Behind the two women, Zack stood about ten feet away. He was pointing a gun at them. The robed woman stepped between Zack and the wounded woman.

The women were positioned between Bree and Zack. Bree had no shot.

Agitated, Zack shook. His hands—and the weapon—trembled hard. His eyes were wide open, and he licked his lips over and over. He was going to shoot again. Bree knew it.

Where was Matt?

CHAPTER THIRTY-THREE

Matt raced down the hall. Without the alarm blaring, the building was eerily quiet, except for the sound of sprinklers still running in the main salon behind him. The sprinklers and audible alarm were not on the same system. The sprinklers would run until someone shut them off. Unfortunately, the fire crew would not be allowed into an active shooter situation.

The last gunshot had sounded from above. Zack was upstairs. Matt ran, hoping Bree would wait until he was in position. Once on the staircase, she'd be an open target.

As he rounded the corner, his wet boots skidded on the tiles. He put a hand on the wall to stop his forward momentum and opened the door leading to the side stairwell.

Matt took the steps two at a time. Pausing at the top, he eased open the door and slid into the upstairs hallway. He could see Zack fifty feet ahead, his back to Matt, his gun pointed toward a woman in a knee-length black robe, her blonde hair pulled back in a ponytail. Next to the robed woman, a spa employee was trying to stop the bleeding of a leg wound.

Matt slowed. What he wouldn't give to have his long gun.

He moved closer. Commercial carpeting covered the upstairs hall, and his boots were silent, but he moved slowly and smoothly, doing his best not to attract Zack's attention.

Something moved just beyond the blonde woman. The top of a head popped over the landing of the spiral staircase. Bree, in position.

A fresh shot of adrenaline burst through Matt's veins. They'd successfully trapped Zack, but the robed woman was in the way.

He aimed Bree's baby Glock at Zack, but the distance was still too great. He could not shoot Zack without endangering the woman. Frustration surged through him. His aim would never be good enough for a shot like this again. Hell, he couldn't be certain he wouldn't hit Bree, not at this distance. He needed to get the woman out of the way so Bree could take out Zack. But how?

Maybe he could distract Zack.

No. Bad idea. The guy was twitchy as hell. Any unexpected noise was just as likely to make Zack pull the trigger. Matt had only one choice. He had to get closer. Much closer.

He had to be the distraction. He had to demand Zack's attention.

He eased farther up the corridor. Now that he was out in the open, his skin itched with vulnerability, like heat rash. If Zack looked his way, Matt was completely exposed. Zack could shoot at him, and Matt couldn't even return fire for fear of hitting an innocent bystander.

Zack walked toward the woman, his gait unsteady. He grabbed her by the ponytail and shoved the gun into the soft flesh under her chin. Was he deciding whether or not to kill her? Or was he dragging out the moment to make her suffer? Was he losing his shit and no longer thinking at all? Didn't matter. Matt couldn't let her die.

Matt called out, "Drop the gun!"

Zack's gun swung away from the woman and toward Matt. Zack released the woman and fired. Matt dove for the floor, shoulder rolling into an open doorway. The bullet hit the doorframe, and wood splintered.

Matt landed on his feet and returned to the doorway, peering around the frame. Zack had turned his back on the robed woman.

"I'm going to kill you!" Zack screamed, advancing on Matt. Zack's face was red, the veins in his neck bulging as if he was going to stroke out.

Matt fired into the wall opposite Zack, well away from the woman in the hall. Zack flinched, but his steps didn't slow. He came at Matt as if he were invincible, or a robot.

Or as if he didn't care if he lived or died.

If that was the case, there would be only one way to stop him.

Behind Zack, Matt saw Bree climb onto the landing. Her gun was drawn, but the robed woman was still in her way.

She passed the wounded employee and yelled at the robed woman, "Get down!"

If the woman in the robe dropped to her knees, Bree would have Zack cold. Hopefully, this would happen before Zack shot Matt through the wall.

The robed woman's head turned. Matt held his breath.

"Zack!"

Who was that?

A black-clad employee stepped between the robed woman and Zack. Steph. She must have come up the center hallway. No doubt her intentions were to save her coworker, but she'd just fucked up everything.

"Please don't hurt anyone else," Steph said, her words shaky. "I'll do whatever you want."

Her hands were raised, the palms toward Zack in surrender. She was clearly intent on de-escalating Zack, but she'd probably just signed her own death certificate.

Chapter Thirty-Four

Steph.

Bree's heart compressed. Instead of leaving or hiding with the others, Steph had come looking for her husband.

Kudos for her courage and loyalty, but shit, shit, *shit.*

Three more seconds and Bree would have put him down. Now they were back in the same situation, with Steph between Bree and Zack.

"Please don't shoot me," Steph said. "I'm carrying our baby. Your baby."

"It's probably not even mine." Zack put his back to the wall. He pulled a second gun from his waistband and pointed it at his wife. The first he kept aimed at Matt.

"I never cheated on you," Steph said. "Ever."

He shook his head. "You lie."

"No! Of course it's your baby, Zack," Steph said, her voice both terrified and hurt. "How could you think anything else?"

"Because you lied to me." Zack's tone was flat.

"No," Steph said. "Never."

Quiet stretched time for a few seconds.

"I don't believe you." Zack's voice—and his aim—wavered. "You packed your shit before you went to work this morning. You're leaving me. An honest wife doesn't do that."

"I was leaving you because you scared me, and I want to protect our baby." Desolation and hopelessness edged Steph's comment. "I can't change the fact that you don't trust me. I've never been unfaithful to you. I've loved you from the very first moment we met. We had something special. But you let your unfounded jealousy come between us."

"You cheated." His face and tone were emotionless.

"No, Zack. I never did."

But his eyes were dark and unbelieving—unforgiving.

"Ever since you lost your job, you've been insecure," Steph said. "You invented failings for me and tried to make them come true. I've done everything I can think of to make you happy. I don't know what else to do. Tell me. What do you want from me?"

"I won't let you leave. You belong to me." Zack never blinked. Nothing his wife said got through to him. His boot tapped on the floor, and his weight shifted back and forth. Nerves and adrenaline fighting for an outlet in a still body.

Bree had seen it a few times before. Zack had decided he'd been wronged, and hearing otherwise didn't penetrate his personal conviction. He'd nursed his perceived wrong. He had nowhere else to direct his anger—and he'd invested so much energy into his belief that he wasn't willing or able to let it go.

Zack pulled the trigger. The gun clicked, empty.

"Steph, get down!" Bree yelled.

But Steph seemed frozen.

Backing partially into the doorway behind him, Zack threw one gun to the floor and transferred the gun he'd been pointing at Matt to his right hand. He pointed it at Steph. Tears ran down her face, her chest heaved as if she'd just run a full-out sprint, but she didn't move. Her gaze remained fixed on her husband.

"Please don't." Steph's hands dropped to hug her belly, as if she could block bullets with her forearms.

Bree ran forward, moving to the side of the hallway, trying to get a clear shot around Steph.

A body charged out of the doorway. Matt. But he was several strides away and an open target. Bree fired a wide shot to distract Zack. He fired back at her. Bree ducked into a doorway. Bits of wallboard exploded as the bullet hit the wall a few feet away. She peered around the frame. "Steph, run!"

But Steph was still rooted in place.

Matt charged across the hall. Zack pulled back into his own doorway. Clicking sounds indicated he was reloading. Matt took Steph down to the floor and covered her with his body. Zack stepped out into the hall. He swung his gun arm in an arc toward Matt and Steph. The muzzle dropped toward his targets on the floor.

Bree cleared the doorway, leveled her weapon, and fired at him. Three shots hit him in rapid succession. Three spots of blood bloomed on his chest.

"Drop the gun!" Bree yelled.

Instead, he raised his weapon and brought it around toward her.

She fired again, the fourth shot landing in the dead center of his chest. He went down to his knees. The gun dropped from his hand.

Bree leaped forward and kicked the weapon away. She moved to the first gun he'd thrown away and kicked that down the hall as well. His vest was bulky, with large pockets. She couldn't tell if he had any additional weapons. She eased closer and pointed the gun at his face. "Show me your hands!"

She didn't think he was dead. The bad guys only died instantaneously on TV, and she'd seen men survive multiple bullet wounds.

"Show me your hands!" she yelled again.

"Police!" Sheriff's deputies carrying riot shields and AR-15s appeared at each end of the hallway. Another team approached from the center corridor.

"Off-duty police officer!" Bree lowered her gun and backed away, but she didn't set it down where Zack could reach it. He'd killed at least one woman and shot at minimum two more. He'd fired at his own pregnant wife. She had no doubt if he was still breathing, he'd try to shoot someone else.

She let her gun dangle, her finger in the trigger guard. She raised her other hand in a classic surrender position. The deputies swarmed her. Bree released her weapon and let herself be handcuffed. She expected it. Standard procedure was to secure everyone involved—especially the armed people—and sort them out later.

Down the hall, Matt and the three women were being taken over by another team of deputies.

Bree could hear the disbelief in Steph's voice over the sound of a dozen deputies and from twenty feet away.

"He pulled the trigger," Steph said. "If the gun hadn't been empty, he would have killed me." Her hands cradled her belly. "He would have killed his own child."

Bree sat on the floor as instructed. She'd killed a man, something she'd never done in more than a dozen years on the Philadelphia PD. She would feel the impact of being the one to pull the trigger tomorrow. She had no doubt that taking a life would profoundly change her.

But for today, she'd grieve those Zack Wallace had killed. And she'd be grateful Steph, her baby, Matt, and Bree had all made it out of the incident alive.

Chapter Thirty-Five

Within an hour, Matt followed the sheriff's department vehicles to the Wallace property. Lights swirled and sirens blared as they drove to the gray saltbox-style house. They parked in front of the detached garage and workshop. Matt and Bree leaped from the SUV and followed the deputies.

Todd had wanted them to go to the sheriff's station and wait to be interviewed, but Matt had refused. Justin was probably dead, but Matt needed to know.

"Check the garage and workshop," Matt shouted. Steph hadn't seen Justin anywhere on the property, but she hadn't been in Zack's workshop in months because the sawdust smell had been making her nauseated. She didn't even have a key to the building.

Todd gestured for them to hold up, and Matt and Bree reluctantly fell back while the deputies used a battering ram to open the side door on the garage. Two minutes later, they emerged.

"It's clear," Todd yelled. He and his men ran for the workshop.

Staring at the building, Matt propped a hand on his hip and rubbed his face. "If he's alive, he has to be in there."

What were the chances?

Bree took his hand. "You'll know in a minute."

"I should be in there. Zack is dead. He's no longer a threat."

"You know this is how it has to be." She gave his hand a squeeze. "There could be booby traps."

Matt was more worried about a dead body.

The deputies used the battering ram again. The workshop door flew open, and they filed inside.

"He's here!" one of them shouted.

A few sweaty minutes later, Todd leaned out of the doorway. "Matt!"

Matt ran inside, past cabinets, workbenches, machinery, and raw boards. In the back of the space, Justin lay on a pallet made out of folded blankets. One wrist was attached to a metal beam by a chain and handcuff. Blood saturated the shoulder of his shirt.

His eyes were open, but his skin was pale gray, his eye sockets were sunken, and feverish spots colored his cheekbones.

Relieved, Matt rushed to his friend's side. "I can't believe you're alive."

It was a freaking miracle. Justin had been shot a week ago and hadn't received medical care. His wound was probably infected.

"Me either. Don't wanna be. Not without Erin." His face was tortured by pain that went deeper than physical, and he wouldn't look at Matt.

Matt dropped to one knee beside Todd, who was unlocking the handcuff. Matt took his friend's hand. "You're OK. We've got you."

Justin's eyes weren't focused on Matt. "He killed her. There wasn't anything I could do. She died in my arms." His voice sounded almost detached.

"I'm sorry," Matt said.

Justin didn't seem to hear him. "He used my dad's gun. I'd left it on the dresser. I heard the shot from the shower. I ran out. She was on the floor." He blinked a few times, as if clearing a vision only he could see. "I heard an engine outside and took Erin's keys. The gun was a few feet away. I picked it up, put on clothes, and ran after him. There was a truck driving away. I followed it." He grabbed at Matt's arm. "I was gonna kill him, Matt. I was."

"I know." Matt didn't know what to say.

Justin continued. "He drove out of town and stopped near the big farm, the one with the hay rides and shit."

"Empire Acres," Matt said.

"Yeah. I thought I was being smart. I hung back where I didn't think he saw me. I was gonna sneak up on him. But he shot me before I could shoot him. He threw me in the back of Erin's truck and brought me here." Justin's breaths quickened. "I wanted to die. It's all my fault. I left the gun out." Justin sobbed. The sorrow and regret emanating from him was as palpable as a cold mist. "Erin is dead because of me."

"No, man. That's not true." Matt leaned in, wrapped his arm around his friend, and held him like a child while he wept. "He had another gun. He would have shot her even if you didn't leave the Sig out."

But Justin was beyond hearing. Another siren signaled the arrival of the ambulance. A minute later, paramedics came in and began assessing him.

Matt squeezed his friend's arm and stepped out of the way. The paramedics and gurney took up most of the space, and Matt retreated from the workshop to give them room. Outside, Bree fell into step beside him.

"What kind of condition is he in?" Bree asked.

Matt glanced back at the workshop. "Physically, he looks much better than I would expect of a prisoner with a gunshot wound. He's lost blood, and he's weak. But he's conscious."

"Why did Zack keep him here, alive?"

"So many questions." Matt handed her the keys to his SUV. "Would you drive my truck to the hospital? I'm going to ride with Justin."

"You go." Bree took the keys. "I'll meet you there."

"Thanks." Matt headed back toward the workshop.

Justin was alive, but his emotional state was precarious.

Maybe survival wasn't everything.

CHAPTER THIRTY-SIX

Tuesday afternoon, Bree shook another hand. The line of people paying their respects seemed to go on forever. The memorial service had been quick. People had gathered around the photo collage and shared memories. Bree had given the eulogy, just long enough to make the kids happy. She barely remembered it. Tears had blurred her vision and constricted her vocal cords, but she'd gotten through it.

"Great eulogy," a stranger said.

Bree nodded. "Thank you for coming."

How many times had she said those words today? She was operating on autopilot; her mouth and body were doing what needed to be done, but her mind had shut down. Her grief was overwhelming, and she hadn't had time to process yesterday's shooting.

She looked for the kids. Luke and Kayla stood in the back of the room with Adam, all three of them avoiding the crowd and looking as exhausted as Bree felt. Grief clung to them all like a virus. Dana hovered next to them, on guard. Matt was not in sight. Bree had asked him to cover the entrance. Under no circumstances was Craig permitted to enter. Bree would not allow him to ambush Luke and Kayla at their most vulnerable moment.

She had arranged for the funeral home to serve coffee in a separate room after the service. Strangers were not invited back to the house. The kids had had enough. Bree wanted to sleep for a week, but tomorrow she had to be at the sheriff's station for an interview. She'd given an initial statement, but Todd had follow-up questions. Since Zack was dead, and there were no charges to be considered, Todd had given Bree today to grieve her sister.

Bree shook another hand. Jack Halo. She was surprised he was there. She'd thought he would have been busy with the aftermath today.

"So sorry for your loss." Jack enveloped Bree's hand between both of his own.

Bree suppressed the urge to punch him. She gritted her teeth. "Thank you for coming."

"Of course I came. Erin will be missed."

Because he'd have to find a new target for his unwanted affections?

Bree wanted to threaten him, but maybe it was better not to give anything away at this time. But she did squeeze his fingers just a little too hard.

"Thank you for everything you did yesterday." Jack hadn't been at the salon during the shooting and had arrived after it was all over. One innocent person had died and another five had been wounded. "It could have been much worse if you hadn't been there."

Bree nodded. She forced herself to be civil, but friendly was not going to happen. Not with the man who'd harassed her sister.

His salon wouldn't be operating for some time. The sprinkler system had caused extensive water damage. Until the salon reopened, he wouldn't have the opportunity to abuse his female employees.

Wincing, he released her.

With a tight smile, Bree moved on to the next guest, but she would not forget about Jack and how he had treated her sister.

Bree had a blackmailer to deal with as well. She considered Craig the most likely suspect, but she couldn't prove it. They'd found no evidence at Zack's that it had been him.

Two people had been missing from the funeral. Justin was still in the hospital undergoing surgery. Bree was relieved that he was alive and innocent. She had dreaded giving the kids any more bad news. Steph had said her presence would shift the focus of attention to her, rather than where it belonged, on Erin and her life. Bree suspected Steph didn't want to face the kids, not after her husband had killed their mother. She doubted they would blame Steph, but they needed time to come to terms with everything that had happened. Steph's presence would have been too much.

Two hours later, Bree opened the door to her sister's house. Dana, Luke, and Adam filed inside. Matt had gone directly from the funeral home to the hospital to see Justin.

Adam carried a sleeping Kayla over his shoulder. Her eyes opened as he eased her onto the couch.

"Can we watch a movie?" she asked.

"Sure." He sat next to her and turned on the TV. Luke dropped down next to them.

Dana headed for the kitchen. "I'll start the oven."

"No rush," Bree said. "I'm not hungry."

Dana waved her off. "None of you ate this morning."

She'd put together some sort of casserole before they'd left for the funeral home. Equally exhausted and restless, Bree went into the kitchen. She wanted to sleep, but she knew she wouldn't be able to close her eyes. While Dana unwrapped her casserole, Bree opened a canister of coffee.

"Let me get that." Dana herded her away. "Your coffee is bitter."

"How complicated is adding water and grounds to a machine?" Bree moved to the window, staring outside.

There were no houses or people in sight. The horses grazed in the pasture. Light snow drifted down, peaceful and quiet. A fresh inch had already accumulated, but the horses didn't seem to mind. Bree sank into a kitchen chair. She watched the scene for a few minutes, with Dana bustling around behind her, the kitchen smelling like a home-cooked meal in the making.

Dana set a cup of coffee in front of her.

"Thanks." Bree tasted the coffee. It was better than hers. "You know what?"

"What?" Dana slid her casserole into the oven.

"I could live here." Bree sipped her coffee. "When I first came back, I didn't think I could. I always thought this town was tainted for me. Too many memories of my parents and their deaths."

"But it's not?"

"I don't think it matters where I am. Those memories are part of me. They will always be with me." If Bree were being completely honest, maybe being in Grey's Hollow had forced her to make a peace of sorts with her past. "Also, I have too many current issues to worry about something that happened in 1993."

"Have you seen the timer?" Dana closed one drawer and opened another.

"No. How long do you need?"

"Forty minutes."

Bree set a timer on her phone. "Is it four o'clock?"

She glanced up at the cow clock on the wall. The hands were stuck in the two-thirty position. She went to the wall and removed the clock from its hook. After setting it on the counter, she turned it over, looking for the battery. "This is weird."

The design was just a frame with clock hands mounted on a drawing of a cow. In the center of the back was a plastic box about two inches square containing the actual clock mechanism with a compartment for a AA battery. An envelope was taped to the back of the clock.

Dana looked over her shoulder. "Erin had a hidey-hole?"

"Looks like she did." Bree carefully removed the envelope. She opened it and removed a stack of twenty-dollar bills. Bree thumbed through the stack. "Looks like two hundred dollars."

"She had a rainy-day fund." Dana pointed to the envelope. "There's something else inside."

Bree turned the envelope over. A mini SD memory card fell to the counter.

"Let me get my computer. I'm pretty sure I saw an SD adapter in the desk drawer." Bree walked to the office for her laptop. Kayla, Luke, and Adam were all asleep on the sofa as she passed.

She booted up the computer as she returned to the kitchen and finished her coffee until the screen came to life. Then she connected the adapter to the laptop and inserted the SD card. But when she accessed the SD card, instead of photos, two audio recording files appeared on the screen. Bree clicked on the first.

"Here it is," Erin said on the recording. The sound of her voice brought tears to Bree's eyes.

Paper rustled. Bree recognized Craig's voice with his very first word.

"Is it all here?" Craig asked.

"It's all I can get today," Erin said. "I already gave you thousands of dollars. My savings are gone."

"It'll do for now."

"I don't have any more money, Craig."

"Then you'd better make some better life choices," Craig sneered. "I want another three thousand next week, or I'll sue for custody."

"I don't have it, and you won't win."

"Won't I?" Arrogance filled Craig's voice. "I'm a minister now. I could get a hundred members of my new congregation to fill the courthouse and testify to my outstanding character."

"I don't have an extra three thousand, Craig."

"Better start working overtime or ask your rich brother for the money. Three grand is coffee money for him. Even if I don't get custody, your attorney fees will cost way more than paying me."

The recording ended. Anger stirred red-hot in Bree's belly. She'd suspected Craig, but hearing him threaten Erin made her want to hunt him down and make him pay that very moment.

Patience.

Dana and Bree shared a look. Bree shifted her anger to make room for some hope. With real evidence, Craig could face felony charges, and it was unlikely that he'd be given custody of the kids. Even he couldn't smooth-talk his way out of extortion.

"I'm almost afraid to listen to the next one." Bree clicked "Play."

"I'm done with this, Craig." Erin's voice sounded firm. "This is the last payment. Take it and go away."

"You aren't making the rules," Craig said.

"I think you're wrong about that."

A click sounded, then the first recording played.

Craig exploded. "You fucking—"

"This proves you were blackmailing me," Erin interrupted. "I hear the courts frown on using your own children for leverage and financial gain."

Fabric rustled.

"Let go of me!" Erin said.

"Give me that recording, bitch."

"I made copies. That's why I didn't play it for you last time."

A few seconds of silence ticked by while Craig processed Erin's statement.

"If you play that for anyone . . ." he said.

"You'll do what?" Erin's voice sharpened. "Stay away from me and *my* kids. Or I swear I will march right down to your church and play this in the middle of your Sunday sermon."

"We are a long way from being done." Craig's tone went full-on menacing.

Then recording number two ended.

"Do you think he continued to harass and threaten her?" Dana asked.

Bree checked the date on the recording. The file was dated the Tuesday before Erin was killed. "I do. He backed off, but not down." Bree paced from one end of the kitchen to the other. "Knowing Craig, he thought of an angle to work. Her call to me came on the following Tuesday, Craig's next day off. I suspect his continued harassment is what she called me about. She would go to Adam for money, but if she felt like she was in physical danger, she would turn to me."

"What are you going to do?"

"Oh, I'm going to fry his ass." Bree rubbed her hands together. She felt almost gleeful. Most important, the kids should be safe with Bree now. But secondly, Bree wanted Craig to get what he deserved. He'd treated Erin like dirt since she was a teenager. "I'll call Todd. Extortion is a felony in New York State, but he'd have to convince the DA to file charges." Bree pulled out her phone. "Looks like I'll be moving up here after all." The grief she'd been saddled with all day lifted just a little.

"Yeah. Family courts frown on dads who extort money from moms." Dana glanced around. "Let me know if you need live-in childcare or a personal chef or whatever."

"You would want to move up here?"

"The fresh air is nice," Dana said. "I woke up at five this morning. Do you know what I did?"

"No."

"Nothing, and it was beautiful." Dana lifted a cookbook from the table. "I read some recipes. I drank coffee. I watched a squirrel in the yard."

"And you'd be content with that? 'Cause I'm going to need a job. I could use the help with the kids."

Dana nodded. "Yeah. I'd be cool living here. I've been working with death and violence for almost thirty years. Peace and quiet is exactly what I need right now." She pointed to the audio recording. "A little revenge would be pure icing."

CHAPTER THIRTY-SEVEN

Matt leaned his forearms on the conference room table in the sheriff's office. He'd finished his interview. Bree was currently in the next room being questioned. As soon as she was done, Todd promised to talk to them both together.

The door opened, and Bree came in carrying a bottle of water. She dropped into the chair next to him. "How is Justin?"

"I haven't seen him today. When I stopped to see him last night, he was still pretty out of it from the anesthesia. But yesterday's surgery went well."

"That's good, right?"

"Yeah. I'll go to the hospital when we're finished here." Matt was more worried about Justin's mental and emotional scars.

She reached across the table and gave his hand a quick squeeze.

They'd saved Justin's life, but he was going to need help to rebuild it. Matt would be there for him.

Todd came in and closed the door behind him. He had a manila file tucked under one arm and a mug of coffee in the other.

"Thanks for your time." Todd sat across from them and opened his notebook. "First of all, we want to thank you. Without the two of you,

Zack would have kept going. He still had more than thirty rounds of ammunition on his person when he died."

"I'm glad I was there," Matt said.

Bree nodded. "Any off-duty officer would have done the same."

"Now where to start. The whole story is just too bizarre." Todd tapped on a page. "We think Zack had been stalking Erin for a couple of weeks. We found a 35mm camera with a telephoto lens in his workshop. He also had notes, spreadsheets, and photographs documenting her daily activity. He'd outlined Erin's whole schedule. He was probably the one who slashed her tires at the salon. The surveillance camera doesn't cover the rear section of the parking lot, where the employees park, but we saw a vehicle that looks like Zack's truck drive past the front of the building that night. Stephanie Wallace flagged a number of calls from her phone to Erin's that she says she didn't make. We assume Zack used her phone. Justin verified that Erin had received numerous threatening calls from Zack, telling her to stay away from Steph and accusing her of trying to talk Steph into leaving him again."

"Erin was not a fan of Zack," Bree said. "She advised Steph not to go back to her husband when they were separated. He wanted his wife isolated and under his control."

"Yes." Todd continued, "He also had some notes on your activity, Bree. He watched your farm a couple of nights. He also spent a lot of time checking up on his wife's whereabouts. He kept detailed notes on everything."

Bree shuddered.

Matt swallowed. He didn't want to think about Zack sitting in front of the farm, possibly armed, with Bree and the kids inside, potentially asleep and vulnerable.

Todd rubbed his jaw. "Surveillance footage from a local sporting goods store shows Zack buying ammunition and the hunting vest last Friday afternoon. He'd owned a Ruger 9mm for many years. We think he brought his own gun to Justin's house the night he shot Erin, but when he saw Justin's, he decided to use that one instead."

Bree sipped her water. "Maybe he thought Erin's shooting would be blamed on Justin."

"And that's exactly what happened, initially." Matt stretched his back.

"So, after he stashed Justin in his workshop, he drove Erin's pickup out to the factory to dump it?" Bree asked.

"That's correct," Todd said. "And then he walked across the field back to his own truck, which was still parked down the road from Empire Acre Farms."

"He chose the factory to dump the pickup because it was convenient," Matt said.

"Seems logical," Todd agreed. "We have clear footage of Zack sitting in the salon parking lot on Monday. He'd already called his wife numerous times. She was expected to answer his calls within three rings. From what we've pieced together, Zack was always controlling and insecure about their relationship, but his mental status began to seriously deteriorate when he lost his job. He became paranoid and suspicious whenever his wife was out of his sight. After she told him she was pregnant, his obsession escalated. On Monday, Steph had packed some clothes and important papers in a duffel bag and sneaked them out of the house. But Zack noticed."

"It seems he would alternately be obsessed with the baby and accuse Steph of cheating," Bree added. "And the thought of her leaving him again sent his paranoia and rage off the charts."

"It did," Todd agreed. "He told her several times that he'd kill her before he let her go."

"Do we know why he kept Justin alive?" Bree asked.

"Not really," Todd said. "Maybe he didn't want to store a dead body. Maybe he wanted someone to brag to. We believe he wanted to use Justin to implicate someone else in Erin's death. At first, he was unsure how to accomplish this. Justin's gunshot wasn't the kind that could be self-inflicted. Therefore, Justin couldn't be framed. But, as I said before, Zack kept detailed notes on all his surveillance. He'd spent some time watching Craig Vance. Erin had told Steph that Craig had contacted her recently about taking her to court for custody of the kids. Zack had photos of Craig's apartment at the church, and he'd begun recording Craig's daily movements. He'd called the church for his office hours and schedule."

"Didn't he have work?" Bree asked. "Steph said he was in his workshop all the time."

"He lied to her," Todd said. "He had no work. He spent all his time in his workshop scheming."

Matt asked, "He had a plan?"

"A detailed one." Nodding, Todd took a breath. "He knew about Erin's life insurance. Steph had told him about it when she first found out she was pregnant. She wanted to buy a similar policy after their baby was born. Zack put the life insurance and the custody issue together and figured Craig had financial motivation to kill Erin. So, he could be framed for her murder. Zack decided to kill Justin, dump his body in Albany, and plant the gun in Craig's apartment."

"An exit strategy," Bree said.

"A smart one," Matt added. "It might have worked if he'd followed through."

"But when he found out Steph was leaving him, he lost it." Todd flattened his hands on the table. "That's all I have today. I'll let you know if other questions come up as we wrap up the investigation."

"Have you talked to Craig Vance?" Bree asked Todd.

"I have excellent news on that front," Todd said. "I drove down to Albany yesterday and shared the audio recording with detectives with the Albany PD. It turns out that Craig Vance did not have everyone in his church fooled. The Albany PD has been quietly investigating him for a couple of weeks for stealing from the youth group ministry fund.

During their investigation, they found additional account discrepancies that they're still trying to trace. A search warrant was obtained for Craig's apartment. While an Albany detective and I questioned Craig at the station, his residence was searched. Officers recovered a burner phone. The number matches the one that interacted with your sister around the times of the cash withdrawals."

Bree looked relieved. "I knew he was up to no good at the church."

"And you were right," Todd said. "Craig is looking at multiple counts of grand larceny and extortion, all felonies. He is going to serve time."

Bree sighed. "I'll bet he was the person who broke into Erin's house the first night I was there. He knew Erin had the recordings. He wanted to find them."

"That makes sense," Matt said.

"Bree, I'd like to talk to you in my office for a few minutes." Todd stood. "Matt, I'm going to the hospital next to question Justin again. I'd appreciate it if you were there when I talked to him. Justin isn't very stable. He could use the support."

Matt nodded. "I'll see you over there."

They walked out the door and down the hall.

Matt touched Bree's arm. "I'll talk to you later."

"OK." She turned. "I hope Justin is better."

So did Matt.

CHAPTER
THIRTY-EIGHT

Bree followed Todd back to his office.

He closed the door.

"Please have a seat." Todd gestured to a guest chair.

Bree sank into it. "Thank you for your help with Craig."

"You're welcome. It was my pleasure. Now I have something to ask you." Todd picked up his phone and pressed one button. "Marge, would you come in here for a minute?"

Todd got up and rounded his desk. He perched on the edge, facing Bree. Marge came in, closed the door, and stood next to him.

Presenting a united front.

Suspicious, Bree leaned back in the chair.

"You and Matt were instrumental in this investigation," Todd said. "Though I'll never be able to publicly acknowledge how helpful you were, people took notice after that video went viral."

The woman in the robe had recorded Bree taking down Zack. The video had gone viral overnight.

"Yes. The video." Bree frowned. She still couldn't believe the woman had pulled her cell phone from her robe pocket and filmed the shooting.

"You seem unhappy about it," Todd said.

"I am."

"Why?" Todd asked. "You looked like a hero."

"And a total badass," Marge added.

Bree searched for the words. "It's hard to explain, but the viral sharing feels intrusive. Frankly, I don't like getting attention for killing a man, even if I had no choice."

She'd played those final moments over and over in her head, and she still saw no other way she could have ended the altercation. Yet, she still wasn't comfortable with what she'd done, nor could she express why.

"I can see that." Todd cleared his throat. "Anyway, Marge and I were talking." They shared a glance.

"You should be the new sheriff," Marge said.

"What?" Bree straightened. She was considering local law enforcement, but running for sheriff hadn't made her radar.

"You're a good fit," Todd said. "I strongly believe we need an outsider to rebuild this department. You have the experience."

"You're honest, and you have roots in this county," Marge added. "From the positive comments on that video, I'd say the public would be all for it."

"I don't know," Bree said, but the idea of taking on the challenge was strangely appealing. She needed a job. She'd be working close to home. But did she really need the stress of politics? Sheriff was an elected position. She'd have to campaign.

"I want to show you something." Marge led Bree out to the squad room. Two deputies typing reports at their desks looked up as they passed by. Marge stopped on the other side of the room. Mounted on the back wall were framed photos of previous sheriffs. Most were formal, professional shots, but Marge pointed to a simple snapshot, enlarged.

"I took this picture. He refused to have a professional portrait session. He said it was a stupid waste of money." She touched the frame. "His name was Bob O'Reilly. Do you remember him?"

"Yes." Bree stared at the picture. In it, a clean-shaven man in his midfifties smiled from behind the big desk in the sheriff's office. He wore a tan uniform shirt and jeans. She couldn't see his feet in the photo, but she knew he was wearing cowboy boots.

The same boots she'd first seen walking down the back-porch steps that cold and dark night when her entire life had changed course. Adam was screaming in her arms, Erin hiding behind her, clutching at her pajamas.

Bree recalled one clear thought at the sight and sound of those boots clumping down the back steps.

Not Daddy.

Daddy wore big-soled work boots. These were the cowboy kind.

Relief had stolen her breath and started her shaking. The man had crouched under the steps and pried loose the board. "It's all right. You're all safe now." He passed the beam of a flashlight over them, then shone it on himself. He wore a jacket with badges. "I'm Sheriff Bob. Come on out, and I'll take you somewhere warm."

His voice was friendly and soft. Erin had crawled right out, and a man wearing the same kind of jacket wrapped her in a blanket and picked her up.

Sheriff Bob turned back to Bree and asked, "Your name is Bree, right?"

She nodded.

"Bree, that baby is cold." The sheriff set the light on the ground and put his arms through the hole. "Why don't you hand him to me so we can get him warmed up?"

Adam's body had gone stiff, his feet pushing away from her. He *was* cold. She was cold too, so cold that her skin hurt. She put Adam in the sheriff's arms, and he cradled him for a few seconds before another man in uniform wrapped him in a blanket too. Bree's whole body went weak. She crawled out and stood in the dark yard.

Sheriff Bob draped a blanket around her shoulders, then took off his thick jacket and wrapped that around her too. It was still warm from his body. "I see your feet are bare." His voice hitched a little. "Would it be all right if I picked you up?"

She nodded, and when he scooped her up in his arms, she hugged him and burrowed her face into his shirt.

"You're safe now, I promise," he said, tucking his coat around her bare feet.

Bree blinked. The sheriff's department squad room roared back at her in a wild sensation of color and light.

Marge was talking. "Bob called me in that night. He said he needed help with three children. I met him here. Bob was a mess. He had a black eye and bloody knuckles. He wanted to get cleaned up. Your brother was asleep when you all got here. Your little sister came to me right away. But you wouldn't let go of Bob. So, he took you into his office and let you sleep on his shoulder while he iced his face and hand. When your family arrived, they had to peel you off him."

"I don't remember being here that night." Bree's gaze swept the room. It didn't look remotely familiar.

"You were half-asleep." Marge smiled.

"Why would the sheriff have a black eye and bloody knuckles? My father killed himself."

"I don't know exactly how the night went down."

Apparently, neither did Bree. She'd always assumed her father shot himself before the police arrived. No one had ever told her otherwise, but then, the family hadn't talked about the incident at all. Bree had never questioned her memories.

Until now.

"Does the department still have the files from 1993?" Bree asked.

"Yes," Marge said. "They're boxed up in the basement. I assume you're thinking about your parents' case."

"Yes. I'm wondering if my memories are faulty."

"Does it matter?"

"I don't know."

"Your parents' case is closed, so there's no reason you can't have a copy of the file. But think long and hard about what will be in those files. Do you really want those images in your head? For the most part, you seem to have put the tragedy behind you. What would you gain by dredging it all up again?"

"That's a good question." And Bree truly didn't know. Maybe Marge was right, and she should let go of the past.

Marge turned to face her. "I believe Bob was the last truly good sheriff to hold this office. I think you taking the job and putting this department to rights would be an excellent legacy to him."

A surge of emotions filled Bree's chest. "Geez, Marge. No pressure."

Marge lifted an unconcerned shoulder. "I never said I played fair."

"I don't even know what's involved with running for sheriff. I'm not a politician, and even if I knew how to run a campaign, I don't have the money for one."

"What if you didn't need to campaign?" Marge asked. "Would you consider the job itself?"

"Maybe."

Marge lifted one pencil-point eyebrow. "The job has been vacant a long time. No one ran in November. You meet all of Randolph County's requirements for office. Special elections are expensive. It would be easier and cheaper to have the governor appoint you as sheriff. Then you would serve out the remainder of the current term before having to actually run for office. You'd have years before a campaign would be necessary."

Bree pressed the heel of her hand against her forehead. "How do I get the governor of New York to appoint me as sheriff?"

"You let me worry about that." Marge didn't blink. "The footage of you shooting Zack Wallace should convince anyone you're the right person for the job."

"I don't think shooting a suspect should be the main qualifier." Bree almost cringed at the visual. She'd briefly seen the news coverage. The media had rehashed her entire family history. Somehow Matt had avoided the cameras.

"You stopped an active shooter," Marge said. "Most folks will think your courage is enough."

Bree didn't agree, but the idea of building something meaningful and protecting the citizens of Randolph County appealed to her. She'd have more daily variety than she did in her current job in homicide, more to her day than death, death, and more death.

Now that she wasn't worried about Craig taking the kids, Bree needed a job in Grey's Hollow.

"If you can get the governor to appoint me, I'll take the job. Tell me how you know the governor?"

"I was his secretary many, many years ago, back when he was a brand-new prosecutor." Her eyes twinkled. "Before he was a big shot."

Marge really did know everyone.

CHAPTER THIRTY-NINE

Matt walked off the hospital elevator. Mr. Moore was sitting in the waiting area at the end of Justin's hall. He was drinking coffee and eating graham crackers.

"How is he?" Matt asked.

Mr. Moore looked like he'd aged twenty years in the last week. "He's exhausted and in pain. Last night, he had a roommate who screamed all night."

Matt put a hand on Mr. Moore's shoulder. "I'm sorry."

"He seems a little better now. They moved him to a private room and gave him more pain meds. He asked me to leave so he could sleep."

"That's good. Why don't you go down to the cafeteria and get some actual food?"

"Yes." Mr. Moore nodded. "I'll do that. Thanks."

"I'll check on him. If he's asleep, I'll hang out here."

"OK." Mr. Moore turned and walked toward the elevator. "His room is at the end of the hall. Number three forty-eight."

Matt went down the hall. He passed the nurses' station and continued to the end of the corridor. Justin's room was dark and quiet, the door ajar. Hoping his friend was sleeping, Matt gently pushed the door open just enough to stick his head through the gap. He waited for his eyes to adjust. An IV dripped into Justin's wrist, but there were no other machines connected to him. His injury, barring infection, wasn't life-threatening now that he was receiving medical treatment.

"I'm awake," Justin said.

Matt walked in. The dark room was depressing, so he flipped on the light.

Justin covered his eyes with his hand.

Matt crossed to the bedside. "Are you allowed to have food?"

"Yeah." But Justin's voice was flat, emotionless.

"Good. I brought you fries." Matt set them on the tray table and rolled it in front of his friend.

"Thanks." But Justin ignored the food.

Someone knocked on the doorframe, and Todd peered into the room. "Hey, Justin. Are you up to answering a few more questions?"

Justin coughed, then winced, one hand going to the fresh bandage on his shoulder. "Sure."

Matt filled his water cup from the plastic pitcher on the tray and positioned the straw to point at Justin.

Todd walked to the opposite side of the bed and pulled a small notepad and a pen from his pocket. "What do you remember about your time with Zack?"

Justin shook his head. "It was really weird. At first, he treated me like we had something in common." His gaze went to the ceiling. "He said Erin had treated us both badly."

"Do you believe that?" Todd asked.

Justin shook his head. "No. Our marriage breakup was entirely my fault, but Zack blamed Erin for all the problems in his relationship with Steph. Erin, who gave Steph a place to go. Erin, who encouraged Steph to leave him. He stalked her and threatened her friends. Most of them stopped communicating with Steph because Zack was such a problem."

"But not Erin," Todd said, taking notes.

"No. Erin didn't give up on her friends." Justin paused to breathe. "She wouldn't stop being friends with Steph because her husband was a prick any more than she would stop being my friend because I'd made mistakes." Justin's voice rasped.

Matt handed him his cup of water. Justin took it and drank deeply.

"You and Erin still had a relationship?" Todd asked.

Justin closed his eyes for one breath. When he opened them, they were bleak. "Yeah. She didn't want drugs in the house. I respected that." He paused, his next breath quivering. "She had faith in me. She believed I could beat my addiction. I wish I could have been half the man she thought I was."

"Zack just talked to you?" Todd asked.

"It was strange," Justin said. "I kept asking him to let me die. The more I asked, the more he didn't want to. It was almost perverse." He paused and exhaled hard. "I wanted to die. I couldn't—can't—imagine living without her." His voice faded, and he began to sob.

Todd pocketed his notepad. "I'll let you get some rest."

Matt didn't know if rest was going to make any difference.

Todd left, and Matt waited for Justin to stop crying.

"I feel bad for the cop," Justin said. "He barely got a few questions in before I fell apart."

"It'll get better." Matt hoped.

"Will it?" Justin's tone shifted to angry. "She's gone. What do I have to live for?" He reached for his IV tubing. "This?"

Matt grabbed the tubing. "Hey, you need the antibiotics."

"They gave me painkillers too." Justin shrugged. "I couldn't even quit with my marriage on the line. I couldn't quit with Erin standing behind me. I couldn't quit for the stepkids I swore to love. How will I ever quit with nothing to motivate me?"

"Those kids still need your love," Matt said. "They lost their mom, and they miss you."

"They don't."

"They do. Kayla told Bree."

Justin didn't respond. Instead, he turned his face away.

"Give it time. You need to heal." Matt would be there for his friend, but would it be enough?

CHAPTER FORTY

Bree hadn't been home more than ten minutes when the doorbell rang. She glanced out the window at the front porch. Steph.

Bree paused. Exhaustion settled over her. She needed some breathing room. But she wasn't getting any until she dealt with Steph. Again.

Bree opened the door.

"I'm sorry." Steph backed away. "I don't want to come in. I just wanted to talk to you for a couple of minutes."

"Sure." Bree stepped out onto the porch. The cold wind blew through the holes in her cable-knit sweater. She rubbed her arms.

"I don't expect the kids to forgive me."

Bree stopped her. "You didn't do anything." But Bree wasn't ready for the kids to interact with Steph yet. They knew that Zack had killed their mother, but Bree had given only the details they'd specifically asked for.

Hell, Bree needed processing time. She wanted a solid week with nothing traumatic to do. OK. Maybe a month.

"My husband killed Erin. I didn't even know." Steph still sounded as if she didn't believe what had happened. "It's been two days, and I still haven't processed it."

"I know how you feel." It still felt surreal to Bree too.

"Anyway, I just wanted to thank you."

"Do you have somewhere to stay?" Bree asked. Steph's house was still a crime scene.

"Yeah." Steph sniffed. "One of the girls from the salon let me stay in her guest room. I'm going to sell the house. I can't ever live there again."

"How do you feel?"

Steph rubbed her belly. "OK, I guess. How do I tell the baby her father tried to kill us both?"

"I don't know."

"I'm sorry. I forgot." Steph covered her mouth with one hand.

"It's OK. We can't change our past, but we do learn to live with it."

That said, Bree hadn't told Luke or Kayla that their father had used them to extort money from their mother. She had to tell them eventually. It would be far worse if they heard about Craig from someone else. But they'd had enough bad news for now, and Kayla wasn't old enough. She didn't know anything about her father. Bree dreaded the day she had to tell her the whole story.

Steph backed toward the porch steps. "Anyway, I just wanted to say thank you and that I'm sorry. Take care of yourself."

"You too."

Steph walked down the porch steps and climbed into her car. Bree waved and watched her drive away. Before she went back inside, Adam's beat-up Bronco turned into the driveway. He parked in front of the house, then opened the cargo hold of his SUV and took out a canvas. She opened the door for him, and he carried the painting into the house. In the living room, the kids gathered around them.

"That isn't the painting you were working on." Bree knew from the size alone.

"I finished that one the day you took the kids back home. Erin asked me a hundred times to paint her a picture of the farm." He uncovered the canvas. "It isn't very good, but I tried."

Bree just stared. In the painting, Erin was holding Cowboy's lead rope, while Luke and Kayla groomed him. Erin was smiling, one hand on the horse's nose. The wind picked up the ends of her dark hair. Behind them, the barn stood surrounded by its flower-dotted meadow. Sun shone from a brilliant blue sky.

"That's the day she brought him home from the auction," Adam said.

Luke stood next to Bree. "Cowboy was a mess. Skinny and dirty, covered in scratches. Mom said he would have been shipped to the slaughterhouse the next day if she didn't take him."

Bree caught her brother's sideways smile and knew without a doubt that Adam had paid for that horse. And probably the others as well. In the painting, the horse was resting, his head hung low, one rear leg cocked, as if he knew he was safe.

Adam had painted from the viewpoint of the back porch—from the viewpoint of an outsider. An uneasy feeling stirred in Bree's gut. Was that how he felt? Like an outsider to other people's closeness?

Most of his work was dark and disturbing, but this . . . This was all the light his other paintings lacked. This was unicorns and rainbows and glitter compared to the inner demons Bree was accustomed to seeing in her brother's art.

"Anyway, I thought you might want it." He shrugged.

"Thank you. Why would you say this isn't good?" Bree thought it was the most beautiful thing he'd ever done, but she didn't say that. He'd be offended, and what did she know about art?

He frowned. "It's not from my mind. I didn't create it. It's just them."

His perspective floored her for a minute. Adam thought because the painting was realistic rather than interpretive, it was of lesser value. He couldn't have been more wrong. Bree took him by the arms. "You created every square inch of this, and I think it's amazing. You captured Erin's essence. You portrayed one split second of her life and managed to show her kindness, generosity, and optimism." All the things that

Bree wanted to remember about her little sister. "It's brilliant. What do you call it?"

Adam turned back to it for a second, his eyes glistening with moisture. "Safe."

Bree hugged him. She was not going to let him retreat into his art again, at least not completely. She would drag him into the light. "You're staying for dinner, right?"

"Um." He stared at his shoes. "I need to start another painting."

"You just finished two."

Dana walked past them and picked up a cookbook lying on the end table. "Of course he's staying for dinner. I made cacciatore."

Adam met Bree's eyes with just a hint of panic. Ha! He didn't know how to argue with Dana, and Bree wasn't going to help him. She gave him a one-armed hug. "The kids need to see you more, so I'm going to expect you for regular dinners."

"Weekly family dinners would be great for the kids." Dana headed back toward the kitchen, cookbook in hand. "Whatever day works best for everyone else. Every day is the same for me now."

While the kids *oohed* and *aahed* over the painting and Adam looked for the best light to hang it, Bree followed Dana into the kitchen. "Did I tell you I was sort of offered the position of sheriff?" Bree filled a glass of water and summarized her talk with Todd and Marge.

"You'd be a great sheriff. You're smart. You're experienced and good with people. Your mouth doesn't run before your brain, and you don't have a dick to trip over."

Bree choked on her water. Wiping her chin with a napkin, she said, "Yeah. If I get the job, that's not going to be one of my acceptance speech points. This sheriff's department has never even had a female deputy."

Dana rolled her eyes. "Seriously?"

"Yep."

"Then you'll shake things up." Dana grinned.

"Now you're making me regret saying yes." Not that Bree thought the job was a done deal. Just because Marge had once been the governor's secretary didn't mean he'd appoint Bree as sheriff.

Someone knocked on the kitchen door. Matt stood on the back porch. Bree opened the door. He held a big white-and-black dog on a leash. As soon as the dog saw Bree, it lunged at her. But Matt was ready and held it on a short leash. Still, Bree jumped backward, her heart trying to race right out of her chest.

"Ladybug, sit," Matt said in a firm voice.

The big dog's ass hit the floor. Its tongue lolled, and huge brown eyes took in the kitchen.

"What is that?" Bree asked.

"Your gateway dog," Matt said.

"What?"

"We talked about this. A dog designed to make you like other dogs."

"Why is it here?"

"Her name is Ladybug. She's from my sister's rescue. You don't have to keep her, but she really needs a foster home, a place to calm down and get accustomed to living in a house. Then my sister can get her adopted and save more dogs."

Bree looked down. Ladybug was pudgy. She was mostly white with a black mask and ears and random black spots on her body. "Why did you bring her to me?"

"You need a nonthreatening dog. She is about as nonthreatening as it gets."

It was true. The chubby mutt looked like one of Kayla's Pillow Pets come to life.

The kids came into the kitchen.

"I told you I heard Matt!" Kayla yelled. "He brought a dog."

Luke and Kayla beelined for Ladybug, who forgot how to sit and jumped all over them. The kids squealed. The dog slobbered. With only a one-inch stump of a tail, Ladybug wagged her whole butt.

"She's a rescue," Matt said. "I'm trying to place her in a home. Do you think you guys could teach her house manners? That would really help."

"Why can't *we* keep her?" Kayla stopped petting the dog, who bumped her hand with her nose in protest.

"That would be up to your aunt Bree," Matt said.

"Mom would have loved her." Kayla hugged Ladybug, who slurped her face. "She looks like a cow."

Vader jumped down off the kitchen counter and walked up to the dog. Ladybug paid him no attention. The cat walked away, jumped back onto the counter, and knocked some mail to the floor, as if upset he couldn't intimidate her.

"I'm going to feed the horses." Unable to deal with the melee—and the prospect of living with a dog on a daily basis—Bree went to the back door and put on a coat and boots. "Would you help me, Matt?"

"Of course." He followed her out to the barn.

The horses were at the pasture gate, ready for their dinner. Bree opened the gate, and they ambled into their stalls on their own. Matt closed the doors while Bree dumped grain into buckets. She checked water and gave them hay.

Then she leaned her back on Cowboy's door and crossed her arms over her chest. "You should have asked me about the dog first."

Matt took up the same position next to her. "You would have said no."

"Probably." Definitely.

"You don't have to keep her."

"You know the kids are already attached, and I won't take her away from them."

"I was hoping you'd say that."

"I don't like it," Bree said. "You should have consulted me."

"It was insensitive," Matt agreed. But he didn't look the least bit sorry.

Bree sighed. What could she do? She would have to deal with her fear, and she wasn't sure how she felt about that. Annoyed. Scared. Maybe even a little relieved she'd be forced to confront the final terror of her childhood. Tomorrow. She'd deal with her feelings tomorrow. Today, she was too damned tired. "OK. I'll do my best. She does look sweet."

"She loves everyone and everything, but I will warn you that she is a terrible watchdog. She'll let anyone into the house, but her complete lack of aggression is why I thought she'd be perfect for you."

Something in his tone made Bree look sideways and scan his face. His eyes were troubled. Had he come straight from the hospital? "How was Justin today?"

The air left his chest in one whoosh. "His shoulder is healing, but his emotional recovery is going to be rough."

"I'm sorry." Bree turned to face him. Without thinking, she wrapped her arms around him and pulled him close. He returned the embrace and leaned his face on the top of her head. They stood like that for a few minutes, until she felt him relax.

"Do you want to talk about it?" she asked.

"No. I really don't. I'll support Justin however I can, but I can't recover for him. He has to do it himself."

"OK. Let me know if I can help."

"I will, thanks." He shook his head, as if putting his friend's tragedy out of his mind, then smiled down at her.

She released him. Their eyes locked. *Damn.* He smelled good.

As if caught in the emotional moment, he lowered his face toward hers.

Bree planted a hand in the center of his chest. "Hold on there, Thor."

317

"Thor?" Matt stared down at her.

"Your beard has filled in again. You look like a Viking."

His mouth quirked. "I want credit for not making a magic hammer joke."

She snorted. He was an attractive man, but it was his sense of kindness and humor that were hard to resist.

"We hardly know each other," she said.

He lifted a brow. "We've worked together day and night. I've saved your butt. You've saved mine."

"And it's a very fine butt," she said. "But—"

He grinned. "You like me."

Bree fought the urge to roll her eyes. "You've been normal all this time. Why are you suddenly acting like a seventeen-year-old?"

"Maybe you make me feel like a teenager." He leaned closer and sniffed her hair. His beard rubbed against her face.

Inside her boots, her toes curled.

"Yes. I like you," she said.

He frowned. "I sense a *but*."

"I have a lot going on here. Those two kids have to be my focus."

"I heard you're going to be sheriff."

"It's hardly a done deal," Bree said.

"Marge told me, so it's going to happen."

She laughed softly. "You have a lot of faith in Marge."

"She gets shit done."

"OK, my point here is that I'm going to be around, and I do like you."

He grinned.

She continued. "But I don't have time for a relationship."

"What about some casual dating?"

"How casual?"

"Dinner now and then," Matt said.

"Maybe I can manage that, as long as our relationship remains casual."

"OK." He shrugged. "You can call it whatever you like."

Despite his easy acceptance of her terms, Bree feared she was not as in control of the situation as she would have liked, and she had a terrifying suspicion that was going to be her new life in a nutshell.

But she had the kids for motivation. She would take on whatever came her way for them. A new job. Three horses. A dog she didn't want. Whatever.

Go ahead, life. Bring it on.

Acknowledgments

It truly takes a team to publish a book. As always, credit goes to my agent, Jill Marsal, for nine years of unwavering support and great advice. I'm thankful for the entire team at Montlake, especially my managing editor, Anh Schluep, and my developmental editor, Charlotte Herscher. Special thanks to Rayna Vause and Leanne Sparks for help with various technical details, and to Kendra Elliot, for pushing me to write on days when I lack motivation.

ABOUT THE AUTHOR

Photo © 2016 Jared Gruenwald Photography

#1 Amazon Charts and #1 *Wall Street Journal* bestselling author Melinda Leigh is a fully recovered banker. After joining Romance Writers of America, she decided writing was more fun than analyzing financial statements. Melinda's debut novel, *She Can Run*, was nominated for Best First Novel by the International Thriller Writers. She's also garnered Golden Leaf and Silver Falchion Awards, along with two nominations for a RITA and three Daphne du Maurier Awards. Her other novels include *She Can Tell, She Can Scream, She Can Hide, She Can Kill, Midnight Exposure, Midnight Sacrifice, Midnight Betrayal, Midnight Obsession, Hour of Need, Minutes to Kill, Seconds to Live, Say You're Sorry, Her Last Goodbye, Bones Don't Lie, What I've Done, Secrets Never Die,* and *Save Your Breath.* She holds a second-degree black belt in Kenpo karate, has taught women's self-defense, and lives in a messy house with her family and a small herd of rescue pets. For more information, visit www.melindaleigh.com.